PRAISE FOR *SAVING RAINE* (THE DRONE WARS: BOOK 1)
BY FREDERICK LEE BROOKE

"…packed full of **intrigue, action, drama, romance and colourful characters**."
— *Simon Jenner, Amazon reviewer*

"Readers of **intelligently plotted and written sci-fi** reads will be thrilled with this book."
— *Roxy Kade, Amazon reviewer*

"…a **fast paced, action packed, intriguing , gripping and thrilling read** which had me hooked from the very first line."
— *Totally Addicted To Reading*

GET *SAVING RAINE* IN PAPERBACK ON AMAZON.
GET *SAVING RAINE* IN EBOOK AT ALL MAJOR ONLINE RETAILERS.

INFERNO

THE DRONE WARS: BOOK 2

FREDERICK LEE BROOKE

INFERNO (The Drone Wars: Book 2)
© 2014 by Frederick Lee Brooke

FIRST EDITION
ISBN-10: 1499769075
ISBN-13: 978-1499769074

Edited by Elizabeth King Humphrey

Interior Design and Layout by Anne Chaconas

Cover Art Design by Anne Chaconas

Printed in the U.S.A.

www.frederickleebrooke.com
Switzerland ● Chicago

Inferno is a work of fiction. The names, characters, places and incidents are products of the author's imagination or have been used fictitiously and are not to be construed as real. Any resemblance to actual persons, living or dead, or actual organizations, is entirely coincidental.

Printed in Book Antiqua font

America will never be destroyed from the outside.
If we falter and lose our freedoms,
it will be because we destroyed ourselves.
— **Abraham Lincoln**

DERRICK SIMS STARED *intently at his control screen, operating the robotic arms with swiping motions of his fingers on a pad. At this shallow depth of 260 feet, on the uneven floor of San Francisco Bay, the submarine mechanics obeyed his commands in real time. He'd trained in deeper water, up to two thousand feet, where sometimes a delay occurred between a swipe and the corresponding motion of the arms.*

The training had lasted for the past twelve months without any of them knowing what their mission would be. Earning triple what Sims had taken home as an officer in the US Navy had taken the edge off the secrecy. In the Navy, you rarely knew where you were headed either. You could be cruising off Hawaii or approaching the Kola Peninsula off Severomorsk in the Barents Sea. It all looked about the same from the inside of a submarine. And you were never far from danger. The kind of danger that could mean the end of the world.

"Handle with care," said Jajackck McLamore, munching on a cold cheeseburger while staring at his own screen, where he followed Sims's manipulations.

"You're in more danger from high cholesterol than from one of those babies going off," Sims replied, keeping his cool. McLamore had always been the coolest head during trainings, but today only constant eating kept his nerves in check. Sims guided the robot arms till they locked on a steel box the size of a small trunk. He lifted the box out of the muck, swiveled the robot assembly, which worked like a small underwater crane, then telescoped the arms to deliver the box into the cargo hold at the back.

"It's that moment when it's right over our heads that freaks me out," McLamore said. He took another bite of his cheeseburger.

"Even if I dropped it, it wouldn't puncture the hull and it wouldn't blow," Sims reminded his partner as box number thirty-six locked down safely in the hold. The robot arms shrank into themselves and came around again. The submersible could carry forty of the two hundred-pound boxes.

When the cargo hold was full, they would make the twenty-mile journey out to sea to offload onto the Nemo. *They could reach the* Nemo *in under an hour, offload in forty minutes, and run back here for the fifth load. The* Nemo *was loading the boxes into a container that would be brought to an unknown port. Surely one of the West Coast ports. They wouldn't risk smuggling this cargo through Panama Canal security.*

"You believe everything they tell you?" McLamore said.

"I have to think they know what they're talking about. We're working to make this country safer."

"Look at the size of that thing," McLamore said. He was pointing at a section of cable from the Golden Gate Bridge, which had been destroyed this morning in a series of timed explosions just as an army convoy was crossing. Everyone had seen it over and over on TV. The convoy had been carrying those 240 steel boxes. The team in this submersible wasn't supposed to know what was in the boxes, but Sims knew, and he knew McLamore knew. That was what made McLamore nervous. A single box, if it blew, would level the entire city and snuff out the lives of all four million inhabitants.

The weird object McLamore was pointing at looked more like a Greek column at the bottom of the Mediterranean than a steel cable with over five hundred strands wound together. He looked beyond the underwater drones that were giving the March22 leaders real-time information on their progress. That cable had to be three feet in diameter. It stood straight up, as if it had bored into the ground when it hit. Thousands of tons of tensile steel could very well bore a hole in bedrock, Sims figured, dropping through seawater like a pile driver. The column rose into the murky dimness about thirty feet off to their right. Cables like this, extending right up to the surface, had to be interfering with surface shipping. March22 had calculated correctly that debris from the bridge destruction would prevent the military from swooping in on the same day to recover their deadly cargo.

Sims smiled, thinking of his year of training. March22 had been prepared. March22 had gotten here first. After waiting offshore, they had guided the submersible into San Francisco Bay and gotten started less than two hours after the bridge was destroyed.

"Damn, this one's stuck on something," Sims said. The robot arm was trying to claw the thirty-seventh box out of a tangle of wires and ropes. He swiped left and then right again, wiggling the box to work it out of the mess. But the box fell and settled down into the tangle again.

"Let the master have a turn," McLamore said. He had finished his cheeseburger.

Sims transferred control of the robot arms to McLamore with the touch of a button. Their orders were clear. They couldn't leave a single one down here. After thirty seconds of skillful maneuvering, McLamore extricated the troublesome box out of the tangle. Sims watched as McLamore manipulated the box to free it from one last thin cable that stretched over the top. The box suddenly fell free again as one of the robot arms lost its grip.

McLamore shifted in his chair, and giant sweat stains appeared under his arms in the dark green uniform shirt.

"Butterfingers," Sims said.

"I went to my lawyer, you know. Wrote my last will and testament," McLamore said. Beads of sweat covered his brow and upper lip as he brought the robot arms down for another try.

"I told you, they're not going to blow," Sims said.

He hoped to God his information was correct.

PART 1

CHAPTER 1

NEAR LOLO, MONTANA
NOVEMBER 30, 2021—11 PM

"Pretty hot girlfriend," the March22 fighter said. "Too bad she ain't on this patrol, keep us all company." When Matt Carney didn't react, the man prodded his shin with the toe of his boot. That was going too far.

The tight space in the back of this modified SUV held eight men, sitting hip to hip on benches along the sides. No more than two feet separated their knees. The man's thick lips curled into a lewd smile.

"Yep, sure has a nice rack. Reminds me of Nina Nardelli."

"I didn't get your name," Matt said. The reference to America's premier sex symbol was offensive. This dude was clearly itching to fight, but did it have to happen during a mission?

"Malone. Just call me Mike," the man said. A large mole stared like a third eye, exactly placed between his bushy eyebrows.

"Listen, Malone, we've got a job to do, here. Why don't you keep your teeth together and focus on that."

Their vehicle was the rear guard for a hazardous big rig load. They'd picked up the big rig from another March22 team east of Spokane before crossing Idaho, and into Montana. These mountain borders out west had no checkpoints. In forty minutes they would hit the highway south to Big Sky Base, where they would offload the dangerous cargo far from any active fault lines.

"What's the matter, first mission jitters?" Malone continued.

Matt's boot kicked up hard, as if spring-loaded. It hit Malone's shin with brute force. People learned not to mess with Matt Carney.

Malone screamed in pain, at the same time exploding out of his seat, fists flying. Suddenly all the men sprang into motion. The tight space boiled over with shouting, grunting men trying to intervene or dive out of the way. Malone landed one blow on Matt's helmet as Matt planted a right in the man's solar plexus. One of the men took Malone's next wild punch in the eye. Everyone was shouting, muscles bulging. Finally the others coordinated their efforts and pinned them both in their seats. Fire burned in Malone's eyes.

"I'll kick your ass, Carney."

"Settle down, Mike," one of the men said.

After that, they just sat and glared. Matt kept his focus on the man's chest, wary of another attack as the SUV rolled down the highway.

Information was highly compartmentalized in March22. That explained why Matt was the only one here who knew those weapons in the big rig was could make the entire Pacific Northwest uninhabitable for the next thousand years. He shouldn't really know the details either, but his twin brother Luke shared information freely with him.

March22 had stolen the weapons from the US Army in a complicated underwater operation under the Golden Gate Bridge two weeks ago. The US Army's idea of good policy had been to move the weapons from one storage facility vulnerable to earthquake danger to another facility even closer to the San Andreas Fault. The March22 leaders, including his father, John Carney, had decided if the US Army wasn't going to keep the weapons safe, March22 had to take over the job.

March22 had its own armed drones in the air above tonight's route. If they picked up hostile activity, the drones would communicate it to the two SUVs leading the convoy. The drones had Hellfire air-to-ground missiles that could take out a tank. To defend the convoy, the Big Sky Base leader, Douglas Winter, had selected twenty men, who carried a variety of weapons.

"He isn't even trained." Malone broke the silence again. "He's the weak link here, a hazard to all of us." The man just couldn't zip it. At least he kept his butt planted. Most of the men went on dozing.

Of course, Malone would have no way of knowing that Matt had singlehandedly killed nine men between November 15 and 23, just getting from Chicago to California. Two with his slingshot, four others with an old AK-47, and another three with an AR-15 assault rifle identical to the one he carried now.

Matt wasn't proud of the killings. It made him sick to his stomach to think of those men dying. But it had been kill or be killed. That was the reality today. That was what they were working to change — together. Maybe Malone was the one who needed more training. He needed to work on his teamwork skills.

Matt's slingshot had ended the life of a man on a Harley with an eight-year-old girl strapped to his body as a human shield. The man had ridden his bike into a giant tent in which eighty people were eating lunch. The assault rifle balanced on his right arm had Pastor Peaches' name on it. The screaming girl's long blond hair had trailed in the wind of the speeding bike, shielding the killer's face and making it harder to draw a bead. Security dudes had come running from all sides, but they'd all held off for fear of hitting the girl.

As the assassin sped past his table, Matt had seen his chance. In one movement, he'd raised his slingshot and let the ball bearing fly, striking the killer square in the temple. He'd registered that clear demarcation between the rounded curve of the girl's scalp and the killer's pockmarked face pressed against it. At ten feet, the man's temple had been an easy target, even through the girl's hair. The ball bearing had gouged a crater two or three inches into the man's brain, cutting enough nerves to end the threat instantly. The bike had rolled another thirty feet before bashing into the stiff tent wall, throwing the dead rider off. The girl had struggled free, her hair spattered with blood and brains, but unhurt.

Pastor Peaches had stood up from the dirt floor, untouched, but trembling visibly at narrowly escaping another assassination attempt.

That day, they'd called Matt Carney a hero.

The SUV continued rolling through the darkness at sixty mph. Matt saw Malone open his big mouth to provoke him once more, but this time he didn't get the chance.

A detonation went off somewhere ahead. The sound was unmistakable. All the men jerked to attention and looked around. The concussion sounded like one of the dirty nukes in the big rig going off, but Matt knew they wouldn't still be sitting here if it had been that. He felt the adrenaline pouring into his muscles as their vehicle hit the brakes and went into a skid.

"Obstruction ahead, likely ambush," said the voice on Matt's comm. All of them had an earpiece in their helmets. It was the voice of one of the commanders in the lead SUV or in the cab of the big rig, high over the road. As soon as their vehicle stopped, the rear doors popped open. Matt and the other March22 men hit on the pavement at a jog, keeping low and moving in formation. The night air was a shock after the stuffy vehicle, but the chilly scent of the pine forest all around felt good on his face. "Take positions for scenario seven, repeat, scenario seven."

This meant that although the convoy had been forced to stop, the threat hadn't been identified yet.

Tearing his gaze away from the fireball five hundred feet ahead, Matt jogged after the other men in his row. Everyone had a specific task. The wide four-lane highway was hemmed in by tall, dense pine forest on both sides, with a wide grassy ditch by the emergency lane. He took a position on one knee in the emergency lane two hundred feet downhill from the stopped SUV. Two other March22 men spread out at hundred yard intervals, covering access from the rear, one of them Malone. Their quadcopter Vipers hovered over their heads, giving them 360-degree vision and thermal imaging early warning via their Jetlinks.

Up ahead, the big rig had stopped in the road, but looked intact. Peering past it, with the fireball far ahead dying down, Matt saw only one SUV standing in the road. With a sickening feeling, he realized they must've blown up the lead SUV. That was the fire. Four March22 fighters had manned the lead vehicle.

His stomach churned at the thought that Raine had pleaded to come on this mission. What if she'd been sitting in that lead SUV? It all happened so fast when it ended. Whoever you were, enemy or friend, everything could end forever in a single flash of light. Raine had only started her training four days ago due to a case of the flu after they had arrived in this corner of Northwest Montana. Luckily, Winter had judged that she wasn't ready.

To Matt's right, Malone and one other March22 man wielded rocket propelled grenades, ready to take out threats from the rear. To his left, an assortment of assault rifles looked ready to go. Scanning the nighttime sky and checking his Jetlink, Matt saw nothing.

They'd been ascending a rise, and he could see two miles down the road, where they'd come from. No traffic approached.

"The drones aren't picking up anything," said the voice on the comm, referring to March22's Predators flying fifty thousand feet above. "The road was mined, or else an IED. Our lead vehicle was destroyed and the crater is too big to drive around. Be alert."

Just then, Matt heard a muted popping sound to his right. He knew the sound of suppressed assault rifles. Both men with the RPGs wobbled on their legs, then tumbled to the ground. Malone lay flat, unmoving, probably already dead. Pivoting in his crouch, Matt next watched two March22 men to his left fall. Goddamn it, nothing from above. His Viper showed a blank. It hadn't picked up a thing. The attack had to be coming from the forest.

"Four men down, rear guard, possible ambush from the forest," he reported into the comm. Now his Jetlink beeped. The Viper had picked up someone directly behind him.

Before he could stand and fight, Matt felt a wet stinging spray in his nose, then strong arms on his shoulders, his own muscles suddenly powerless to resist. The lights went out.

MATT WOKE TO the high-pitched whine of an engine. His body bounced face down on the back of what looked like an ATV. He struggled, but couldn't move his arms or legs or his head. At least they hadn't blindfolded him.

Multiple strips of duct tape pinned his left wrist to the fiberglass housing. His angle of vision allowed only a limited view of the forest spinning along behind them as the ATV exhaust stung his nostrils. Something held his body fast against the fiberglass, probably rope, but with every bump, he floated an inch in the air before slamming down hard again on the brutal surface. His hipbones and shoulders took the worst of the beating as the ATV sped over rocks, branches, and uneven ground.

He tried again to free his hands, but the tape made it hopeless. It was a good thing the dark green March22 uniforms featured padding in the groin area. He'd have to give a pat on the back to whoever thought of that. His head throbbed even though his helmet protected him from the jolts.

"Hey, where the hell are you taking me? Let me go!" he yelled.

He was sure the driver must've heard him over the whining ATV engine, but no answer came.

The ATV sped through the pitch dark pine forest, presumably headed away from Route 90. This didn't appear to be a proper trail. They bounced over rough ground and zigzagged through pines and larches that receded into the background, curved around boulders, jumped up and over rises. The ATV tilted precariously each time it reached the top of a small hill, for a fraction of a second dangling in midair, close to tipping. Maybe he could throw his body weight enough to roll it over.

He couldn't raise himself enough to turn and face front. There must be a rope wound over the padding at the back of his neck. But sometimes, now that he had full command of his senses, Matt could feel whenever the ATV was struggling up a rise. The engine screamed as they accelerated. When they reached the top and left the ground momentarily, his sense of balance measured the angles changing. Timing was everything. After their vicious attack, this driver was in a big hurry. Sometimes the ATV teetered to the right when the wheels left the ground, sometimes left.

The next time he felt the vehicle speeding uphill, he strained every muscle in his body to pull it left. It was the only way he could tip it, thanks to his position. He strained against the ropes and the duct tape and tried to throw his weight to the left. But the ATV tilted to the right during the brief airborne moment, and his effort was wasted.

This was probably pointless anyway.

A minute further on, Matt felt the four-wheeler accelerating up another hill. He strained all his muscles and flung his weight left again, just at the moment the wheels left the ground. This time it was working. He pulled left over and over as the whole vehicle tipped over in midair.

The ATV came down hard on its two left wheels, bouncing and twisting and practically out of control.

"Goddamn it," the driver yelled. It was the first time Matt heard his voice. He felt the wheels churning the ground as the driver gunned the engine, wiggling crazily and dropping speed. The spongy ground had absorbed the messy landing. The vehicle came to a stop, and Matt heard the driver getting off.

Without warning, a powerful blow struck Matt's back. The crunching jolt between his shoulder blade and spine came so hard he saw stars.

"I have orders to get you there in one piece, Carney," the man said, breathing hard. "Try any more shit, and I'll really make you pay. Got it?"

"Who the hell are you? Where are you taking me?"

"No questions. Just be a man."

With his body pinned like this, he didn't have a hell of a lot of choice. If he'd been able to put the driver out of commission in a crash, he might've freed himself. Then again, he could easily have had his own head split open in a crash, like a melon thrown at a boulder.

He tried to relax his mind, his body bouncing and jostling on the fiberglass top. Not exactly ideal conditions. His twin brother, Luke, had coached him in the technique over the last eight days, since they arrived from California.

Matt concentrated on blocking out all thoughts and sensations. He blocked out the memory of the March22 men falling to the pavement, the spray that had overcome him, this bumpy ride. After a few seconds he felt himself rising slowly, then magically floating above his body, calm and placid, aware of the ATV racing ahead below, but focusing inward now.

Shit, that hurt like hell, Luke said. Matt heard the voice in his mind, thin and reedy and distant, but distinct, like a voice in an empty room. Still floating above the speeding ATV, he focused on his answer. He was so lousy at this. Luke had said the key was relaxing. And believing.

What hurt?

My back, moron. Felt like a frigging sledgehammer.

They didn't actually speak aloud. Luke would be sitting in his room back at Big Sky Base now, probably looking at dirty pictures on the Internet. It didn't matter how much distance separated them. The special link between the two brothers was as simple as sending thoughts back and forth.

You guys f—, Luke said. Matt missed the rest. He often missed the end of what Luke said. It was as if some kind of silent static drowned out the last word. But he could usually finish Luke's sentences anyway.

We were ambushed. I'm tied to the back of an ATV riding through a forest. This idiot clobbered me before. Did they steal our cargo?

They didn't even touch—. The rest faded out.

What? Why not?

How the hell should I know? Killed eight of our men, spared you for some reason. They didn't give the big rig a second look. Where the hell are you?

Can't you see me?

Luke could see things on the ground through the eyes of a drone at fifty thousand feet. Using his extraordinary programming abilities, Luke had stolen more than a thousand armed drones right out of the air from Homeland Security. Even more amazing, he had given March22 the capability of flying them without Homeland Security detecting them. Matt hadn't understood the explanation. Something to do with how numbers were rounded off, something normal mortals like Matt Carney, lousy at math since about third grade, would never grasp.

If you're in a forest, we won't see jack, Luke said. *The rest of them are backing the big rig back down Route 90. Nobody mentioned you weren't with them.*

Great, nobody noticed I was missing?

Eight men dead. I don't have identities yet. They loaded up the bodies and took off, back the way they came. You got lost in the —.

Listen, they shot the guys on either side of me. They could've easily shot me too, but instead they knocked me out. Next thing I know I'm lashed to the back of this ATV like a deer carcass. Maybe you want to report it or something.

ATV —? was all Matt caught of Luke's answer. Luke had said practice would make it better, and the communication already worked much better than at the beginning, when he could only catch single words. Somehow, as long as he could get himself into this relaxed state, sending was easy. Receiving still gave him trouble.

Yeah, big old four-wheeler. Hey, we're coming out on a road now.

The ATV took the turn on two wheels onto a narrow gravel road. Some logging road, the kind they often jogged on as part of the March22 training. In the moonlight, clouds of dust kicked up in the wake of the ATV. They headed downhill spitting gravel, making good speed, and curved around to the right before making a ninety-degree left turn on another gravel track. He floated effortlessly above the ATV and just below an unbroken canopy of pine branches.

Well, not much of a road, come to think of it, Matt said. *Don't know if you guys can spot anything on these logging roads.*

Those forests have vast networks, Luke said. *We need him to come out in the open to —.*

What happens then?

How the hell should I know? Maybe we'll send someone in to recover our lost asset.

Thanks.

Or maybe we won't. Not my decision to make alone.

Thanks a lot.

Right, I'm getting input from the leaders. No one has a clue why anyone would kidnap you. Do you have a secret bank account or something?

Screw you.

Do they look like US military?

Not this one guy.

So maybe a militia. But they didn't touch the bombs, go figure. Killed a bunch of our guys, and kidnapped you, but left the cargo —.

I guess that's good news, all in all.

Damn straight.

Matt knew March22 wanted to bring the dirty nukes to a safe place and never use them, maybe even destroy them. The government had proved it wasn't capable of safekeeping the bombs. His father said they couldn't be trusted not to use them.

They came around a sharp curve, after which the gravel road joined a two-lane asphalt highway, where the driver gunned the engine. The moon cast bright reflections on the trees sliding by.

Hallelujah, Matt said. *We hit a proper road.*

Tell me if you see any kind of sign, Luke said.

Speed limit sixty-five, Matt said.

A highway marker would be more helpful, moron.

Damn it, how many ATVs can there be ten miles from the point where our convoy stopped? Matt had no precise way of measuring how long the journey through the forest had lasted. Ten miles seemed like a good guess.

Hold on, looks like we might've spotted you, Luke said.

At that moment, the ATV veered across the deserted highway and entered an open paved area off the road. An airfield. They swung around in a wide arc, and stopped next to a white, two-engine plane.

"End of the line, Carney." The driver climbed off as three other men jogged up, accompanied by two Vipers hovering overhead. The propellers on the plane started to turn, first one, then the other.

"He awake?" grunted one of the men.

They're putting me on a plane, Matt said. *Two engines, propellers.*

How close are you to the — ?

Twenty feet.

I see the plane. Too close. You might be on it by the time we could take it out. We'll just try to keep —.

Tell Raine I'm fine, okay?

You're not fine. You're dead booty.

Just do it.

What other lies should I tell your girlfriend? That you're good in bed?

As of right now, I'm fine, okay? It's not a lie.

"Get him down," an unseen man said. "Cuff him before you untie the feet."

"Who the hell are you idiots?" Matt demanded. He had returned effortlessly to his own body. Heavy hands stripped away the tape that pinned his hands to the ATV. "You aren't putting me on that plane."

"Why not, Carney, fear of flying?" The man speaking came into his field of vision, a large, broad-shouldered dude in a Hawaiian shirt with a heavy leather jacket. The man had bushy dark eyebrows and cradled an AR-15 in his arms. Matt saw a pistol crammed into his belt as well.

"More like nervous about getting shot out of the sky. How do you dickheads know my name?"

"Are you going to walk like a brave soldier or do we have to drag your ass?"

"HAVE YOU GOT a name?" Matt asked the man in the Hawaiian shirt who sat directly across the aisle. The plane had left the runway and was skimming the treetops. Two other bodybuilders sat in the seats behind, keeping an eye on Matt, as if the Vipers buzzing around the low ceiling weren't enough.

"Thomas Paine," the man said.

"Where are you taking me, Paine?" Matt glanced out the window on his side, noticing they were still flying low. It looked like they were flying two or three hundred feet above the forest. The moonlight reflected off the silvery pines, like waves in the ocean. He had seen the ocean for the first time in his life only eight days ago, after taking off from San Francisco Airport.

"You'll find out soon enough," Paine said.

"Does this pilot know what he's doing?"

"Dudley? I would hope so."

"Looks like he's the one with a fear of heights."

Paine leaned across the aisle, fake whispering, "Under the radar. Pilots worth their wings get off on it. They tell me it's better than sex."

"Makes me fucking nervous," said one of the bodybuilders.

"Try not looking out," Paine snapped.

"What's the point of kidnapping me? You killed eight men. Why not me?"

Paine's eyebrows went up. "We can trade your ass for something, Carney, isn't it obvious?"

"What the hell are you talking about?"

"You're a *Carney*, aren't you?"

"It might help to know who you are."

"Never heard of Dark Fiber?"

"The militia? Sure, I've heard of it. You're Dark Fiber?"

Paine smiled. "The one and only."

"Why didn't you go after what was in the big rig?"

"You're not a very good listener, are you?" Paine said.

"I heard you before."

"We didn't want whatever stupid cargo March22 was hauling. We have more weapons than we know what to do with. We wanted you. Almost too good to be true, especially since someone handed us your ass on a plate."

"What?"

"Never mind, you don't need to know about that," Paine said. "Just sit tight. You want a glass of milk to help you sleep better?"

Matt didn't know a lot about militias, and almost nothing about Dark Fiber, but he'd never heard anything so crazy. He'd only joined March22 a few short weeks ago. He had certain skills, like his slingshot prowess, but that wasn't worth an operation like this. People had died back there. Who would've handed his ass to Dark Fiber on a frigging plate? That was such a bizarre notion, he didn't believe it for a minute.

"Big shot, most wanted March22 boy," Paine went on. "The wanted posters say you're a predator."

"That's bullshit!"

"Your own stepbrother? Is it really true you like fourteen-year-old boys?" Paine wrinkled his nose.

"Just shut up."

"I know another guy who likes them young, but he's in jail."

He gave up trying to reason with this militia idiot. Paine was obviously provoking him, trying to see how much abuse it took to make Matt Carney explode. He wasn't about to give him the satisfaction.

He gazed out the window, remembering how he'd been provoked worse than this. Much worse. Only three weeks ago he'd still lived under the thumb of his stepmother Wanda, who never strayed far from her Red Label bottle, and his stepbrother Robert and stepsister Marissa, both useless potheads. The three had never missed a chance to remind him he was on his *third* try as a junior in high school. Wet Wanda always taunted him, saying he wouldn't even get a job at the post office.

"You should treat Matt with more respect," his fourteen-year-old stepbrother, Benjy, had said at the table one night. It had been Matt's kill. After shooting it, Matt had gutted and skinned and butchered it himself. Benjy was his only voice of support in the house whenever John was gone, but being the youngest, and so straight, Benjy didn't get much respect himself. "We wouldn't have this delicious meat if it weren't for Matt."

"It's better than any of the meat we get from shadowmarkets," his father had added, taking another bite of the fresh venison slathered in gravy. The praise had filled him with pride. That had been shortly before his father's arrest.

In the middle of the night of November 1, the FBI had come with their drones and guns and three vehicles. They'd searched the house and dragged his father out in handcuffs. The next morning, Matt had gone to school just like normal, trying to pretend his father would be there when he arrived home in the afternoon. Two weeks had gone by with no word from John Carney. Matt's calls to the FBI had been met with stonewalling, until finally they blocked his number. As the days dragged on, and the others hassled him for every little thing, he'd felt more and more abandoned and alone. One day, after a fight with Robert, Wanda had demanded that Matt move into a small, unheated room in the basement. She had taken away his bedroom, his only refuge.

The secret message he'd found while cleaning out his belongings that night had filled him with hope once again. His father had dropped a computer chip in a can on his shelf, probably just before being arrested. In the short video, his father urged him to quit school, leave home, and get himself to California any way he could. He'd said Raine was in extreme danger. Something was about to happen at Stanford University. His father couldn't say what, or when. Matt simply had to get her out of there. He couldn't tell anyone about it, otherwise he'd be arrested and sent back. Suddenly filled with purpose, Matt had left Chicago the same night, saying good-bye forever to that nightmare of a home.

All that was before he'd learned that his father was one of the leaders and founders of March22. His father had in fact brilliantly staged his own arrest in order to throw everyone off the track, especially Wanda. He knew now that the main reason his father had given him that mission had been to get him started with March22.

Matt went on gazing out the window as Paine slept. It was unsettling flying just above the treetops, but the moonlight reflections had a hypnotizing effect. He'd been looking forward to sleeping with Raine tonight, back at the training camp in northwestern Montana, with the intoxicating smell of fresh pine penetrating even the bulletproof windows of the March22 safe house.

They'd been reunited so recently, it stung to be separated again. He'd pictured himself falling into bed after coming back from convoy duty, nestling against her warm body, waking her up or not waking her, whichever happened—that had been his only wish for tonight. He would've been content just to lie beside her soft, warm body, safe in the knowledge of her love. Closing his eyes and letting the vibrations of the plane relax his muscles, he lingered on an image of Raine's red tresses crazily spread across the pillow, and her sleeping face.

CHAPTER 2

"MR. PRESIDENT, THAT operation at the Golden Gate Bridge I briefed you on after you were sworn in..." began Secretary of Defense Reese.

President James Jeffers didn't have to search long in his mind. Of all the cockups and catastrophes he'd witnessed in the fifteen days he'd been president, this one alone brought that old coppery taste to his mouth. The taste he'd first gagged on during pitched battle many years ago, with men screaming and falling around him, their limbs blown off or their guts spilled out and burning.

The Golden Gate Bridge had been blown up, leaving only the two towers standing, just as an army convoy had been crossing into Marin County. More than two hundred soldiers had lost their lives. They'd perished in the initial explosions or when their vehicles hit the water, after plummeting 220 feet. What was worse, the cargo had gone to the bottom of the bay, where it sat for more than two weeks. Debris from the shattered bridge—mainly, torn cables lurking just below the surface that would tear a hole in a side of any ship—had made any passage through the waters impossible. It had taken two weeks of work clearing debris with special equipment before they could get correctly equipped salvaging teams into the area.

He looked at the two quadcopters floating near the ceiling. One went everywhere with Reese, while the other was a Secret Service device.

"Do we have to have those damned drones in here for this?" Jeffers stood and walked to the door as Reese deactivated the Department of Defense drone with his Jetlink. He signaled to the Secret Service agents outside the door.

"Listen, it's just Secretary Reese and me. Get that damned drone out of the room so we can hear ourselves think." The agent hesitated, looking at him with unblinking eyes. "That's an order, Sergeant."

Once the room was cleared, Reese went on with his report. The highly decorated general gulped like a kid admitting he'd stolen his dad's condoms.

"Last night, our ships were finally in place. Last night and all today, they searched the floor of the bay. Twenty divers. The cargo is gone."

Reese was one of the toughest soldiers Jeffers had ever worked with, and he had gone pasty white. Reese had authored books on guerilla warfare in megacities. His guiding principle, Jeffers knew, was that wars were won and lost because of psychological pressure, more than weapons advantages or even training. Jeffers felt the blood draining from his own face.

"You can't be serious."

"Jim, I wouldn't shit you. I've spent the last eighteen hours yelling at my people. They're the best in the world at what they do. With the best technology money can buy at their fingertips. If they can't find the bombs, they're not there."

"Didn't we have something guarding the bay?"

"We positioned a sub off the point within twenty-four hours of the incident," Reese said. "Nothing came in or out."

Jeffers himself had been secretary of defense until fifteen days ago, when President David Burns and the next five in the line of succession to the presidency had been assassinated simultaneously. He knew all about those bombs. He had supervised their development and their storage. Massive arguments about the secret project had rattled the walls from the beginning. Some had opposed building such weapons, concerned that they could fall into the wrong hands. Some had questioned why the United States would even produce such weapons. The naysayers generally had little idea how the world really worked. Very few people knew about the program, but those who did were a damned fractious bunch.

As secretary of defense, Jeffers hadn't been happy knowing such dangerous weaponry was stored near the San Andreas Fault, but under the Burns administration, the decision of moving the bombs had stayed mired in bureaucracy for years. Finally David Burns, God rest his soul, had broken the logjam. By a freak coincidence, the convoy had finally moved out on the day of the man's assassination. Jeffers had felt immense relief, up until he'd heard the news about the inferno that took out the landmark bridge. Then, he'd felt sheer panic as the entire convoy—trucks and jeeps and armored personnel carriers and their secret cargo—had gone to the bottom of San Francisco Bay. That same night, he had been sworn in as president. Now the problem of those bombs was coming back to haunt him.

"Who the hell got down there and how?"

Reese didn't look away. The man actually had tears in his eyes. "I just hope to hell it's someone we can work with."

The statement shocked Jeffers, but after a moment's reflection, he knew Reese was right. Someone now had a firm grip on their collective balls. One day soon, they were going to start squeezing.

He swallowed hard against that coppery taste. It was times like this you started considering prayer as a valid approach.

"Any contacts from anybody? Any footprints, any traces? Did they go out to sea? Did they come up on land?"

"Not a damn thing," Reese said.

"I need to reflect," Jeffers said. "Brief Dave Knopfler and Hal Holsom. Get Tom Underwood in the loop, but not the Vice President. We need Homeland Security to find those damned bombs. Otherwise, this one stays quiet. Keep me updated."

CHAPTER 3

NEAR RED LODGE, MONTANA
DECEMBER 1, 2021—2 AM

"EIGHT MEN DEAD," John Carney railed, on the secure chat. His father always railed, Luke thought. It was his chief mode of expression. Always some damned thing to rant about. "Senseless killings, and they weren't even interested in the load!"

"This operation had a horrendous cost," Sander McIntyre agreed. "They died by fire. We had to back the load up all the way to St. Regis and take Route 135 to Route 200, and from there on down. The country can be thankful the bombs are now safely stored."

"Safe as we can make it," Douglas Winter said.

"The country doesn't know a thing about their existence," Sander said. "But at last they're in a safe place. Wyoming, your work with that submersible and financial support have once again made all the difference."

"Damned shame about those losses," Wyoming Ryder said, ignoring the praise. "We can't take that lying down."

Luke knew the Hollywood star was so loaded he hadn't batted an eye at the price tag for the four-man sub and all its support equipment. Over the last eighteen months, he'd helped the man's lawyers and accountants make countless transactions and ownership records completely vanish. Wyoming Ryder was clean as a whistle. Bank networks were among the most secure on earth, but they'd managed it. Fortunately there were island countries in the Pacific not fully integrated into the global banking system. Learning by doing.

Luke imagined himself sitting on some beach, his toes digging into the sand pleasurably, palm fronds swaying in the breeze, the sun rising as wave after wave rolled in. And a beautiful, curvaceous female in a string bikini coming out of the water, dripping wet, smiling, maybe one part of her top slightly askew...

"Damn right," his father said.

"We have to find out who was behind it," Wyoming said.

"We will. And we'll show them what happens when March22 gets mad," his father said.

Luke felt his irritation flaring higher each time his father's rough voice cut in. Men *died* in violent conflict. All soldiers knew they might die; otherwise, they had no right calling themselves soldiers. If the *leaders* couldn't stomach casualties, they didn't deserve to be leaders.

This secure chat, Luke thought during the silence that followed, was as protected as he knew how to make it. He'd written a protocol with fourteen discrete protective features, like a castle with fourteen walls, so that no unauthorized person could hack in. And he'd coded another that deleted all traces as they went along, within five seconds of the spoken word. This darknet address was one of billions that would exist for the duration of the chat and then cease to be traceable, swallowed into a black hole of endless re-routings and looping false paths.

"What about Matt?" Sander asked.

"His body wasn't among the dead," Winter said.

"Thank God," his father said.

"He didn't come back with the rest, either," Winter went on.

"Matt is alive," Luke said through his voice synthesizer, speaking for the first time. "This was a Dark Fiber Militia operation. They've kidnapped Matt."

Suddenly everyone was speaking at once.

"Kidnapped?" his father exclaimed.

"Dark Fiber?" Winter said. "Is that who's behind this?"

"How do you know?" Wyoming said.

"Why would Dark Fiber kidnap Matt?" Sander echoed. Luke knew Sander sat in his farmhouse in Iowa.

"Matt told me they want to use him as a bargaining chip," Luke said.

"Bargaining for what?" Wyoming asked. He and Winter were here with Luke at Big Sky Base, although Luke sat in his own room. The only light came from his laptop screen. He liked his privacy. His round-the-clock aide, Corinne, was in the next room if he needed anything.

"They're sure as hell not bargaining with us," Winter growled.

"The word is the militias are projecting a Homeland Security crackdown," his father said. "Dark Fiber is the biggest militia by far. They think they can stave it off somehow by dangling Matt."

"What birdbrain came up with that idea?" Winter said.

"How much does Matt know?" asked Wyoming in a worried tone.

"Very little," his father said, inaccurately, as usual. His father would never overcome that hubris. Luke wondered if it would lead to his downfall, like Julius Caesar and Napoleon and so many other leaders throughout history.

"This is guesswork," Winter reminded the group. "We don't really know why they did it. How are they going to contact us?"

"I'll set something up and inform Matt," Luke said. "Who wants to be the designated hitter?"

"How are you communicating with Matt?" his father asked. "Didn't they take away his Jetlink?"

The renewed silence went on a few seconds. This was why Luke detested group chats. His father kept ignoring the wall between them, always probing, always trying. Sander jumped in. "Luke, tell us how you plan to get through to Matt."

Time to drop a different kind of bomb, Luke thought. Time the rest of them knew, including his father. "When Matt and I were reunited eight days ago, we discovered that we were blessed with a special communication link."

"What kind of link?" Wyoming asked.

"Telepathic," Luke said. "Something to do with us being identical twins, and being separated in early childhood."

"Are you shitting me? You have a telepathic link?" Wyoming said.

"That's impossible," his father said.

"How does it work, Luke?" Sander asked.

"How about you give us an example," Winter said.

"I just did," Luke said. "I told you what Matt discussed with his kidnappers in the last sixty minutes. Things Matt told me. He doesn't have his Jetlink. They told him they were Dark Fiber. I did some research on the man he's talking to, and it checks out."

"What name?" Sander asked.

"Guy named Thomas Paine, from Missoula," Luke said. "One of the three original founders of Dark Fiber."

"I've heard about him." Winter was himself a Montana native. "That one's got a few loose screws."

"Do we know where Matt is now?" Wyoming asked.

"In a twin-engine plane flying over eastern Montana at an altitude of three hundred feet," Luke said. "Paine and two other men on board with him, plus whoever's in the cockpit,"

"Jesus," his father said.

"I'm still trying to get my head around this," Wyoming said. "This isn't with Jetlinks? You can talk telepathically to him while he's on that plane?"

"Piece of cake," Luke said.

"It's simply extraordinary. I've never heard of such a thing. When did you boys discover this?" his father asked.

Luke kept silent. Firstly, he'd already answered that question. It should also be obvious the telepathic link couldn't have worked before they both knew of each other's existence. This got to the heart of his grudge.

When their mother had separated them as babies, the John Carney half of the family had ceased to exist for her. Through her occasional indiscretions, Luke at least had learned that he had a twin brother. And, more than just knowing, he had occasionally *experienced* him. Matt, on the other hand, since he had grown up with their idiot father who kept Luke's existence a secret, had never known a thing.

"I want to meet my brother," Luke had said one of those times, after his mother had mentioned something.

"Over my dead body," she'd retorted.

She was afraid of arrest. Luke was all his mother had, and if he contacted Matt, she feared their father would find out where they lived, then ride in and steal him away again, leaving her with nothing. A classic divorce battle over the kids, lasting seventeen years. The parents' relationship ended on a stalemate, one twin each. The kids were the losers.

At fifteen, he'd finally managed to get away from Belinda Carney, and started studying advanced math and physics at MIT. At the same time his mind started exploding with rapidly multiplying ideas and theories—he actually pictured it as a controlled nuclear reaction—so intensely that he would go for a week without even sleeping, and as he discovered with infinite excitement that he possessed an uncanny and ever-expanding ability to see through impossibly dense thickets of complexity, all the muscles in his body had started to freeze in place.

He'd been tempted to contact Matt many times in those years. But when you discover you have ALS motor neuron syndrome, and your body fails you to the point where you end up in a wheelchair, dependent on others for your bodily needs—for your survival—it wasn't as easy as picking up the phone. Within a year of his diagnosis, Luke had gone nowhere without an aide.

In those days he'd been too damned dependent to strike out on his own. Factor in the harm that would come to their mother... the potential consequences of that one call had been more difficult to predict than any coding challenge he'd ever faced. Owing to his father, Luke had been denied the pleasure of knowing his twin brother all the years of his childhood, even though he'd been aware that he had one. Even though they were the two halves of the same person.

"So they're keeping under the radar," Sander summarized. "Heading east. We'll just have to wait till they land to learn more."

"I have eyes on them," Luke said. Naturally he had a drone shadowing the plane from fifty thousand feet.

"Luke, enough of this ridiculous silence," his father spluttered. "Answer my questions. Do I need to remind you that we're fighting on the same side?"

Luke said nothing. His father should understand better than most why he was immune to begging.

"Maybe Matt's case of meningitis at the time of their early separation triggered the phenomenon," Sander said. "But how does it manifest?"

"I can send him thoughts. He answers with his thoughts," Luke said.

"Anytime?" his father asked.

"Can you do this anytime you wish?" Sander echoed after a few moments.

"It didn't work when I had a fever a few days ago," Luke said. "Otherwise it works pretty much whenever we both feel like it. He answered me as soon as he realized he'd been abducted."

"Identical twins often have some level of concordance, or even communication," his father said. "This sounds like a turbocharged version."

"All right. We'll talk about that again. For now, if you all agree," Sander went on, "we'll have Luke set up a way for Dark Fiber to contact me with their demands, whatever they may be. You'll tell Matt, Luke, so he lets them know?"

"Sure thing."

"Once you find out where he is, and what their security setup is, we can make a plan to go in and extract him," Winter said.

"Guns blazing," his father said.

"Would be interesting to know more about that special communication link," Wyoming said.

"I'm researching it," Luke said. "So far, no similar cases found."

"They'll try to debrief him for a day or two," his father said. "So we'll have to wait for them to contact us. Let's push on with other business."

"Agreed," Wyoming said. "Tomorrow I'm turning myself in. Wish me luck."

"Everything's ready," Winter said. "Just don't expect us to visit you in the slammer."

When the men laughed, Luke thought, it sounded like a bunch of old men laughing. The idea of the skirt-chasing movie star in a prison cell set them all off. Sander, Winter, and Wyoming, he could work with. His father's raucous braying reminded him of a donkey.

"I may be incommunicado for a while," Wyoming said. "Who can take over supporting Abba?"

J. Paul Abba was their drone base commander in Georgia. Luke knew what Wyoming meant. Unlike Winter, who had military experience and was in charge of Big Sky Base, Abba was a businessman. He was wealthy, and totally committed to March22, but he needed support in the area of security, especially now that they had shifted their backup command and control to his purview.

"Leave it to me," Sander said. "I've met him. I can coordinate anything he needs with Luke and the rest of you."

"Sounds good to me," said his father.

"I have another announcement," Sander said. "Matt had a brilliant idea when he spent the night with us in Iowa two weeks ago. When I told him we were making a new March22 drone for our big launch into the political arena, he suggested we stylize it as a bluebird. Matt has a thing about bluebirds. We needed a catchy meme. I decided to give it a try, and it came out truly eye-catching. Dan Creighton loves it. We went ahead and programmed it into the 3D printer profile. You'll all be receiving prototypes tomorrow."

"Has Creighton prepared everything so it's ready to go?" Winter asked.

"The House of Representatives will look like an aviary Friday afternoon," Sander smiled. "Keep it on your TV wall."

"I don't mean to stab Matt in the back," his father said, "but that bird meme is going to remind people of Twitter. Do we really want to go with a symbol that's associated with a defunct social media tool? Remember tweeting and all that?"

"I thought the lighthearted aspect made a good counterpoint to our serious aims," Sander said.

"Twitter was instrumental in bringing down repressive governments," Luke added. "Don't forget Egypt, Libya, Tunisia, or Turkey." He doubted anyone noticed that his brain had automatically generated the country names in alphabetical order. He also wondered if his father's objection to the drone design in fact had a more deep-seated basis. His father had made several comments lately casting doubt on the idea of March22 going legit.

"Luke is right," Winter said. "In fact, it's perfect."

"I just don't like it," his father said.

"Want to suggest an alternative, John?" Sander asked. "We've already delivered five hundred of them in Washington. It's late in the day."

"I'm feeling blindsided, here," his father said.

Always the renegade, Luke thought. It was one thing building up an organization and putting the elements in place. That work was done. They had everything they needed now. They had agreed it was now time to let March22 take its place in the halls of power, and help steer the country by embracing the normal political process, rather than fighting from outside. Leave it to his father to have second thoughts at the last minute.

"If you all agree, I suggest we start with the bluebird, since they're already produced," Sander said. "Because of the tight schedule. Creighton already has the birds. Wyoming's turning himself in. See what I mean? If we want to change the symbol in six months or a year, we're free to do that."

"Agree," Winter said.

"Second," Luke said.

"Luke's argument about toppling governments is convincing," Wyoming said.

"You're all nuts," his father said.

"I've got something to run by y'all, too," Winter said, jumping into the uncomfortable silence that followed. "You remember those two fellas I told you about, the ones whose hog farm was blown sky high when the drones first went up?"

"We've now secured the video," Luke finished Winter's thought.

"What video?" Sander asked. "I remember you telling us about this attack, but what's the video?"

"The military always videotapes drone strikes," Luke explained. "It took some hunting, but I found it on a Department of Defense server. Nobody knows about that strike. It's up to us to make it public."

"Good going, Luke," Sander said.

"Luke and I were thinking of sending those two hog farmer guys down to Bozeman," Winter said. "Mel and Phil Grady. They could do an interview on the ABC television affiliate. They're the victims here. The administration is lying to the American people about how they're using drones. With a TV interview and this video, we'll give human faces to the travesty."

"We have to choose the most opportune moment," his father said.

"Yes," Wyoming said. "Let's watch and see what happens. Let the media focus on me for a couple of days. Then stoke them all over again with your sensational video on TV — which I'm sure will be picked up nationally."

"Show the world what filthy liars they are," his father said.

"Did you all know Mel and Phil also happen to be the founders of the Prove Your Patriotism movement?" Winter said.

"Those hog farmers?" his father said.

"Of course," Sander said. "They were bacon merchants. Their farm got smoked."

Winter and Wyoming groaned at the pun.

"Their Facebook page has over a million likes, and counting," Winter said. "Everywhere you go, you get offered bacon treats."

"A million likes," his father marveled. "Can we co-opt it as a March22 page?"

"They *are* March22 now," Winter said. "We can do what we want."

"Luke, can you add a bluebird to the page?" Sander suggested.

"Let's talk about that in a week," his father said. "You guys are really jumping the gun with that silly bird."

"We'll wait with that, then," Sander conceded, needlessly. Luke added to his mental list the task of decking the Facebook page with bluebirds. When he was done, it would look like a Valentine's Day card festooned with hearts.

"I'm concerned about Dark Fiber kidnapping Matt," his father went on. "I wasn't reckoning with anything like that."

"We're all concerned," Sander said. "Luke, you'll keep us posted?"

"Sure thing," Luke said.

They all signed off. Luke checked to make sure the last traces of the conversation had vanished from their unique, well-concealed address. He then switched to another screen, which showed a nameless woman in a tank top in the wind, her dark hair partially hiding her pouting face.

CHAPTER 4

SIERRA NEVADA MOUNTAINS (NEAR TUNEMAH PARK) DECEMBER 1, 2021—7 AM

ROONE FRANZEN STOOD in the pristine blue stillness of the Sierra upland and surveyed the scene around him. Tunemah Peak rose in its eerie beauty to the south. The smooth, wind-rounded expanses of untouched snow reminded him of a sleeping woman's bare ass. That was a memory from his younger days, when he was still inclined to charm the local pretties.

Using drones in this pristine corner of America was a perversion of nature, but he had a job to do. The six quadcopters flew far ahead and up the mountain face. Equipped with metal detectors and thermal imaging, among other features, they would alert him to evidence too small or distant for the eye to catch.

At first, he'd had no stomach for the job. Literally, nothing in his stomach. He'd spent the last six weeks trading old mountaineering equipment for enough spuds to make one meal a day. No tourists booking snowshoe tours for the second year in a row. No planes flying. Too tough just getting to this remote section of the Sierra Nevada.

A man couldn't live on potatoes and a few bacon treats cadged upon entering stores. All the stores in town recognized him now, and sent him out hungry. This bacon-treat thing had started a couple of weeks ago, without anyone knowing what it was about. *Prove Your Patriotism,* they exhorted, as if anyone could think Roone Franzen wasn't a patriot. He just craved meat, and bacon was meat. It was bound to die down again soon anyway.

When the urgent message had come two weeks ago from his brother in Montana, he'd scattered the f-word around as noun, verb, adjective, and adverb in his flaming answer. That big shot March22 commander never had understood the realities of today's world.

That same night, Franzen had been offered a drink, something that hadn't happened in years. From a stranger. The dim barroom was filled with the sweet, companionable scent of all the doobies being shared around. Most folks had hair as gray as his, and all minded their own business. Everyone except the stranger. In this bar, not a single personal drone buzzed around and spied on folks, thanks to the sign on the door.

"Bring this man a beer," said the bearded stranger, a cap pulled low over his eyes. The man hardly looked thirty and he wasn't smoking. Franzen made no comment, being suspicious by nature, but also reluctant to venture out of his hard-earned zone of tranquility.

The beer arrived. He didn't touch it because even touching it would be an acknowledgment of the offering, and oblige him to listen. The younger man sat nursing his own beer for a few minutes, looking at him. Finally the man spoke again.

"I received a message from Winter," he said. "They need you to get your ass up to that GPS spot he gave you. There's no one else with your skills. No one else they trust. Oh, and this." The man reached in an inner pocket of his army coat and pulled out a thick sheaf of gray ration coupons. "It's ten thousand."

Franzen took the ration coupons without hesitation. You didn't turn down ration coupons. He wasn't that crazy. He hadn't had steak in months. A man had to eat. He was glad they had gone back to paper coupons, after the initial electronic ones distributed via Jetlink had proven vulnerable to forgery. He liked the feel of the thick bundle in his hand. People around the bar turned to look.

"Tell my brother..." Franzen hesitated, toying with various curse words. Ten thousand in ration coupons was a convincing statement. Ten thousand in ration coupons made a man agreeable to swallowing large piles of steaming shit. Where the hell had Winter gotten so many ration coupons? "Tell him I'm grateful. I'll be up there by daybreak."

The young man had gotten up instantly, leaving most of his own beer for Franzen to enjoy.

The next morning, Franzen had arrived at the GPS spot when it was still dark. He'd found what Winter wanted him to find, and covered it up. Two weeks had passed. Keeping it covered till the snow melted in June was included in the payment.

Franzen trudged ahead on his snowshoes, ignoring the jets of his own breath. He tried to think when he'd last seen his brother, who had gone by the name Winter since the assassinations in 2015. He'd asked him one time where the hell he got the idea of changing his name, and Douglas had said, "I read a good book, *Winter in the Blood*. Spoke to me." Douglas had always bossed his ass around. Now he was a cocky old coot. With a different name, he didn't feel so much like a brother. Who ever heard of taking a new name from a book at age fifty?

Franzen kept his eye on the myriad faces of Tunemah. The rising sun shimmered low in the morning sky, causing vapor to rise in swirling cyclones of snow dust that settled down as quick as they started.

Tunemah Lake lay six hundred yards ahead, hidden under twenty feet of powder. Stunted trees poked out of the snow where the layer was thinner, due to wind or slope.

Franzen searched for a flash of color, like a seat cushion, or the glint of metal in the sunlight. They were worried someone might find that wreckage. An airplane blown apart by a missile didn't hit the ground in one or two pieces, more like a few big ones and a thousand little ones. On detonation, all those fragments had rocketed downward at four hundred mph. They'd gone into the snow like bullets streaking out of the sky. With six feet of new snow during the last two weeks, nobody would find much till summer anyway. You might find pieces on both sides of a mountain like Tunemah, but so far this morning he hadn't found diddly.

Three hours later, Franzen stood on the ridge near the summit and spied what he was looking for. A thousand yards down the south side of the mountain a giant piece of silvery metal stuck out of the snow. Using his field glasses, he looked for pockmarks and disturbances in the smooth white surface, but found none. Damn thing hadn't stuck out like that three days ago. Wind currents off the mountain must have carved out a bowl around it.

Traversing down on his cross-country skis took less than ten minutes. He removed from his pack one of the paper-thin, white Mylar cloths he'd brought along. Unfolded, the cloth measured thirty-five feet square, plenty to cover the wing section.

He anchored the ends with special white plastic rods that had a butterfly attachment at the bottom. After sinking the rod three feet into the snow, he pressed a button. He couldn't see them, since they were three feet down, but that made four plastic flaps snap out like feathers on an arrow. They would swivel ninety degrees then lock in place, deep under the snow. The flaps down below would anchor the cover through all wind and storms. He tied white twine from the tops of the rods to plastic eyes along the edges of the Mylar cover.

When he was done, he trudged on snowshoes back up to the top of Tunemah Peak. Even his knowing eyes could not make out the covering job.

Franzen headed up the ridge, which was the shortest way to Blue Canyon. The plane had been streaking east when it was hit. He filled his lungs with the frozen crystalline air as he trudged forward. Why March22 didn't want the wreckage found was a mystery. Everything about Douglas Winter was a mystery.

In Blue Canyon, he found thirteen more pieces sticking out of the snow, big enough to warrant covering. He'd brought along different sizes of Mylar and a good supply of tie rods.

Franzen was just finishing when he heard the chopper. He couldn't see it, which meant it was still beyond the line of the mountain. Helicopters in this part of the world could mean only one thing. With a few strong lunges, he dug himself a shallow grave. He lay down and dragged the piles of snow over himself. The chopper was just coming over the ridge from Tunemah Peak when he pulled the last bit of snow over his facemask. He estimated the layer shielding him must be six inches thick. Their thermal imaging wouldn't detect his body heat.

He heard the chopper circling for two minutes. Must be just reconnaissance, not equipped with trekkers, otherwise they would have set down. Maybe they'd seen something, maybe they hadn't. Maybe they'd noticed the snow had been worked, contrasted with the pristine untouched snowfields all around. On the other hand, beneath them stretched a massive expanse of whiteness that hurt the eyes. They'd be taking photos and video of the site and relaying that back somewhere.

He'd done the best he could.

CHAPTER 5

NEAR RED LODGE, MONTANA
DECEMBER 1, 2021—7 AM

THE INSISTENT KNOCKING on his door startled Benjy Robson awake. He sat up, rubbing his eyes. "Come in!"

Raine burst in, panic written in her face. "Matt didn't come back last night. Someone said a lot of men got killed."

"What?" Like a panther, Benjy rolled out of bed. Quickly he pulled on the jeans he'd tossed on the floor last night. He felt her fear reaching for him like a contagion. Matt couldn't be dead, he just *couldn't*. Not after all they'd been through.

"They said eight men killed." Raine started crying as she moved closer. Dressed in his T-shirt and jeans, in bare feet, Benjy let her hug him tight. Even though Raine was five years older, same as Matt, Benjy was taller. He felt her shuddering in his arms.

"Raine, listen, they would've woken us up. They would've told you something. They wouldn't just let us sleep till morning if he'd died."

"You think so?" Raine drew back, searching his eyes through a mess of tears and snot. He reached to the night table for a tissue.

"Sure. Remember when that guy died last week during training? They came and woke up his buddy in the middle of the night."

There had been a midnight run for half the camp. More of an obstacle course, really. Most of the first half had been uphill, through the forest, in the total darkness, then along some cliffs, then scrabbling down the cliff at a point where you had to pick your way through boulders the size of kitchens and cars—glacial leavings—then around a lake and back through another forest. All in the pitch dark, with the light of the stars only filtering through the cloud cover sporadically. They aimed to train your night vision as well as your endurance.

Toward the end of the run, there had been another drop-off. That was where Chad had taken a curve too close. Benjy had been running ten steps behind the guy. He'd actually seen it happen, though the camp commander had also reviewed video from one of the Vipers that accompanied them. They'd all been clumsy with fatigue by then.

Chad's right foot had come down on something unstable, a stone, or maybe the crumbly edge itself. His feet had gone out from under him. He'd slipped over the edge with a frightened yelp, like a dog being beaten. Benjy would never forget that last sound Chad made.

Then everyone was shouting and staring over the edge, clamoring for a response from Chad. Two or three participants had shined bright lights down. The guy had lain there without moving. He'd fallen at least fifty feet, and at the bottom was another gigantic rock pile. Even if Chad hadn't fallen directly on his head, he must've banged it on those unforgiving granite surfaces. He couldn't have suffered long—at least that.

"When Chad died last week," Benjy went on, "the first thing they did was wake up that guy he came with from Texas, Mike, remember? Just out of consideration. They would've done the same with you. Both of us, in fact. We would've heard from John."

"I guess so," Raine said, still sniffing. "But Matt's not back."

"Who told you? Who did you talk to?"

"I don't know his name. It was downstairs, in the entry. One of the junior leaders. He was going out. He said I had to talk to Wyoming or Winter."

"Let's go find one of them," Benjy said.

Downstairs in the entry, one of the other March22 soldiers informed them that Winter was arriving from Big Sky Base in twenty minutes and they should wait in the kitchen.

"What is it? What happened?" Raine pleaded, but the soldier dashed out without answering, accompanied by a Viper over his head. "Why won't they say anything? Everyone knows but me."

"Come on." Benjy took her arm and they went in the kitchen.

Raine busied herself making hot chocolate for him and coffee for herself.

"We've had such a beautiful time the last ten days." Raine's green eyes went dreamy as they sat at the table. It was easy to see why Matt was in love with her. "It's really hard work, this training. I never knew places like this camp even existed. At least we were together during the night. Most nights, anyway, when he wasn't out on one of those midnight runs."

"You were separated what, four months?" Benjy knew exactly how long it had been, having heard it from Matt about two hundred times. But talking seemed to calm Raine.

"God, when I left for Stanford that was about the hardest thing I've ever done. Saying good-bye to Matt. He didn't even come to see me off, because we both knew I wouldn't go if he were the one to put me on the bus. We said good-bye the night before."

"I remember that," Benjy said. "Although I didn't see much of either of you that night. How many buses were in your convoy?"

"Like thirty, I think they said. And about twenty security guards in six or seven other vehicles, all heavily armed."

"Those convoys are something else," Benjy agreed.

Ever since airplanes had been grounded more than two years ago, due to the coordinated attacks with shoulder-fired missiles all around the country, the safest way to get across the country was in a bus convoy with armed protection. The convoys made it through the checkpoints with no hassle, since everyone was scrutinized and documented before departure. Any militias intent on kidnapping people or stealing valuables were guaranteed heavy casualties. These days, bad things happened on the highways.

Benjy had seen a big rig shoot a missile right out of one of its trailers, blowing up a patrol helicopter in midair. As the helicopter had plummeted in flaming pieces that slammed into the highway, the companion chopper had retaliated with two missiles. One missile had exploded in the rear trailer of the big rig while the other had turned the cab into a ball of fire. The twin explosions had catapulted four or five other cars twenty feet in the air as they tried to speed past, killing their occupants as well.

He and Matt had witnessed that on the highway leaving Chicago on the first night of their trip, barely escaping the inferno themselves.

"I still can't believe you guys made it across the country the way you did," Raine went on.

Benjy opened his mouth to speak, but decided to keep silent. They sat at the table huddled over their mugs, waiting for Winter's arrival. How could he begin to tell her about the nonstop series of attacks and ambushes and explosions they had somehow survived? An obstacle course more dangerous than any March22 training. The whole purpose of it had been to get to California and save her. If Raine knew the true extent of what they'd gone through, he imagined her going catatonic.

"I thought I knew Matt inside and out before the separation," Raine went on. "But everything I've heard about your trip to California, and the last ten days together, have shown me there's another whole side of Matt that I didn't know before."

Benjy gulped. "I don't know what he's told you... all the details, but an experience like that would probably change anyone."

"He said his father told him in a secret message that he had to get to California as quick as possible and get me out of there."

"That's right."

"That was before anyone knew John was one of the leaders of March22."

"And one of the founders."

"Matt is so incredibly proud of him."

"He's a great man," Benjy agreed. "I hope we can achieve at least some of his goals."

At that moment, Winter strode into the kitchen, followed by a small Viper that rose to the ceiling and hovered in place. Without removing his leather jacket, Winter came to the table, turned a chair around, and sat facing both of them.

"I believe we've met once. Name's Douglas Winter," he said, extending his hand first to Raine, then Benjy. His eyes were pale blue, and he wore his white hair down to his shoulders. Everyone said he was younger than the hair made him seem.

"What's happened to Matt? They said you could tell me," Raine said. She had that panicked look again.

Winter met her eyes. "Matt's been kidnapped. A militia called Dark Fiber ambushed our convoy last night. Should never have happened, the way we swept the road before coming through. They're nimble bastards."

"Kidnapped?" Benjy exclaimed.

"We don't know exactly why," Winter said. "Too early to tell. They killed eight of our men and took Matt. They put him on a plane and headed east."

"But why? Who are these people?" Raine pleaded. "Why Matt?"

"Largest militia in the country," Benjy said. "Mainly the alcohol shadowmarkets." Winter smiled confirmation. "I know my militias," Benjy said, feeling the color go to his face. When would he learn to keep his big mouth shut?

"No, you're absolutely well informed. How old did you say you were?"

"Fourteen."

Winter shook his head in disbelief. "Anyway, they didn't touch our cargo. They killed without mercy, taking out all the men around Matt. They really did it just to snatch Matt. *Why* we don't know yet. We have to wait for their contact now."

"But he's safe?" Raine asked.

"We know he's safe, at least for the moment," Winter said. "Going to all that trouble and showing such *fierceness* makes me think if they wanted him dead, he'd be dead already. If that's any comfort."

"What in the world did they kidnap him for?" Benjy said.

"How about you do a little more of that research you've obviously been up to," Winter said. He rose from his chair. "Seems like you've got a knack for that. And you, pretty lady, just be brave. I'll keep you posted, or else Luke will."

Benjy watched him exit and realized Winter was actually a very small man, with narrow shoulders and hips. He figured he was probably an inch taller than Winter. Maybe that was why the commander always kept that big leather coat on.

CHAPTER 6

NEAR ANN ARBOR, MICHIGAN
DECEMBER 1, 2021—9 AM

OUT OF HABIT, Matt found himself checking and rechecking his wrist, but of course they'd taken away his Jetlink. He'd noticed it was gone when they put him on the plane. He had no way of telling the time, and no way of communicating with Raine or anyone else. Except, of course, Luke.

Sometime long in the early hours of the morning the plane had landed, after which other Dark Fiber people in two pickup trucks picked them up. They'd kept Matt's hands bound, but allowed him to see. Driving down a two-lane road in the darkness, they'd passed a sign advertising Michigan blueberries, then another announcing Ann Arbor city limits.

The only reason he knew anything about Ann Arbor, Michigan was because Raine once talked about the possibility of going to a university here. Instead, she'd ended up in California at Stanford. Practically the end of the world in today's United States, as he had discovered so arduously.

He wished he could call her now, let her know he was fine. He hated to think of her reaction when she found out he'd been kidnapped. Who even knew what garbage Luke would feed her?

The pickups pulled to a stop at a big two-story cabin in the middle of a very dark forest. In one night he'd gone from a forest in Montana to another in Michigan. As they got out, the men formed a perimeter around the vehicles. They aimed their guns at unseen threats.

"This way," Paine said.

"Why did you say someone handed you my ass on a plate?" Matt asked. "What does that mean?"

"No questions, Carney."

Matt jerked away from the hand on his arm, but followed Paine's tacky Hawaiian shirt. What choice did he have, with all these guns on him? The other men fell in behind as they walked through a doorway into a kitchen. Dirty dishes covered the counters, pizza boxes with half-eaten pizza on the floor, and the place reeked of rancid oil and spilled beer. He followed Paine down a narrow stairway.

The basement had a concrete floor and thick wooden posts supporting the ceiling. Couches and armchairs formed a circle at one end. Five men and one woman watched as the group filed in. He saw holstered guns everywhere he looked, and all eyes on him.

"So here he is," Paine said. "You sit here, Carney."

Matt lowered himself into a straight chair, bound hands in his lap. The men on the couches looked young, some with fluff and scruff in place of real beards. The lone woman had short brown hair and brown eyes that fixed him in an intense gaze. Her leather pants, black turtleneck and combat boots made her look like some kind of revolutionary. She lifted the hem of her sweater to reveal a pistol on her hip.

"You killed eight of our men just to fly me across the country to this rat's nest," Matt said. "What the fuck?"

"You're going to be our guest," one of the men on the couch said. He had dark red jeans with a gray hooded sweatshirt. "You're insurance."

"Like hell I am," Matt said. "You think March22 is just going to roll over and take it?"

"They won't have a clue where to find you," red jeans said.

"You underestimate March22. Really, you're just wasting everybody's time. They'll have me out of here within a day, and I'm sure they'll take their revenge for the loss of life."

"We'll take our chances with March22," red jeans said. He turned to Paine. "You guys have a good trip?"

"We survived," Paine said.

Matt felt his anger rising. "You expect me to just sit around here doing nothing? What's your timeline, anyway? Not that it's relevant."

"There's a TV wall down here, there's food, drinks. You can work out. You can read books. You just can't leave this basement," red jeans said.

All at once, Matt saw flashing red signals on the Jetlinks of every person in the room.

"Shit, we've got company," red jeans said.

"Take your men upstairs and prepare to defend," Paine said. "We'll back you up. Claire, you stay down here with Carney. You're the last barrier."

"Got it," the woman said.

All the men jogged across the room and ran up the stairs. Matt heard the door at the top of the stairs slam, then a bolt being thrown. Great, so they were locked in down here.

He and the woman were both standing.

"What's happening here?"

"It's a rival militia." She opened a switchblade. With one swipe, she cut the plastic bracelet, freeing his hands.

"How do you know it's not March22 coming to rescue me?"

"You're actually more of a jackass than anyone thought, aren't you?"

"You didn't answer my question."

"Because we know their cars, stupid. We know their faces." She held up her Jetlink and showed him an image of several cars coming to a stop outside the cabin, men with assault rifles jumping out. Dark Fiber must've had early warning drones positioned up the road.

At that moment, the shooting started. Even with the door closed at the top of the stairs, the noise was deafening. After a few seconds, the smell of cordite tickled his nostrils. The woman stood by the couch, studying her Jetlink.

Something banged at the top of the stairs, startling Matt. It sounded like somebody's body being thrown against the door.

"I don't like this," the woman said. "We're tougher, but there's a lot of them."

"Feels like a death trap to me," he said.

"Follow me," the woman said.

Matt didn't need to be asked twice. "What did you say your name was?"

"Claire." He followed her into a room with a washer and dryer, and ducked under clotheslines. Claire slammed the heavy wooden door, turned a key in the lock, and left the key there. Through a transom, he saw the first hint of gray in the eastern sky. The sounds of automatic rifle fire from upstairs continued unabated.

"Maybe you could fit through that window, but not me," he said.

Claire stood by a tall metal cabinet, fitting a key. She was a head shorter, and couldn't weigh more than a hundred pounds, tops. After opening the cabinet to reveal an impressive collection of weapons, she handed him a 9mm Beretta and two extra clips. He checked to see if there was a bullet in the chamber. Claire relocked the cabinet, and went around to where it stood against the wall.

"Help me," she said. She gripped the back of the cabinet in the narrow space between it and the wall. Matt crouched down low and took hold with both hands. "On three," Claire said.

With all those weapons and ammo he'd expected serious weight, and in fact on the first try the cabinet didn't budge. Persistent banging came from the door at the top of the stairs, plainly audible through the thick laundry room door.

"Again," Claire said.

This time Matt planted both feet against the wall and used his whole body. With a noisy scraping, they managed to move the cabinet out three inches. His forehead covered in sweat, he set up for another pull. Working together, they managed six inches more. He had his doubts about how much Claire was contributing, here. With his back against the opposite wall, Matt could now work with his thighs, giving the cabinet one last shove with his feet.

"What the hell's in this thing?" he panted.

"Concrete lined. Fireproof, obviously."

Claire used another key to open a small metal door in the wall behind the cabinet. Matt had to stoop to get in. She activated the light on her Jetlink, illuminating a crude tunnel barely big enough for a person. Thick lengths of wood supported a tin roof. While Claire locked and barred the door behind them, Matt inched ahead. His boots made no sound on the packed clay floor.

"Where does this lead to?"

"Just walk."

It didn't go far, maybe forty feet, and straight as a bullet's path. They reached a metal ladder bolted to the far wall.

"Me first," Claire said. When she put out the light, he suddenly felt like he was in a tomb. His eyes picked up nothing.

Matt heard Claire's cautious steps going up, leather soles on steel rungs. "Be perfectly quiet," she said.

He heard her fiddling with a latch. The tunnel entrance would be in some hidden place in the yard or the surrounding forest. She seemed so sure the attackers were another militia group. But what if this was March22 coming to rescue him? She'd rejected that possibility out of hand. It did seem a bit too quick, but then these people had no idea about March22. Maybe Luke had whipped up a swift response team that had followed them from the plane to this cabin.

Matt now made out light from above, the graying sky, and he saw Claire's shape at the top of the ladder. He started climbing and kept an eye on the opening about ten feet above.

As he reached the top, he smelled the rotting leaves and wet branches before he saw them. It smelled just like home, near Chicago, where he always hunted. Standing next to the hole, ten feet inside the edge of a forest, he watched Claire silently replace the trapdoor. She took care to spread sticks and leaves over it. Across the yard, through the first line of trees, the cabin stood silhouetted against the star-filled sky.

Claire tugged on his hand. "Come on. We've got to get away."

Two men were exiting the house at the front, walking away, followed by a pair of red Vipers. Matt didn't recognize them. Of course, he wouldn't know the faces of any local March22 men.

"Do you want to die, or are you just stupid?" Claire insisted, yanking on his hand. The men were jogging toward the cars.

Matt stared at her, his heart filling with rage. He'd had just about enough of this small, flat-chested, cheeky woman, who first called him a jackass and now stupid. Nothing pissed him off more than being called stupid. What if those *were* March22 men?

A colossal explosion filled the sky with fire. He was thrown to the ground as a giant fireball rose over the cabin. The heat wave slammed into them, lying in the leaves. He felt his eyebrows scorching, even with the cover of the trees. They would be lucky if they didn't catch fire themselves.

"They blew it up. That's their hallmark. They blow everything up. You'd be dead if it weren't for me, so are you satisfied?" Claire said. He hardly heard her over the roar of the fire. "Would you please move your ass? I've got a motorcycle parked this way."

They trotted through the forest as the eastern sky gradually went to iron gray. The cabin burning behind them blurred in the distance through the trees, until finally he saw it no more. He'd been in a house that was burning to the ground. No fire trucks would get to this isolated spot in time to save it. Even in that locked laundry room, they would've quickly died of asphyxiation. Claire knew the people around here. She knew their ways. She might be his best bet at the moment, after all.

After jogging twenty minutes, they came to a small gravel parking lot in the middle of the forest, where three cars and a motorcycle were parked.

"Get on," Claire said.

"Pretty big bike for a woman your size."

"Just shut up and get on."

He did what he was told.

CHAPTER 7

NEAR ANN ARBOR, MICHIGAN
DECEMBER 1, 2021—8 AM

MATT HAD RIDDEN a motorcycle many times, but this was his first experience as a passenger. His back rested against a leather seatback, his boots pressed against footrests, while with his hands he gripped a thick chrome bar under his thighs. He wasn't about to put his arms around this bitch.

The wind whipped in his face as Claire passed car after car on the two-lane highway headed into Ann Arbor. Off to the east, the sun hung just above the horizon, cutting first rays of warmth through the thin mist over the fields. The temperature had to be well above freezing, but still he wondered if the pavement might be too slick for such acrobatics. Maybe Claire's gonzo riding style helped her forget her slight stature.

She slowed when they entered the city, doing just under fifty as they passed shuttered storefronts and dingy apartment buildings. He tried to get a feeling for the geography, in case he had a chance to take off on his own. Without his Jetlink, he would be handicapped. At least he had a gun, and they hadn't bothered to take away his slingshot.

"No need to prove yourself on the bike," he shouted. "You already saved my life. Be a shame to lose it like this."

"Do me a favor. Zip it!" Claire shouted back.

"Where are we going?"

She slowed way down as they rounded another corner. Two blocks ahead, fire trucks and police cars with lights flashing crowded the street. Flames leapt from the windows of a building in the middle of the block. Emergency workers hauled hoses and shouted orders as a group of onlookers pressed against a barrier.

"Shit," Claire said.

"Take a parallel street."

Claire stopped, engine idling. Her gaze never left the burning building.

"Those assholes torched my house," she said.

"You live there?"

"I did until now."

"Who did this?"

"Black Widow. Same ones who attacked us at the cabin. They burn everything down."

"Who's Black Widow? Some other militia?"

Claire nodded. "We control the alcohol business. They're trying to intimidate us. They have the meat, what more do they want?"

When he started to climb off, Claire instantly clicked the bike into gear and swung around. She headed back the other way at full throttle. Matt was nearly thrown to the pavement.

"Would you mind telling me what you have in mind?"

"We have a safe house not far. I'm taking you there. I'll get with my people and regroup."

"Where is this safe house?"

Claire didn't bother answering as she ran a red light, still accelerating. No one was coming from either direction anyway.

It would be suicide to jump off at this speed. Maybe Luke could spot this safe house if Matt gave him indications from the highway signs. After another mile, he spotted a small white sign indicating Route 23.

They drove ten minutes, headed south out of town, and ended up at a farm out in the cornfields. The main house was set back from the road at least five hundred feet, with a long driveway that wound through a stand of trees. A big red barn and some other outbuildings sat to the west of the house. In the glare of the early sun, Matt saw a mist-covered pond, and two men fishing out of a rowboat. At this hour of the morning, the fish might be biting.

"What is this place?" Matt asked.

"A safe house, I told you. Follow me." Claire walked up the steps onto the wide porch, but before she could ring the bell, the door opened. A woman with gray hair and a deeply lined face stood in the door.

"Claire, so nice to see you."

"Hi, Gram. This is Matt Carney. We need to get inside."

"Of course you do. Hello, Matt, welcome." The woman extended her hand as they walked inside. She had a strong grip. She gave no indication of whether or not she recognized his name.

"You don't look old enough to be Claire's grandmother," he said as she closed the door.

"I'm not anyone's grandmother," the woman said. "Never had any kids of my own. Everyone just calls me Gram, and you can too. Anybody hungry?"

Fifteen minutes later they sat at the table with pancakes, bacon, and coffee while Gram did something in another room. Matt ate hungrily, his last food having come before convoy duty, late yesterday afternoon. He had to let Luke know where this place was. Maybe they could give him a signal to get out, and then blow the place off the map with a Hellfire missile.

"You're on the most wanted list, you know," Claire said. "Your picture's hanging on a cash register in every store across the country."

"Whatever they say, I didn't do it," he said. This was quickly becoming his standard answer.

Claire's intense brown eyes studied him over her coffee mug. They were a deep, rich shade of brown, but her staring made him uncomfortable. She had a small, pointy nose with a sprinkle of freckles, and thin lips that curved into a permanent frown. "I don't know how this is going to play out exactly, but I do know one thing. It wouldn't help either of us if the cops picked you up."

"I'll tell you how it's going to play out," Matt said. "You killed eight of our men back in Montana. March22 will fight fire with fire."

"We probably lost that many this morning, too," Claire said.

"That's not our problem."

"Okay, so March22 is mad at Dark Fiber, I get that."

"And they're going to come and extract me, sure as this is shitty coffee."

"What are they, some kind of mind readers?"

Matt smiled. If the woman only knew. "I don't know about that, but I would say you've underestimated us. There's no point in getting too chummy. As soon as they get here, I'll be working against you."

"Well, I'm just saying, I decided the best strategy was to trust you with that gun and untie your hands. Until your superhero friends actually show up, the best way to demonstrate your intelligence would be to keep out of sight of the law. That's how I'm in a position to help you."

"Paine told me Dark Fiber wants to trade me for something. Is that just because I'm on that stupid most wanted list?"

Claire stirred more sugar into her coffee. "They heard the government is talking about wiping out the militias. The leaders thought the Matt Carney operation was a good idea."

"But not you."

"I'm the leader in this small city in Michigan, not a national leader. I have to support their decisions whether I agree or not."

"Why did they bring me here, to your neck of the woods?"

"The big cities are too hot, too much interdiction. Too hard to keep you safe."

"And keep me locked up."

"Maybe that, too, I don't know. I wasn't in on the rationale. I only found out two days ago that they were planning something. I didn't know it was you till first thing this morning. I was told to get a few things ready."

"Like that house in the woods?"

She nodded. "That was one of our safe houses."

"Not exactly safe when your enemies can firebomb it."

"Nothing's safe when they go to those lengths. Those people are pyros. They just love to see shit burning."

"How did they find out we were there?"

Claire shrugged. "Most likely someone traded information for ration coupons."

"You don't have much discipline in your group if that's happening."

She fixed him again with her eyes. "People are hungry."

He knew it was true. The whole country was reduced to scrounging and bartering. A few days ago, Benjy had received a shocking video from a school friend in Chicago. The friend had secretly filmed Benjy's mother—a very unwashed-looking Wet Wanda—on the street somewhere trading an old junky lamp for a bag of potatoes. After completing the deal, she was attacked by two other boys, both a head shorter. While they tried to jerk the potatoes away, Wanda pulled a knife with her other hand and cut the nearest boy in the face.

He'd been stunned to see the level to which his stepmother was reduced.

"So what's next?" Matt asked.

"I'll get an update from my people, see who our casualties were. Maybe we'll have a meeting tonight. Maybe we'll keep you here, maybe we'll move you."

"I need my Jetlink."

"You think I'm stupid?"

"You have it?"

"Of course. Thomas gave it to me when you arrived. I'll give it to you at the appropriate time."

"You give me a gun but not my Jetlink."

"Matt, after what happened, I might need your help in a fight," Claire said. At first he thought he hadn't understood properly. Like he was going to shoot people who attacked his kidnappers. She certainly wasn't very logical. Not wanting to lose the gun, he kept the thought to himself.

"Well, I want it. Now is the appropriate time."

He stood up quickly, but she had her gun leveled. "I won't shoot to kill, but I have orders to shoot," Claire said when he hesitated. "You'd look dorky with your shoulder in a sling for the next two months, and no good to March22 or anybody. I'm an expert marksman."

Matt took his seat again, a wry smile forming. Claire sure was a tough bitch. Guns, fast bikes, red lights... anything to boost her self-image. All he really wanted his Jetlink for was to let Raine know he was all right. If he wanted to communicate with March22, he could do it through Luke.

"Pretty please?"

"Matt, you saw what happened this morning. The danger is real. Work with me a little. Trust me."

"You just said your plan was to hand me over to Homeland Security. Why would I even think about trusting you?"

"That's not happening any time soon. That was just someone else's vague concept. Trust me for today, maybe tomorrow. I'll do my part for you."

"You mean you'll help me escape if Dark Fiber decides to turn me in?"

She blushed. "I didn't say that. You can see how the situation is in flux. Thomas might be dead, I don't know. The other leaders need time to figure out what's next. I have to get an update. I'm only a local leader, but I'm in charge of you right now. I'll have some say. I'm just trying to convince you that if you walked out of here on your own, you'd be picked up within two hours. Everyone out there, and I mean *everyone*, is your enemy. You're safer sticking with me."

His stomach full of pancakes and coffee, Matt felt his eyelids drooping, and left the table. He hadn't slept much on that plane. The guest room Gram had assigned to him had a sagging double bed, an old wooden night table, and a mirror on the wall next to the door. Dark circles had formed under his eyes. Claire thought he was safer here, but what did she know? He needed to get back to Raine. He gazed out the window as Gram drove away in her white Impala. Claire would stay here to keep watch over him, but at some point she had to sleep as well.

Conscious of every creak in the floor out in the kitchen, he slept fitfully the rest of the morning and into the afternoon. When he woke—or half woke, still in that place somewhere between sleep and wakefulness, only dimly aware of the sun shining in through the curtains—he heard a familiar voice in his head.

Hey moron, Luke said.

When are you guys going to come and get me?

When the time is—. Luke's voice faded out again. Somehow they had to fix that problem.

When the time is right? What the hell does that mean?

What progress have you made on your mission?

What mission?

Infiltrate Dark Fiber. Find out more about how they work.

I didn't know anything about that. What kind of a crazy idea is that?

All right, that's your mission.

You know I can't do that. I want to get back to Montana.

No dice. You're staying put.

Forget about it. I don't know how to do anything like that.

That's an order, soldier.

Who decided this? You?

The gang of five, Luke said. *Your idiot of a father, Sander, Wyoming, before he left, Winter, and me.*

Tell them I'm not doing it. By the way, he's your father, too.

Don't remind me.

Matt didn't get what Luke meant, but he decided to let it go for now. Luke seemed to have a strong tendency to put down their dad. *Anyway, you can forget about me finding out anything about this stupid militia.*

Matt, use your brain for once. We have an opportunity here.

Shut up about my brain. Everyone was always dissing him for his lack of intelligence. Even if it was true, people had no right to go there.

Eight of our men were killed. We want to send them a fitting answer when the time comes. Don't you want to be part of that?

He had detested Malone, the idiot who couldn't keep his mouth shut on the convoy, but the man hadn't deserved to die. Four March22 men had perished when their vehicle hit an IED on the highway, and snipers had picked off four others. Cowardly killings, all for the purpose of kidnapping him. Sure, that had to be avenged. He owed it to the dead men, even Malone. He did want to be part of it. March22 ought to wipe this militia off the face of the earth. Plus, it was what his father expected.

But I don't even know where to start.

I've been researching them. In a few hours, I'll have some information that might be useful. In the meantime, play friendly. Do what they say.

What about Raine?

Little boy miss his — ?

Come on, butthead, does she know I'm safe?

I've been giving her the occasional update. I think I saw her kissing one of the other — .

Stop being an idiot, Matt said after waiting some moments for the rest of the sentence. Luke had no idea of what had happened at Stanford. The truth was Matt had been forced to rescue his girlfriend from more than one kind of danger.

What about that babe you're with there?

She's not a babe, and I'm taken. Get that through your hyperactive head.

I guess I'm more of a grab-the-opportunity kind of — .

Wide awake now, Matt realized he was ravenous. In a flash, he fell out of the relaxed state, distracted by powerful hunger pangs, and the conversation was cut off.

In the shower, he started regretting what he'd said to Luke. He'd half-promised to try and carry out their mission, but the more he thought about it, the more convinced he was they were crazy to depend on him. He wasn't trained for this sort of work. Spy work.

If they weren't going to extract him, he'd have to try and escape on his own, work his way back across the country. Back to Raine. He'd done that kind of trip once before now. He could hitchhike, or steal a car and take the back roads. In two or three days, he'd be back in Montana again.

When he returned to the kitchen, Claire was sitting at the table with a cup of tea. She gazed at him with unblinking eyes.

"Wait a minute, I've got something I can heat up for you," she said.

He ate the macaroni and cheese without speaking, feeling her eyes upon him. *In the meantime, make friendly,* Luke had said. How the hell was he supposed to do that with this irritating woman? Claire only spoke again once he'd finished.

"So we've got your basic needs taken care of. Sleeping, eating. This is a nice place, isn't it?"

"Thanks for lunch," he said. "Listen, when they come for me, I don't want you to get hurt. You've taken care of me, and I'd hate to see you get shot or something."

"I can take care of myself."

"I'm just saying. They won't care who gets hurt."

Claire leaned forward over her mug. "Matt, you have real problems with reality and fantasy, don't you? March22 isn't coming."

For a second, he had the crazy idea that Claire might've somehow managed to listen in to his chat with Luke. Which was impossible. She'd simply convinced herself this farmhouse was off the grid.

"How did Black Widow find out about that cabin, if we're so safe here?"

Claire shrugged. "No place is absolutely safe. We have a lot of places, a lot of people. Some jerk must've ratted us out. Hopefully he was one of those killed."

"So, we're just going to sit around here for weeks and weeks?"

"The leaders of Dark Fiber are considering the options. Things don't always happen overnight. We have to wait for their instructions."

"I'm just supposed to sit around watching TV for weeks on end?"

She smiled. "Why don't you just relax? What's it like being part of March22?"

"You think I'm going to tell you about that?"

"God, I'm just making conversation. You don't talk much. Are you always such a bundle of nerves?"

It was the first time anyone had ever called him a bundle of nerves. He certainly wasn't going to get any information out of this woman if they were both so tense. He took a deep breath and started over.

"A few weeks ago I was sitting in my high school class staring out the window at explosions in the distance, wondering what the hell I was doing there."

"Really? You look older."

"Nineteen."

Claire gave him a funny look, wrinkling her nose. Matt knew that look very well. People reacted this way when they learned he was still in high school at nineteen, but didn't dare ask for details.

"I'm twenty, sophomore in college. University of Michigan at Ann Arbor."

"So you're in college but you're also the leader of Dark Fiber here?"

Claire nodded. "Good at time management. Plus I'm not very interested in school right now."

"I guess we have that in common."

"Not with all this shit going on around us."

"How did you become the leader?"

"You mean because I'm a woman?"

He shrugged. "More because of your age, I guess."

"Partly through attrition. We've lost a few members in the last twelve months. I acted like the leader when there was a crisis, and became the leader. It's not a big deal. I don't just decide everything by myself."

"So is Dark Fiber pretty big, or just, like, big in Michigan?"

"Our operation to kidnap you took place in Montana, so you know it's not just Michigan. As far as I know, Dark Fiber is active in forty states, with about five hundred local chapters."

"Five *hundred* chapters?"

"Surprised?"

"I don't know much about militias, that's all. You train with weapons and all that?"

"Sure."

"How many in each chapter?" Maybe Luke wanted this kind of information. Maybe he could find out a few nuggets after all before hitting the road.

"Small ones might have only twenty members, but big ones would number in the hundreds. Detroit, for example, has about five hundred trained members."

"That's a lot of personnel."

"A lot of mouths to feed," Claire agreed.

Claire suddenly went quiet, and they didn't talk anymore. Matt had no idea what had set her off. Maybe she had a friend she missed in Detroit. Maybe she was thinking about the guys who got killed this morning. When she left the room, he went to the sink and washed his own dish.

CHAPTER 8

ANN ARBOR, MICHIGAN
DECEMBER 1, 2021—3 PM

"THINGS WENT SOUTH over here," Thomas Paine said on the secure link. He sat in his car in a Denny's parking lot. A lone, armed guard with an AR-15 assault rifle and a Viper hovering six feet above him stood outside the restaurant entrance, watching him.

"Report," Pluess said.

"We brought Carney to a safe house to hand him over to the local chapter. Claire Tenneman's the leader here."

"I remember."

"Black Widow chose this morning to make a move in Ann Arbor. Today of all days, before sunrise. They attacked the safe house where we were meeting, less than a half hour after we got there. We fought them off, but they firebombed it."

"Did they know about Carney?"

"No indication of that," Paine said. "Just shitty luck."

"How bad?"

"I'm the only one who got out alive."

"What?" It took a lot to get a reaction out of Cedric Pluess. Paine still had soot on his face from this morning. When he looked beyond the Jetlink at his hand, he realized he was still trembling.

"Seven of ours dead, including Claire. Carney is dead."

"Goddammit," Pluess said.

"They blew up the damned cabin," Paine said. "I was only spared because at that moment I was chasing one of their men in the forest behind the property. After I took care of him, I turned to go back, and the cabin blew up in my face."

"You're sure Carney was inside?"

"We left him locked in the basement with Claire while we engaged the attackers. There was no way out."

"Shit," Pluess said. "So much for that whole plan."

"I'm sorry, Cedric."

"Thomas, I've got to say, you fucked this one up bad."

Paine had no words for that.

CHAPTER 9

JACKSON HOLE AIRPORT (JACKSON, WYOMING) DECEMBER 1, 2021—9 AM

OPERATING ON FIVE hours of sleep, Wyoming Ryder stood on the tarmac in his knee-length leather jacket with fur lapels. His Gulfstream 650 gleamed in the morning sun on the tarmac behind him. He had just flown in from Montana. The sun-tipped peaks of the Grand Tetons reached for the heavens in the distance beyond the airfield as the cameraman signaled ready.

Wyoming wondered how long until the posse arrived.

"I still can't believe you're alive, Wyoming. I had to see you with my own eyes to believe it," said Farrah Clark, the cute reporter from KCQK, the ABC affiliate in Jackson. Her cameraman stood off to one side, his little camera on a drone that he controlled with a tablet.

"We're rolling," the cameraman said.

"I'm here live with Wyoming Ryder at Jackson Hole Airport in Jackson," Clark said. "Live in every sense of the word. Wyoming, eight days ago, authorities said your plane went off the radar over the Sierra Nevada. They showed video of the explosion in midair. Millions of fans mourned your passing. I'm so happy to see the rumors that you'd survived were true. Can you tell us what really happened?"

He waited a dramatic moment. "The rest of us smoke normal weed. I don't know what they're smoking over at Homeland Security. I spent that night in my suite at the St. James Hotel. Most of the night, anyway."

"The St. James in San Francisco?" Clark asked.

"That's right."

"We saw video," Clark said. "Homeland Security confirmed it was your plane."

He turned and gestured at the gleaming white G-650 on the tarmac behind him. "I had a smooth flight in. I was planning to do some fishing today."

"Homeland Security also reported you were accompanied by First Lady Amanda Jeffers, and she's still missing."

"She was kidnapped," Wyoming said. "We were sleeping. Suddenly there were men with guns standing around us. They zipped her into a duffel and carried her out."

"Are you saying the First Lady was kidnapped in San Francisco eight days ago?"

"Yes."

"Why didn't you call the police?"

"After the others took her away, two men stayed behind and held their guns on me while I dressed. They took my Jetlink. They drove me to the airport at gunpoint. They made me get on my plane and leave. They threatened to torture and kill my children if I talked to the police."

"The First Lady has Secret Service protection. Where were they?"

Wyoming smiled. "We sort of gave them the slip. Amanda wanted that. I thought we'd be safe in the St. James."

"Do you think the police are going to arrest you now?"

He shrugged. "I've taken the necessary measures to safeguard my children. I hope they wait until I'm back from fishing, though."

"Why did you wait so long to come forward?"

"Two children in different cities, two ex-wives to negotiate with. You know what I mean?"

The reporter smiled and then renewed her focus. "Who were these men? Can you give any indication of who they were or why they kidnapped the First Lady?"

"They had motorcycle helmets and assault rifles," he said. "They didn't make any speeches. I was glad they didn't kill us on the spot. I was awful sorry for Amanda, though. I'm shocked that she hasn't been found yet. I hope she's all right."

"Homeland Security confirmed it was your plane that exploded. Why would they put that on TV if they weren't sure?"

He made as if to ponder the question before answering. "Don't get me wrong, I think those Homeland Security folks are doing a great job protecting all of us. I guess they make mistakes, too, like other people." He turned and gazed again at his plane. "I'm just sorry for my fans. They had to go on all this time thinking I'd moved on to the great movie studio in the sky."

"If it wasn't your plane, what exploded?"

"I guess that's a question for the experts. Maybe they got the video switched with some other explosion."

"So they aren't going to find any wreckage in the Sierra Nevada?" Clark persisted. "The search has gone on for eight days with no results."

Wyoming saw three police cars and a couple of black SUVs speeding toward them from the other end of the airport with red-and-blue flashing lights. A fast reaction indeed. Other agencies around the country would be scrambling —Secret Service, Homeland Security, the US Army. He imagined people shouting orders in offices far away. He was in for a long day of questioning. Maybe more than one day. His lawyers were en route from L.A.

Hopefully the FBI office would have decent coffee.

"Certainly not this plane," he smiled, gesturing again at his jet. "But the main thing now is to find Amanda. I'm so concerned about her."

"Is that why you came forward?"

"Absolutely, she has to be found. It's a terrible thing for our country. If I can help the authorities in any way, that's what I'm here for."

"Thank you, Wyoming Ryder," Clark concluded. "Millions of fans can rest easy, knowing Wyoming Ryder is alive and well, and his plane didn't explode over the Sierra Nevada. Meanwhile, the search for Amanda Jeffers continues."

Car doors opened, and black-suited men and police officers poured out of vehicles. Wyoming saw them crouching behind doors, guns pointed. It was just him, a cameraman, and the cute reporter here. As men spread out in a circle behind the plane, he saw a dark suited man in a white cowboy hat adjusting the controls on a drone.

"Orrin, keep the live feed going," Clark said to the cameraman. "It looks as if the authorities are now going to detain Hollywood star, Wyoming Ryder. Wyoming, were you expecting the police to show up?"

"You never really know what to expect these days, do you?"

It was all he got in before the drone loudspeaker kicked in.

"Wyoming Ryder, this is the FBI. Lie down on the ground with your arms and legs spread wide. Get down, now!"

"I've got to get down on the ground?" He had his arms high in the air, but reached down to finger his silver belt buckle. "This was a present from John Wayne, you know. Don't want it scratched."

"Wyoming Ryder is being detained by the FBI and they're telling him to lie flat on the ground, here at Jackson Hole Airport," Clark reported.

"Get down on the ground now!" The FBI chief yelled so loudly, feedback whistled from the drone. Several sharpshooters stood on either side, keeping Wyoming in their sights.

Slowly Wyoming sank, first to his knees, then down on his chest. Flat on the pavement, with his head turned to face the cameraman, he slowly moved his arms and legs, as if creating a snow angel.

"We have live coverage of Wyoming Ryder being detained on the tarmac of Jackson Hole Airport like a common criminal," Clark said.

"Turn it off, folks," the FBI chief said, moving in. Followed by six other agents, one of whom stuck his hand in front of the camera lens, the FBI chief now stood over Wyoming. Another agent grabbed the actor's arms and handcuffed his wrists behind his back. A third felt around in his jacket for weapons, around his hips, and up and down his thighs and calves. Did they really think he would be dumb enough to come to this party armed?

Wyoming watched the scattering of agents facing away from the drama, ready to defend their perimeter with heavy weapons. Maybe they were expecting March22 soldiers to ride up on motorcycles, like in *Easy Rider.*

"We have the right to film what's happening here," Clark said.

"Like hell you do," the FBI chief said. "If I see that camera on again, I'll have my agents destroy it."

"The boots?" an agent said.

"He hasn't got anything in his boots," the FBI chief said. "Get him in the car."

"Why are you arresting me?" Wyoming asked.

"I ask the questions around here," the FBI chief said. "Just so you know, I don't watch your trashy movies, either. Never seen a single one of 'em."

"My lawyers are on the way, but they won't be here for a couple of hours," Wyoming said.

"Is that so?" the chief said. "Get him in the car."

"Get up, movie star," said another agent, prodding him in the kidney with the toe of a polished black shoe.

Wyoming decided on a mild form of protest. He remained in position, jaw resting on rough pavement, hands cuffed behind his back. No one had read him his rights. He wondered if he had any rights. The fact that he had mentioned his lawyers meant they couldn't legally start questioning him until they arrived.

"I said get up," the agent said, impatience showing.

"He's not moving."

"Sir, for the record, why are you arresting Wyoming Ryder?" Clark asked, stepping closer. The FBI chief ignored her.

"Get up and walk, you commie idiot," the chief said.

"We might as well wait here for my lawyers. Fresh air and everything," Wyoming said. Surely the cameraman would be recording this.

"All right, pick him up," the chief said.

Five agents grabbed him by the arms, the ankles, and his belt with the buckle from John Wayne. He kicked just enough to make them swear, to strain their lower backs, not enough for an assault charge. One agent lost his grip as he kicked, and then another, and suddenly his two-hundred-twenty-pound body weight was distributed among three men instead of five. For a second, he thought they were going to drop him on his face. Wyoming looked forward to watching the whole thing on TV.

They managed to hold on, at least till they reached one of the black SUVs. They dropped him none too gently on a yellowish foam rubber pad that covered the floor of the vehicle.

"Commie pig," an agent said.

Wyoming let it go. Anyone who thought he was a communist was poorly educated in the best case.

When the SUV drove off, he had one last view of his plane on the tarmac. He hoped he'd be able to fly out again within 24 hours. Although, having kept them waiting for eight days, and with the First Lady still missing, that could prove overly optimistic. They dropped a black hood over his head and shoved him back down on the foam rubber.

CHAPTER 10

NEAR ANN ARBOR, MICHIGAN
DECEMBER 1, 2021—9 PM

MATT FOUND HIMSELF wandering around the house alone. A boring afternoon stretched into an evening in which he'd repeatedly caught Claire staring at him for no reason. He then watched the Dark Fiber leader take off somewhere on her motorcycle. Gram, who hardly showed her face in his presence, had disappeared somewhere upstairs. He had noticed the stairs creaked noisily whenever anyone went up or down, and she hadn't come down in two hours.

Matt sank into a comfortable chair and closed his eyes, shutting out the sounds of the birds filtering through an open window, the kitchen's lingering smell of dinner, and his own thoughts. He concentrated on a simple, pleasant image, as Luke had coached him. He imagined himself lying in the grass looking at the blue sky above. Blue above, green below, and the scent of freshly cut grass, and not a care in the world.

All at once, the compartment in his mind clicked open like a magic box. A thought formed, and he focused.

There's a safe here somewhere, he said. *Can you get it open for me?*

Why, what's in it? Luke answered immediately.

As Luke had explained it a week ago, under the right conditions, Matt's question would appear in Luke's mind just as quickly as it formed, and Luke's answer came to him just as instantaneously. In practical terms, how it happened—how their thoughts and whole sentences traveled instantly over great distances—was something Luke was still researching and pondering.

You told me to look for Dark Fiber correspondence.

I need to know some info you can read off the side of the safe to know if I can hack into it. Like, if it's —.

Matt stood in the living room studying the walls. He knew Luke had intended to say *on a network.* He felt the words even though they hadn't come through. Plus, it was logical. Practically everything was on a network these days—whether ovens and toasters, the sound system, the TV wall, or the garage door opener. Why people would want their safe on a network, he had no idea. But what did he know?

Peeking behind a painting of a barn, he found only blank wall. A glass-covered print of some old cars from the 1950s yielded the same result. He threaded his way between a couch and an armchair to get at what looked like a family portrait. A bunch of old people, a row of young adults, plus children and babies placed before a burgundy studio background.

Behind the portrait, a metal line showed through a cut in the wallpaper. He carefully lifted the picture off its hook, revealing a wall safe about eighteen inches square.

Found it, he said without thinking. To his surprise, standing here and focusing on the cut in this wallpaper, even while depending on his ordinary sense of sight and touch, it seemed he was able to keep the channel open with Luke.

What does it look like? Luke asked.

It's covered with wallpaper.

So rip the – .

This was easier said than done. Fortunately, the wallpaper was old and dry. It came off in thin strips and left most of the metal exposed. If anyone looked at the safe now, his handiwork would be discovered instantly. Luckily the clean cut along the outer edges made it possible to tear strips that ended precisely at the edge. Once he replaced the picture, the damage would be hidden.

Okay, it's sort of grayish-green.

Not the color, dickhead.

Excuse me for breathing. It has a keypad. You have to put in a code.

Just numbers, or – ?

Numbers and letters.

Okay, look around the edges of the keypad. There should be the name of the manufacturer and some other numbers, etched real small.

Kryptonase, Matt read. Then he read off a long string of letters and numbers, like a serial number.

Okay, give me – , Luke said, fading out.

Bringing the wallpaper fragments, Matt went to the kitchen to wait. Did Luke always fade out because he started concentrating on something on his computer before he finished speaking? Maybe it wasn't a problem at the receiving end.

Through the kitchen windows, he'd see anyone driving in. If he had to, he could replace the picture in ten seconds. No creaking noise from the stairs. Maybe Gram was sleeping up there. He found a plastic bag and put all the torn strips of wallpaper in it, then stuffed the bag in a pocket of his camouflage pants.

Next, he took a notepad, and wrote a note.

Claire, I got bored and went for a little walk. Back in an hour or so.

Did it work? Luke said.

Matt ran back into the living room. The safe door stood open an inch. *Brother, you may be the world's biggest geek, but you amaze me sometimes.*

Handicaps have their —, Luke said.

Ever thought of robbing banks?

Not enough of a challenge. What's in the safe?

Matt strapped his Jetlink on his wrist and powered on. Then he pulled out a sheaf of papers. One was a contract with "Mortgage" written at the top. Underneath it he found a bunch of certificates held together by a paper clip. Investments of some kind. The rest of the papers looked like contracts of one sort or another.

Looks like it's all personal stuff, he said. *Stuff that has to do with this house, nothing to do with Dark Fiber. This is just somebody's house.*

He peeled off two thousand in cash and an equal amount in gray ration coupons from the bundles, then closed the safe. Being kidnapped surely entitled you to some freedom money.

"What's going on here?"

The voice startled Matt as if he'd touched a live wire. Slowly he turned, the gun in his right hand. Gram stood inside the doorway, arms crossed over her chest. Clearly she had seen everything.

"I know how to use this, and I won't hesitate," he said.

"You're a well-known killer," Gram said, the corners of her mouth curling down. "Are you going to kill me, too?"

"Come in here and sit down. Take off your Jetlink," he said, moving a step in her direction. He waved the gun at an armchair inside the doorway. Gram handed across her Jetlink as she sat down.

"That's a fine way to treat your host," Gram said.

"That's a nice way of putting it," he said. "They kidnapped me. I've got nothing against you, but I'm being held against my will."

"She trusted you with that gun," Gram said. "I guess she was mistaken."

"All I need is a head start. I'll send you back your Jetlink in a few days. That's the best I can do. Now give me the keys to your car."

"They're in the kitchen, by the coffee machine."

He locked the door to the living room with Gram inside, confident that Claire could find a way to get her out when she got home. This hadn't gone quite as smoothly as he hoped, but he was glad he hadn't been forced to hurt the woman. Grabbing the car keys, he left the house and ran down the porch steps to Gram's white Impala.

As he was driving out the driveway, lights darkened, Luke chimed in again in that special compartment in his mind.

I told the gang what you said about the Dark Fiber numbers. We need to know about their weapons and communications. Especially weapons, since I'm —.

That's ridiculous. How do you expect me to find out about their weapons?

He turned north onto Route 23 as he waited for Luke's answer, flicking the lights on as he upped the speed. As far as the eye could see, no car was coming from either direction.

At last, he was on his way back to Raine. March22 had decided to abandon him here. They were ignoring his kidnapping and content to leave him idling in some Michigan farmhouse. Well, he knew how to get across the country, in spite of the checkpoints, Homeland Security drones, assassins and wanted posters.

The March22 leaders could take their mission and shove it.

We don't care much about Claire Tenneman, Luke said, finally coming back after Matt had covered two miles. *Local lightweight.*

You can say that again.

But, she might know what weapons they have and where. For instance, we think maybe they have the missing shoulder-fired missiles locked up somewhere. We'd love to get our —.

Do you think Dark Fiber was behind that?

Almost had to be. Dark Fiber is the biggest of the militias, and one of the early ones. Shooting down all those planes made the whole country switch to shipping cargo by truck rather than by air, giving the militias easy targets to hijack.

What makes you think that bitch is going to tell me stuff like that? Matt asked.

Use your prodigious charms, Luke said. *If you can't find out from her, she may lead you to the bigger fish. Let them recruit you if they want to. Don't make it seem obvious. Be sure to —.*

You don't understand. I can't do shit like that, Matt said.

Why not?

For a moment, Matt had no idea what to answer. He was certain he couldn't charm or trick Claire into telling him any Dark Fiber secrets, but he couldn't think why. Suddenly a very satisfactory answer occurred to him.

I'm too damned honest.

Like hell you are. You just took your Jetlink out of —.

Hearing this from Luke hit him like a hammer blow to the face. How did Luke know he'd lifted the Jetlink? Luke had his nosy eyes on so damned much.

You are a real pain in the ass sometimes, he said at last.

Probably a good thing. I just hope you don't get any dumb ideas.

Like what?

Like trying to escape from Dark Fiber, when March22 needs —.

All right, all right, you already said that about a hundred times. He had to hope Luke didn't have some drone circling above at fifty thousand feet, zeroing in on his Jetlink and revealing that he was now six or seven miles north of the farmhouse, and approaching Ann Arbor.

Listen, I think I'm going to hit the hay. Thanks for the chat.

Sleep well, little brother, Luke said.

"Little brother" was priceless coming from that super-geek, with his sticklike arms and shrunken paralyzed body.

Raine would be wondering all this time what had happened to him. He speed-dialed her on his Jetlink. Who knew if it would even be possible later? Within seconds, her face appeared, radiant on the screen.

"Matt, is it really you? I'm so glad you're safe!"

"Did they tell you what happened?"

Raine nodded. "Where are you? Do you know when you're coming back?"

"They want me to stay here for a while. Listen, I can't stay on long." He didn't mention it was because Luke was probably following the whole conversation. He didn't mention that in fact he was on his way back to her already. "I love your bones, Raine. I'll be back as soon as I can."

"Stay safe, Matt. I'll be waiting for you."

He powered off as he entered Ann Arbor. He hated these short bursts of conversation with Raine. He had more to say, and Raine always had ten times as much that she wanted to say to him. Over the last week, they had lain in bed every night and talked, sometimes for hours, in between rounds of athletic lovemaking. After their four-month separation while she was at Stanford, they'd had a lot of catching up to do. Now, damn it all, thanks to those Dark Fiber idiots, they were separated again.

Well, he was on his way back, whether it suited March22 or not.

Claire had said there were five hundred chapters of Dark Fiber around the country. The smallest had twenty members and the biggest numbered in the hundreds, as he had told Luke. She'd said Detroit had five hundred members. Five *hundred.* He decided to busy his mind with calculations as he searched for a suitable place to exchange the Impala.

If the top ten cities each had five hundred members, that made five thousand Dark Fiber idiots right there. If there were another hundred cities that each had one hundred members, that would be... one thousand? No, ten thousand. Ten thousand plus five thousand was fifteen thousand. That left almost four hundred smaller chapters. If they each had twenty members, that would be... damn it, he was so bad at math.

Luke had probably done these calculations in half a second, adding them in perfectly lined up columns on the inside of his eyelids, while plotting strategy with the other leaders.

Four hundred times twenty had to make eight thousand. So eight thousand plus fifteen thousand made twenty thousand. If Dark Fiber had twenty thousand trained members around the country, it was one big-ass militia. That was more like a standing army. He'd always thought of these militias as small local groups of twenty or thirty people. It shocked him to think they could actually be big organizations.

Even if Dark Fiber was the largest, Matt could think of ten or twelve other militias he had heard about on TV. There were explosions, hijackings, and assassinations of well-known people around the country every day, assuming that only the most sensational ones were reported. If you heard about them on the news, they probably weren't rinky-dink groups.

He slowed at the sight of a small strip mall with an auto repair place, a darkened restaurant, a gas station, and several other stores. The auto repair lot had six or seven old cars, and the light was dim. With no other cars driving past, Matt felt creepy, as if he were the only person out on the street, but such was life in 2021. People generally stayed indoors unless they absolutely had to go out. They gawked at *Faking It with the Nardellis* on their TV wall, they got high, or they sat around doing nothing. Inside was safe, as long as the FBI or Homeland Security didn't come and break down your door. Outside was dangerous.

He parked the Impala next to an old blue Toyota Celica and left Gram's Jetlink on the front seat. They only wanted $10,000 for the Toyota. The side was dented, the passenger mirror was missing, but this model always had a reliable engine. No antitheft drones hovered around it.

The doors didn't yield when he tried them. Feeling around in the wheel wells didn't produce a key, either. Not for the first time in recent weeks, Matt thought with admiration what uncanny vision his father possessed. Not every father taught you how to steal a car and get it running, even without a key. Matt peered around once more to make sure he was alone, and lifted his leg high. In one swift motion he kicked in the passenger-side window. It took two tries before the glass crumpled inward, and his boot got stuck awkwardly in the jagged hole, but at least no alarms went off.

Ten seconds after extricating his foot, he sat in the driver's seat working on the plastic housing that covered the ignition mechanism. With a little brute strength, it finally came free, revealing a neat bundle of colored wires.

When the engine started, the gas gauge moved to about half full. He could cover three hundred miles on that much gas, and he had plenty of money and ration coupons when that ran low.

He swung the Celica onto the road, headed into town. No one came running across the street shaking a fist. In fact, no one—and no drone—appeared to be around as he flicked the lights on and drove off. Gram's Impala receded from view in the parking lot. He had left her Jetlink on the front seat. No hard feelings.

This road would take him into the center of Ann Arbor, and from there he could head west, back toward Indiana and Illinois. He would stay off the Interstate, keeping to two-lane county roads, where no checkpoints existed.

The dashboard display read eleven o'clock as he entered the city, looking for signs. Here in town, the occasional car met him at a stop sign. He was almost happy for a sign of other living people. Still, the only company he truly desired waited in Montana. His own personal paradise. He could almost taste her kisses.

He would get well away from Ann Arbor, and then stop for food in a couple of hours at some friendly looking place. *As long as they don't have a wanted poster with my picture on the cash register,* he thought with a pang of fear. Could it really be true that they were all over?

Maybe a drive-through restaurant would be smarter. Some places still had drive-through windows, though now always with bulletproof glass.

On the other side of Ann Arbor, having found Route 12 heading west, Matt caught sight of a motorcycle catching up at high speed. With a sickening feeling, he stepped on the gas. The Celica engine screamed as he jammed the gas pedal to the floor. Slowly the old car crept up to seventy, then eighty mph. This car wasn't built to outrun a high-powered bike. He saw in the mirror exactly who it was. How the hell had she managed it? Had she tried all the roads leading out of town? The woman seemed to have a sixth sense.

Claire came alongside, matching his speed easily. Her face was a mask of fury. He took it down to fifty mph and cranked the window open.

"Just out for a late-night drive," he said.

"If you pull over right now, I won't shoot out your tires," she yelled over the whipping wind.

He pulled over and waited for her to dismount. His right hand crept down to the pocket in his camouflage pants where he kept his slingshot. He could end her life in a split second, before she even had time to draw her weapon. She didn't even know about the slingshot. He could surprise her.

After a moment's hesitation, he left it there. This woman had saved his ass from a burning building. She'd trusted him with a loaded gun. She didn't deserve to die on this ugly stretch of road, just so he could escape.

Maybe Claire's finding him meant it was his destiny to stay here and carry out the March22 mission. His father would be pissed if he didn't try.

"How the hell did you find me?"

"I stuck a GPS tracker in your Jetlink." Claire wasn't smiling. "I guess I overestimated your intelligence. Smart enough to get into the safe, dumb enough to try to get away. And threaten Gram. You have some explaining to do. Now get on."

In silence, Matt rode back to the farm on the back of her motorcycle, rage burning in his chest.

CHAPTER 11

THE **FBI** CONFERENCE room was not nearly big enough for twelve people, but half stayed standing. He was the movie star, and they let their gazes linger. Three drones hovered around, presumably live-streaming the proceedings somewhere. Wyoming had no trouble with people staring. People stared at him everywhere he went.

The two guards had stared at him in his cell last night.

"You want an autograph or something?" he'd said through the bars. For some reason, that had sent them running. Usually people fought for his autograph.

His lawyers, Karen Vixen and Mark Knox, hadn't made it in till this morning, which delayed the whole thing. He'd had thirty minutes to plan strategy with them before this meeting began.

"Your story at the St. James Hotel checks out," Agent Knight said. A tall, angular man with graying temples and deep sunken brown eyes, Knight looked like a man who slept too little, drank too much coffee, and rarely had sex. Wyoming wondered why a man would ever want to work for the FBI. "I want to know more about why you felt you could just flee the scene of a crime. A crime involving the First Lady."

"I didn't flee the scene, I was forced at gunpoint. There were six of them," Wyoming said. "Motorcycle helmets, leathers, assault rifles. When they zipped Amanda into the bag, four left with her while two others held their guns on me. We were held at gunpoint the whole time. They threatened my children. They forced me to get dressed, get my things and go to the airport."

He had been practicing this story with Amanda, Winter and John for the past week, nailing down the details, brainstorming interrogation questions, honing answers down to their essence. Amanda had turned out to be a quick study. After watching her in the role plays, Wyoming hadn't been surprised to learn she had done drama in college.

"Describe this bag," Knight said.

"Big black rubberized duffel with a thick zipper. The kind you'd carry scuba gear or something in."

"What did they say to you?"

"Short commands, like, get dressed now. Move. Hurry up."

"Accent?"

"I didn't notice anything special."

"Did they all speak, or just one?"

"Just one spoke most of the time. When he spoke to the others, they mostly did what he said without answering."

"He didn't have an accent?"

"No. Normal English."

"High voice, low voice? Rough?"

"Low, normal voice. Nothing special about it."

"How tall was this leader? Was he thin, fat, broad shoulders?"

"Not especially tall. Normal height. They were all broad shouldered and muscular."

"All men?"

"I think so. I couldn't swear to it. They were covered up the whole time and kept their helmets on. The ones with Amanda were gone after five minutes."

"Who carried the bag?"

"Two of them together. Each took a strap."

"What was she wearing?"

Wyoming imagined the president watching this video later. He adopted an expression that said he couldn't do anything about it, calculated for maximum effect. "Amanda, ah, was naked."

The FBI agent remained stony-faced. "So, they made her get dressed before they put her in the bag?"

"Yes."

"What did she put on?"

"A pair of jeans and a blouse. She also had a sweater."

"Shoes?"

"I guess so. I... yes, now I remember. Sandals." He wondered if questions like this were to test his credibility or if they simply wanted to know whether they would find her dressed or undressed later. Maybe FBI agents got off on details like this. Karen Vixen, his lawyer, was the only woman in the room.

"Did she have her Jetlink on?"

"They took it away." That would be logical for a kidnapping victim. Otherwise, she would've been able to send an SOS from inside the bag.

"When did they take it away exactly?"

"When she got out of bed. She was naked, they saw the Jetlink, and they told her to give it to them."

He gazed at the three drones hovering near the ceiling in different corners of the room. No doubt recording and live streaming everything. Probably taking measurements of his breathing, heart rate, pupil activity. Dozens of people would analyze it all. Lie detector specialists from the FBI would study the video.

"She slept with her Jetlink on?"

"Don't you? How else would you know how you slept?" Wyoming was genuinely curious. Jetlinks measured your REM sleep. For men, more importantly, it measured the number and duration of your erections during sleep. But that probably wasn't high on Agent Knight's list of priorities.

The FBI man ignored the question. "You said they held you at gunpoint while you dressed and packed your things."

"That's right."

"Then you left the hotel room. Where did they take you?"

"Down the elevator to the garage."

"No one saw this. We have no witnesses that saw four men leaving with a big bag or two men leaving with you."

"I didn't see anyone else, either."

"They held their guns on you in the hallway and the elevator?"

"Yes."

"What if someone had walked out of their room?"

Wyoming shrugged. "Nobody did."

"And no one else was on the elevator? No guests coming home late? No employees?"

"It was four in the morning."

"And then they put you in their car?"

"In the garage, yes."

"What kind of car?"

"Some big SUV with tinted windows."

"What make?"

"I don't know."

"You don't know if it was a Lincoln or a Lexus or whatever?"

"I'm not a car guy."

Knight shook his head. "What color?"

"Black, I think."

"You think?"

"That's what I remember. I guess I was a little shaken up, you know?"

"Who rode where?"

"The guy who did all the talking drove. The other guy sat in the back with me and held his gun on me."

"They didn't cuff you?"

"No."

"Didn't they stop at any lights? Didn't you think about jumping out?"

"He was holding a gun on me. He threatened my children. Don't you have children, Agent Knight?" Knight went on without acknowledging the question.

"Did they tell you they were taking you to the airport?"

"Yes."

"When exactly?"

"When we were in the car. Driving out of the garage."

"You said they put you on your plane. What about your pilots? Were they already there, or did you call them?"

"They made me call them from the car, while we were driving. I guess that's why they told me where we were going."

"The pilots met you at the airport."

"They arrived fifteen minutes after I did."

"One thing I don't understand," Knight went on, "is why they went to the trouble of bringing you to the airport. Did they say why they did that?"

"No."

"And you didn't ask?"

"I asked several times where they had taken Amanda, but they weren't exactly inviting questions."

"Okay, so now we're at the airport. Did these two men just stand around in motorcycle helmets while the pilots did their work? Flight checks, filing the flight plan, all that?"

"They file flight plans electronically, you know," Wyoming said. Agent Knight didn't look insulted at all. "Yes, they stood there pointing their guns at me. I instructed the pilots to get us off the ground as soon as possible, and not to try any emergency calls."

"Did you know the airport was closed when your plane took off?"

"My pilots came and told me while we were standing in the hangar," Wyoming said. "My attackers said we had to take off, or they would shoot us all. I asked the pilots if they thought it was safe."

"There was a battle royal raging at the north end of San Francisco Airport. You must have a guardian angel. No one can understand how you got off the ground alive."

"What I don't understand," Wyoming said, "is why Homeland Security claims my plane exploded over the Sierra Nevada. Why did they doctor that video?"

"We're not here to talk about that."

"It's a question of my reputation," Wyoming said. "Why did they lie to the American people?"

"I'm sure the explanation will be clearer when we find the wreckage," Knight said.

"If you haven't found the wreckage after, what, nine days, are you ever going to find any? Not if there was no explosion," he answered his own question.

"Do you realize we could lock you up for the rest of your life for not reporting the disappearance of the First Lady?" Knight asked.

Wyoming's lawyer, Mark Knox, spoke for the first time. "My client made a difficult choice when his own and his children's lives were threatened."

"We could throw the book at him," Knight said.

"You're welcome to try," Knox said. "Surely it's in the your interest to focus all efforts on finding Amanda Jeffers, not retribution against my client for a difficult judgment call."

"The FBI is perfectly capable of working on two parallel tracks," Knight said testily. "I want Mr. Ryder to acknowledge the gravity of the situation. Nine days have gone by. Nine days."

"I fully understand the gravity," Wyoming said. "I care about Amanda. It tore me to pieces to watch her being kidnapped."

"Yet you didn't defend her," Knight said.

"Six men with assault rifles," Wyoming said. "They knew my children's middle names. They knew their addresses, the addresses of their schools. They said they would torture and kill them if I went to the police. Yet I'm sitting here with you. I'd like to do my part to help you find Amanda. I think we're on the same side, here."

"So why did they take you to the airport?"

"I told you, I don't know."

"But you see my problem?" Knight grilled him with those deep sunken eyes. "Why not just leave you in the hotel room? Why not take your Jetlink, tie you up, gag you, and leave you there?"

"Beats me," Wyoming said.

"Think of all the things that could go wrong. They couldn't have known you'd encounter no other guests or employees in the hall, the elevator, or the garage. They took extra risks to get you out of the hotel and bring you to the airport. They could've had an accident. They could've been stopped for speeding. They could've had a flat. Your pilots might've called for help. See what I mean?"

"I do, but I don't know the answer."

"It really bugs me," Knight said. "It's not logical. It doesn't fit."

"I guess they wanted to get me out of town."

"How did they know about your plane? How did they know which hangar to drive to, which exit to take off the highway?"

He had the feeling the FBI agent might answer his own questions, but the silence expanded. The agent obviously didn't know where to go with it. Based in a quiet Western state, Knight had to be a second stringer in the FBI. It surprised Wyoming that Homeland Security and the FBI hadn't confronted him with higher level officials yet, given that this was about the First Lady. You had to assume they were dealing with it this way for a reason.

"How did they know which suite we were in?" Wyoming said at last. "How did they know Amanda was with me? They obviously *knew* things. I guess they could've somehow found out my plane was there."

"Allow me to sketch out a different scenario," Agent Knight said, ignoring him. "All six men left with Mrs. Jeffers in the bag. You got scared and decided to run to the airport and fly away. Which is why we suspect you of fleeing the scene of a crime."

Wyoming had to work to keep the smile off his face. "You can talk to my pilots. They'll confirm the story."

"Rest assured, we already have, Mr. Ryder," FBI Chief Knight said.

At this point, warning that they would be back in thirty minutes, the law enforcement officials—followed by their drones—filed out of the room, leaving Wyoming alone with his lawyers.

"Do you know what's amazing to me?" Karen Vixen showed them both a note when the others were all gone. Clearly, they couldn't talk freely. They passed the note back and forth, keeping it covered with their hands while reading.

"What?" Mark Knox wrote.

"Up until three hours ago they thought Amanda Jeffers was dead. Everybody's been talking about a funeral for her."

"That's because the President thought he'd killed her," Wyoming wrote.

"Maybe they're still in a state of shock," Karen Vixen wrote.

"Tell Nina Nardelli I need to see her in person," Wyoming wrote. He scribbled the reality star's private telephone number and watched Vixen copy it onto her Jetlink.

Then the lawyer removed a lighter from her purse and burned the note, dropping it on the floor when the flame reached her fingers.

CHAPTER 12

JACKSON, WYOMING
DECEMBER 2, 2021—2 PM

THE LACK OF witnesses, except for a single room service waiter, bothered FBI Agent Gordon Knight. He knew teams were going through the hotel suite with high-tech tools while he interrogated Ryder. They'd already found hairs that came from Amanda Jeffers's head and her DNA on a champagne glass.

He'd never visited the St. James Hotel, but the website revealed it as a large, old hotel with a modern tower, and the older landmark building rebuilt after the great earthquake and fire of 1906. Ryder had stayed in the Hollywood Suite in the tower, on the fortieth floor. A direct elevator reached the garage, but it seemed so unlikely that not a single night bellman or guards would've seen any of them exiting.

The lone waiter who had seen the pair, a twenty-year employee named Fred Jones, signed a statement saying he had delivered dinner on a cart to the suite and had seen Amanda Jeffers and Wyoming Ryder. He'd received a fifty-dollar tip and left the suite immediately. Jones still had the bill, and Wyoming Ryder's fingerprints were on it. The cart had been left in the hall. Another employee later picked it up and did not see Ryder or Jeffers. Jones, a resident of South San Francisco, was married with two grown children. He worked full-time, and had no police record.

It worried Knight that he could see how the defense team would build their case, if it ever came to a trial, better than he could see the government's case.

Rumor had it that Wyoming Ryder was involved with the March22 organization. That bothered Knight as well. What if Ryder had simulated the kidnapping with some March22 accomplices? What would anyone accomplish with such an action?

And what was his plane doing on the tarmac at the Jackson Hole Airport, if it had exploded over the Sierra Nevada?

Knight spoke a command into his Jetlink, opening a direct line to Lance Windward, an agent he knew in the San Francisco office. Windward had been on the force with him back in Jersey.

"Gordon, what's shaking with Wyoming Ryder?" Windward asked. It was the only case anyone was talking about today. It was only a matter of time, Knight knew, before the interrogation would be moved to the much larger and better-equipped San Francisco office.

"He's lying about something," Knight said. "Something doesn't feel right."

"We're still waiting for final analysis on the physical evidence from the hotel suite," Windward said. "But you know it's gonna check out as his and hers. There's plenty of fingerprints and hairs and shit."

"No sign of a struggle?"

"No, none of that. Six men held them at gunpoint. How do you want them to struggle?"

"Any woman would struggle if you zipped her into a bag. Even at gunpoint," Knight said.

"So what? She struggled, she didn't struggle. She's gone. We did find signs of imprinting on the carpet in their suite that could've been made by a rubberized bag containing the weight of a body. At least we know she didn't die in a plane crash."

"That's another thing I don't get," Knight said. "I saw his plane with my own eyes. What the hell is going on with that?"

"Looks like our Homeland Security friends have some explaining to do," Windward said. "We've got some top guy coming out from Washington, apparently. He was more than pissed off."

"What about? The garage?" Knight went on. Bad blood between Homeland Security and the FBI was nothing new. "How many cars went out of there at four in the morning? What about video?"

"The video monitors on the fortieth floor and one of the elevators were defective that night. Also in the garage. Exactly the ones we need."

"Don't you find that a little odd?"

"Sure I do. But what does it prove? What's your theory, buddy?"

"I don't know. Just way too much coincidence, if you ask me."

"Listen, we've got these angles covered over here. A couple of agents flew out your way two hours ago. Like I said, there are people flying in from Washington, too. Not FBI people."

Knight rubbed his temples and wished he could take a nap.

KNIGHT WATCHED THE movie star across the table, trying to parse the man's quick glances at his Jetlink, the staring into space, the rolling eyes. Ryder was an enigma. His perfectly tanned face and arresting blue eyes marked him as a movie star. He probably paid five hundred dollars a pop to get that wave in his rich brown hair. With a net worth of about one billion dollars, Ryder had made forty movies in the last fifteen years. Comedies, Westerns, action thrillers, artsy-fartsy movies. He produced the movies he starred in now, meaning he bankrolled them and earned even more money. You would've expected him to have more than one billion dollars, but with a lifestyle like that, who could tell?

Knight wondered what it must be like going from one movie project to the next, donning a role, embracing it, making it real. Wyoming Ryder had a reputation as a character actor. When you watched his movies, you forgot you were watching an actor. He was that good. Knight had seen a few of the man's movies himself, even if he'd lied about it during the arrest.

Did the thrill of making movies and being a star get old? Was that why Ryder had an affair with the First Lady? Could that explain a celebrity's involvement with a terrorist organization?

Smith and Garagiola from the San Francisco office had arrived, and were now observing the interrogation. They were getting live updates from the St. James Hotel and the San Francisco office while Knight continued the questioning.

"Tell us about your relationship with the First Lady."

"We met a year ago at a dinner in Washington," Ryder said. His face revealed nothing. Was the award-winning actor playing a role or telling the truth? "We sat next to each other. I was there to receive a medal. We chatted for a couple of hours. I didn't think too much of it, considering her position. When she asked for my number, I gave it to her."

"You don't give out your number frequently?"

"Certainly not." Ryder smiled faintly.

"What was her husband's position at the time, Mr. Ryder?"

"He was secretary of defense."

"Did you meet him, too?"

Ryder shook his head. "He didn't attend."

"So you gave her your number. Did you expect her to call?"

"You never know."

"Mr. Ryder, it's a yes or no question."

"Sorry. I guess what I meant to say was I found her attractive. We laughed a lot. But I never expected her to call."

"Did she give you *her* number?"

"No."

"Okay, so that's when you met her. Now how did this meeting at your house in Malibu come about?"

Ryder smiled. "Fast forward a year. Out of the blue I got a message from Amanda."

"What did it say?"

"'Do you remember when you invited me to come to California anytime? I could use a little vacation.' That's what she wrote," Ryder said. I happened to be doing absolutely nothing that night. I saw her message and wrote back."

"What was your message?"

"Oh, something along the lines of dreams coming true," he said.

"Did you know she was no longer the wife of the secretary of defense but the First Lady?"

"Her message came completely out of the blue, and I answered her a minute or two later," Ryder said. "That only occurred to me afterwards. My first thought was the memory of what a lovely time we'd had at the awards dinner."

"Did you imagine at that moment that Mrs. Jeffers would have an affair with you?"

Ryder steepled his hands. "Forgive me, Father, for I have sinned. Is that what you want to hear?"

"No," he said. "I want to hear if it occurred to you that you might have an affair with her."

"Yes, it did," Ryder said.

Thus far, Knight could not detect the slightest discomfort in Ryder's facial expressions, his hands, or his body. Either he was telling the truth, or he was a phenomenon in the evasion of lie detection.

"So, you planned to seduce her?"

A funny look on Ryder's face. "That's going too far. I imagined it briefly. I decided I'd be open to it, based on what I remembered. That's it. In my experience, you don't plan these things."

"Is it fair to say you've had multiple affairs? Hundreds of affairs?"

"Mr. Knight, is this really relevant?" Karen Vixen interjected.

"It's okay, Karen," Ryder said. "I'm not ashamed of my lifestyle, Mr. Knight. I've had a ton of affairs. At my age, I wouldn't want to start counting."

"Then what happened?"

"I made a couple of calls, then sent Amanda another message that I would pick her up the next day."

"With your private plane."

"It's the only way to get around, these days."

"The Gulfstream 650."

"That's what it is."

"A sixty-million-dollar plane." He watched Ryder keep his lips pressed together, not commenting. "You then flew to Washington."

"That's right."

"Was it just you and Mrs. Jeffers on the plane?"

"This is taking a lot of time," Ryder said.

"I'm asking the questions, here," Knight said, showing annoyance of his own. "Was it just the two of you?"

"We also had Bessamy Belluccio on board," Ryder said. Another movie star, Knight thought. Christ, the man was golden. Bessamy Belluccio was one of those gorgeous Hollywood leading ladies who made thirty million dollars a picture. She was all over the billboards with her perfume line. "She'd been in New York on business. When she found out I was picking up Amanda, she took the train from New York to Washington and met us at the airport."

"How did she find out you were picking up Mrs. Jeffers?" Knight asked.

"We happened to be chatting that morning, soon after I'd heard from Amanda."

"So you and Bessamy Belluccio picked up Amanda Jeffers at Dulles Airport at four o'clock on November twenty-second. Then you took off and flew back to L.A. on the same day."

"Exactly."

"What did you talk about with Mrs. Jeffers on the plane?"

"Talk about?"

"Yes. Subjects of conversation."

"Let's see," Ryder looked at the ceiling. Or was he just rolling his eyes? "What it's like to be a movie star. What it's like to be the First Lady. Oh, and we talked about Nina Nardelli."

The eyes of a couple of the agents in the room opened wider. Knight remained cool. "You talked about Nina Nardelli?"

"You see, Bessamy had been in New York to talk to Nina about doing a cameo on her show. That's how the conversation got started. Then we also watched her video. You know, the original one, *Having Sex with the Devil?*"

"You watched *Having Sex with the Devil* with Bessamy Belluccio and the First Lady on your plane?" Knight remembered the video vividly for its raunchy portrayal of a beast-like devil raping and sodomizing the reality star. The video had inspired countless copycat rapists in real life.

"We did, and then we had a threesome," Ryder said.

"Excuse me?" Agent Garagiola said, speaking for the first time. Knight glared at him.

"We had a threesome. You know, Amanda, Bessamy, and me."

"You had a threesome on your plane with the First Lady?" Knight echoed.

"And Bessamy," Ryder said. "It's a five-hour flight, you know."

Knight decided to play angry. "Mr. Ryder, do you think this is some kind of farce? Do you think there's anything funny about the First Lady being abducted and held captive?"

"You're asking what happened on the plane. Do you expect me to lie?"

"I expect the truth."

"Well my plane wasn't shot out of the sky, as you now know, and Amanda and I were not killed, and we did have a threesome on the way out to LA. That's the truth, so deal with it."

Knight cleared his throat. "Was there in your opinion any coercion used in the threesome?"

"Is he serious?" Ryder looked around the table at all the spellbound faces. "Three consenting adults."

"It might be helpful to know where you're going with these intimate questions," Karen Vixen interjected.

"Tell us about after you arrived in LA, Mr. Ryder," Knight continued, as several men adjusted their neckties.

"My chauffeur picked us up at the airport and drove us to my house in Malibu. Bessamy had someone else picking her up, so we said good-bye there. When we got back to the house, Amanda and I had a quiet evening."

"What about the next day?"

"The next morning we had armed intruders."

"Ah, armed intruders at your house in Malibu? Tell us about that."

"This is happening more and more in Southern California. All my friends have experienced the same thing. I don't know if it's the dreadful food shortages, or what. One of my employees rushed into my bedroom at four in the morning to tell me that a gun battle was taking place in the yard."

"Who were these intruders?" Knight asked.

"I don't know."

"What did they want?"

"I didn't stick around to find out."

"Did you know five Secret Service agents lost their lives on your property on the morning of November twenty-third?"

Ryder's face transformed into a mask of shock.

"Did you know that?" Knight persisted.

"Secret Service?" the movie star said. "What happened?"

"We'll come back to that. Was Mrs. Jeffers with you in the bedroom?"

"Yes. We barred the bedroom door and went up on the roof, where I had a helicopter waiting."

"A helicopter?"

"The same employee who came and warned us had alerted my helicopter pilots at the first sign of trouble. The chopper was warming up when we came out on the roof. We flew to Van Nuys Airport and transferred to my plane."

"You didn't think anything of the fact that a gun battle was taking place in your yard and your house?"

"I have my own people for protection, Agent Knight. I let them do their job. Plus I had the First Lady with me. I felt responsible for her safety."

"The Secret Service had arrived to bring her home. Your people overpowered the agents in the house, and when reinforcements arrived, they fought them in a pitched gun battle."

"I'm sure it didn't happen that way at all," Ryder said. "All I knew was that there was a gun battle going on down on the ground floor. I had no idea who was attacking us. All I knew was we had to get out, for our safety."

"You claim you were thinking only of the First Lady's safety."

"We had been planning to fly to San Francisco anyway, you know. My son lives there and Amanda wanted to go. I just didn't think we'd leave quite so early in the morning."

"We'll come back to that morning. Tell me what happened when you arrived in San Francisco."

"We transferred to the hotel."

"It must have been pretty early still," Knight said. "Was the room ready?"

"I stay in the Hollywood Suite when I go there," Ryder said. "They knew I was coming. We caught up on our sleep. Later that morning, Amanda took a bath."

"What about meals?"

"We ate lunch in the room."

"All right. And the afternoon?"

Wyoming thought about it. "We stayed in the room and watched TV."

"All afternoon?" Knight asked.

"Pretty much. I think Amanda got interested in a movie. I kept dropping off."

"Weren't you going to see your son in San Francisco?"

"Yes, but he couldn't."

"Oh? What happened?"

"He had school and then he had his piano lesson. His mother said no dice, not today. She was right. I kind of sprang it on them, this visit."

"How old is he?"

"Fourteen. He's pretty good on the piano."

Knight arched his eyebrow to show displeasure at the irrelevant comment. "And after the movie and the TV, did you go out?"

"We went out on the balcony."

"But not sightseeing."

"Amanda wanted to, but for me, you know, it's difficult. I don't like wandering around in crowds."

"They recognize you."

Ryder hung his head, as if thankful someone understood.

"Some people might have recognized Mrs. Jeffers, too."

"True, true."

"At dinnertime you ordered room service, correct?"

"Yes. Dinner, champagne. We watched another movie, then went to bed."

"You had room service at lunch and at dinner, but only the waiter at dinner appears to have seen you. Nobody saw you at lunch."

"Haven't we covered this?" Karen Vixen interjected.

"We weren't dressed, so we had them leave the cart outside," Ryder said with a perfectly straight face.

"Were you planning to fly back to LA the next day?"

"Yes, that was the plan."

"Until Mrs. Jeffers was kidnapped."

"That's right. It's so terrible. I'm so worried."

After another exchange of a procedural nature, Knight stopped the proceedings. He'd gotten word that they were moving the interrogation to the San Francisco office.

The man was lying about something, Knight felt sure of it. Something to do with his plane, and this whole kidnapping scheme. Knight's instructions were to leave the subject of the shootout in Malibu to the Homeland Security and Secret Service investigators who were flying to San Francisco. They wanted their chunk out of Ryder as well.

Knight felt he'd gotten nowhere with the man. But this wasn't over yet. Not by a long shot.

CHAPTER 13

NEAR WHITE RIVER, SOUTH DAKOTA
DECEMBER 2, 2021—10 AM

AMANDA JEFFERS LAY blindfolded on the carpet, hands and feet bound tightly, unable to see a thing. Her thirst had grown into an evil monster. She had to distract herself and not think about it.

They'd driven eight hours through the night to get here, and then left her in the early hours of the morning. It had still been dark when they gave her one last drink and put the blindfold on. Wyoming and Winter had told her it could be six hours, twelve hours, even, in the worst case, twenty-four hours. How was she expected to hold her pee for twenty-four hours? She knew they wanted her to pee in her jeans. So she had. At some point, she had just given in. They wanted her to look thirsty and starved and messy. It was all part of the ruse.

It was part of her plan to hurt Jim.

Nine days ago, she never would have thought herself capable of joining forces with a terrorist group. When your own husband gives the order to kill you in cold blood, the equation changes. Wyoming had saved her life. Her husband had tried to kill her. Simple as that.

With this elaborate plan, she could return to normal life at the White House and be with Penelope again. They'd assured her that the chip in her breast was undetectable. She imagined herself a modern-day Amazon, a secret female warrior.

She swallowed dry. As if you could call life at the White House normal.

On her second day there, she'd watched Secret Service agents shoot a man repeatedly at point-blank range. Surely he had died after the first eight or ten bullets. The very next day, her husband had barely escaped assassination when Senator Zachary Lincoln, head of the Liberty Party, had pulled a gun during a meeting. When Jim dove out of the way, four shots had struck Russ Harris, the president's chief aide. Her sweet Russ.

On an impulse, while still in shock from the news about Russ, she'd sent a message to Wyoming Ryder, inviting herself to California. She'd had the idea of getting away. Too many bullets, too many killings, and right inside the White House. Wyoming Ryder, in person, had arrived with his plane the next day. Her life had started a new chapter.

These random memories whirled around her brain as she lay here blindfolded in her clammy, smelly jeans.

All of a sudden, Amanda heard gunshots. At first, she thought she might be remembering another hail of bullets, like an replay in her mind of events that had happened a week ago. But no, that was machine-gun fire right here, all around her. She heard a man scream and others shouting. She shut her eyes tight under the blindfold. That was why they'd laid her down on the floor. *Please shoot high.*

The shooting continued without interruption for two or three minutes. More shouting, punctured by screams. She smelled smoke. She wondered if the house might be burning or if that was from all the guns. How many men did March22 have here? She hoped no one would be killed, but that was obviously an illusion. They were dying for *her.*

In the midst of the shooting, the door burst open with a bang. Then more shouting.

"Cleopatra, we have Cleopatra," shouted a man. Involuntary tears came to Amanda's eyes. It was going to be over. Clomping feet, the floor vibrating beneath her, and then more men. She felt hands on her body, on her face. A strong, thick finger pressed against a spot on her neck.

"Mrs. Jeffers, are you okay?"

"I... I think so," she stuttered. "Thank God you're here. What took you so damn long?"

"We're going to get these bindings off you," the soldier said. When the blindfold came off, she blinked and saw he was dressed from head to toe in camouflage. His helmet had a camera. Three or four drones buzzed around the small room. Somewhere outside, people were still shooting.

"Where am I?" She remembered the all-important question they'd told her to ask.

"South Dakota," the soldier said. First he cut the bindings on her hands, then her ankles. "Just stay right where you are, ma'am. You're looking a little pale. Thirsty?" She drank from his canteen. It was water, but laced with something.

"What the hell is this?"

"Just healthy isotonic minerals, Mrs. Jeffers. Take it slow. How long have you been lying here?"

"They gave me a shot. I don't remember anything after that."

"Okay, just stay real quiet now. You want to try sitting up?"

"I wet my pants."

The soldier shrugged, supporting her back with a strong hand as she struggled up. "I've seen worse than that, ma'am."

"The First Lady does not wet her pants. What's your name, soldier?"

"Sergeant Briggs, ma'am. Army Rangers."

"If you breathe a word about my accident, I'll have your ass discharged with twelve kinds of dishonor."

"My lips are sealed, ma'am," Sergeant Briggs said. "Soon as we get this shack secured, we're going to put you in a chopper and get you on your way back home."

It was lucky she'd done drama in college. The tears came easily. She worked it up to a good sob, making a mess of her face to equal the mess in her jeans. The soldier fed her tissues. Real feelings fueled these tears, rage at Jim, who'd tried to kill her, no different from some mafia boss in a movie. Tears of joy at the kindness of Wyoming, even if he'd had ulterior motives. Wyoming, after all, was deeply involved with March22. Up to his neck with the group. She didn't care about his motives. It wasn't as though he'd recruited her. She'd invited *herself* out to California. Wyoming liked her genuinely, and it was beautiful.

Twenty minutes later, the soldiers walked her out of the little house. Her thighs chafed as she walked in these cold, damp jeans. She saw a few other uniformed soldiers standing around, but they must have removed the bodies. A pine forest surrounded the house. The speeding white SUV she rode in, with Sergeant Briggs on the seat next to her, wound around and around on a gravel road that went on for miles before coming out on a paved road. All the while she heard a chopper overhead. How in the world had the Army Rangers found the place?

Forty minutes later, she was strapped in on a huge army helicopter with two rotors, bound for some air base, where a plane would ferry her back to Penelope. She hoped she would still see her daughter before she went to bed.

THE PLANE WAS much bigger than Wyoming's private jet, and Amanda was pleased to see it had a bedroom with a double bed. How she would've liked to lie down and shut her eyes. Sadly, they weren't allowing naps. A woman soldier named Sergeant Janice allowed her to wash in private, but before Amanda could put on more than her underwear, the woman examined every inch of her body. She had some kind of wand in her hand.

"You're not touching me," Amanda said.

"Just checking to see if they planted anything on you," Janice said. "I'm going to wave this over you."

"Go easy on that. My grandmother and one aunt died of breast cancer."

"I hear you, Mrs. Jeffers," Janice said. She held the wand an inch from Amanda's bra in front, then in back, keeping one eye on her military-style Jetlink. Amanda waited for some kind of beep or alarm as Janice waved over her breasts, but none came. Wyoming had promised, promised, *promised* it would be undetectable. The chip must be made of special materials or coated with something, however those things worked.

"I don't know what those criminals would've planted on me. Radishes, maybe?" Amanda said.

"Now your mouth," Janice said. The woman had about as much sense of humor as a block of wood. Amanda opened wide while Janice examined her dentistry with a miniature wand. "You said you were drugged. You wouldn't have any idea what they did to your body."

Dressed, Amanda followed Janice out to the main cabin. Janice handed her off to a friendly looking officer in camouflage. He had big, kind brown eyes that looked right into her, and short hair graying at the temples.

"I'm Major Nance," the soldier said, extending his hand. "It's a pleasure to meet you, ma'am."

"I wish I could say the same," Amanda said. "I just want to get home and see my daughter. How long till we land? Are those for us?" A large platter of crackers and cheese sat on a table. The food supply on the chopper had been limited to cookies and one stick of beef jerky donated by one of the pilots. She could only imagine the jokes he would tell for the rest of his days about the First Lady eating his beef jerky. She hadn't cared.

"About two hours, I'd guess. Shall we sit?"

Sitting to her right, he crossed his legs and smiled, appearing relaxed. A few other soldier-types sat some distance away. Two small drones hovered near the ceiling, no doubt filming, listening, measuring her heart rate or whatever. Sergeant Janice asked what she would like to drink with her meal.

"What're you having?" Amanda asked the major.

"I'll have a Coke," he said.

"Same for me," Amanda said. "Put a little rum in it, could you, honey?"

After Janice brought the drinks and a tray of hot food for her, Major Nance spoke. "Well, how does it feel to be a free woman again?"

"What are you, some kind of psychiatrist?"

The major smiled. "You guessed it. But, listen, don't think about my job. Dr. Smith checked you out and said you were healthy. I'm just here for a little chat, really."

"That's a laugh. That woman checked every inch of my skin as if she thought I had some disease. I'm fine, really. Just tired." She spoke in between bites of fish, rice, and vegetables with cheese melted on top. A piece of strawberry cake waited.

"We're here to protect the First Lady," Major Nance said. "Were you afraid?"

"I hate guns. I hate shooting. When I heard them shooting in that house where I was, I almost peed in my pants again. I thought I was going to die."

"So you were awake?"

"I woke up before the soldiers came. Just lying there."

"Do you remember anything before that?"

"When?"

"From the last nine days?"

Amanda put a blank look on her face. They'd spent hours coaching her on this part. "What do you mean, nine days?"

"You were abducted from a suite at the St. James Hotel nine days ago."

She laughed. "You're joking, right? I thought that was... well, wasn't it yesterday?"

"I'm assuming they kept you under. Unconscious."

"For nine days?"

"It's possible. We don't know who did this, do we?"

"No idea."

"Or why?"

She shook her head, holding his gaze. "I can't believe it's been nine days. That's impossible."

"Check it on your Jetlink, why don't you?" the major said.

She checked the date, and indeed it was December 2. She kept the expression of astonishment while looking at him and shaking her head in disbelief. After a moment, Major Nance went on.

"Suppose you tell me what happened in the hotel that night."

"We were in bed sleeping. All these men burst in the door. They all had machine guns. Suddenly I had three machine guns pointing at me."

"Machine guns or assault rifles?"

"What's the difference?" She hated all guns. Major Nance waved the question aside.

"So you mean they broke down the door?"

"No, they had a card key. They just walked in."

"What did they say?"

"I had to get out of bed. Then I had to get dressed while they pointed their guns at me, whatever kind they were. Wyoming had to stay in bed. They ripped the covers off and took away his pillow. I guess they thought he might've had a gun or something."

"And they had helmets on?"

She realized the major was fully informed. "Like motorcycle helmets with dark visors. You couldn't see a thing. They could've been robots, for all I know."

"Then what happened?"

"They made me get in a bag."

"How did that feel?"

She stared. "How would you feel getting into a bag and then someone zips you up in it?"

"I've never tried it. Claustrophobic, I'm guessing."

"I thought I was going to die. But then I told myself, I'm the First Lady. They wouldn't kill me. They wanted to trade me for political prisoners in some country somewhere or for ransom. If they wanted to kill me, they could've just shot us both in bed."

"Right," the major said. "You were thinking rationally."

"I always think rationally."

"Sometimes in high stress situations the rational mind gives way to emotional reactions."

Like when you find out your husband just gave the order to murder you, Amanda thought. The major sure was right about that.

"When I was a kid, I was walking my dog one day," Nance went on. "His name was King. Golden Retriever. I loved that dog. He ran out into the street after a squirrel and a car hit him. What did I do? I ran right out into the street without looking. The car that hit King had stopped, but another car was going around it at high speed. I barely got out of the way. I almost got killed."

"You were focused on your dog," Amanda said.

"I knew the rules, but the emotional mind takes over. Rational thinking is out the window."

"Makes sense."

"They took off your Jetlink before you got in the bag, correct?"

"Yes."

"Yet you were wearing it when we found you."

"I was?" She looked at it. "I guess I was."

"They must've put it back on you at some point. I wonder why," the major said.

"Is that strange?" She hoped her acting was convincing. In fact, the March22 leaders had known that the Secret Service would be able to track her whereabouts, and had deactivated the Jetlink the day they had flown to Montana. When she'd re-activated it in the chopper flying out of South Dakota, an endless list of unanswered messages had scrolled down the screen.

"It seems risky. What if you'd been able to loosen your binds?"

"I tried. I couldn't."

"But why would they take the risk?"

She met his gaze, trying to appear thoughtful. "I guess you're asking the wrong person."

"Courteous kidnappers?" the major suggested.

"Those guns weren't courteous," she said. "It's not courteous to zip the First Lady into a duffel."

"Nor to drug a person unconscious for more than a week," the major agreed. "Another thing. Did they gag you when they put you in the bag?"

"No."

"Did you realize they were carrying you out of the hotel suite?"

"Yes."

"Did you know you were getting on the elevator?"

She pretended to think back. "Yes, I heard the little bell ring. I heard the doors opening and closing."

"Why didn't you scream?"

"They said they would shoot me."

"Who said it?"

"The one guy. One man did all the talking."

"In the suite he said this?"

"Before they zipped up the bag."

"What did he say exactly?"

"He said, 'If you make a sound, we'll put a bullet in you.'"

"And you believed him."

"Should I have doubted him?"

"It was a public place. Hotel corridors, elevators. Video surveillance. He would've taken a big risk firing shots there."

"I didn't think of that."

"Who could blame you?" The major smiled.

"I was, like, paralyzed. I thought they were going to shoot Wyoming. I was afraid I'd never see Penelope again."

"I was going to say the emotional mind took over," Major Nance said. "But those are rational thoughts. Very interesting."

Amanda held her glass up and looked around. She could only hope this officer would be satisfied with her answers. She caught the eye of Sergeant Janice, who instantly stood up. "Could I get another one of these?"

CHAPTER 14

NEAR ANN ARBOR, MICHIGAN
DECEMBER 2, 2021—4 PM

"LISTEN, MATT, COULD we call a truce?" Claire looked across the table with those intense brown eyes. When he didn't speak, she said, "I'm still pissed at you for trying to escape, and what you did to Gram. You're pissed off because we kidnapped you. I understand that. Anyway, so we're kind of even. Can't we just make the best of it, for the moment at least?"

She had made grilled cheese sandwiches to die for, and when he finished two, she made him three more. She couldn't fit more than three in the pan. Gram had jars of homemade sweet pickles, and they were washing the food down with Coke.

He needed to talk to Luke again. It just wasn't fair that they left him here, expecting him to carry out some vague mission. That idiot Malone had actually been right when he said Matt wasn't fully trained. How did they expect him to get useful information about Dark Fiber? What was the point? This was his second full day in captivity. He just wanted to get back to Montana and be with Raine. Was that too much to ask?

"I've got a confession to make," Claire said. "I enjoyed my work with Dark Fiber up until yesterday. I enjoyed the shadowmarkets, the logistics, the hijackings, and the fights with Black Widow and other militias. But yesterday morning something changed. I don't know what it is. I just don't know if I can go on."

"You're thinking about quitting?"

"Oh, he actually talks. Very good, Matt."

"Shut up."

She shrugged and looked away for once. "You know what they say. Never waste a good crisis."

"What does that mean?" He hated it when people talked in riddles. He was always the last to understand.

"Well, I was thinking about what happened at the cabin, you know? I realized something. They've been contacting me from Dark Fiber, you know, but I haven't answered. Not once. Because I was thinking, hey, what if they all think I'm dead?"

"Why would you think so?"

"The cabin blew up, right? If anyone from Dark Fiber survived the explosion, they knew we were in the basement. They would assume we didn't get out in time."

"They didn't know about the tunnel?"

"A couple of my local members knew about it, but they weren't there. I don't even know if anyone else survived."

"I guess I owe you my life or something," Matt said. He wasn't wild about being in this woman's debt, but they clearly would've died without her quick thinking. All because of some other militia group that kept attacking Dark Fiber.

"So for some reason it's a turning point," Claire said. "I can feel it. I don't know why, exactly, but I feel like it's my chance to get out of that rat race. Do you think I should answer them, or just get out and stay quiet as long as possible?"

He looked at her, clueless about what the right answer could be. How could he possibly know what was right for her? He didn't even know her.

"I mean, sometimes things like this point the way for you, don't you think?"

"I guess so."

"Maybe getting out of there alive while everyone else died, and then having my apartment torched, and then being stuck here with you — everything, you know? Maybe it's all pointing me to the exit, my graceful exit from the militia life."

"You don't have any place to go now," Matt said, realizing the gravity of her situation.

"Gram would let us stay here as long as we need," Claire said. "I think she even sort of forgave you. But yeah. I lost all my stuff, I lost my place. Maybe I lost a friend or two there, too. I don't know who got out in time, or what. I just don't feel like being in touch with people right now. Maybe I'm just happy I survived it myself. I'm sort of content just not existing, at the moment."

"That's not the same as quitting the militia. Giving up being the leader in Ann Arbor and everything."

"I know, but it's not like I'm depressed. Just the opposite. It's more like I see this door in front of me and the door suddenly opened, and all I have to do is step through it."

"What kind of a door?"

"You know, not a real door, an imaginary one. I just can't see what's on the other side. In order to see what's there, you have to have the guts to step through. Does that make any sense?"

"No," Matt said. She laughed, and he smiled with her. "Well it doesn't. Who would ever walk through a door without knowing what was on the other side?"

"We all do it all the time, if you think about it," Claire said. "Like when I opened the door to the tunnel."

"That was different. We had some bad shit happening behind us. We had to get out."

"One good reason for going through the door is because of all the bad shit you have to get away from," Claire said. "You know how bad it is. That much you know. That's bad shit back there, I have to get away. Here's a door just waiting for me to pass through. Even not knowing what's on the other side is tolerable then, because anything is better than the shit you're escaping from. See what I mean?"

"That makes sense," he agreed.

"So that's what I'm saying with Dark Fiber. On the whole, there was a lot of bad shit going on. It couldn't be sustainable. I always knew it was a temporary thing for me. I knew it deep down, but I didn't think about it. I focused on the work we had to do every day, we did it, and we did it well. It's dangerous, illegal, and violent, and, eventually, people die under those conditions, you know what I mean? I don't want to die at age twenty."

"I don't blame you."

·Her idea started him thinking how it had been at home before he left for California—the hassles from his stepmother, Robert, and Marissa, their constant insults and lack of gratitude for all the work he did putting food on the table. Was he their slave? When Wanda had demanded his room, claiming to need it for her home business, he'd been so furious he'd been ready to leave right then. His father's secret message had given him the perfect excuse to get out.

"When I left home, my stepmother actually took a shot at me," he said.

Claire's eyes widened. "Your own stepmother?"

"With a shotgun. Thanks to my little stepbrother she missed."

"Why? What did he do?"

"She was about to shoot at me from the porch as I drove by in my truck. Benjy was watching out of his bedroom window. He sent down a drone and crashed it into her head just as she was pulling the trigger. She did get a shot off, but she missed me."

"My God," Claire laughed.

"I guess that would qualify as bad enough shit to get me through this door you're talking about."

MATT RESTED ON his bed in the early evening, letting his mind wander. No sound came from the rest of the house. Claire was as bored as he was and had proposed watching a movie later. For now, he wanted to be alone.

Anything to report? Luke asked, almost as if his twin brother had been waiting for this moment.

Not a thing.

Was she mad?

Why?

When you tried to escape?

What the hell do you know about that?

First, there was your Jetlink, Luke said. *I figured you were up to something. Then, I saw you on a motorcycle. I felt your anger. More like rage, like a burning fire in my chest. I felt it as if it were burning me up.*

Luke had said this phenomenon was not unheard of in identical twins. Luke sometimes experienced Matt's emotions, especially when they were powerful, negative ones like fear or rage. This phenomenon among identical twins was apparently much more common than their ability to communicate in real time over long distances, which Luke said was unique.

Yeah, she caught me. She was pretty pissed.

We need you to stay there, Matt.

I know, I know.

So, is she hot? Tell me about this babe.

Shut up.

No, just do me a favor and tell me. Big breasts?

You're a real idiot, you know that? Luke was incredibly hard up. It bugged Matt to be pestered about stuff like this.

Corinne's got pretty big breasts, so I really can't complain.

Why are you so obsessed with breasts?

I'm a man, moron. After a while, fake stuff on the Internet doesn't cut it. When Matt said nothing, having no idea what to say, Luke went on. *Did you think just because I'm handicapped I don't have needs? Urges?*

I never thought about it. Now that you're talking about it, I'm trying especially hard not to think about it.

Corinne shows me her breasts, you know, and then she makes me — .

Matt thought he knew exactly how Luke must've finished the sentence, and he was so shocked he couldn't speak. The idea of Luke and Corinne... Luke's wheelchair... Corinne opening her shirt and taking off her bra. Anyway, what could possibly happen next? The whole idea made him nauseous.

Your dick is not a muscle, by the way, Luke continued, as if reading his mind.

Do we really have to talk about this?

What are you, some kind of modern-day Victorian prude? It's one of my great blessings, for lack of a better word. My dick functions just fine. Corinne just has to whip out her boobs and up goes the old tent pole. I live for that, buddy, just imagine. Try to understand instead of just judging me. The problem is Corinne's just doing her job. I can't get that out of my mind, and sometimes it's downright demotivating. She doesn't love me. She probably doesn't even like me.

When they said she was there for your bodily needs, it didn't occur to me that sex was included. How did we even get on this topic?

I inquired politely about Claire Tenneman's boobs.

Oh, yeah.

So, what about it? Can you describe them?

I'm not telling you that.

Why? Didn't you bonk her yet?

Man, you are so weird. You are such a geek. People of the opposite sex don't always hop in bed just because they happen to meet. You know very well that I have a girlfriend. I'm in a relationship, all right?

You are a Victorian prude, I knew it, Luke said. *Either that, or she has tiny breasts.*

Matt felt himself blushing. *I'm not interested in Claire for multiple reasons, for your information. Not a single one has anything to do with the size of her breasts.*

Raine's got really nice breasts, I've got to say.

You shut up about Raine.

All right, don't get pissed. Just a scientific observation, more or less. I'm not going to steal your girl or anything.

You've got a lot to learn if you think breasts are so important. That's all I can say.

Why, what else is there?

Matt was in the midst of considering his answer when he suddenly became aware of knocking. Claire was knocking on the door. It sounded timid, totally unlike Claire. He imagined her standing there, ear to the door, trying to be considerate, wondering if he was sleeping.

"Matt, the movie is starting. You still want to watch it?"

"Be there in a minute," he said.

Luke would have to wait. It felt good to leave him hanging.

CHAPTER 15

WASHINGTON, DC
DECEMBER 2, 2021—7 PM

"THIS IS OFF the record," Jeremy Overman said. "You don't name me or my agency."

"You said you have a story," the white-haired journalist said. Dirk Greenwood had written feature stories for the *Washington Post* for thirty years, but on the side, he wrote political exposés. He had produced seven bestseller books. The managing editor at the *Post*, a younger man named Jenkins with gelled black hair, and a female lawyer named Kahan sat at the other end of the table watching. It was dinnertime and they sat in a private room in a Washington restaurant. Every NSA employee had a tracker implanted, ever since the Edward Snowden affair in 2013, even Holsom. The snoops would have a record of him here, when he'd arrived and when he left, but it would look like an ordinary dinner.

"Those are my conditions."

"We agree to your conditions. What's the story?"

Jeremy checked his Jetlink once more to ensure it was powered off. You couldn't be too careful. He knew it better than most. People powered off from time to time, for various reasons, for example in restaurants. That he could explain away. He'd also insisted on no drones in the room. No video.

He was risking his life being here. As his father always said, there were things worth risking your life for. His father had succumbed to prostate cancer the year before. Dad would've been proud to know he was doing this.

"When the American Prison Corporation had its software glitch on November sixteenth, and the doors of fifteen hundred prisons opened all across the country, a national crisis of unprecedented proportions started," Jeremy said.

"Two million inmates walked out scot free," Greenwood said.

"It happened the same night President Burns and five others were assassinated. President Jeffers was sworn in."

"You're telling me the assassinations were linked to the prison break?" Greenwood said.

"I don't know about that. The story I have for you is about what happened afterward."

"The drone decision?" You could almost see Greenwood salivating.

Jeremy nodded. "In his first decision as president, Jeffers opted to activate military drones for surveillance purposes in order to help round up the escaped prisoners. I was at the meeting."

"Who else was there?"

"My boss was there."

"Holsom?" Greenwood named the NSA chief.

Jeremy nodded. "The attorney general. The president's chief of staff, his press secretary, the secretary of defense, plus a few aides."

"Let me guess, the attorney general and the press secretary before Petra Bedrosian were opposed," Greenwood said.

"Correct. Which is why the president promoted her and is now vetting other candidates for attorney general."

"All right."

"So, they started putting drones in the air. By daybreak, we had six hundred flying. Twenty-four hours later we had about three thousand drones flying, covering most of the country."

"This is not news. I mean, we didn't know the exact numbers. Maybe there's a story in the numbers."

"What happened next is your real story," Jeremy said. His mouth had gone dry as dust. What he was about to do took courage. He popped a stick of gum in his mouth before going on. *You are a brave man,* he thought. "Homeland Security started losing drones within the first twenty-four hours."

"What do you mean, 'losing drones'? They crashed?"

"No, they were stolen."

"The drones were stolen? By whom? How?" Sitting straighter in his chair, Greenwood looked alert.

"By electronic means. The drone controllers reported the same phenomenon again and again. Their computers would crash. By the time they logged on again, the drone was gone. Invisible. Gone from the radar. Taken over in midair by a rogue controller."

"Holy shit," Greenwood said. At the end of the table, Jenkins and the lawyer started murmuring. "Are we talking *armed* drones?"

"The first three thousand went up armed," Jeremy affirmed. "There was a misunderstanding about that. Whenever they came in, over the next few days, the missiles were removed, but the first wave that went up, they were armed."

"How the hell did someone steal them? Do we know who to point the finger at?"

"Nobody has claimed responsibility, but we think this operation has the fingerprint of March22."

"Not a foreign power?"

Jeremy shook his head. "No drones have left our airspace."

"How would you even know, if you can't see them?"

"We have redundant electronic perimeters controlling American airspace up to two hundred miles offshore. We're confident that we would've picked up any drones leaving our airspace. Unless of course they were loaded onto ships. But that's impossible, due to the sheer numbers."

Greenwood was making notes on his Jetlink. "How many drones have been stolen?"

"One thousand, two hundred and ten," Jeremy said.

Greenwood just stared. "Armed?"

"All of them," Jeremy said.

Greenwood looked at his editor for a long moment. "Times like this, I really need a cigarette."

"Be my guest," Jeremy said.

"Don't even think about it," Kahan, the lawyer said. Greenwood stuffed the pack back in his breast pocket. "Please go on, Mr. Overman."

"All right, just out of curiosity, what was the president's reaction to the missing drones?" Greenwood said.

"As you all know, President Jeffers was secretary of defense before becoming president two weeks ago," Jeremy said. "He was in charge of the country's drone program when they were still being deployed in Afghanistan, Pakistan, Yemen and other countries. Just when production of new UAVs was ramped up. You can imagine how furious he was."

"Have you made any progress in finding them? Or finding out who was responsible?"

"As I said, it's reasonably certain March22 is behind it," Jeremy said.

"What makes you think so? Are you speaking for yourself or for the NSA?"

"This is the government's position. That being said, we are still not one hundred percent certain."

"Damn, this *is* a story," Greenwood said.

"We could not locate the drones on any radar or by any electronic means, but we surmised there must be a command and control that was directing the overall operation. On the third night of our search operations, we isolated a series of microburst signals emanating from the Bay Area. They went dark and then they would send again. It took us a few more days, but we finally nailed the coordinates. The Navy sent in a wet team, and we covered them with stealth choppers."

"Don't tell me this was that business at Stanford University," Greenwood said.

"Right again. Early in the morning on November twenty-third."

"So there was no virus outbreak?"

Jeremy shook his head. "A ploy we hatched with Centers for Disease Control's cooperation to get everyone off campus so we could go in and take out March22's command and control."

"So, what happened?"

"Our elements on-site commenced their attack, but ten minutes later they were called off. They received new orders to interdict a terrorist attack at the Presidio, twenty miles away. The people in the command center escaped."

"Wait a minute. Why were those units called off in the middle of an operation?"

"March22—if it really was them—was able to give orders that appeared genuine. Choppers, jeeps, about fifty men. They left Stanford University, believing they were following genuine orders."

"How the hell did they do that?" Greenwood's voice was tinged with awe.

"What about traitors within the US military?" the lawyer asked.

"We've got a lot of people working on it, twenty-four-seven," Jeremy said. "Someone stole our drones. Someone redeployed our troops, even in a super-secret operation like this. So far, we've found no evidence at all that it's coming from inside the military. If it is March22, we've clearly underestimated them till now."

"You said they escaped."

Jeremy nodded. "You remember what happened at the San Francisco Airport?"

"That was the same morning. Of course," Greenwood said.

"Our theory is that they created a diversion at the north end of the field. Ten remote controlled big rigs, a hole blasted in the perimeter fence. Our tanks and other assets were stationed at commercial aviation, guarding the kerosene supplies, when they received orders to move to the north perimeter to fight off an incursion. All the assets moved up to the north end of the field."

"That was a hell of a firefight," Greenwood said.

"Not really," Jeremy said. "We took out the trucks easily. When we went in to inspect the damage, there were no bodies. The big rigs were operated by remote control. That's when we started to smell a rat. Then we had a private plane taking off, even though the whole airport was closed due to the firefight. One plane."

"Don't tell me. Wyoming Ryder's plane."

"Correct," Jeremy said.

"Which went down in the Sierra Nevada."

"Which we shot down."

"Get out of here," Jenkins said from the end of the table.

"Have you got proof?" Greenwood said.

"I've got video. The president gave the order himself."

"Holy Christ," Jenkins said. "The president ordered Wyoming Ryder's plane shot out of the sky? Can you get us that video?"

"I have it right here," Jeremy said, putting a memory stick on the table. The other three in the room eyed it greedily.

"Any objection to watching it right now?" Greenwood said.

"My Jetlink is off. You'll do the honors?" Jeremy gave the stick to Greenwood, who plugged it into his Jetlink and aimed his projector at the near wall.

When the video activated, it showed images taken from far above. A red circle enclosed the private jet, which was hard to distinguish because of the clouds beneath it. After a few seconds, the picture zoomed closer to the private jet, and then slowed to two frames per second. From the left of the screen a projectile streaked into the picture and slammed into the engines at the tail of the plane. The plane exploded in a fireball. When the picture cleared, only clouds could be seen.

"This happened ten days ago."

"Wyoming Ryder's plane, yet he appeared on TV yesterday, standing in front of his plane," Greenwood said.

"We're not sure what the explanation is," Jeremy said. "We know this was the plane that took off unauthorized from San Francisco Airport. We followed it on radar from the moment it took off. The president assumed the drone control elements that had been holed up at Stanford were on board."

"On Wyoming Ryder's plane."

"Yes."

"Yet he denies it. He denies that his plane was even shot down. He's alive and well, and we saw his plane on TV."

Jeremy nodded. "He claims to have been in his hotel suite that morning in San Francisco with the First Lady when six men came in and kidnapped her."

"Jesus, this is hairy shit," Greenwood said. "What about the wreckage? You find the wreckage, you'll know who died in the crash."

"We haven't located the wreckage. It's a very rugged and remote area."

"And Ryder claims the First Lady was kidnapped out of their hotel room."

"Right."

"But we just watched the video. And you guys know it was his plane, what, from the markings?"

"And the transponder."

"And the First Lady? Who grabbed her?"

"We don't know. But we picked up some chatter during the night last night and raided a house in South Dakota late this morning."

"South Dakota?"

"Army Rangers rescued her. Mrs. Jeffers was safe and sound, but doesn't remember a thing, can't tell us who the kidnappers were or why they kidnapped her. She should be back in Washington by now."

"What kind of chatter?"

"You know, key words, that kind of thing. We're good at that sort of thing."

"I get it. Telephone, email, or Jetlinks."

"Right."

"Why kidnap the First Lady? Who would do that? What are they trying to achieve?"

Jeremy shrugged. "Not for money, presumably. We didn't get any ransom demand. Nobody claimed responsibility. She was just gone for nine days, and then she turned up again."

"What about this chatter, what can you tell us?" Greenwood said.

"Sometimes you get lucky," Jeremy said. "We picked up some key words. We located the signal. They got sloppy."

"Or they led you there," Greenwood said.

"I doubt that," Overman said.

"But not so lucky with those drones," Greenwood went on. "Where the hell would you hide a thousand drones? How the hell does anyone outside the military even know how to fly them?"

"Very good questions," Jeremy said.

"I have another question," Greenwood said. "You put yourself at risk tonight. Why did you come forward with this?"

"Look, there's something I didn't get to yet," he answered. Time for the big revelation. "Back at the San Francisco Airport, our tanks started getting hit with missiles from above. In fact, after taking out the big rigs, all six of our tanks were destroyed from the air."

He watched their faces transforming as the reality of what he'd just said sank in. All three looked deeply shocked. It made his own skin crawl.

"Explain," Greenwood said simply.

"Stolen drones took out all the tanks that morning at San Francisco Airport," Jeremy said. "Hellfire air-to-ground missiles. It was a real mess. It was over in five minutes. We had our own drones in the theater as well, but we couldn't see the stolen drones. They can fly them, but we can't detect them."

"And they fucking know how to aim missiles," Greenwood said, low.

"Now you know why I came to you," Jeremy said. "It worries me."

The look on their faces was that same look of complete shock people had had on 9/11. No matter how many times you saw it on TV, it didn't go away. It was the initial shock, but it was something more as well. It was the realization that the world had become a more dangerous place.

Jeremy thought they all looked suddenly ten years older, gray, the lines in their faces deeper. Greenwood, the star journalist, shook out a cigarette, lit it, and blew out a long rope of smoke. The lawyer at the other end of the table, Kahan, said nothing.

Strange how Jeremy felt better now.

CHAPTER 16

WASHINGTON, DC
DECEMBER 2, 2021—7 PM

TOGETHER WITH NSA Chief Holsom, Dave Knopfler from Homeland Security, Defense Secretary Reese, and Chief of Staff Tom Underwood, President James Jeffers watched raw video of an army major talking to Amanda.

"Reactions?" he said.

"She looks a little out of it," Knopfler said. "You'd expect that from a person held captive."

"We'll find out more in the debriefing," Underwood said.

"One thing that was strange," Knopfler went on. "That house in South Dakota where we found her, it was rigged with remote control, wall-mounted guns. Bunch of miniature drones flying around giving someone visual input."

"What do you mean?" Underwood said.

"They were firing at our rangers via remote control," Knopfler said. "This is March22 at work. I'd stake my life on it."

Jeffers looked from one man to the next, as they all digested this news. Knowing your enemy was the first step to vanquishing them.

"This whole thing stinks of March22," Jeffers said. "It started with the drones, then that fiasco at San Francisco Airport. Someone stole our bombs, and I'd bet my last dollar it was March22. That was Wyoming Ryder's plane taking off that morning, dammit. What are we doing to squeeze that jackass?"

"We moved him to San Francisco," Knopfler said. "The local FBI chief got things started. Our investigations of his business empire are on overdrive. We need to go to work on him now."

"You need to study the money flows," Tom Underwood pointed out.

"Is Penelope prepped?" Jeffers asked, moving on.

"Are you sure you want to do this, Mr. President?" Holsom asked.

Jeffers fixed him with a stare. "It's a matter of national security. Amanda will share things with our daughter that she would never reveal to me. Maybe not today or tomorrow, but give her time. I know her, gentlemen." He left it at that. He didn't need to say the rest.

"I'M GLAD YOU'RE safe." Jim looked into her eyes and squeezed her hands, then kissed her on the cheek. Amanda's cheek burned where his lips touched it. This was the man who'd given the order to kill her nine days ago.

"Where's Penelope?" Amanda asked. It was seven in the evening in Washington, but her daughter was neither in the dining room eating nor in her bedroom studying. After landing at Dover Air Force Base less than an hour ago, they'd rushed her to the White House under police escort. She hadn't even stopped to pee.

"At my mother's in Alexandria," he said. "She's been there for a week. Under the circumstances —"

She didn't let him finish. "I need to see her. I miss her so much."

"We'll bring her back in a few days, Amanda. Let her enjoy her evening."

"You don't understand. I thought I was going to die. I have to see her right away and give her a hug."

"You didn't give me a hug."

Amanda smoldered behind her smile. Was Jim ever going to admit what he'd done? He hadn't tried to hug her, either. He didn't try now.

"I'll go and call a car," she said.

"Amanda, no," Jim said. "They have to debrief you."

"They did that the whole way home on the plane."

"That wasn't a debriefing."

"How do you know what it was?" He'd obviously been listening, but getting Jim to admit it would be like moving rocks.

"All this is standard operating procedure. Like when our agents spend time behind the lines, so to speak. They have to be debriefed. It happens right away. Before you sleep."

"What do you mean, behind the lines?"

"You were missing for nine days, Amanda."

He was fishing, just as Major Nance had done. It was almost as if they knew something. Yet if they really knew, she would be in handcuffs now. "I'll collapse if I have to answer any more questions."

"No you won't. You're my Amanda." His expression softened and he took her hands again. "Did you at least have a good time before the kidnapping?"

What a ridiculous question. Where was he going with this? "It was a relief to be away from this rat race," she said honestly.

A knock on the door interrupted the awkward silence. A white-gloved Secret Service agent stepped in.

"Mrs. Jeffers, if you could come with me," the boy said in a high voice. She almost laughed. He couldn't be more than twenty-one.

"Please, stay for dinner. What's your name?"

The agent glanced at the president.

"She's going with you, Sergeant. Just a little shy," Jim said.

The conference room Amanda walked to, against her will, turned out to be yet another room in the White House she'd never seen before. The red leather couch looked inviting, but so did the big armchairs with plump pillows. A fire crackled in the fireplace. When the uniformed man standing in the corner turned, she recognized Major Nance from the plane. These people worked long hours.

Then a man stood up in the other corner. She hadn't seen him at first. This man had longish blond hair that looked anything but military style, and he was dressed in Armani jeans and a black turtleneck. He wore sneakers, a gold bracelet, and had a small tattoo on the back of his hand.

"You again," she said to Major Nance. "They said there was food here."

"We can order whatever you like," the major said. "Mrs. Jeffers, may I introduce Riley Johnson from Homeland Security."

They shook hands. "Homeland Security? I guess you want to know about my kidnapping. I've already told the major here everything."

"Mr. Johnson is fully apprised of our conversation, to spare you the trouble of repeating," Major Nance said. "This time I'm just going to listen."

"And watch me in case I'm lying?"

"I'm sure you wouldn't lie, Mrs. Jeffers. Please don't be suspicious. You're the First Lady, and we don't know why they kidnapped you. We don't know who it was. We're trying to gather bits and pieces that might lead us somewhere. You want to find out who did this, don't you?"

I want to hurt the man who tried to kill me. She left the question unanswered and sat down on one of the armchairs.

"I'm starving. Could you get them to bring me a green salad and a steak with fries or something? And some red wine?"

Major Nance spoke low into his Jetlink as Johnson took a seat in the other armchair and crossed his legs, never looking away from her face.

"Do you want to catch whoever did this to you?" Johnson asked. "I didn't hear your answer."

"It's a really dumb question," Amanda said.

"It's an important question."

"Of course I want you to catch them. Do you think I liked being tied up and blindfolded?"

"You must be tired," Johnson said. "Hopefully the food will do you good."

"I can see I'm going to lose my appetite with your questions."

"Oh, I don't think so. We already have a large part of the story, so maybe we won't be here all that long. Let's see, I was wondering if you could tell us anything more about how you first met Wyoming Ryder?"

"There was an awards dinner in Washington last year," she said. "Jim couldn't go, but I wanted to. I happened to be seated next to Wyoming."

"What did you talk about?"

She put on a sweet smile. They'd gotten off to a bad start, but this was easier. "What would you talk about with America's biggest movie star of the last twenty years? What it's like to be a star. Living in California. His ex-wives, his children, his house."

"Did you talk about yourself?"

"I don't like to talk about myself much."

"So he didn't ask you what it's like to be married to a career army officer?"

She made as if to reflect. "Certainly not. We mostly talked about him, but I guess we also talked about the environment."

"The environment?"

"I think we even argued about it, now that I remember."

"What about?" Johnson prodded.

"Oh, I don't know. I think it was something to do with oil drilling. You know those people in California. They're against any kind of drilling. Where do they expect us to get our oil if we don't drill for it? I continued to remind him of the benefits of being energy self-sufficient. He kept talking about bird habitats."

"He's a well-known environmentalist. Owns a large amount of land in northern California and insists on keeping it undeveloped."

"I guess so. At least that's what he said." She wondered why Johnson hadn't mentioned the places in Montana. Maybe Wyoming owned them through some foundation. Maybe the government wasn't aware of them. Well, Montana didn't exist in her story anyway. She'd been zipped into a bag in San Francisco and rescued in South Dakota. Unconscious to everything in between.

"Did you talk about the environment when you saw him in California?"

"No, I don't think so."

"Not once?"

She shrugged. "Maybe he was trying to avoid an argument."

"Would you mind telling me what you did talk about?"

She sighed. "Listen, this is a huge invasion of my privacy. Are you going to ask me about *everything*? What is the point of this anyway?"

"It's like Major Nance said," Johnson answered. "We don't really know what we're looking for. You were there, and we have to reconstruct it through your impressions. Anything you can share might be helpful. Anything at all."

"Well, he has a nice plane. I liked it better than any plane I've ever been on."

"What was so nice about it?"

"I don't know, just so sleek and white. He opened a bottle of champagne. We watched a video. It was so relaxing. Maybe it wasn't the plane, just the company."

"This was on your trip from DC out to LA?"

"Right."

"But you took his plane again, didn't you?"

"Yes, we flew to San Francisco. It seems like yesterday, but they told me I lost nine days out of my life. God, that was such a shock."

"Why did you fly to San Francisco?"

"I think I told Major Nance already, didn't I?"

"Not sure," the major said.

"Well, Wyoming Ryder's son lives there. That's why we went."

"When did you leave?"

"It was very early in the morning. Oh, golly, yes, now I remember. We were still sleeping when some man burst into Wyoming's bedroom. One of his staff. He said there was shooting in the yard. Some kind of a shootout."

"You were sleeping when this happened?"

"He woke us up. So after he went out again, Wyoming barred the door, and then we ran into his bathroom and up a ladder to the roof. There was a chopper waiting on the roof, and we flew right to the airport."

"Did you find that strange?"

She looked for a hidden meaning in Johnson's eyes. He had beautiful blue eyes, but she sensed a deep coldness. He was trying to trick her, despite his friendly demeanor. Homeland Security prick. That would be a fitting title for Johnson.

"Of course I found it strange, what do you think? I could see them shooting each other as the helicopter took off. I hate guns. I hate shooting. There's way too much of it everywhere, like an epidemic. We managed to stamp out diseases like polio, but people go right on killing each other every hour of every day with guns, as if that were the most normal thing in the world."

"I meant strange to have a gun battle in the home of a Hollywood star."

"What did I just say? I don't think it should happen anywhere. Yes, I found it highly strange in every way."

"Did you receive a message from the president that morning?"

"Yes. He told me to be at LAX at seven. He wanted me to fly back to Washington."

"And you answered him."

"I told him, no dice." She had no doubt that the messages had all been recorded somewhere.

"But the president didn't *ask* if you wanted to come home, Mrs. Jeffers. He ordered you to come home." Johnson's cold blue eyes never wavered.

"He may be the president, Mr. Johnson, but he's also my husband. I don't always do what he tells me. It was unreasonable. I'd just arrived."

"Didn't it occur to you that it might be dangerous to take off in Wyoming Ryder's chopper and fly away?"

"I thought it would be dangerous sticking around with a gun battle downstairs. Wyoming wanted to get away from the shooting."

"Do you know who was shooting or why?"

"I have no idea."

"Didn't Mr. Ryder tell you?"

"He didn't know it himself."

Johnson made a dubious face. "In fact, we came to bring you to the airport ourselves, but were denied entrance at the front gate. When our agents used force to open the gate, Ryder's people started shooting. We lost five Secret Service agents that morning."

"Coming for me?"

"Yes, you."

"Why were they coming to get me? Why did they need to use force?"

"Those men getting shot, they were your ride."

Amanda was taken aback. Five Secret Service agents had died for her. Men with families, men with whole lives up to that moment. Wyoming's men had traded gunfire with the Secret Service while she flew away in his chopper.

"I'm very sorry for them. Really, I am. I had no idea they were our people. My God, what a mess. How could I have known? Jim didn't say anything about a ride in his message. He just told me to be at the airport by seven. I answered him. That was it. Sometime after that, we had that guy burst into our bedroom and announce there was shooting downstairs."

"Did you know there were four Secret Service men in the house with you while you slept?"

"I knew they were there," Amanda said.

"Did you know that Mr. Ryder's staff overpowered them and locked them in a walk-in freezer in the early hours of the morning?"

She made her mouth into a large O. "Of course not. How shocking!"

"Didn't Wyoming Ryder give the order to do that?"

"Certainly not, Mr. Johnson. If you're suggesting he had anything to do with this mix-up, you're absolutely mistaken."

"If he didn't give the order to lock them up, who was it? Are you saying you think someone on his staff did that without Wyoming Ryder knowing it?"

"This is the first I've heard of it. If you tell me it happened, I guess I have to believe you. As far as I'm concerned, that's the only explanation."

"Were you with him all the time?"

"Of course."

"All right, so you boarded the plane and went to the St. James in San Francisco, right?"

"That's right."

"You spent the whole day in your hotel suite, correct?"

"The meeting with his son didn't work out. We were both worn out from all the things that had happened. It was a relaxing day, actually."

"Did he check in with his staff back in Malibu?"

"Not that I know of."

"Did he make any calls while you were with him?"

"I suppose he might've. I didn't notice."

"I need you to think carefully, Mrs. Jeffers. When he left Malibu, his house was under attack, correct? He escaped with you in a chopper and then you flew to San Francisco. Wouldn't he have wanted to know how it turned out? Five men were killed on our side and the same number on Mr. Ryder's staff. Plus, a fair amount of damage to the statues in the yard and the house itself. Don't you find it odd that he didn't check in? Are you sure he didn't say anything about his own people dying?"

"Look, maybe he checked in while I was in the bath. How should I know? He didn't say anything to me about it. You're asking me about things I'm not even aware of. It doesn't help you much if I just invent answers you want to hear, does it?"

"No, I don't want you to invent anything. But didn't you ask him about the gunfight in his yard, later in the day?"

"No." She shuddered.

"Why not? You said you saw it from the chopper. Weren't you the slightest bit curious about what happened?"

"Mr. Johnson, I already told you. I hate guns. I hate shooting. It's like an allergic reaction. I didn't ask him. Maybe I was trying to put it out of my mind."

A sharp knock came on the door. A waiter entered with a tray. The inviting aroma of steak fries carried across the room, and she eyed the big glass of red wine greedily.

"Finally, my dinner," Amanda said. "Are we finished here?"

"Fifteen minute break." Johnson checked his Jetlink.

SHE ATE IN silence, the two men sitting like statues, not watching. She wished she could get in a car and be whisked to where Penelope was. She wanted to crush her daughter in a hug. She wanted to explain the ways of the world. But Jim had pulled presidential authority, and she wouldn't see her daughter till tomorrow.

Wyoming and the others she'd met had given her many warnings and tips on interrogations. They'd coached her on likely questions and the answers she could give. She had to sound credible without seeming like a changed person. That was the hardest part. She *was* a changed person. How could an experience like finding out that your husband tried to blow you out of the sky not *change* you?

"Did you enjoy your dinner?" Johnson asked, fingering a long lock of blond hair away from his forehead.

The alcohol warmed her mood. "They do a good job with steak fries."

"I find it curious that the wife of a career military officer hates guns," Johnson said.

"What's weird about it? I'm just afraid of them, that's all."

"But you've been married for many years." Johnson smiled. "It would be like someone hating movies while married to an actor."

"People are different," Amanda said simply.

"I want to talk about you and Mr. Ryder," Johnson said. "You had sex with him."

"What is this?"

"Let me finish. You had sex and, so my question is, do you feel an emotional attachment to him?"

"What in God's name has this got to do with my kidnapping?"

"Mrs. Jeffers, excuse me, but it's my job to ask the questions. It's your job to answer."

"Why do I feel like I'm on trial?"

"I don't know. Why would you?"

"Because you're asking me personal questions, you moron."

Johnson smiled. Major Nance looked impassive. "I need to know if you're emotionally attached."

"Do you realize what an insulting question that is?"

"Yes, I see that."

"I'm the First Lady, and I do not have to answer your insulting questions."

"I'm afraid you do, Mrs. Jeffers. Listen, you're looking a little tired. I'm sure you'd like nothing better than to go back upstairs and go to bed. The sooner we can get this done, the sooner you can go."

"What kind of a woman do you think I'd be if I had sex with someone without an emotional attachment? What do you take me for?"

"Good, so the attachment is there. Do you love him?"

"Go to hell, Riley."

"Mrs. Jeffers, these are things we need to know."

"If the president wants to know things like that, he can ask me himself."

Johnson ignored her response, but moved to a different question. "Are you planning to see Mr. Ryder again?"

"I don't even know if the man is alive. How do I know?"

Johnson had a quizzical look. "What makes you think he might not be alive?"

"The last time I saw him, I was being zipped into a bag while several people were pointing machine guns at him, okay?"

"He is alive. He went to the FBI and informed them of the kidnapping. Unfortunately, he did so after an inexcusably long delay."

"So, he's alive?" She allowed a look of relief to flood her face.

"You'd like to see him again?"

"If the occasion presented itself, I'd be happy to see him," she said honestly. Wyoming had said the more questions you answered honestly, the better you came off. "Right now, my first priority is to see my daughter."

"How do you think your daughter will react to the news of your affair with Mr. Ryder?"

"That's *really* none of your business, Mr. Johnson. You know very well our daughter is off limits." Actually, Penelope had been jealous when she told her she was going to California. Every woman in the country would be happy to get an hour alone with Wyoming Ryder. Amanda had enjoyed eight days.

"It is my business, Mrs. Jeffers. Do you think she'll feel ashamed of you?"

"Certainly not."

"Do you think she'll be angry that you betrayed her father?"

"Only a nincompoop would think so." The Homeland Security officer was ignoring her demand to leave Penelope out of it. The March22 leaders had warned her they might try to use Penelope to get to her. She hadn't believed them.

"Do you think the president was happy about your affair with Mr. Ryder?"

"He doesn't give a damn," Amanda said. "Besides, I don't think he does 'happy.'"

"Do you think your affair reflects well on him?"

"I can see what you're trying to do," she said. "You're never going to make me feel guilty. You should be asking the president about his betrayal of me, not the other way around."

"What do you mean by that?"

"Well, for one thing I never even see him. For another thing, he never gives me a second thought, much less spending any time with me, caring about me. That's a kind of betrayal, wouldn't you say?"

"Isn't it possible Mr. Ryder himself was responsible for your kidnapping, Mrs. Jeffers?"

"What kind of ridiculous theory is that?"

"What if those were *his* men in the hotel suite? Why did he turn against the Secret Service agents who were sleeping in his house? Why did his staff use deadly force keeping other agents out, when the First Lady was in his house?"

"I guess you have to ask him, if you really think it happened that way," she said. "That's not what happened at all. I was there."

"Did Wyoming Ryder say anything to you about March22?" Johnson asked.

"March22?"

"Yes, the terrorist group."

"Where do they come into it?"

"Did he mention March22?"

"No. For Heaven's sake, what next?"

"Nothing at all?"

Did they think she was stupid? "Which part of the word 'no' didn't you get, Mr. Johnson? What's March22 got to do with it, anyway?"

"The events at San Francisco Airport lead us to believe he's involved with March22," Johnson said. "His plane flew out of there when the airport was closed and under attack by a convoy of March22 big rigs. Then there was the destruction of our tanks. There are other things I can't mention here. He was either in the wrong place at the wrong time, or he's involved. Hugely involved. I don't believe in coincidences that big, Mrs. Jeffers."

"You obviously know much more about all these things than I do," she said. Johnson seemed to know what he was talking about. She hoped the worry she felt inwardly didn't register. At least the March22 leaders who were listening to this would know just how well Homeland Security was on to them. "I have no knowledge of the things you're describing. Personally, concerning Wyoming Ryder, I'd say you're barking up the wrong tree. The man shoots pictures, reads scripts, does publicity appearances, and meets his fans. How could he ever be involved with March22? Where do you guys come up with this stuff?"

"Where were you for the last eight or nine days, Mrs. Jeffers?"

She drained the last of her wine and looked plaintively at Johnson. "Either this is done, or you get me another glass of wine."

Major Nance spoke into his Jetlink.

"We're not done, Mrs. Jeffers. Not by a long stretch. Wine is cheap and so, it seems, is the truth." Johnson's eyes had that cold glint again.

The questions kept coming for the next three hours. Where she found the energy to fend them off, she had no idea. Maybe they thought plying her with wine would get her to reveal something incriminating, either about herself or Wyoming, but she knew her tolerance for alcohol. She consumed it slowly and on a full stomach. Her strength was born out of righteousness. Her own husband had tried to kill her. She wasn't about to forgive it.

CHAPTER 17

NEAR RED LODGE, MONTANA
DECEMBER 2, 2021—8 PM

"DID MATT EVER tell you about the night we met Sander's sons, Walt and Tom?" Benjy asked. Raine set down her fork, thinking. They were having dinner in the kitchen of the lodge, just the two of them. Most of the others had left camp in a hurry this afternoon, with no one saying why. The two of them were leaving tomorrow morning with Winter. No one had heard anything from Matt or Dark Fiber today.

"He never mentioned those names. Sander is the leader who lives in Iowa, right?"

"Exactly," Benjy said. "His sons live in northern Illinois. At first we thought they were the enemy, but then they saved our lives."

"Why, what happened?"

"This was that first night. Matt had escaped from home with a bunch of UMC guys being killed and then we'd gone through a checkpoint and watched a helicopter get shot out of the sky. We'd already seen a lot."

"I'll say you did," Raine said.

"It was the middle of the night, probably two in the morning, and we were on this narrow county road in northern Illinois, heading for the Mississippi River. Matt saw a dead deer lying by the side of the road, and we got out to load it in his truck. Then, a few minutes later, this red Chrysler came driving up behind us really fast, flashing their bright lights in our mirror, and they made us pull over."

"That must've been scary."

"It was like we were the only ones out there, for miles around. Matt had his slingshot out, but he decided not to shoot the guys for some reason. I think because there were two. He might've gotten the first, but then the second would've shot us faster than he could reload. Instead, we started talking to them. They demanded the deer, since we were in their territory, but then they surprised us. They gave us an assault rifle and a whole bag of ammunition in exchange, as if they did that kind of thing every day. They sent us on our way."

"That's amazing," Raine said.

"We thought so too. We were still kind of raving about it a few minutes later when we saw two motorcycles catching up behind us. This time it didn't go so well. They pulled us over and made us get out at gunpoint. I thought we were goners."

"Who were they? Friends of the guys who gave you the gun?"

"Not at all. They were after me. My mom got in contact with the UMC in Chicago and got them looking for us. That's where they caught up with us. They told me to get on the back of one of the bikes, and Matt had to get in the truck. Otherwise they were going to shoot him."

"My God, I can't believe all the brutal stuff you guys went through," Raine said. Her face had gone pale.

"I guess we had a guardian angel that night," Benjy went on. "While we were still standing there in the road, Walt and Tom came roaring back in their red Chrysler. When the one UMC guy was distracted by the oncoming car, Matt shot him with the AR-15."

"Oh no," Raine said. Her eyes filled with tears.

"The other guy had his gun on me, but the Chrysler smashed into him before he could react. They didn't even slow down. The guy flew about fifty feet in the air, and died on the spot."

For a minute, Raine just stared. She looked like she was about to cry. Benjy couldn't quite believe he was sharing these details with her. He hadn't told anyone about the events of that night. Maybe that was the problem. Maybe he just needed to let it out.

"They rescued you," Raine said. "But how did they... how did they know?"

"Tom and Walt had left a drone behind to follow us for a while. Then they saw the motorcycles race by when they were driving back the other way. They had a bad feeling and decided to turn around and make sure we were all right. When they saw us stopped by the side of the road with those guys pointing guns at us, they knew what to do."

Raine let out a big sigh and rested her head on her arms on the table.

The whole scene had replayed in Benjy's mind a hundred times. He knew he would never forget the sight of that big red Chrysler speeding towards them like a runaway train, catching the UMC dude standing in the middle of the road. A car's front end could serve as a deadly weapon just like anything else.

"They took us back to their house," he said. "We spent the night there, and the next day they gave us another car so we wouldn't be recognized so easily if any other UMC guys came after us."

"Why was the UMC after you? I don't understand."

"Earlier that night, my mom had told them to ambush Matt when he was skinning a deer, only Matt got the jump on the guy and shot him with his slingshot. Then there were those other UMC guys that came after Matt as he was leaving the house. They came to avenge the first one. Five of them died. The local Chicago UMC people were pissed, and they obviously had my mom feeding them information."

"I never realized it was so incredibly bad at home."

"It was always bad, but it really turned rotten after John left. You know how Matt has always idolized John."

"Of course."

"John taught him how to shoot a gun when he was twelve. Even before that, he got him started with the slingshot. Matt would go out in the forest for hours and practice with his slingshot. In those days he used to take the bus to get there."

"I knew they spent a lot of time together when Matt was younger."

"But you know what Matt did that night before he left?"

"What?"

"This really tells you something about Matt," Benjy said. Now that he had gotten started, it felt so natural talking about his stepbrother. "He was responsible for our food, you know? Especially the hunting, so we would always have meat, but also the ration coupons. So, instead of just leaving on the spot, he took the time to go hunting. He took his truck out to the edge of the city, where he knows he can usually get a deer, and he killed two deer with one shot."

"Two? How do you kill two with one shot?"

"Wait, there's more. This is what I was telling you about before, that first UMC guy. Matt brings the deer back to that old abandoned garage near the house where he always skins them, right? What he didn't know was my stepmother had sent a drone to spy on him. As soon as she sees him in there, she calls up the local UMC office, tells them there's a guy skinning a deer, and gives them the address. Next thing you know, Matt is ambushed in there by a UMC guy with a gun."

"He didn't tell me this."

"He's so modest, he would never tell you. The guy was ready to kill him for that fresh meat, but Matt surprised him with his slingshot. He shot him in the wrist and then took his gun away."

"My God," Raine said.

"But he knew he had to get out of there. Those guys are vicious, and they look out for each other. Matt threw the one carcass in his truck, leaving the other one hanging there, and drove home. Within five minutes, he was in and out of the house. He told my mom he was going to New Orleans, to throw her off his track, even though he was headed to California."

"Matt is so smart. People don't give him credit for that."

"I'll say he is. Wait till you hear the rest. Matt saw on our TV wall that my mom had a drone in the garage. My mom had watched the whole thing. He really blew up when he saw it. That's why she got so mad. Her plan got messed up, and he found out about it."

"I never knew she was so underhanded," Raine said.

"She sent me up to my room when Matt went out the door. I watched him drive across the road to the CVS drugstore just as three UMC cars came up Ashland from the south. I was thinking, my God, that's the end of Matt. All I could do was watch out my bedroom window."

"How did he get away?"

"He hid behind the CVS for a minute. Two of the UMC cars drove into a trap that either John or Matt set up, I'm not sure."

"What kind of a trap?"

"They had bolted a big gun to the top of a telephone pole in the CVS parking lot. When the UMC cars drove into the line of fire, Matt pulled the trigger, using an app on his Jetlink."

"Matt did that?" She was obviously shocked to hear about Matt killing all these people.

"They were going to kill him, Raine. He was smart enough to realize it, and brave enough to fight. That's why he's still alive today."

Raine's eyes filled, and then tears were running down her cheeks. She hadn't eaten another bite. Maybe he shouldn't have upset her with all the gory details, after all. If Matt hadn't told her these things, maybe there was a good reason.

Benjy had always admired Matt in spite of everything Robert, Marissa, and their mom had said. His siblings spent their entire high school years in a perpetual high. The smell of drugs polluted the house for everyone. His mother was chained to her Red Label. She could go without food for days, but not without her whiskey.

Matt, on the other hand, never touched alcohol or anything that could be smoked. Almost singlehandedly, when he wasn't in school, Matt had taken care of procuring food for the family of six during the past two years. He might be lousy in school, but Matt knew how to handle a slingshot, guns, and cars.

Benjy dreamed of building his muscles. He might never look like Matt, and he might never learn to handle a gun like his stepbrother, but the training in this March22 camp was already having a noticeable effect.

"Maybe I shouldn't have told you all that stuff," he said when Raine had calmed down. "Maybe Matt wouldn't have wanted you to know it."

"I want to know all of it." Raine's eyes flashed. "If he didn't tell me, there could only be two reasons. Either he's too modest, or he didn't want to hurt me. Neither one is good. He tries to put me on a pedestal but I'm much tougher than he thinks. I miss him so much. I need to hear all this stuff in order to know the real Matt."

"I guess so," Benjy said.

"You said two cars got shot up in his trap. What about the third one?"

"He said there were two UMC guys in each car. One guy got out and ran away when they drove into the kill trap. The other three guys were dead. The third car steered away from the trap and chased Matt around the back of the CVS. Matt came roaring out and passed the house once more. My mom was out on the porch waiting. That's when she took a shot at him with our shotgun."

"After all that, he still had to get shot at by her." Raine shook her head, looking at him through tears. She was absolutely right, Benjy thought. It was beyond comprehension, your own stepmother shooting at you at the same time you were trying to outrun a bunch of UMC killers.

"I was watching out of my window. I just said to myself, this is not happening. I sent my Viper down and crashed it into her head just as she was pulling the trigger."

Raine's eyes filled again, but she was laughing. "You hit her in the head with your drone? I can't believe it."

"She was so pissed off, I thought she was going to shoot *me*," Benjy said. "I kept my door locked for a while, till she went away to find her drink. Then I snuck out, got on my motorbike, and took off after him."

"How did you find him? How did you know where to go?"

Benjy smiled. "That same drone I crashed into my mom's head? I sent it after Matt so I could follow where he went. It can go eighty miles an hour and has a range of twenty miles. I saw when he escaped the third chase car. I saw when he got on the tollway. Those checkpoints can take a long time, so I caught up to him. It took some convincing, but finally he let me get in the truck and ride with him."

"Benjy, that is the most amazing story. It tells me so much about Matt that I didn't know. I mean, I always felt there was that depth in him, that courage, that toughness — but I didn't really know it before."

"I admire him a lot."

"And you know, it tells me a lot about you, too. You're a pretty brave guy yourself."

He felt his face going hot, the way Raine was looking at him.

CHAPTER 18

NEAR RED LODGE, MONTANA
DECEMBER 3, 2021—3 AM

THEY'D ROUSED HIM out of a sound sleep only ten minutes before, but Benjy felt wide awake as he got into the back seat of the red Ford van. He and Raine had each gone to their rooms soon after dinner, and he'd gone right to sleep. Raine looked worse off, her hair in tangles, her face blotchy. He could well imagine she'd had trouble falling asleep, after all he'd told her.

They were leaving earlier than planned. A man named Renny drove. Winter, the white-haired commander, sat in the front passenger seat. Two motorcycles and another van, carrying the last remaining residents at the camp, followed behind.

"Sorry we had to get you kids up before the sun," Winter said as they sped down the gravel road. Benjy, who had run along this road in trainings, knew it wound downhill for over five miles before meeting up with Route 93. "We just got information that they're on their way and gonna raid the house at daybreak."

"Cuttin' it kinda close," Renny said.

"Who's going to raid the house?" Benjy asked.

"Oh, Army Rangers, Homeland Security, some such," Winter said. "Not sticking around to find out."

"Where are we going?"

"It's a long drive," Winter said. "Won't get there till tomorrow afternoon some time. If you wanna go back to sleep, be my guest."

"I'm not tired," Benjy said. "I'd like to understand things better. Has anyone heard anything from Matt?"

"I was just going to ask," Raine said.

"Radio silence, for the moment," Winter said. "But we know he's okay."

"How do you know that?" Raine asked.

"Luke's in contact with him," Winter said. He didn't elaborate, but that was how Winter usually talked, Benjy thought.

"Do you know where he is?" Raine asked.

"Michigan," Winter answered. "Pretty part of the country. Not as pretty as this, of course, but still."

"Why did Dark Fiber kidnap him?" Benjy asked.

"They haven't told us yet," Winter said. "But don't you worry. Matt's pretty good at taking care of himself, from what I've seen."

"You can say that again," Benjy said. "I've seen it firsthand."

"Your stepdad told me a few things about that," Winter said. "Your trip west. You boys did a good job of staying alive. He's real proud of you, you know."

Benjy didn't look at Raine, though in the darkness of the car she probably wouldn't notice his blush anyway.

In the silence that followed, Benjy started thinking about the few days he and Matt had stayed in a Bible Party encampment headed by Pastor Peaches — first in Des Moines, then in Denver. They'd eaten well, and they'd done work for the group. Sander had worked out a plan with Pastor Peaches to get them to San Francisco, traveling with the tour.

When Matt's face had appeared on national TV during a live broadcast of Pastor Peaches giving one of her sermons, they'd had to leave in a hurry. Pastor Peaches had given them her turbocharged Porsche and a couple of contact addresses on the route between Denver and San Francisco. John had appeared on a secure link before they left. Benjy remembered perfectly what he'd said. "Pastor Peaches will help you, boys. She's one of us." The statement had left him more than a little confused.

"There's one thing I'm still trying to understand," Benjy said in the noisy darkness of the speeding van.

"What's that?" Winter said.

"Ten days ago the Bible Party joined in a coalition with UMC and the Corporate Party. But aren't the UMC our enemies?"

While Winter hesitated, the van turned off the noisy gravel road and joined Route 93, heading south. The air quality in the vehicle immediately improved. Benjy hadn't even realized how the gravel dust was coating his throat.

"Let me put it this way," Winter answered at last. "UMC are the worst of the lot, and in power now. Before them we had the UN Party in power, and before David Burns it was Edward Cornell from the Corporates. The president doesn't decide everything himself, of course, but he has the bully pulpit, and he appoints cabinet members. The party that's in the White House has tremendous power. Now, March22 has enjoyed a grassroots surge for one reason and one reason alone, due to the failures of all three parties that have been in the White House in the last five years.

"Their policies have created a mess that touches every citizen across this great country. The chaos and the constant danger we have to put up with now stems from their lack of focus on the real problems of the country."

"Like food shortages and shadowmarkets?"

"That's a big one," Winter said. "Also moving freely across the country, getting in your car and driving to another state. That used to be a thing no one thought twice about. Nowadays, you get into one of those checkpoints, and they're liable to take your car apart before they're done, then confiscate your money and ration coupons and anything else of value."

"The politicians would say those measures are necessary because of homegrown terrorism. For instance, March22," Benjy said.

"I know they would," Winter said. "But if you think about it, March22 was born as a reaction to terrorist actions that were already happening, primarily instigated by UMC people."

"You mean the assassinations on March 22, 2015?"

"Exactly. March22 didn't even exist when those six Democrats and seven Republicans—all the primary candidates—were wiped out in one massacre, leaving no viable candidates to run for president in 2016. With that one action, UMC created a tremendous vacuum in the political landscape. All the splinter groups ran like hell into the vacuum and formed their own parties, following UMC's lead."

"March22 formed after that?"

"Some of the members of Anonymous got together after that. They decided to set up Anonymous as a political party and March22 to do the dirty work. We could see where UMC was heading. They were strong, appealing to people's fears, and they wanted to rule the country, with laws that would take us into a dark age of ignorance, anarchy and suffering. We formed March22 as an alternative vision."

"Who were the founders?"

"Well, there was your stepdad, Wyoming, Sander, Rory MacGregor—who you'll meet tomorrow—and myself. There were a few others who are no longer with us."

"The Anonymous militants who were executed?" Benjy asked.

"What?" Raine said. Benjy hadn't even realized she was still awake.

"Now, where did you hear that story?" Winter asked. "I been chattering in my sleep or something?"

"Sander gave us a little of the history when we passed through Iowa," Benjy said.

At that moment, they all heard a helicopter overhead. The loud noise of a chopper rotor sounded as if it were directly above them. Renny was peering up through the windshield, trying to spot it. In the darkness, Benjy saw nothing. Maybe the chopper was blacked out. Winter was studying his Jetlink, then talking.

"Luke, how many choppers are there?" Winter asked.

"Just the one."

"Can you tell if they've got any missiles armed?"

"Checking now."

Benjy recognized Luke's machine-synthesized voice. It must be a secure link. Luke must be following the situation through the optics of one of the March22 drones.

"Well, I don't like this," Winter said loudly. "Blow his ass out of the sky, before he takes us out."

"Missiles not armed. I'm checking who it is," Luke said. The van continued at seventy mph down Route 93. As the silence from Luke's end lengthened, the chopper easily kept pace, shadowing them. Winter had said the camp was due to be raided at sunup. What if they arrived early? Benjy could only assume they looked like a small but suspicious convoy from the air, with the two motorcycles and the tail car close in line behind them.

Then Luke spoke again. "Joke's on you guys. It's my ride on one of Wyoming's birds. They're bringing me and Corinne to Iowa. Ha, ha, ha!"

"Luke, this is no time for a joy ride," Winter said angrily. "Get the hell away from here before the feds arrive. Wacko!"

In the lights of a lone oncoming car, Benjy saw beads of sweat on the commander's face as he cut the connection.

CHAPTER 19

MASSIVE DRONE THEFT BAFFLES GOVERNMENT EXPERTS
First Lady Kidnapped in California, Rescued in S. Dakota

Over one thousand armed military drones were stolen from the US government in the early days of their deployment, according to a confidential source with access to sensitive information. Government officials became aware of the thefts as they were taking place, but were powerless to stop them, the source said.

The government, according to the source, is convinced that no foreign power or organization is behind the theft. The lead suspect is the homegrown terrorist group March22, as they are known to have significant hacking capabilities. However, until now, March22 has never been suspected of an operation this complex and immense.

"Whoever stole the drones knows how to fly and control them, how to shoot and aim the missiles they are armed with, and in addition, has sophisticated facilities in which to store them," the source said. The government suspects that the stolen drones have already been deployed, and fired missiles, in the San Francisco Airport battle of November 23, 2021.

In that confusing battle, ten big rig trucks smashed through the perimeter fence at the north end of the field as tanks fired on them, repelling the incursion. No sooner were the trucks, operated by remote control, eliminated, the tanks began to be hit by air-to-ground Hellfire missiles. All six tanks were destroyed. Thirty-six soldiers lost their lives, with another twenty wounded.

The details of the San Francisco Airport battle have not been publicly explained, and no group has claimed responsibility. One government theory was that the big rigs came to the airport in the hope of stealing kerosene to fuel the stolen drones.

When the fighting began, Homeland Security closed the airport, but one private jet took off, defying the restrictions. The plane reportedly belonged to film star Wyoming Ryder and may have been carrying First Lady Amanda Jeffers. That plane reportedly exploded twenty minutes later over a remote region of the Sierra Nevada Mountains. No survivors and no wreckage have been found to date.

Yesterday, in a surprising development, Mr. Ryder emerged in Jackson, Wyoming, to give a live television interview. Ryder told KCQK, the ABC affiliate in Jackson, a story about having been surprised at gunpoint in a San Francisco hotel suite. The First Lady was then kidnapped, and he was threatened, along with his family.

Mrs. Jeffers was rescued yesterday from a remote location in South Dakota, where she had been held captive for the last eight days. Mrs. Jeffers was flown back to Washington and is recovering at the White House.

The stolen drones are now unaccounted for. Even worse, according to the source, they are undetectable to military and Homeland Security drone controllers when flying. The authorities have not been able to decipher how the theft took place and how the UAVs can be rendered undetectable.

Wyoming Ryder is currently in detention and being questioned by the FBI as a person of interest, due to the coincidence of his plane illegally taking off from San Francisco Airport while stolen drones were firing on US military assets.

CHAPTER 20

WASHINGTON, DC
DECEMBER 3, 2021—7 AM

"LET'S GET THIS meeting started," President James Jeffers said. Within three seconds, the voices died down to nothing. His lack of patience was familiar to these people. Since David Burns and the next five in the line of succession were assassinated in coordinated attacks, three new people stood in for their former bosses whom the president had fired in the last eighteen days.

Jeffers looked around the table in the White House Situation Room and considered the team assembled. Hal Holsom, the white-haired NSA chief, was a straight shooter, but he and his best cracks still hadn't figured out how the drones could be stolen or made undetectable. That was unacceptable. Dave Knopfler, deputy chief of Homeland Security, seemed to need less than three hours of sleep a night, yet still had not dealt with March22 effectively. Reese, his secretary of defense, was something of a career plodder but brilliant in strategy. Perry, acting attorney general, was only a placeholder while the new candidates were vetted. Vice President Bianca Orlando was loyal, and that was the main thing. Press Secretary Petra Bedrosian had exhibited admirably feistiness in these hard times.

Jeffers had also invited Mark Sullivan to the meeting, head of the Federal Aviation Administration.

"We have an article in this morning's *Post* which literally puts our genitals on display," Jeffers went on. "I don't know about you, but I would've preferred to find the goddamned drones and stamp out March22, and only then have the shit hit the fan. How the hell did this information get out?"

To their credit, when he shouted, no one averted their eyes. No one was admitting to being the *Post*'s hallowed source. And, in all probability, it hadn't been one of the people in this room. More likely one of their trusted aides.

"When we find out who leaked this information, we will crucify them," Jeffers said. "I want an accounting from each of you within two hours of who, on your staff, had access to the information in that article. We will then employ the Defense Intelligence Agency to interview them and analyze their devices, their movements, and their communications over the last seven days. Is that clear?"

Murmurs of agreement from all present.

"Now, the press conference is scheduled for ten a.m., is that correct?"

"Yes, Mr. President," Bedrosian, the press secretary, said.

"Our aim right now is to nail down her talking points. Before we get to that, I want an update from each of you. Knopfler, you first. What are the latest numbers from Homeland Security on the mass breakout?"

"Mr. President, we've rearrested almost ninety-six percent of the convicts,. Slightly more than four percent remain at large."

"That's still eighty thousand criminals."

"How many are being captured per day at this point?" Tom Underwood, chief of staff, asked.

"One or two thousand a day," said an aide. "Trending down, of course."

"I guess those are the ones with an IQ over eighty," Knopfler said. "But we'll get them."

"NSA?" said Jeffers.

"We're picking up chatter and taking out an average of four March22 camps or safe houses per day, in close cooperation with the FBI and Homeland Security," Holsom said.

"What happens then?"

"Often there's no one there. Everything cleaned out, no prints, no data, nothing. The few people we've arrested, when we get them into a room, they don't know anything," Knopfler said. "March22 is highly compartmentalized. More sophisticated than you'd expect. In most cases, we end up not charging them."

"What the hell are they doing in those places?"

"Target practice, typically," Knopfler said. "At the camps, they practice shooting. In the metropolitan areas, it's telephone boiler rooms. Mass mailings. Various fundraising activities. They're raising money and building a grassroots network."

"How do you get wind of them?"

"They have their private networks, Mr. President," Holsom explained. "A lot of secure mesh networks, but they also take chances on the internet. Every time we get in and catch a key word on any kind of network, we pounce. We also have some evidence that they're feeding us key words to test our capabilities."

"What evidence? Why would they do that?"

"Are they leading us off the track?" Underwood suggested.

"The evidence gets into very technical areas," Holsom said. "I don't know why they would do this intentionally. In my book, every bust is another success."

"How many of these training camps do they have?" Underwood asked.

"Impossible to say," Knopfler said. "Six months ago I would've said ten or twenty. Now, based on the number we're shutting down, I'd revise that into the hundreds."

"Hundreds of training camps and safe houses? I don't like it," Jeffers said. "What about the drone signatures?"

"There too, we're making progress, but no breakthroughs," Holsom said. "Our guys are trying to figure out how they can make the stolen drones undetectable. We've tried some really abstract approaches, but so far no results."

"Maybe they're so small, four camps a day is a good success rate," Vice President Orlando suggested.

Jeffers seethed at the comment. Those drones had been missing for almost two weeks. Where did you park more than a thousand drones without anyone noticing? Where did you stash two hundred and forty high-tech dirty bombs? There were people in this room who knew nothing about the missing bombs, but sooner or later that was going to come out, too. He was beginning to think he was surrounded by incompetents. That would explain how the country had found its way into this cesspool of overlapping problems.

"What about their laptops, their Jetlinks, their personal drones?" he pressed.

"We take everything apart, but no breakthroughs, like Hal said," Knopfler reported. "Sooner or later we'll catch them making a mistake. That's what we're waiting for."

"Mrs. Bedrosian, tell us about your chat with that *Washington Post* lawyer," Jeffers went on. He craved good news.

"Mr. President, their lawyer sent me the story last night at one a.m. Ten minutes later I contacted them, and they would only let me talk to the lawyer. She insisted that the source was genuine but gave me no hints about his or her identity. I told them the *Post* was compromising national security with these revelations, not to mention risking the reputation of the paper, but she wasn't intimidated."

"Can we close down the *Post* for this?" Jeffers asked.

"That would get ugly, constitutionally," Underwood said. "Definitely more trouble than it's worth. The *Post* is not our real problem."

As usual, Underwood was on the money. Everyone in the room knew it. The more he heard, the stronger his conviction grew that it was that damned March22 that somehow stole the bombs.

"All right," Jeffers continued. "Now you may be wondering who the red-haired fellow is, next to Vice President Orlando. Everybody, meet Mark Sullivan who heads up the FAA. I asked Mark to be here because of my next proposal. We have our pants down, we've been the victim of a massive drone heist, and now it's time to move the story forward. I want to take control of it. I want to give the American people something positive. We talked about this, didn't we, Mr. Sullivan?"

"Yes we did, Mr. President."

"Why don't I turn it over to you?"

"Right. Well, as you all know, commercial aviation has been grounded for more than two years, due to the shoulder-fired missile attacks in September 2019, and the fact that around six thousand missiles with launch assemblies were stolen. The president and I discussed the possibility of using Homeland Security drone coverage to guarantee the safety of the skies for commercial aviation once again."

"That's a great idea," Vice President Orlando said.

"How would it actually work?" Defense Secretary Reese asked. "Because I hope nobody here really believes shoulder-fired missiles can be intercepted by a Hellfire before they take out a plane under three thousand feet. That's just not happening."

"That's not the idea," Jeffers said. He cued Sullivan to continue.

"It's more the idea that whoever is stupid enough to launch a shoulder-fired is going to get blown to kingdom come within sixty seconds," Sullivan went on. "We have redundant drone coverage over the entire lower forty-eight states. We could easily protect all seventeen thousand airports, even minor ones. Of course, we would focus most of our attention on the five hundred that handle all commercial and cargo flights. Only one hundred and twenty of these are actually served by commercial airlines. If an attack occurred, we would lose the plane, but the terrorists would pay for it with their life. Every time."

"You're comfortable with the idea of losing a few more planes, sounds like," said Perry, the acting attorney general.

"It's a deterrent effect," Dave Knopfler said. "I'd fly commercial, knowing that deterrent was there."

"So would I," said Vice President Orlando.

"You're thinking logically," Perry countered. "I'm guessing anyone crazy enough to shoot down a commercial plane isn't playing with a full deck, like you."

"Who the hell stole those missiles and why haven't we found them?" Jeffers shot back. They stared at him, and he knew why. He'd been secretary of defense when it happened. The shrinkage had occurred on his watch.

"Life today is filled with risks," Underwood offered. "We're never going to achieve an absolutely risk-free environment. The deterrent reduces the risks. Correct me if I'm wrong, but we've also built up much more effective security in a three-mile perimeter around those hundred and twenty busiest airports now, as well." Knopfler nodded agreement. "So, the risk is much lower because of that, to begin with. The benefits of getting commercial aviation in the air again would be huge."

"Oh, yes," Knopfler said. "There's a good chance they wouldn't get any missiles launched in those zones anyway. We have surveillance and quick-reaction teams on the ground. I would underline that those hundred and twenty airports you mentioned are the only interesting targets for a terrorist."

"While you gloat over the political benefits, consider an opposing idea," Acting Attorney General Perry said. "The rationale for the deployment of the drones was to round up the escaped convicts, right? That objective is nearly met. Now we have stolen drones in the air, *armed* stolen drones, controlled by terrorists. What if we took the high road, here? If we took all of our drones out of the air, any terrorist event that occurred would get blamed on March22."

Ideas coming out of left field always irritated Jeffers. He liked to know what was coming in advance. The silence in the room was indicative of the sneaky intelligence of Perry's idea. A naive intelligence, to be sure. He looked at Underwood.

"I see the beauty of it," Underwood said. "But I liked the idea of getting commercial aviation going again. We can't convince the public of the safety of that without giving them something tangible, like the drone deterrent. By the way, getting planes in the air again would significantly weaken the hold of the militias on our food supply. The reliance on truck cargo helped sow the seeds for the militias taking over food distribution in so many areas. If we can get planes shipping produce from California again, the militias go bust."

"They're not our focus today," Jeffers said, thinking of the missing bombs. "March22 stole the damned drones, and who knows what else? Keep the focus on March22."

"Unless they're the ones that stole the shoulder-fired missiles," Perry warned. "What are the chances of another attack?"

"That's the rationale for the deterrent," Underwood said. "That and the beefed up security around the airports. We all know we carry a heavy responsibility here. But I think we're good."

"Right," Jeffers said.

"What if they used their stolen drones to attack our drones to cover the terrorists on the ground carrying out the shoulder-fired missiles?" Perry demanded. "Has anyone run that scenario? After all, they can see our drones, but we can't see theirs."

Jeffers showed nothing in his face, but that coppery taste surfaced in his mouth at Perry's words. Such a scenario was theoretically possible. The safest solution would be to find the goddamned stolen shoulder-fired missiles. Better yet, take down March22. That had to be possible.

"Another thing," Underwood went on, pointing the finger at Perry. "What good does it do anyone, just knowing who to blame? We could take the high road you suggest, but ultimately the administration would still get the blame for letting March22 continue to exist."

Underwood would make a better attorney general than the acting attorney general, Jeffers thought. That position was now reserved for a Bible Party candidate.

"I want that damned group eliminated," Jeffers said. "This country is beset by lawlessness. March22 is enemy number one."

"We have principles," Perry said. "We have an opportunity to show we stand for what's right."

Jeffers shook his head. "I see that day coming, son. Right now, we've got work to do, and we need our drones to do it." He turned back to Sullivan. "How much lead time do you need to get the planes flying again?"

"The airlines all have contingency plans," the FAA chief answered. "We can start in a week. That gets things rolling again a couple of weeks before Christmas. It'll be a popular decision."

"I like that. All right, talking points." Jeffers looked at Bedrosian. "One, we're mobilizing all our resources to recover the stolen drones and hold those who did it accountable. Two, our drones will be used to help guarantee the safety of commercial aviation, which will start up again on December tenth."

"I'll get working on it right away," Sullivan said.

"Three," Jeffers continued, "the executive order of two weeks ago gave us legal means to let Homeland Security use drones for the stated purpose for ninety days. We anticipate extending the order for an additional year. That will require a bill in Congress. However, it is the intention of this administration to take the drones out of the air as soon as the security of the homeland can be assured without them."

"Any other input?" Underwood said, looking around the table. "Okay, people, let's go. Mrs. Bedrosian, good luck at ten o'clock."

"I'm looking forward to it," the press secretary said.

Jeffers thought she looked like she meant it.

CHAPTER 21

WYOMING RYDER MASSAGED his neck, watching the FBI team march back into the room, accompanied by their fleet of Vipers. Flanked on either side by his lawyers, Karen Vixen and Mark Knox, he felt confident that today, after two nights in the lockup, they would declare him a free man. The authorities clearly felt provoked. March22 had gotten their attention, but they were still clueless. So they would be watching him. It was clear he couldn't go back to Montana anytime soon. He would have to get working on another picture. John Carney had been right about that.

"Let me introduce Riley Johnson from Homeland Security," Agent Knight said. He gave the floor to a man with shoulder-length blond hair and a Marine Corps tattoo on the back of his hand.

"'Your story at the hotel checks out, Mr. Ryder," Johnson said. "Except for one thing."

"Oh, what's that?"

"You said there were six men."

"Six people. They didn't all speak, so I can't be sure they were all men."

"Six people. We found no traces of any other person in that room. We've been over every surface with some very high-tech gadgets, believe me. No saliva, no hair, no bits of skin matter, nothing."

"But I told you, they were all covered up. Motorcycle leathers, helmets, gloves. I guess these were professionals."

"No video from the floor you were on, nothing from the elevator, nothing from the garage."

"You mentioned some of the cameras weren't working that night."

"I have no evidence those six men existed, Mr. Ryder."

"Well, you have the First Lady." He had seen it on the news. Amanda was back in Washington. No doubt they were grilling her just as mercilessly. "You don't have to take my word for what happened. Talk to her."

"We're working on the scenario that you and Mrs. Jeffers made up this whole scenario," Johnson said.

"That's ridiculous," Wyoming said. "Who in their right minds would come up with an idea like that? Working together how? What for? I hardly even know the woman."

"You escaped from your home in Malibu when the Secret Service tried forcibly to gain entrance and bring Mrs. Jeffers back to Washington. Your staff locked up the four agents who were sleeping in the house. They were the lucky ones. Your staff killed five Secret Service agents who tried to enter at the front gate."

"They were defending me and my guest."

"How does locking up our agents in a deep freeze constitute defending yourself and Mrs. Jeffers?"

"I didn't know a thing about that," Wyoming said. "It seems to have happened while we were sleeping. All I can think is that they had some kind of disagreement with my staff."

"This is not a joke, Mr. Ryder. Five agents are dead. I could throw you in jail for the rest of your life right now."

"There's no need to make empty threats, Mr. Johnson," Karen Vixen said.

"It's hardly an empty threat," the blond man shot back. "Do you think we're going to sit by and watch agents get shot down in cold blood?"

"Then arrest him. Problem is, you know you can't possibly convict Mr. Ryder with the evidence you've got. That's because it's just a string of coincidences, with my client being in the wrong place at the wrong time."

"Five of my people were killed that morning, too," Wyoming said, adding a tinge of sadness to his voice. "Otherwise we could ask them what happened with those agents in the deep freeze."

"You mentioned that we should check with Amanda Jeffers," Johnson went on. "Indeed we've been talking with her. She said she was carried out of your hotel room in a zipped-up duffel."

"That's right," Wyoming said.

"I asked her if she knew where she was when she was in the bag. You know, when they carried her out of the room, down the hall to the elevator, getting on the elevator, things like that. You know what she said?"

"I'm sure the First Lady told you what happened," Wyoming said.

"She said she heard the little bell ring, indicating the elevator was arriving," Johnson said. Johnson's meaningful look wasn't lost on him. In a flash, Wyoming realized Amanda's mistake. He knew the St. James Hotel intimately. He didn't change his expression of mild curiosity. "You know why that bothers me?"

"Something bothers you?" Wyoming said.

"There *is* no elevator bell at the St. James. We checked. We talked to the hotel manager. The noise used to disturb guests. It's been deactivated for years."

Wyoming spread his hands. "This bothers you?"

Johnson leaned forward. "Why does the First Lady tell me she heard a little bell when there is none?"

Wyoming smiled. "I'm no psychologist, Mr. Johnson. But it doesn't take an expert to come up with some possible explanations."

"Such as?"

"Maybe somebody's Jetlink beeped. Maybe she imagined the bell. She was zipped up in a duffel, panicking maybe. I wouldn't let a detail like that bother me."

"That's the difference between you and me, Mr. Ryder," Johnson said. "She *invented* the bell. It doesn't exist, but it made her story seem more real. That makes me think the rest could be invented, too."

"Get to the point, Mr. Johnson," Karen Vixen said. "This is the third day we've tolerated your fishing expedition. My client is fulfilling his civic duty by answering your questions, yet you continue to attack him."

"We haven't arrested Mr. Ryder for a different reason," Johnson went on. "We believe there's a bigger conspiracy. We had a big fiasco with four soldiers dying on the quad at Stanford University. We had Mr. Ryder's plane taking off when the airport was closed due to a battle going on, with missiles raining down on our tanks. We've got the Golden Gate Bridge in pieces at the bottom of the bay. We are looking for more than a thousand stolen drones. We had the First Lady missing for nine days, supposedly kidnapped. You, sir, seem to be at the center of all that."

Wyoming laughed out loud, not holding back. He ignored Knight's grim face, directing his mirth at Johnson. "I see all this stuff on the news, just like you. It makes me sick. You're sitting here saying I blew up the Golden Gate Bridge?"

"Maybe you put up the money for it," Johnson said.

"We're wasting our time, here," Karen Vixen said. "Either charge him with a specific crime or let him go."

"We have warrants to search your homes and confiscate your computers and files, and access your bank accounts," Johnson said. He handed a thick pile of documents to an aide, who brought it around the room and laid it on the table in front of Wyoming's lawyers.

"There are a few things I'd like to get to the bottom of," Wyoming said. "You showed a video of my plane exploding and put out the lie that I was dead. I was in a hotel in San Francisco watching that replay on TV over and over, and I was thinking, what the hell? Who is screwing me over here and why? Is it because I didn't vote for UMC in the last elections?"

"We haven't found the wreckage, but we will," Johnson said.

"How can you say that? My plane is intact. Amanda's been rescued, thank God, and I'm alive and well, too. Why are you guys doing this smear campaign against me? Why is Homeland Security trying to destroy Wyoming Ryder?"

"Nobody's trying to destroy you," Johnson said. "But the government will most certainly destroy March22. Mr. Ryder, where was Amanda Jeffers for the last nine days?"

Wyoming waited a beat. "Is this a rhetorical question?"

"It's a direct question. I think you know the answer."

"South Dakota?" he said in a guessing tone. He could play games with these people. He wasn't the least bit nervous.

"Her system did not show any signs of an incapacitating drug over a period of days. She didn't get any such drug infusion. We examined her intestinal flora, her blood sugar, and her hormone values. She was eating and drinking normally somewhere for nine days, and I'm guessing it wasn't that shack in South Dakota rigged with remote control assault rifles. You know, Mr. Ryder, it had all the hallmarks of March22."

"What are the hallmarks of March22, Mr. Johnson? That would interest me."

"Stupidity. Delusions of grandeur. Good computer skills."

Wyoming smiled. "The first two describe me well; you only have to ask my ex-wives. But I still don't know what this all has to do with me."

"Charge my client with a crime and back it up with evidence, or let him go on his way," Vixen repeated. "Mr. Ryder has been in detention for three days, first in Jackson and now in San Francisco. He's a busy man."

Johnson leaned forward again. "It's not going to happen that way, counselor. We're keeping Mr. Ryder locked up while we search his homes, files, and finances. I'm sure we'll have enough within forty-eight hours to charge your client with high treason and murder, among other things."

"You may be within your rights to search and seize," Karen answered. "You will find that my client is not in possession of any conceivable incriminating evidence for the simple reason that you have the wrong man. When the truth comes out and Wyoming Ryder is vindicated, Homeland Security will look like real dopes. And if it takes more than two days, Mr. Johnson, you're going to be facing a civil suit and more stinky publicity than you can imagine."

"I have to stay in jail?" Wyoming said.

"The judge will throw it out," Karen Vixen said.

"Something to tell your kids about thirty years from now, if you don't fry in the electric chair first," Johnson said. The officials all stood and filed out.

Wyoming felt depressed. Luke had covered the tracks of his business holdings so well, he was confident they would never find Big Sky Base. Even if they did, the runway was invisible from the air, covered by a high-tech organic net that gave off the same heat signature as the surrounding scrub. They would never find the drones, or the bombs. They would never see where all the money had gone. He might as well get used to living in a jail cell.

They'd been ninety-nine percent certain it would go this way anyway.

CHAPTER 22

DAN DONOVAN, A UN Party member from Illinois, watched one of the bright blue drones execute a tight circle over his head, no doubt using facial recognition to identify him. Everyone around him had an identical blue drone landing on his desk and most members looked equally bemused. Drones were ubiquitous in the chamber, of course, but he had never seen a whole flock of them.

The vast room was in an uproar as the blue drones continued dispersing over them, high in the rotunda. It almost looked like... a flock of bluebirds. Off to his left, Dan Creighton of the Anonymous Party was rising to his feet with a mischievous smile. Then all seventeen members of Anonymous stood up and turned slowly with one arm out, like synchronized swimmers, pointing at the drones and taking responsibility for the prank.

Creighton was probably the wealthiest man in a room full of wealthy men. A hedge fund guru in his earlier days, the man had cashed out an early stake in J. Paul Abba's freight empire ten years ago for well over a billion dollars. The little blue drones were zipping down across the vaulted space in different directions, one drone to each of the members. Everyone was talking at once, ignoring the rapping gavel of the Speaker as he called for order.

Donovan had come to Washington six years ago, after twenty years building a chain of auto dealerships in the Chicago suburbs. The twenty-million-dollar fortune he'd amassed didn't come close to Dan Creighton's pile, but Donovan would never go hungry. There was a saying for mountain climbers who didn't make it to the summit: the view is also pretty awesome from seven thousand feet.

Donovan secretly took pleasure in spending weeks at a time away from Denise and the kids. Sharing the condo in Georgetown with three other members was almost like a second bachelorhood. It wasn't that he had a Rainbow Party-type preference for men.

Family life just wasn't Donovan's thing. Most of the men came back just to sleep, anyway, so it was a little like living in a hotel, only not quite so impersonal.

Sadly, the UN Party had taken a beating in the last twelve months, with polls sinking month after month. There were voices asking if the UN Party had any reason left to exist, their support had declined so dramatically. Voices Donovan respected. It was enough to make any man of character work longer hours talking to colleagues, listening to constituents, and slaving over compromises that got the bills through committees. Late at night, when Donovan collapsed in bed for the six hours of rest he allotted himself, he went to sleep within seconds. He slept well in the knowledge that he would never give up the fight to give back to the American people, who had been so good to him in his business.

The little bluebird drone sat on his desk and carried on its bottom, attached by a clip, a paper with the official seal of the House of Representatives. He freed the paper and smoothed it out to read.

THE ANONYMOUS PARTY HEREBY ANNOUNCES

The Anonymous Party has legally changed its name, effective immediately, to March22, and officially represents all like-minded constituents.

March22 is committed to fighting for the *preservation* and/or *restoration* of the following rights of all Americans:

1. Congress shall make no law respecting an establishment of religion, or prohibiting the free exercise thereof; or abridging the freedom of speech, or of the press; or the right of the people peaceably to assemble, and to petition the Government for a redress of grievances.
2. A well-regulated Militia, being necessary to the security of a free State, the right of the people to keep and bear Arms, shall not be infringed.
3. No Soldier shall, in time of peace be quartered in any house, without the consent of the Owner, nor in time of war, but in a manner to be prescribed by law.
4. The right of the people to be secure in their persons, houses, papers, and effects, against unreasonable searches and seizures, shall not be violated, and no Warrants shall issue, but upon probable cause, supported by Oath or affirmation, and particularly describing the place to be searched, and the persons or things to be seized.

5. No person shall be held to answer for a capital, or otherwise infamous crime, unless on a presentment or indictment of a Grand Jury except in cases arising in the land or naval forces, or in the Militia, when in actual service in time of War or public danger; nor shall any person be subject for the same offence to be twice put in jeopardy of life or limb; nor shall be compelled in any criminal case to be a witness against himself, nor be deprived of life, liberty, or property, without due process of law; nor shall private property be taken for public use, without just compensation.

6. In all criminal prosecutions, the accused shall enjoy the right to a speedy and public trial, by an impartial jury of the State and district wherein the crime shall have been committed, which district shall have been previously ascertained by law, and to be informed of the nature and cause of the accusation; to be confronted with the witnesses against him; to have compulsory process for obtaining witnesses in his favor, and to have the Assistance of Counsel for his defense.

7. In suits at common law, where the value in controversy shall exceed twenty dollars, the right of trial by jury shall be preserved, and no fact tried by a jury, shall be otherwise re-examined in any court of the United States, than according to the rules of the common law.

8. Excessive bail shall not be required, nor excessive fines imposed, nor cruel and unusual punishments inflicted.

9. The enumeration in the Constitution, of certain rights, shall not be construed to deny or disparage others retained by the people.

10. The powers not delegated to the United States by the Constitution, nor prohibited by it to the States, are reserved to the States respectively, or to the people.

Looking around him, Donovan observed some members shouting, some laughing, others looking apoplectic, turning purple and waving their arms. Everything in this room was broadcast live on a number of TV channels. UMC Representative Hamilton of Virginia slammed his blue drone to the floor and crushed it under his thousand-dollar Bruno Magli shoe.

"It's just the Bill of Rights," Donovan said to Representative Patricia Maxwell, a fellow UN member from Iowa. "What's the point? Why do they think these rights need preserving and restoring?"

"All I know is they're a bunch of terrorists," she said. "They were before, and they still are. Just trying to dress it up nice and fancy, I guess."

"Those members aren't terrorists." Donovan pointed at the grinning Anonymous members, who still stood with their arms out as the last of the bluebird drones circled down. "Those are elected representatives who somehow won elections in their districts around the country."

"Sure, maybe not those particular people," Maxwell agreed. "But they write here that they represent all like-minded March22 constituents. What do they mean by like-minded? Don't you think that means they represent terrorists?"

"If March22 commits terrorist acts, yes. They're either taking a huge risk, or they know something we don't. Maybe March22 isn't responsible for all the things they're accused of."

"It's just a publicity stunt for the cameras," Maxwell said. He could see she was thinking about what he said. If March22 really were a terrorist group, the Anonymous members were opening themselves to prosecution. How likely was it that they would take such a risk?

"The Anonymous announcement is out of order," said the Speaker for the fourth time. This time some of the members seemed to pay attention. "We have taken note of your stunt. The appropriate bodies will report on the legality of your name change. We will ignore the other nonsense. Let's move on with business."

"They're going legitimate," Donovan said, half to himself. The noise in the room drowned out his voice, and Maxwell wasn't listening anyway. He wondered if there was any way of learning how big March22 really was. How much grassroots support did they have? In one fell swoop, March22 would have representation in the House and Senate. How many seats would they gain in the midterm elections next year, and which coalition would they join? Those were the big questions.

With one more rap of the gavel, it was on to the next vote.

CHAPTER 23

ALEXANDRIA, VIRGINIA
DECEMBER 3, 2021—5 PM

THE SECRET SERVICE agents and their Eliminator drones swarmed around the car as Amanda arrived at the old brick house in Alexandria where Jim's mother lived. Carol Jeffers had her own Secret Service protection, of course, but in the wake of Amanda's kidnapping and with Penelope here, the agents and their drones stood around everywhere. Five agents had died in Malibu because of her. She felt their bitterness and avoided their eyes as they made a cordon for her up the front walk.

"Is Mrs. Jeffers expecting you, ma'am?" asked an agent on the porch.

"Of course." Amanda stabbed the doorbell with her finger. It was a travesty that Jim insisted on Penelope staying in Alexandria a few more days. He was purposely keeping them apart.

Penelope opened the door.

"Mom," she said, her face brightening. Penelope had already changed into baggy sweatpants and a sweatshirt, her typical after-school outfit. She wore wooden bracelets that some boy had given her, and she was barefoot. They hugged in the open doorway. Penelope came nearly to her height, but she was stick thin and looked so cute. They headed for the kitchen and sat at the big wooden table.

"Where's your grandma?" Amanda asked.

"In the bath. She always takes one before dinner."

"Does she have any coffee?"

Penelope stood up and studied the machines on the counter. Amanda rose with her, found a capsule in a little bowl beside the espresso machine, and switched the power on.

"How can you drink that stuff?" Penelope made a face.

"It's an addiction," Amanda said. "Some addictions we embrace, like chocolate and coffee."

"Speak for yourself," Penelope said, going back to the table.

"Did you go to school today?"

"We had a history test."

"How'd it go?"

Penelope made a face as if this were a dumb question. "Have I ever flubbed a history test?"

"I guess you're pretty good at just about everything." Penelope got her academics from her father. Amanda had never been very good in school. Boys had been the main attraction for her, even before she was fourteen.

"Mom, there's a bunch of kids at school who are raising money to support March22. There's a car wash this Saturday and everybody's going. Can I go?"

Amanda was genuinely surprised, and let it show. She felt like laughing. "Kids are raising money for March22?"

"They're having a fund drive. We're charging forty dollars a car, inside and out. We're aiming to raise two thousand dollars."

"But that's a terrorist organization, honey."

"No, it's not. That's just what the government wants everyone to believe."

"What about the Golden Gate Bridge attack?"

"Mom, that wasn't March22. That was probably some foreign terrorists, or else the militias. The militias are the ones that blow up bridges. Don't believe everything you read. Can I go? Everybody's going. It's like a party."

"What about the fact that they've stolen all those drones?" Amanda persisted. She wanted to find out how well-informed Penelope was, and she wanted to see how she would defend Wyoming's group. "You can't very well say a group that steals drones from the U.S. military is harmless."

"What I read is they did that to prove they could," Penelope said. "It's like an advanced form of hacking. Hackers release viruses in order to call attention to weaknesses in the system. Besides, they don't know for sure if it was really March22."

"When is this car wash?"

"Tomorrow, Mom. Everyone's going. If I don't go, it just looks ... so lame."

She knew what Penelope meant. It would look like Penelope had to do everything her parents told her. Well, there were advantages and disadvantages to being the First Daughter.

"Do they have these car washes often?" she asked.

"It's a national event. I think there's something like eight thousand locations this Saturday, all around the country. Last month they had a big nationwide recycling drive."

Inwardly, Amanda was amazed, but she showed nothing. Eight thousand school classes organizing car washes. Wyoming hadn't said a thing about this. "Honey, you're the daughter of the president. I don't think your father would be very happy to know you're sympathetic to March22."

"They're for the environment, Mom. They're for education. They're for investing more money in scientific research and the arts, and less on defense. They're for returning freedoms of the press and speech."

Amanda shook her head, but couldn't wipe the smile off her face. It was news to her that March22 had outreach in the schools. In Penelope's private school, of all places. And to know that they were reaching out all over. It was astonishing to hear Penelope talking so excitedly about them.

"You'll have to get your father's approval," she said. "I'm not taking the heat for this one."

"But you'll support me, won't you?"

"Honey, I personally don't like them, but I'm so proud of you for getting involved. That's the important thing." When they hugged, Amanda felt a tingling feeling at the back of her neck that spread out to her face, then her arms and even her legs. Penelope was growing up. "You'd have to have Secret Service there, watching every move," she pointed out when they came out of their embrace.

"They don't bother me," Penelope said. "There's one of them, he's actually kind of cute."

"Oh, Penelope."

"Mom, what was it like being kidnapped?"

Amanda changed her expression. "Don't remind me. Oh, the horror! They pointed their huge ugly guns at me, and I had to get into a duffel bag. They zipped it up and carried me out of the hotel."

Penelope listened with rapt attention. "But they didn't hurt Wyoming Ryder? You were with him, weren't you, when it happened?"

Amanda felt the blush coming into her face. "Yes, honey."

"Didn't he defend you?"

"There were six of them. They all had assault rifles. He couldn't do a thing to help me."

"I saw him on TV."

"Yes, I've heard he was on TV talking about it."

"What's he like, Mom?" Penelope sounded so strange with a sultry voice.

What in the world did you say to your daughter? She couldn't very well tell her about Wyoming's expert hands that knew how to electrify a woman's body, or that he possessed an almost clairvoyant sense of when to go slow and when to shift into high gear. Amanda stared at the ceiling. "He's rich and glamorous, just like you'd expect.

He has a huge house in Malibu, with two cooks and a bunch of other people on his staff. Oh, and on the plane to California, we also had Bessamy Belluccio hitching a ride."

Penelope's eyes went like saucers. "You rode in the plane with Wyoming Ryder and Bessamy Belluccio? Oh my God, does she dye her hair?"

"Nope. Natural blond," Amanda said.

"How do you know?"

"We talked about it. And guess where she was coming from."

"Where?"

"Bessamy had been in New York to talk to Nina Nardelli about doing a cameo on her show."

Even for jaded Penelope, this news was too much. Her daughter had gone speechless. The idea that her mother was hanging around with the A-list Hollywood celebrities, including people who knew Nina Nardelli personally, made Penelope glow with admiration.

"Now, your father's not too happy about all this, so we're not going to talk about it anymore, okay?"

"Mom, is it true that Wyoming Ryder's involved with March22?"

"Where did you get that idea, honey? You're really interested in March22, aren't you?"

"It's all over the Internet, Mom. Don't you ever read anything? He gives them money and lets them use his houses."

"He did mention he supports a clean environment, but I don't think he's involved with March22," Amanda said. "You yourself said not to believe everything you read. For some reason, people are giving him a bad rap."

"Where there's smoke, there's fire," Penelope said. "I think he'd make a great spokesman for March22. When he's not making movies, I guess."

"I'm sure you're mistaken," Amanda said. "I spent less than two days with him before I was kidnapped, but I would've sensed something fishy."

"They said his plane blew up over the Sierra Nevada Mountains," Penelope said. "They even showed this video, taken from a drone or something. They kept saying the whole time he was dead. This was while you were gone, Mom. Everyone thought you might've been killed with him. That's why Dad sent me over here, to Grandma's. It was all so horrible, and then there were all sorts of rumors that you were both alive after all. I really didn't know what to think. Then yesterday Wyoming appeared on TV in front of his plane. They said he was dead, but it's all just smoke and mirrors.

"They tell you anything they feel like, just to serve their needs. That's what I mean about freedom of the press. They just use the media for propaganda."

"Honey, this is your own father you're talking about." Amanda longed to tell Penelope that her father had ordered the plane shot down on which he believed Wyoming and she were riding. That this plane had indeed been shot out of the sky, and that a March22 trekker was employed in the rugged Sierra backcountry to keep the wreckage covered up. She longed to tell her they had actually flown out of San Francisco Airport ten minutes later on a second plane, which had not appeared on radar due to a programming trick of one of the March22 hackers.

Her daughter was so smart, her brain so turned on. How she longed to tell her everything about March22, what hard workers and how organized they all were. But Penelope was only fourteen. A girl her age shouldn't be burdened with such heavy secrets, especially when they created a gigantic and permanent rift between her parents. Besides, given that this was the President's mother's house, these rooms probably had bugs and cameras stashed in every conceivable hiding place.

One day Penelope would know the truth, but not now. Not here.

"I'm sure your father has the country's best interests at heart," Amanda said. "Different people believe in different approaches. That's what makes this country great, don't you think?"

"I'm not so sure, at the moment," Penelope said. "If you read what March22 is all about, you realize all the freedoms we've given up over the last few years. People don't want to live in a police state, Mom. People don't want to depend on ration coupons and barter on street corners and risk their lives at shadowmarkets. March22 didn't cause any of those problems, but they want to help solve them. Why can't the government figure that out?"

"That's way beyond my ability to comprehend, honey. I just wish you were back at the White House so we could see each other more."

"Dad said I have to stay here indefinitely. Why don't you stay here, too?"

Amanda stared at her daughter. Why hadn't she thought of that herself?

CHAPTER 24

WASHINGTON, DC
DECEMBER 3, 2021—5 PM

DAVE KNOPFLER FROM Homeland Security sat with Hal Holsom from NSA and their aides and listened.

"*Now, your father's not too happy about all this, so we're not going to talk about it anymore, okay?*"

"*Is it true that Wyoming Ryder's involved with March22?*"

"*Where did you get that idea, honey? You're really interested in March22, aren't you?*"

"*It's all over the Internet, Mom. Don't you ever read anything? He gives them money and lets them use his houses.*"

"*He did mention he supports a clean environment, but I don't think he's involved with March22. You yourself said not to believe everything you read. For some reason, people are giving him a bad rap.*"

"*Where there's smoke, there's fire. I think he'd make a great spokesman for March22. When he's not making movies, I guess.*"

"*I'm sure you're mistaken. I spent less than two days with him before I was kidnapped, but I would've sensed something fishy.*"

"*They said his plane blew up over the Sierra Nevada Mountains. They even showed this video, taken from a drone or something. They kept saying the whole time he was dead. This was while you were gone, Mom. Everyone thought you might've been killed with him. That's why Dad sent me over here, to Grandma's. It was all so shocking, and then there were all sorts of rumors that you were both alive after all. I really didn't know what to think. Then yesterday Wyoming appeared on TV in front of his plane. They said he was dead, but it's all just smoke and mirrors. They tell you anything they feel like, just to serve their needs. That's what I mean about freedom of the press. They just use the media for propaganda.*"

"*Honey, this is your father you're talking about. I'm sure your father has the country's best interests at heart. Different people believe in different approaches. That's what makes this country great, don't you think?*"

"I'm not so sure, at the moment. If you read what March22 is all about, you realize all the freedoms we've given up over the last few years. People don't want to live in a police state, Mom. People don't want to depend on ration coupons and barter on street corners and risk their lives at shadowmarkets. March22 didn't cause any of those problems, but they want to help solve them. Why can't the government figure that out?"

"That was weird," Knopfler said, after they'd listened a second time.

"He could actually be wrong about her," Holsom said.

"Sounds damned genuine to me," Knopfler agreed. "All relaxed and everything."

"I'd be more worried about the daughter, from the sound of it."

"Anyway, it's good you got those bracelets wired," Knopfler said.

CHAPTER 25

AMES, IOWA
DECEMBER 3, 2021—3 PM

"W HAT DID YOU think of that?" Sander asked.

Six hours after arriving in a helicopter, Luke had set up the secure chat with Sander, Winter, his idiot father, and himself from the bunker room at Sander's farm. Winter's group, including Benjy and Raine, had arrived in Nevada. The chip implanted in Amanda's breast had allowed them to follow all her conversations, including one with her daughter.

"She's doing a good job holding up under pressure," John said. "But they're never going to tell her anything that's of any use to us."

"You're probably right, John," Winter said. "But I like having ears in the First Family. We took a risk sending her back there. So far, it looks like Wyoming was right."

"It was a risk," Sander agreed.

"I want to talk about Matt," his father said then. From that moment, for some reason, Luke had a strong premonition of evil. He pricked up his ears. "He's in the hands of Dark Fiber now. What are we going to do with that?"

"We said we would leave him there," Sander said.

"He can lead us to those stolen shoulder-fired missiles," Winter added.

"Let's assume they have the missiles," his father went on. "Let's assume we get that confirmed. How are we going to get our hands on them?"

"Wait a minute. We said we were in a new phase," Winter said. "When we get our hands on them, we give them to the government. The new March22 is officially part of the government. The new March22 makes the administration look good, when it suits our purpose."

"Right," Luke said. "We've got a political party now. This is our moment."

"The possibility of getting those missiles from Dark Fiber and handing them over to the government seems like serendipity, with Matt's kidnapping," Sander said.

"It's not serendipity," his father said. "I think it's time you all knew. I sent an anonymous message to the Dark Fiber leader in Montana letting him know Matt would be along for the ride on Route 90."

"You what?" Winter exclaimed.

There was a silence. For a moment, Luke could only see numbers spinning in his mind, like numbers spinning on a dial—long numbers rounded to the thirty-second place, to the sixty-fourth place—very precise numbers scrolling in his mind. Then he snapped back to reality. This was no time for a distraction exercise.

Their father had betrayed Matt. He had invited the Dark Fiber Militia to kidnap him, or worse. He couldn't have known they wouldn't kill Matt on the spot. Judas came to mind. Or Brutus and Gaius, who sank their knives into Julius Caesar.

"John, explain please," Sander said.

"I knew you all wouldn't agree, so I went ahead and did it, for the good of March22," Luke's father said. That was always his excuse. "I sent an anonymous message to Thomas Paine. He couldn't possibly trace it. I let him know that one of the country's ten most wanted men, Matt, would be accompanying a convoy on Route 90 three nights ago."

"Your own son, John," Winter said. "You took a hell of a risk."

"I have a high tolerance for risk, as you all know," his father said.

"I still don't understand why," Sander said. "What were you hoping to gain?"

"Exactly what we have gained," his father said. "Get him into the hands of the Dark Fiber leaders. Get confirmation about the shoulder-fired missiles. Get our hands on those missiles to put March22 on the map as a force for good and to shine a spotlight on the true forces of evil in the country."

"It's astounding to me that you were ready to take such a risk with any of our men," Sander said. "Especially Matt, for God's sake. Did you tell Matt?"

"No," his father said.

"I'll say this," Winter said, speaking more slowly than usual. "We can't be a functioning group if someone is too chicken to get their ideas signed off by the rest."

"It worked, didn't it?" his father said. Luke thought it sounded childish.

"We can't function that way, John," Sander said. "I second Douglas's opinion. It's a question of trust."

"How long have we known each other?" his father said.

"Thirty years," Winter said. "That's exactly the point."

"Your actions may have been successful or may turn out that way, but the way you went about it gives me a heavy heart," Sander said.

"He's my brother," Luke said simply. He hesitated, then added, "Nobody turns on my brother like that. Makes me feel like a giant puke." That his body wasn't even physically capable of emptying its stomach contents was beside the point.

"I understand how you feel, son," his father said — such a monstrous lie. The man who sent his own son into the hands of a vicious militia claimed to have feelings. Like, for example, family feelings? It was the ultimate confirmation of something Luke had known for some time. His father was the world's biggest egotist, thinking only of himself.

"For the record, we're sticking with the plan to rehabilitate March22 with the recovery of the stolen missiles, if we can do it," Sander said. "We'll give the missiles back to Homeland Security. We've established our political party in Washington starting today. And we've got that video of the drone strike on the hog farmers we can deploy, just to keep the pressure on the administration."

"And we've got the dirty bombs," Winter said. "But I don't know if I want to give those back just yet."

"In a trampling," Luke cut in, "John Carney would be the one hauling himself up on other people's shoulders, pushing them down, and even stomping on their faces, even if it were his own sons, just to get out alive."

"That's not fair, Luke," his father said.

Luke made a mental note. He had to find some way of blocking his father's access to Big Sky Base, where the dirty bombs were stored. This was urgent. The idea hit him like a cannonball in the face.

"We aim to be a force for good, John," Sander said. "Keep that in mind."

He had to tell Matt so they could talk about what to do. Sander was right. The outcome of their father's secret move might end up being positive for March22 and the country, but the risk had been much too high. Matt could've been killed. The same outcome could have been achieved through different means. The idea could have been shared with the other leaders and together they could have come up with a plan. Now the trust was truly broken.

Their father had to be isolated, at the very least. For that to happen, Matt had to know the truth.

PART 2

CHAPTER 26

DENVER, COLORADO
DECEMBER 3, 2021—6 PM

Iᴋᴇ Mᴜʟʟɪɴ ᴘᴜʟʟᴇᴅ the new black turtleneck over his head and studied himself in the mirror. He liked the way it hugged his thick neck and made his tummy look smaller. "What do you think?" he asked.

"Waste o' money," was all his former cellmate and best buddy Tranny Ng had to say. Glued to the TV, Tranny hadn't bothered to glance at him.

"Only seventy bucks," Ike said.

"Always tryin' to impress that chick, you're wastin' your time, not just your money," Tranny added.

"You're just jealous 'cause you're still in maintenance," Ike said. In this Bible Party encampment outside Denver, people were assigned to different types of work according to their abilities. "Nasreen told me she personally requested having me in security after that dude died a few days ago. Don't worry, buddy, I'll make sure you get a spot in security, soon as another one opens up."

"Thanks, but when it comes to that chick, you're dreamin', man," Tranny said.

"She sure is worth dreamin' about," Ike said. He pictured Nasreen's waves of dark brown hair, her long spindly legs, her womanly curves. Mostly he thought of the way she had smiled just for him and given his hand a special squeeze — twice already — when saying goodnight.

Five minutes later, Ike stood a few steps back from the door of Nasreen's bus, waiting for it to open. He couldn't wait to see what Nasreen would wear for her VIP dinner. Nasreen and Pastor Peaches were eating downtown in some swank restaurant with the VIPs who'd arrived.

The amazing change in his and Tranny's fortunes in less than three weeks made Ike's head swim. For the last nine years, they'd shared a cell at the medium-security penitentiary in Warrenville, Missouri. Both had been serving sentences of twenty years to life. One night just after ten o'clock, their cell door had slid — and remained — open, jammed in that position.

Surprised to find no one guarding them, they had joined the procession of orange-suited inmates jogging to the main gate and into the fresh, free air. They'd made their way to Joplin, Missouri, in a dump truck Ike had hotwired. There they became acquainted with a man named Shipton, who had tested their courage with a special mission and then set them up with cushy jobs in the Bible Party tour with Pastor Peaches.

Ike had developed a serious crush on Nasreen, Pastor Peaches' assistant, the second he'd laid eyes on her. Since then, a steady series of encounters had given him hope that one day he might get Nasreen in the sack.

When you'd spent as much time in the joint as he had, you lost the ability to believe in miracles. Every day was a tortured mix of boredom, stress, boredom, fighting, and more boredom. Most people in the world thought time went by too fast. Their lives were filled with work obligations, family, chores around the house, and, if they had any time left over, maybe a hobby or a sport. He remembered that from the few years he'd lived on the outside. He'd been married once. There were never enough hours in the day, and you ended up fighting with each other over things that hadn't been done. She nagged you, she was never satisfied, and, on top of it, you never got enough sleep. In prison it was just the opposite. Time dragged on far too slowly. Every day was the same and every day felt like a whole lifetime, till you wished it would just end.

Yet here he stood, on the outside again. That was the first miracle. He'd seen something on TV saying the prison doors had opened because of a computer error, of all things. Then meeting Shipton, who had found a way for them to stay safe on the outside. That was a miracle, too. Now, Ike was putting all his faith in a third miracle with Nasreen. Maybe Tranny was right. Maybe it would never happen. But who would've put money on those first two miracles happening? Why not a third one? Was it true miracles only happened when you didn't expect them? Anyway, it was sure fine dreaming about it.

The bus door opened with a hiss, revealing the beautiful Nasreen in a silvery skirt that hung reached just below her knees. Her green silk blouse was open just far enough to hint at the paradise underneath. The white shawl around her shoulders gave Nasreen a look of innocence that he hoped was an illusion. After all, he'd seen her cradling an assault rifle just a week ago, the night that other security dude was killed.

"You're always right on time. In fact, you're early," Nasreen said, smiling just for him.

"Jes' doin' my job." Ike stepped forward and offered his arm as she placed her feet, caressed by cream-colored high heels, on the packed gravel.

As Pastor Peaches appeared behind Nasreen, two other security men joined them. The three of them accompanied the women to their SUV. Assassins lurked everywhere, it seemed, and Pastor Peaches, being such a famous person, was a target. Ike opened the door for Nasreen, who was driving. Unfortunately, one of the other security men was assigned to the women's car. Ike would've liked to sit in the back seat and watch Nasreen as she drove.

Instead, he rode shotgun in the tail car with a dude named Rocker. They followed a few car lengths behind Nasreen on the highway leading to Denver.

"So, where you from, Ike?" Rocker asked.

"Indiana, originally. But I've lived all over." He didn't mention that he'd spent the last nine years in the lockup in Missouri and a few years before that behind the forty-foot walls of the Indiana State Prison near Gary. "What about you?"

"I come from hell itself," Rocker said. "Born and raised."

Ike glanced at the old English lettering in green ink on the man's neck: DIFSOON. Ike had seen Rocker snap both arms of a UMC assassin who'd snuck into the encampment a few nights ago, hoping to kill Pastor Peaches.

"What do you mean?" he asked, not knowing if Rocker was joking. Rocker stared as if Ike was the one joking.

"Man, you serious?" Rocker said. "I'm just lucky I found this security gig and got money coming in to supplement the ration coupons. I've got to feed three kids, my wife, and her three sisters and two brothers. You think a single one of them assholes got a job?"

"I guess not, you say it like that," Ike said.

"Hell no, bunch of worthless fucks. I got them mooching at our place all hours of the day. Problem is, my old lady don't know how to say no."

"You mean she gives 'em food?" Ike said.

"That's right, and dresses their wounds," Rocker said. "She's a nurse, even though she ain't working right now. They're always getting into fights down at the shadowmarkets, getting cut or beaten up, the women just as much as the men."

"What was that you said, *shadowmarkets*?"

"Say, Ike, what planet did you say you been living on?"

Ike swallowed hard. "Got outta the slammer a few weeks ago, got right into this Bible Party tour. You make it sound like I mighta missed somethin'."

"Damn straight. Shit, at least you get three good meals in jail."

"I ain't goin' back in for nothin'. I'd rather die," Ike said.

"Stores don't have shit on the shelves anymore," Rocker said. "Even if they did, it's so fucking costly, hardly anyone can pay for it. So people's taken to buying their food at shadowmarkets, which is a lot cheaper. Then they go trading on the streets for whatever they still need."

"What're you talkin' about, man?" Ike was perplexed. This sounded like another world. "We was at the Safeway a week ago. Okay, the shelves did look a little empty." He suddenly recalled seeing whole aisles of empty shelves in the massive store. They'd been told to buy forty cans of tuna fish and only found six, cleaning the store out. Come to think of it, a lot of other things had been impossible to find as well, especially meat items, coffee, and bread.

"All depends on the locality," Rocker said. "I come from Oklahoma City. Man, it's like a wasteland. Them militias got total control over the food supply in OK City. Even the restaurants get their shit from shadowmarkets."

"I never heard of them shadowmarkets," Ike said. "When did that all start?"

"I guess a coupla years ago, back in 2019. It all went real fast. All those missile attacks on the planes, then they shut down everything—no planes flying since then, and checkpoints popping up on all the highways. Didn't you guys have TV in the joint?"

"One thing I hate is watching the news," Ike said.

"Well, it spiraled downhill real fast. People constantly getting shot at shadowmarkets. Militias in shootouts in the cities and college campuses. Restaurants getting robbed, not for the money, but for the food in their storage. That's when it got so dangerous."

"So your in-laws are livin' on the street?"

"They all got a place to stay, pretty much, just nothing to eat. I remember my sister-in-law Patricia, man, she used to be heavy. Our scale went up to three hundred pounds, and when she weighed herself the needle got stuck on the maximum. Now that woman's thin as a rail and she don't look healthy."

"No shit?"

"I kid you not."

Ike was feeling even luckier to have ended up in this Bible Party tour. "Remind me to bypass Oklahoma City on my next trip."

Rocker looked pissed off. "That ain't funny, man."

THE MEN FOLLOWED Nasreen's SUV off the highway and were cruising through downtown streets. Tall buildings rose up on both sides. Ike saw two old men on a street corner when Rocker stopped at a red light. As one held out a bag with bottles in it, the other handed him a bill. All of a sudden, as the light turned green and Rocker stepped on the gas, the two men started shouting at each other. When he looked back, Ike saw they were throwing punches.

He didn't remember seeing anything like that in his pre-jail days.

When Nasreen's SUV pulled over in front of the fancy steak restaurant, Ike climbed out while Rocker stayed behind the wheel. Ike's job was to escort the two ladies into the restaurant while Rocker and the other man parked the cars.

A doorman flanked by two goons with assault rifles gave them the once-over. Drones hovered ten feet above them.

"Reservation for the Bible Party," Nasreen said. The doorman stepped aside as Ike followed Nasreen and Pastor Peaches in the door. In the crowded entryway, a hostess came right up to them with a platter of bacon treats.

"Prove your patriotism while you wait?" the hostess said.

"Oh, this is always so amusing," Pastor Peaches said as she took one. "What are these?"

"Bacon-wrapped potato slices," the hostess said.

"None for me," Nasreen said.

Ike snagged a toothpick in each hand. "I'll eat hers."

He stood back as Pastor Peaches and Nasreen chatted with the hostess. Armed security men stood in two corners of the dining room. Waitresses crisscrossed the restaurant and a big crowd stood at the bar, laughing as if they didn't even notice the man behind the bar with the assault rifle. Ike didn't want to join those cheerful people at the bar. He just wanted a roll in the hay with Nasreen.

"Follow us, Ike," Nasreen said.

Pastor Peaches marched after the hostess, who threaded her way through the tables. Ike kept one eye on the back of Nasreen's skirt while surveying the seated diners in their path, looking for any sign of a threat. Pastor Peaches had been on national TV many times and people looked up, instantly recognizing her. But nobody asked for an autograph, and nobody aimed a gun.

At the back of the dining room, the hostess opened a door, revealing a private room. Ike caught a glimpse of some men inside. Pastor Peaches led the way in. Ike followed Nasreen and scanned the faces of the men, who stood up and kissed the ladies and shook their hands. All these men in suits looked like they would ooze money if they smiled any harder. Briefcases lined the walls and the men already had drinks.

The hostess was taking the ladies' drink orders. When she came to him, Ike said, "Nothing for me, thanks."

Nasreen came over as the hostess went out. "That'll be fine, Ike. They're going to free up a table just outside this door for the three of you. No one else comes in the room except this waitress, clear?"

"Got it."

"Order yourselves a nice dinner," she said. "It's on our tab."

She squeezed his hand before turning away again. Ike was walking on air as he left the private room.

Forty minutes later, the three guards sat at their table right outside the private room. Ike had polished off a twenty-ounce filet mignon with a baked potato nearly the size of a football. He was sipping coffee. Rocker and the other security dude, whose name was Jerry, sat across from Ike as all three continued to scan the restaurant and its patrons. Cindy, the waitress, had entered and exited the private room six times with drinks and appetizers.

Cindy arrived again now, followed by two busboys carrying trays full of food. She opened the door to the private room and the first busboy moved to follow her. Ike sprang up.

"Hey, you," he said. "You ain't going in there. Set up those trays out here, and she can bring it in."

The first busboy ignored him, marching in behind Cindy with a big tray balanced up high on his left hand. Ike cut in front of the second busboy and followed, heat rising in him. He didn't take kindly to being ignored. When Ike saw the man's free hand snaking into the pocket of his black trousers, alarms went off in his head. Then he saw the pistol.

Ike grabbed the gun arm without thinking twice, spinning the busboy around. Having lost his balance, the busboy shoved the falling tray with six plates of food in Ike's face. Ignoring the heavy plates raining down on him, Ike stayed focused on the man's gun. He tightened his grip on the man's wrist as plates battered his shoulders and chest. Ike held on tight as the man tried to spin away. He yanked the wrist backward and down. Ike heard something crack in the man's shoulder. The gun bounced away on the carpet as he wrestled the man to the ground.

When Ike looked up, Rocker had leveled a pistol at the second busboy, standing three paces away. Jerry stood in the doorway. The second busboy slowly lowered the tray of food he was carrying, set it on a preparation table, and raised his trembling hands in the air.

"Get their wallets," Nasreen said.

Ike fumbled in the downed man's pocket and handed the wallet to Nasreen.

"UMC member since 2016. Surprise, surprise," Nasreen said. She bent down for a closer look at the busboy's face. "Open your eyes and look at me, swine. Don't you watch TV? Tell your boss the Bible Party and UMC are in a coalition together now. The news obviously hasn't reached the rank and file."

Ike let the man get up. The UMC assassin cradled his left arm in one hand and spat at Ike's feet before sauntering out of the room without a word. Ike slipped the man's gun in his own pocket.

The second busboy, a genuine employee of the restaurant, was not affiliated with UMC. He left the room while Cindy served all the food he had brought. Then the waitress went out to put in replacement orders for the rest.

Ike stood in a mess of spilled steaks and vegetables and sauces. Food and sauces dripped from his clothes. Nasreen's secret smile was all the thanks he needed.

CHAPTER 27

DENVER, COLORADO
DECEMBER 3, 2021—9 PM

NASREEN'S FACE LOOKED serene as Ike deposited her at the bus. Pastor Peaches had already gone in to retire for the night.

"Come inside for a minute. I want to show you something," Nasreen said. She touched her Jetlink, making the bus door hiss.

"Sure thing," Ike said.

To the left as you entered the bus was a small office with laptop stations, all dark at this time of night. Beyond those, a tiny kitchen and a living room with a couch and several armchairs. A thick white rug made their steps soundless as she led him toward the back.

"We have to be quiet. She's in the bathroom," Nasreen whispered, touching her Jetlink again, which opened another door.

Ike's heart pounded at the thought that Nasreen was inviting him into the private quarters. Spots of food still covered his black turtleneck. He probably stank of sauce, but Nasreen's musky perfume was making his head spin.

They stood in a narrow hallway. Nasreen pointed at a door at the back. That must be the bathroom, where Pastor Peaches would be. Nasreen opened a door on the left and beckoned him inside. They stood in one of the smallest bedrooms he'd ever seen. The bunk bed had a desk squeezed in underneath. A folding chair leaned against one wall. A tall cupboard, in which she probably kept her clothes, stood against the back wall.

"I wanted you to see this." She pointed at a painting on the front wall.

He saw roundish blue shapes in the picture with white spots here and there. It looked like one of those pictures of space you sometimes saw, with space clouds swirling around and a smattering of stars. Darker shades of blue intermingled with light blue, grays and white. Then he noticed little curving lines in black that seemed to disappear into the darker blues.

He could've sworn the clouds in the painting started moving, even as he stared at the scene. When Nasreen dimmed the light, the picture suddenly appeared three dimensional, the layers rising and separating from each other, black receding into dark blue, and tiny white lines the thickness of hairs coming out the other side. He started to feel dizzy and looked away.

"What is it?" he asked wonderingly.

"It's called *Blues*," Nasreen said. "I love it, don't you?"

"I really do." He had never seen a painting that moved before. He looked at it again, then tore his gaze away. "I can see why you put it up here."

"It relaxes me," she said. "I don't need many objects. We live a life without *things*, here on the tour."

"I see why." The size of her room made collecting anything impossible.

"I just had to show it to you," Nasreen said.

He could swear she was looking at him the way women did when they wanted a kiss. He wanted nothing more than to kiss this woman. *You're dreamin'*, Tranny had said. Yet here he stood in Nasreen's bedroom, with her face only inches from his.

Nasreen, almost his height in her heels, was quicker. He felt her hand squeezing his again. Her face moved even closer, and then their lips touched. Ike hadn't kissed a woman in so long, he'd almost forgotten his technique in the black hole of his nine-year abstinence. A man could always get his rocks off in the joint, if he felt like it, but kisses had become a deeply buried memory. She pressed her lips against his, and, in a flash, he realized Nasreen's lips had parted. When he probed with his tongue, her tongue came out to meet his. He felt her arms come up around his neck, and she pulled him tight against her.

The kiss deepened as they swirled tongues, tasting each other. All his dumb brain could think of was Tranny. This would sure make a believer out of him. To think they had been incarcerated less than three weeks ago. Now look at him, locking tongues with the beautiful Nasreen.

Nasreen's fingers combed through his hair, massaging his scalp, bringing Ike back to the blissful here and now. "I've had my eye on you, you know," she said in a low voice, pulling back.

"I think I mus' be in Heaven."

"You're a good man, Ike."

Their faces were so close he felt her soft breath on his cheeks. Her dark brown eyes were radiant with light, as if the light came from within. Her body hadn't moved away from his, and she kissed him again, hard. She wanted more. When she pressed her hips against him, the realization of what she had in mind hit him like a freight train.

He kissed harder and rolled his hips a little. Nasreen didn't shy away at all at the feel of his manliness. He disengaged from the kiss, nuzzling downwards along her neck, drinking in her glorious scent as Nasreen threw her head back. She seemed to like him breathing on her neck. He licked her skin and kissed ten different places softly, eyes shut tight, picturing her beautiful face in his mind.

"Ike, could you... help me with these buttons?" Nasreen was breathing faster. Her hand found his behind her back, and he realized that was where her silk blouse buttoned. "Start at the top."

Still kissing her neck, he reached up with both hands and found the top button. His fingers were so damned fat and clumsy. Normally he had no trouble with buttons, but these were very tiny ones, and a whole line of them, all close together. With an extra effort, he got six or seven of them undone before she pulled away.

"I'm getting food all over your nice clothes," he said. He looked at the light-colored blobs that stained his front.

"Let's get that off you." Nasreen grasped the hem of the turtleneck around his waist and, in one movement, unrolled it over his head, leaving him standing in his sleeveless undershirt. "That too," she insisted. She tossed his clothes on the floor behind him. He tried to suck in his tummy, but it didn't help much.

"Been meaning to lose a few pounds."

Nasreen laughed. "I like a big man, don't worry." She turned her back and wiggled out of her blouse, even though the bottom half was still buttoned. After laying the blouse on her desk, her hands reached behind her back and she undid the clasp of her bra. Ike felt a little wobbly as she turned to face him and moved in close again, pressing her breasts into his bushy chest hair.

"Surprised?" Nasreen asked, then planted another long, sucking kiss on his mouth, not letting go for a long time. He grunted affirmative without breaking off, then realized she was tugging on his belt. *I'm a lucky, lucky man,* he thought as her fingers fumbled with the clasp. Who would've thought the beautiful Nasreen would ever go to work on his belt? Another miracle. Miracle upon miracle. Finally she had it undone, and then she undid the top button of his trousers.

A moment later, they were on the carpet—Ike on his back with Nasreen on her side next to him. She touched him, running a hand over his chest while keeping one of her exquisite, naked legs draped over his leg. They were kissing in this position when a sharp tap came on the door.

"You need help with those buttons, Nasreen?" Pastor Peaches asked through the door.

"I'm good, PP. Goodnight," Nasreen called.

There was a pause before Pastor Peaches answered. "Okay, night."

What happened over the next two hours, complete with the ultra-thin purple condoms Nasreen supplied out of nowhere, fulfilled all of Ike's fantasies from the last nine years and longer.

CHAPTER 28

OUTSIDE ANN ARBOR, MICHIGAN
DECEMBER 3, 2021—4 PM

BY THE THIRD day of his captivity, depression weighed on Matt. Raine had said she and Benjy were no longer in Montana, but she wouldn't say where they'd gone. She said she wasn't allowed to say. They'd almost had a fight. Today they hadn't talked at all. Now, assuming he managed to escape, he didn't even know where to go. It was almost as if they were *both* being held against their will. If this was what life was going to be like in March22, he wanted no part of it.

He sat on the bed and contemplated his next move. For three days, he and Claire had alternated between news programs and Nina Nardelli on TV, eating, and not going outside. Claire turned out to be a *Faking It with the Nardellis* freak.

He thought about the fact that Claire had refused contact with Dark Fiber people since the attacks. That was fine for her, but it meant nothing was being decided about the Matt Carney question. The March22 leaders wanted him to stay put, while the Dark Fiber leaders didn't even know they had to think about what to do with him. This was how it felt to be blocked on all sides.

After the excitement of being kidnapped, escaping from a burning house, and being dragged back to the safe house on the back of Claire's motorcycle, sitting around doing nothing was becoming a torture. This farmhouse was so still and silent, all you heard was the occasional creaking floor.

In the late afternoon, he decided to go out to the kitchen for coffee. He was supposed to be finding out more about Dark Fiber's weapons and the shoulder-fired missiles. Maybe he could find a way to quiz Claire about those things after all. Anything would beat sitting in this bedroom staring at the walls.

"Hey, Matt." Claire turned in her chair. As usual, Nina filled the TV wall.

"Do you mind minimizing that window?"

Claire smiled. "What've you got against Nina Nardelli?"

"It's all just ... big breasts. I feel like it's just her breasts talking when I watch that stupid show."

"There's much more to it than that," Claire said. "Hey, are you hungry? Can I fix you a ham sandwich?"

"Sure." He fell into a seat at the table, ready for an argument. He didn't object to Claire fixing him food. He knew she was as bored as he was. He just couldn't comprehend how she could go on and on not making some kind of decision.

"I think the physical aspect is part of her larger message," Claire said as she took things out of the fridge. "Everything is fake, phony, lies. You have to see through the lies to get to the truth. Especially in the media."

"Where did you get that idea?" He wasn't interested at all, just trying to make conversation. Claire spread mayonnaise and mustard, piled a thick portion of ham on top, and brought him his sandwich on a plate.

"Like when she did that spoof on jellies and jams, how they actually have no fruit in them at all?"

It took a second, but then he recalled the episode. "That's exactly what I mean. She's having breakfast with this guy she spent the night with, and she spills strawberry jam on her cleavage. Then the guy has to go and lick it up."

Claire laughed. "He was saying how much he loved pure strawberry jam, and it was even better eating it off of her boobs, then pow! She comes out with the chemical specifications and tells him all the synthetic garbage he just ate. The label actually said a hundred percent pure strawberry jam, made from sun-ripened strawberries. All lies."

"Yeah, but why does he have to lick it off of her breasts? That's exactly what I mean. Why is it always about Nina Nardelli's breasts?"

"It was funny, Matt. It's just a way of dramatizing it."

"Why couldn't they eat strawberry jam on toast, like normal people?"

"Who wants to watch people eat toast on TV?" Claire said. "Eating fake fruit off of Nina's surgically enhanced breasts ... it's just a way of revealing all the fakeness and lies around us. Hey, Matt." She gave him such a long, searching look, with a little ghost of a smile, he wondered if she liked him or something. It was different from her intense stares over the past couple of days.

"What?"

"It's nice to hear you actually talking again."

"I don't mind talking."

"You feel like doing some shooting?"

He actually put his monster ham sandwich down for a moment, not sure what she meant.

When he'd finished, she took him out behind the barn, where a path led into the forest. The setting sun shone through the bare trees and felt good on his face. Claire's boots crunched on the rotting leaves as she walked ahead of him. They came out in a large clearing, at the far side of which stood a line of stumps that had been set up for target practice.

"We stay together," Claire said, heading across the clearing toward the stumps. Matt counted out his paces.

"Afraid I'm going to shoot you?"

She turned and looked at him. "Matt, I know you're not that vapid. You have no reason to shoot me. I hope I convinced you that you're safer waiting it out in this place than going out on the road and risking getting caught."

"I'm still here, aren't I? Maybe I am vapid, whatever that means." It sounded suspiciously close to *stupid*.

"No you're not, so stop saying that."

"You said it yourself."

She grinned. "You're smart enough to get into Gram's safe. You still haven't told me how you managed that."

He kept silent. He wasn't about to tell her anything about Luke, and it was probably good if he kept her off guard. He counted out two hundred paces to the stumps, a good little distance, he thought. Must be five hundred feet. Claire went around behind the stumps picking up crumpled and half-destroyed cans and setting them up. When she was finished, they walked back to the other end of the clearing.

"You first," Claire said, arms crossed over her chest.

"What is this, some kind of competition?" Matt took out the 9mm Beretta she'd given him. He flicked off the safety, lined up the first can, and pulled the trigger. The can flew in the air. Ridiculously easy.

"One for you," Claire said. She turned her back to him and took aim. Her can flew off the stump as well.

One by one, they knocked off all the cans.

"I guess you're no beginner," Claire said.

"Have you got any coins or anything?"

"I was just going to say." Claire dug in her pocket and handed Matt a small handful of pennies. They set up two pennies on each stump, a total of twenty. It wasn't hard getting them to stand up. You just had to find a little crack or split in the wood to fit the edge of the coin into.

"I was thinking of introducing this as a place to bring new Dark Fiber members for training. We have other places, but this would be the biggest. Where did you learn to shoot so well?" Claire asked, walking back.

"My dad."

"Same here. I got my first BB gun when I was eight. My mom was appalled."

"These days, it's a useful skill to have."

When they had shot off half the pennies, each one flying into the air with a loud ping, Matt reached into the pocket of his camouflage pants for his slingshot. Just to make things interesting.

Then he hesitated. Maybe it was better if Claire remained ignorant of his alternative weapon.

Back in the kitchen, Claire was chatty as she set to work making instant mashed potatoes and seasoning steaks for dinner.

"My dad is a weapons freak, ever since he got out of the army," she said. "It drove my mom batty. She's completely antigun. He kept everything locked up in a fireproof cabinet in the basement. The basement door was always locked, too, but she always thought we were going to come home in a hearse."

"Safety first," Matt said.

"Of course, and he taught me that every time we practiced. He even made me wear ear and eye protection, as if that ever happens in the real world."

"Right," Matt agreed.

"What about you? Why did your dad teach you about guns?"

The question took him by surprise. He'd never asked himself why. When your dad invited you to go out and shoot a real gun, you didn't ask why.

"I don't really know."

"Well, how old were you?"

"I guess about ten or eleven. I don't remember how old I was, but I remember the first time. We went out to this farm he knew about, where there was target practice in all different kinds of settings. It was really cool. He started me off on a 9mm Beretta just like this."

"Really? When you were ten or eleven? Most people start out with a .22 rifle or something."

"I was always big for my age. We worked with rifles, pistols, and later assault rifles—just about everything."

"So, what do you remember about that first day?" Claire asked. She was stirring the mashed potatoes as the water came to a boil. He stood next to her at the stove, watching.

"I was a good shot from the beginning," he said. "I have good eyesight, and good breathing, he said. We started out on an ordinary course, shooting at targets. I scored pretty high. Then he took me out for pizza. We had pepperoni and mushrooms."

"You remember what kind of pizza you had?"

"That was kind of the high point, I think." He smiled at the memory. Going out alone with his father had always been the high point, ever since he could remember. When food had been offered, that naturally catapulted it into a kind of memory hall of fame.

"At this other place," Matt went on, "I remember you had to shoot out of a cave. We were aiming at targets from the depths of this cave as they flashed by outside. That was really cool. You were fifty yards in and you had to adjust for the bright sunlight at the cave entrance. Something would rush by and you had to decide if it was a friend or foe. If it was the enemy, you had to shoot it before it went by. That was really good training."

"That sounds kind of dangerous, shooting out of a cave. Was that with live ammunition?"

"Yeah, sure, but the conditions were controlled. You entered from the back. Outside the mouth of the cave, there was this complicated mechanism of moving targets that went around on a pulley. Everything was scored on a computer that was hooked up to the targets."

"How did you recognize the enemy?"

"That was the toughest part. All the targets were human-sized puppets dressed in clothes and hats and everything. The enemy targets had a little red sticker somewhere on the body. The sticker was the size of a dime."

"Man, that sounds like fun," Claire said. "I wonder who dreamed that up."

"We went there pretty often. My dad was friends with the owner."

"When you were ten or eleven," Claire looked at the ceiling, thinking, "that would've been before March22 was founded."

"Really?"

"Sure, because March22 was founded in late 2015. Didn't you know that?"

He shook his head. "I'm a new member. Not even fully trained. That's why it makes no sense that you guys kidnapped me."

"Your dad was a founder and you didn't even know about it?" She looked like she didn't believe him.

"I was thirteen in 2015, okay?" She didn't have to know he had only found out about his father's involvement in March22 three weeks ago.

"Okay, you don't have to get upset."

"I'm not upset. Don't look at me like that just because I didn't know something. I'm not a huge expert on history or current events or anything."

"But you did get into Gram's safe," Claire said. "I have to know how you did that."

He smiled at the thought that Claire actually believed he was going to tell her anything. The woman was deluded. "I have my strengths," he said.

"It's a really secure safe," Claire said. "I would never have thought anyone could crack it. Come on, you have to tell me. I'm losing sleep over this."

"Sorry, that secret is going to the grave with me."

Claire scraped her chair, moving three feet closer. She was suddenly so close he became uncomfortable.

"I just want to look at your eyes," she said. He forced himself to look at her for a few seconds, then looked at the ceiling. "You have really nice gray eyes, you know. Do you have brothers and sisters?"

When she didn't move away, he scraped his chair and moved back a few inches. He actually had blue eyes. Claire leaned forward in her chair. She sat on her hands and looked at him. She had freckles across her nose and cheeks. Her short brown hair stood straight up in places. It was just plain messed up in others. She seemed to like that look.

"I've got a brother, two stepbrothers, and a stepsister," he said. "What about you?"

"Big family," Claire said. "Us, it's just me and my two kid sisters. When did your parents split up?"

"I was still a baby then," he said. "I don't even know my mother."

"Because she died?"

"Not that I know of." His father would've told him.

A look of surprise came over her. For a minute, Claire looked like she wanted to say something, then finally said, "Man, that must've been weird. You don't know her at all? No contact? All the time you were growing up?"

"No memories at all," he said. "I wouldn't know her if she bumped into me on the street."

Claire's hand moved from under her leg and, before he could move away, came to rest on his hand on the chair's arm. She left her hand there for a few long seconds, saying nothing. He felt a kind of electricity at her touch, like when you touched two live wires together. Claire was so weird. He gripped the chair arm and toughed it out. Finally, she looked away. A moment later, she took her hand away.

"I'm not especially close to my mom," Claire said. "I was trying to imagine not knowing her at all. Like, if she were dead or something. Like, if she died before I even knew her. I can't imagine it. She's my mom."

"Well I do have a stepmother," he said.

"Is she nice?"

"The last time I saw her, she shot at me," he said. "That was after she sicced a bunch of UMC killers on me. She's a real evil bitch, if you want to know."

Claire's face filled with sadness, and he turned away. He knew what she was thinking. First, his mother had abandoned him, then his stepmother turned out to be even worse. He couldn't stand it when people sympathized. Of all the feelings in the world, nothing grated on him more than sympathy. The way Claire had moved closer with her chair, tried to touch him, and kept staring at him, he had to wonder where she was really going with this.

"Listen, don't worry about me. I'm over all that," he said. "I've got my brother and my dad. And my little stepbrother. Everything's fine. Or at least it would be if I weren't being held captive halfway across the damned country."

As he said it, a pain formed in his chest that spread out to all the muscles in his body. To his surprise, he felt his throat tightening and his eyes filling. What the hell? He probably wasn't over it, in fact. He wasn't over it at all. No kid should have to say he didn't know his own mother. No kid should have to hear that his own mother had abandoned him as a baby.

He looked down and savagely wiped a hand across his face.

The next thing he knew, Claire was hugging him. He sat tensely in his chair as she wrapped her arms around him. He felt her breath on his neck. He didn't respond, but he didn't push away either. A kind of paralysis overwhelmed him — while inside him a hopelessness and darkness he hadn't even known was there started expanding, quickly finding every corner of his soul with its tentacles.

"Try not to think about it," Claire whispered. He felt her settling her weight on his lap, her legs draping over his right thigh. She was a lightweight, all right. She had her arms wrapped tight around his neck. The side of her face was pressed against his face. A fragrant, flowery perfume wafted from her skin. He hadn't noticed it before.

This was all wrong. Why had he opened his big mouth? He didn't want Claire's sympathy. He didn't want it from anyone. He didn't want some other girl's arms around him. He ached to just go home and be with Raine.

"I think I'm going to go to my room for a while," he said.

When Claire rose and walked to the sink, he got up and walked stiffly in the direction of his room. This place was getting to him.

CHAPTER 29

DENVER, COLORADO
DECEMBER 4, 2021—7 AM

IKE MULLIN WOKE in his own bed in the camper he shared with Tranny. His first thought, even before he opened his eyes, was the memory of Nasreen's beautiful face, her long dark hair, and her voluptuous breasts with dark nipples. To his surprise, his excitement developed all over again in the tight confines of his boxer shorts. After all that exercise of the previous night, a man could use a rest. But there were certain things he had no control over.

He got out of bed, made coffee, and sat in the tiny living room daydreaming of the things Nasreen had said. *I like a big man,* she'd said. *Just let me know when you're ready for an encore,* she'd said a little while after their first mind-blowing romp had come to a gentle finish. After a half hour of cuddling, they'd gone for round two in Nasreen's bed, with her on the bottom.

It amazed him that she genuinely liked him. It seemed as if they'd talked for hours while Nasreen circled her warm hand around his big white gut.

"Where the hell'd you disappear to last night until three?" Tranny said while they ate breakfast. "You missed a double feature of *Resident Evil* on TV."

"Starred in my own movie," Ike said.

"What the hell?"

"A romantic movie," Ike said, winking. "The beautiful, intelligent Nasreen."

Tranny stopped chewing. "No shit, man?"

"No shit."

"Well come on, gimme the dirt."

"I ain't givin' you no dirt."

"You're tellin' me you spent last night till three in the morning with that hot chick?"

"I did indeed."

"You can't hold out, man. What'd you do, get her shirt off or something?"

"Not just her shirt, Tranny-boy. And that's all I'm gonna say."

"Hot damn." Tranny gazed with pure admiration. Ike went on spooning his cereal, careful to keep his mouth closed as he chewed. He hadn't thought about his table manners for many years, but now he had a reason to make the effort. Tranny had gone to bed as a nonbeliever and woken up a convert. All at once, Tranny's expression grew serious.

"You don't think she'd be interested in sharing a bit of that romance around?"

The cereal went chalky in Ike's mouth. He hardly believed his ears.

"What'd you just say, Tranny-boy?"

"You know, piece of the action for me, too, type of thing?"

"If you come within ten feet of that woman, I'll have to kick your ass."

Tranny stood up, flexing his trapezius muscles. "Like to see you try."

Ike shrugged. He knew very well that Tranny could whip his ass if it came to that. In prison, Tranny had beaten him up three times. Once, Ike had spent a night in the prison infirmary with a busted collarbone and three broken ribs. Most guys in the slammer had learned to avoid Tranny, but when you bunked together, a few fights were inevitable. All things considered, he preferred being friends.

"Since you and me're buddies, I'm surprised you'd even get the idea to steal my woman," he said. Words were his best weapon with Tranny, who sometimes took a while to catch on.

"I'm just sayin' if that chick likes you, it stands to reason she'd like me, too."

"What the hell kinda logic is that?"

"We both spent time in the joint, didn't we?"

"That ain't got nothin' to do with her liking me," Ike said. "She don't even know about that."

"She knows we're friends, don't she? Maybe she just gets off on big, strong working men that've been in prison for a while."

"Just find your own woman, man."

"I can do that anytime I want," Tranny said. "I'm just sayin,' if she's available."

"She ain't available. That's what I'm tryin' to tell ya."

"How do you know? She was available to you. She don't even know you."

"She knows me. We've been getting to know each other. Besides, in the restaurant, I saved her life." Ike told a short version of incapacitating the phony busboy. Tranny was impressed.

"See what I mean?" Tranny said. "She probably felt like she owed you a quickie. That's how come she invited you in like that."

They split up after breakfast, Ike headed for security detail while Tranny headed to maintenance. The discussion left Ike grumpy. Why couldn't Tranny get it through his thick skull that they truly liked each other? Was that so hard to believe? Especially since he'd been dreaming of it and working on Nasreen since the day he met her. *I've had my eye on you,* she'd said.

On the other hand, what if Tranny was right? Certain unpleasant thoughts kept nagging at his brain. What if Nasreen slept with all the new guys, like some kind of nympho? What if all those nice words and laughing together had been an act she'd practiced hundreds of times? She'd want to move right on to the next lucky chump. Maybe even Tranny. A hot young thing like Nasreen wouldn't be satisfied going months at a time with no nooky.

At least he'd proved she was no lesbian, one of Tranny's early theories. Tranny had gotten the idea when that UMC motorcycle assassin had ridden into the tent with his assault rifle. After that young security guy, Matt, had shot the killer dead with his slingshot, everyone noticed how Nasreen lay spread-eagled on top of Pastor Peaches. Tranny interpreted that to mean she preferred the ladies, and maybe Pastor Peaches did, too.

Ike struggled to put both of these arguments out of his mind, but he couldn't help wondering if his quick action in the restaurant hadn't created a feeling of obligation in Nasreen. Wouldn't she have mentioned it? During their four hours together, she hadn't breathed a word about his heroics. Still, women didn't always say what was on their mind. He knew that from his own failed marriage.

When he reached the security tent, Nasreen was already there, making a speech to about fifteen other guys. She stopped talking to check something on her Jetlink, then fixed Ike with an icy look.

"Good morning. If you want to stay on the security team, you will show up to the morning briefing on time, not seven minutes late."

Ike felt the heat rising to his face, and lowered his gaze by way of apology. Was that the way you greeted your lover? Not "Good morning, Ike," with a smile, just "Good morning," all cold and distant? A pain burned in his chest, like an icicle in the heart.

"We've got a full day ahead of us, with visiting VIPs," Nasreen went on. There's a group this morning at ten and another this afternoon at three. "

As Nasreen rattled on with instructions and assignments, Ike's mind wandered back to Tranny's theory. Maybe Nasreen took her pick every few nights, sweet-talking some hard up stooge like him. Like a drug addict needing a fix. Maybe it had just been her way of saying thank you. Maybe it was already over, the morning after.

He'd met a few women like that in his time. The more he thought about it, the more either scenario seemed possible.

"You, there, in the green shirt. Are you even paying attention?" Nasreen was glaring at him again.

"Sorry, what was that again?" he asked with an innocent smile.

"I do not have time to repeat myself every time some bozo starts daydreaming. Get your assignment from one of the others here."

With that, Nasreen turned and headed for the tent entrance.

Ike's muscles felt sluggish and heavy. He trudged out of the tent, trailing behind the two other men, hardly hearing their chatter. *Some bozo.* His shoes made strange indentations in the gravel, one foot after the other. The gravel clearing in front of the buses, the ratty collection of cars all painted pink and green with the Bible Party logo, people milling about with cups of coffee... it all looked so drab and depressing. The buses were closed up tight, as usual. No Nasreen anywhere.

CHAPTER 30

DENVER, COLORADO
DECEMBER 4, 2021—10:30 AM

NASREEN KHADOUR KNEW her seat at this table was due to her loyalty to Pastor Peaches, dating back to the days when PP had presided over a Lutheran church in Ames, Iowa. As a student at the university, Nasreen had studied religion, history, and philosophy. Raised Muslim in Los Angeles, her Iranian parents had been crestfallen when she told them of her church visits.

"Just tell me you're not converting," her mother had said.

"It's water under the bridge," Nasreen had answered. Her father had shook his head. They hadn't broken off relations, but they weren't close anymore. It made her sad to think of her parents growing older, putting up with traffic, food shortages, and violence outside. She visited each year in the summer and all her mom wanted to do was sit in the living room with her feet up, eat sweets, and chatter about Nasreen's cousins, who were all married with children. Every last one of them.

Every cousin had married another Persian but one, Ravi. Ravi had married a Jewish girl, of all things. Ravi and Sarah had met at UCLA, where both studied business. After college, they'd started a company servicing drones and robots. People didn't have time to fix their robots when something went wrong, and the business had grown even faster than their family. Ravi and Sarah had four children. Everyone in the family had accepted Sarah without recriminations, even though she insisted on raising the children Jewish, which gave Nasreen a warm feeling in her heart. Differences could be celebrated in a marriage, and Ravi and Sarah were the living proof.

Nasreen knew that nothing would make her parents happier than if she settled down and had babies. They believed marrying and raising children lay on the direct path to true happiness. You couldn't attain happiness without putting in your time as a wife and mother. In her heart, she believed it herself. It was just that, at the moment, Pastor Peaches had such incredibly important work to do for the Bible Party. And PP depended on her. She wasn't going to abandon PP, just when all their dreams were starting to look like they could come true.

"We're here to answer any questions you might have about the new coalition with UMC," Pastor Peaches opened the meeting.

Nasreen studied the Bible Party politicians who'd flown in from Washington. Senator James Humphrey looked like he drank a lot of bourbon. His bright red face contrasted with his curly shock of white hair.

"Sounds like you're giving us marching orders, flying us here on short notice," Humphrey said. "I don't take marching orders from you or anyone else."

"I understand, Senator," Pastor Peaches said. "It was a sudden meeting, and I'm grateful you cleared your schedules. This is a very secure room. I'm sure you can appreciate that there are things we can't talk about even on secure chat."

"What could be that hot?" Senator Humphrey asked.

Nasreen imagined a woman in a negligee. She had an image in her mind of a blond woman, much younger than the senator. She saw the woman's pouting expression, heard her pleading. In an instant, Nasreen knew with absolute certainty why the senator was so irked at having to fly to Denver for the day. It had nothing to do with his work schedule. The meeting with Pastor Peaches had forced him to cancel a tryst with this blond woman—Nasreen was sure of it.

At odd moments she had these visions, and they often turned out to correspond exactly with reality. Where she had obtained this power, Nasreen had no idea. She had never mentioned it to anyone, not even PP.

"We will have the chance in the very near future to handpick not just one, but two Supreme Court justices," Pastor Peaches said, getting to the point. "We can't speak publicly about this just yet. But this coalition means we will have support from UMC and the Corporate Party for Bible Party nominees. We'll have more than enough support."

"It's about abortion," Humphrey said.

"Of course. This is our golden chance, gentlemen. Our justices will tip the court for the next twenty to thirty years. Roe v. Wade will go on the ash heap of the most infamous decisions handed down by the Supreme Court. That, by itself, would be reason enough to give our wholehearted support to this coalition and make sure all our Bible Party colleagues in the Congress and the Senate vote accordingly. Do you disagree?"

"I wouldn't say I disagree," spoke up Congressman Nat Jacobs from Virginia. "However, number one, there's going to be a hell of a big fight over those nominations, I don't care how much support we've got. Number two, people have a strange tendency to modify their views once they get on the court. We've seen it happen repeatedly. How are we going to protect ourselves against that?"

"I'll second that, and raise him one more," said Congressman Ham Larson of Tennessee. "There's real nasty stuff coming out of committee these days, and this coalition means I have to vote for it. My constituents did not elect me to put military drones in the skies over America. Now they've gone and gotten themselves in a real shitstorm about those thousand drones stolen by March22. I've received more than four thousand messages from angry constituents about that."

"The drones are there for a good purpose," Pastor Peaches said. "Think of them as a tool for rounding up the last of the thousands of escaped prisoners. They've been a godsend in solving that problem."

"And now the administration wants to use them to protect commercial aviation," Larson retorted. "This country has become a war zone."

"Well, we need commercial aviation to get the economy back on track," countered Senator Humphrey, who had switched from the Corporate Party to the Bible Party only three years ago. "Surely you have no argument with that."

"The bill coming out of committee would create a legal framework for leaving them there for a year, which in the real world could mean permanently," Larson answered. "The president legitimized their use for the emergency with an executive order. That gave him ninety days. I could live with that, even if my constituents couldn't. I could even live with another ninety days. But not by an act of Congress, where you know it's going to get attached to some other big bill every year and get rubber-stamped on into the future." He shook his head in disgust.

"That's not what we should be talking about here," Jacobs said. "March22 is today a political party with marginal representation in Washington. My staff has been studying some demographics, including social media trends. If they play their cards right, we're projecting they could triple their number of seats less than a year from now. March22 has a lot more support than people realize."

"I personally don't have a problem with that," Pastor Peaches said.

"What makes you so sure they won't take away Bible Party seats?" Jacobs asked.

Pastor Peaches hesitated, and Nasreen wondered how far she would trust these political hacks. "Because the Bible Party has its finger on the pulse of this country," PP said finally. "The UN Party is lagging. The Rainbow Party is complacent. The Liberty Party is regrouping and unlikely to rally additional support in time for next year's midterm elections. If March22 gains seats, it takes them away from those parties, not us. We're projected to keep growing as well, last I read."

"I wish I were as sure as you," Jacobs said.

"Besides, how is March22 a threat to our programs?" Pastor Peaches asked. "I think I'm pretty well informed. All March22 really wants is to return the country to a safer, freer place like it was just six or seven years ago."

"The jury's out, as far as I'm concerned," Humphrey said. "Our March22 colleagues in the Senate will be fortunate not to be led out in handcuffs, from what I've been hearing. If they're going to be the mouthpiece of the folks who blew up the Golden Gate Bridge, they'll have to take responsibility for it."

"I'm not here to *defend* March22," Pastor Peaches said. "What I'm saying is, we need to vote together with UMC and the Corporates, even if it means holding our nose. That's the only way we can keep them in line when it comes to our priorities."

"I have no problem with the Corporates," Jacobs said, glancing at Humphrey. "With UMC, I not only have to hold my nose. I have to put on a gas mask."

"We could debate this all afternoon," Pastor Peaches said. "But I think you see the political realities. We want those Supreme Court seats. They also promised us attorney general. Pastor Wiggins, who will be put forward by the President, has a law degree from Georgetown and practiced law in Washington for fifteen years before taking up the ministry. We're on a roll, gentlemen. With the coalition with UMC and the Corporates, we'll have a Bible Party attorney general and two Supreme Court seats. Then nothing can stand in our way."

"Those things certainly have value," Humphrey said. "With this perspective, I can commit to keeping my colleagues in the Senate in line."

"I see the value too," Larson said. "I just worry about the high price we're paying."

"We stand for re-election every two years," Jacobs said.

"That means you need to get with your constituents now," Pastor Peaches jumped in before he could continue. "And use your formidable rhetorical skill to help them understand the rationale behind the coalition. Everything has a price, gentlemen. We paid a low price for what we're getting in return. They needed our support. UMC and the Corporate Party had no one else to turn to. They were desperate. We'll continue to press them for more. Right now, I need every coalition member to do his part whenever it comes to a vote."

Nasreen never failed to be impressed at the way Pastor Peaches built her arguments. She had a unique gift, which she used every day, whether talking to VIPs or ordinary people who didn't want to admit how they had failed their spouse.

Her parents had seen Pastor Peaches on TV and they'd been impressed, too. "You work for that one?" her mother had said, wide-eyed as they watched Pastor Peaches end an inspirational sermon.

"I'm her top assistant," Nasreen had said.

"Her right-hand man," her father had said, then smiled his patented goofy smile that she loved so much.

CHAPTER 31

NEAR ANN ARBOR, MICHIGAN
DECEMBER 4, 2021—5 PM

"You can't say where you are, I can't say where I am. This is ridiculous," Matt said. "Why do we have to accept this?"

Raine nodded, her image filling the small screen on his Jetlink. "I'm in Nevada. They told me you've been here before."

"Ah, okay, sure. I'd be able to find that place again. That is, if I ever get out of here. I'm stuck in Michigan."

"Michigan!"

He laughed. "Yeah, pretty close to home, or at least where home used to be."

Raine's face grew serious again. "Matt, Benjy told me some of the things you experienced on your way to California. I had no idea."

"Why, what did he tell you?"

"I guess just about everything. He told me about Walt and Tom. He told me about those UMC guys outside your house in Chicago. He told me about what happened on the river. And the biker you shot with your slingshot."

Matt felt his face catching fire, and a deafening rush in his veins. "He told you all that, the little stinker? He had no right."

"Matt, don't be mad at him."

"Why'd he have to go and tell you all that stuff?"

"Don't you think it's better that I know? That's part of you now, Matt. That's a part of you I didn't know before. It's nothing to be afraid of."

"It's not that I'm afraid of it. It's just..." He didn't know what he wanted to say. Maybe he *had* been afraid of telling Raine he'd killed so many men. Maybe he'd been worried about her reaction. After all, who wanted to find out their boyfriend was a killer?

"Anyway, I wanted you to know it's okay."

"You probably think I'm some kind of cold-blooded monster."

"No, Matt, not at all." Shaking her beautiful head.

"Assassin. Predator. That's what my wanted poster says, you know."

Raine didn't smile. "It was self-defense, Matt. It was kill or be killed. Benjy told me everything. Everything he knew, everything he saw. I know you're no predator, Matt, stop it."

He had that sick feeling in his stomach, the feeling he got every time he thought about the people who had died. Why did it have to be so violent? It might be okay for Raine, but would it ever be okay for him?

"Maybe I didn't tell you because I've got a problem with it myself," he said. "It's not like I enjoyed it. We did what we had to in order to survive."

"Can I tell you something?" Raine said.

"Sure." She was always good at changing the subject.

"I've been training with guns ever since we got to Nevada. There's a shooting range underground. Rory says I'm a natural."

"You've been shooting?" He was shocked. "Last I heard, you hated guns."

"I used to hate them," she corrected. "That was before I knew what was going on in the world. I was just afraid of them. People are afraid of what they don't understand, Matt, it's natural. I never touched a gun before three days ago."

"Jesus, I hope you never actually have to use one," he said.

"I hope so, too. But if I had to defend you or myself—our children or whatever—I think I'd at least be capable of it."

Our children, Raine had said. *Our children.* He'd been standing the whole time, but he felt his leg muscles going rubbery. Slowly he sank down on the bed. Raine wanted to have children with him. Obviously they would have to wait a few years, but still, just the idea made his head swim with happiness. Children whose mother would stay put. Whose father would be a lot like Matt's father—tough, often silent, self-sufficient.

"Raine, I'm... I'm really looking forward to having children with you."

She smiled. "See that you live long enough to do it, buster. And we need to keep in practice, if you know what I mean?"

He laughed. "My highest priority is getting back home to you. Home is where you are, Raine."

After they said good-bye, he lay in a semi-dream state for some minutes, imagining children that looked like Raine. A little girl running around the yard, maybe a little boy. A house somewhere out in the country, like in Montana, far from all this mayhem. He could hunt in the forest and keep meat on the table. They could plant a vegetable garden. Ration coupons would cover their other needs, like coffee, milk, salt, and sugar. Raine would never have to shoot a gun. A simple life, a life without people killing each other.

With his eyes closed and no sounds from outside, it was easy to stay in this fantasy, seeing images of Raine with a big belly, then a baby crying, then changing diapers, or giving the baby her breast... .

Hey loser, wake up, Luke said, opening the channel.

I'm awake, super geek. Where've you been the last couple of days?

I'm going to tell you, I've been working and slaving, and you're not going to believe what I found out.

Hard to imagine you working and slaving.

I don't even know where to start. Okay, so here goes. You know Thomas Paine, the Dark Fiber leader?

Hawaiian shirt?

The one who kidnapped your ass.

Right, a real idiot.

All right, guess who sent that idiot an anonymous message that Matt Carney was going to be on convoy duty on Route 90 on the night of November thirtieth? I'll give you a hint. An even bigger idiot.

What the hell are you talking about, Luke?

You heard me. Thomas Paine got an anonymous tip. That's how he got the idea to kidnap you. It gave him all the information he needed.

Even though Luke's words were coming through loud and clear, this time with no gaps at the end of the sentences, Matt was having trouble making any sense of it.

What do you mean by anonymous tip?

Handing over your ass. Basically, inviting those idiots to use you any way they saw fit.

You've got to be joking. Who would do a thing like that? Was it the UMC? How would they even know — ?

You're cold. It wasn't any UMC idiot.

I was just trying to think. Who did I piss off? My stepmother?

Even colder. Although, in a way, warmer.

Warmer, colder — just shut up and tell me what this is all about.

Are you ready for this, Matt? Our father sent that bastard the message. He gave Paine the coordinates of where the convoy would come through and the approximate time.

Dad? You're crazy, Luke. You're always attacking Dad.

So I am, and with good reason.

Luke, do you expect me to believe this shit? It doesn't even make sense. I don't even know what you're talking about.

Don't even think about not believing me, brother. Our father confessed his deed in a secure chat with the leaders two days ago.

Matt was too stunned to answer. The idea of his father writing a message to that Dark Fiber prick that led to him being kidnapped and freighted across the country and landing in a Michigan safe house with Claire — it was all too much to comprehend.

He said it himself?

I wish I were kidding. It boggles the mind, no?

But why? Why would he do a thing like that?

Here comes the working and slaving part, Matt. After he told us, I still had trouble getting my head around it.

Why did he do it?

He said his aim was to get you into Dark Fiber so that you could find the stolen shoulder-fired missiles. We want to hand those over to Homeland Security publicly as part of our initiative to show March22 aims to be a force for good in this country.

It's just so crazy to rope me into this. I'm not qualified. Are you sure he said what you think he said?

First, because they could've just executed you on the spot, like they did some of the other March22 men that night, Luke said. *Of course, I agree with you on every level. That's why I had to know more. Thus the working and slaving. When people stop talking,* Luke starts surfing. *There's always more to the story than people own up to, and such is also the case with our father.*

What do you mean?

I hacked into Thomas Paine's emails and saw what they were planning. They definitely have the shoulder-fired missiles, by the way. I haven't had time to run down that angle yet. I was concentrating on their exchanges after they received the tip from our father.

What exchanges?

The Dark Fiber leaders first had to sort out who you were exactly. You're not exactly well-known, even if you are on the most wanted list. Congratulations on that honor, by the way.

Thanks a lot.

So there were a few messages back and forth asking what's the point, what's the value of this guy, and so forth.

I ask myself the same questions every day, Matt said.

Behold, my brother has a sense of humor.

Especially here in this stupid safe house.

Hold on, the best is coming. The interesting part is when they tried to figure out who sent the anonymous tip, and why.

What did they come up with?

Our father routed the message back through sixteen different servers all the way back to one at the Chicago Public Library, Ashland Branch. Does that ring a bell for you?

Ashland rings a bell. I never went to libraries much.

Your stepmother lives on Ashland Avenue, does she not?

Sure. So, you're saying it was her?

No, dickhead, our father made it look like it was her. The original email traces back to that Ashland Avenue branch, two blocks from the family house. He wrote a program that made it look like someone sat in that library and sent the message, routing it through sixteen other places around the world. Any duffer could've followed it back to Ashland Avenue. So the Dark Fiber techies took one look at the location of that IP address, put two and two together with your stepmother's street address — her name is Carney, too — and deduced it was your stepmother who sent the mail.

She is a good Dark Fiber customer, with all the Red Label she drinks.

Don't you see the point, Matt? Our father betrayed your ass, but he wanted Dark Fiber to think it was her that did it.

I don't get it. You've totally lost me.

They went and knocked on her door, Luke said.

Why? Why go to all that trouble?

Think about it. They get one anonymous tip with what turns out to be a tantalizing offer. For people like that, it's like winning the lottery, you know? Too good to be true, but also too good to ignore. It could've been a trap of some kind, so they had to satisfy themselves. Our father understood all that. He thinks like they do. They weren't going to set up a complicated and dangerous operation without knowing more. Wanda was only too happy to confirm what a devilish little twerp you are. I saw it in their messages to each other. She swore up and down she never sent the anonymous tip, but they didn't expect her to admit that part of it. Who would ever admit it? Her very existence and the things she said about you convinced them to go ahead with the kidnapping. All because of the diabolical way our father sent it.

My God, that all sounds pretty sick.

That's how much trouble our father went to in order to put your ass in harm's way.

How could he put me in danger like that? I mean knowingly.

You mean why didn't he use someone else?

Well, yeah, I guess so.

My guess is he saw a way to convince them it was real by using Wanda, and just went with it. He got his ass reamed in our secure chat. Nobody saw it his way. The other leaders were more than pissed off. For all of us, the main issues were trust and working together as a group. He went ahead with this secret operation without consulting anyone, then presented it to us as a fait accompli.

What? What's that?

It's like when something's already done and can't be undone.

Like the fact that I'm already here, deep in the heart of Michigan.

Deep in the heart of Dark Fiber, is right, Luke said. The complication is, our father's plan has worked so far. You're safe, we've learned they have the missiles, now we just have to find out where they are and steal them.

Jesus, that's a tall order.

No, but I mean the problem is that our father feels vindicated by the success so far. What you're doing there is the best thing that could happen to March22. But it's wrong for him to feel what he did was acceptable. That's my problem.

The walls, the ceiling, the room swam around him, thinking of the connection between his father and Thomas Paine. The Dark Fiber leader had acted so smug on the plane. All of a sudden, Paine's comment that someone had handed his ass to Dark Fiber came back to him. His own father.

The realization stung.

He could've asked me, Matt said. *He damn well could've asked me.*

CHAPTER 32

"YOU'VE GOT A visitor," the guard said.

Wyoming Ryder stood up from his cot, where he'd been watching a video, and waited while the guard unlocked the door. The face that greeted him as the door swung inward was nothing short of amazing.

"Nina!"

"Thirty minutes," the guard said.

"Hope you enjoyed the frisk," Wyoming said good-naturedly. The guard looked as shocked as if Wyoming had pulled a gun on him.

Unsmiling, Nina marched into his cell. She held her biggish nose high and looked right and left, as if expecting trouble. This wasn't a suite in the St. James, but at least he had a separate toilet, complete with a decent shower. The clothes closet contained hangers made of cheap plastic, the kind that floated in mile-wide garbage piles in all the world's oceans, choking dolphins and myriad other creatures, but at least he could hang up the clothes Karen Vixen had brought.

Nina Nardelli bent forward for a kiss, and Wyoming pulled her into a hug. He needed one right now. Nina wouldn't care if he smudged her makeup. She was wearing a hooded sweatshirt and designer jeans, three-inch spike-heeled boots and about ten different metal bracelets that clinked and clanked on her wrist.

She pulled him close again and whispered, "Your lawyer told me to come. Can they hear if we talk like this?"

"I doubt it," he whispered back. They were barely mouthing the words. They stayed in the embrace.

"I paid that guard and the guy at the front desk a thousand dollars each to keep my name off the visitor record."

"Let's hope it sticks," Wyoming said. He had his doubts whether ordinary men would keep secrets about meeting Nina in person.

"Tell me everything," Nina said. "This is the most bogus, trumped up conspiracy in the entire history of the United States. I know exactly what you were thinking. It's perfect for my show."

Over the next twenty minutes, Wyoming summarized the events leading up to his own arrest, leaving nothing out. He had confided a few details about March22's aims in the past, whenever they crossed paths. Nina had a brilliant mind, and he knew he could trust her completely. He told her about the stealing of the drones, the Battle of San Francisco Airport, the kidnapping of Amanda Jeffers, and about March22 discovering that the dirty nukes were being transported through the city of San Francisco and across the Golden Gate Bridge. He told her about Dark Fiber kidnapping Matt Carney.

"How did we steal the drones?" Nina asked when he was finished. He loved it that she said *we*, as if it were the most natural thing in the world. "How do we keep them undetectable?"

"We have technology superiority." He purposely left Luke's name out of it. Some things were sacred. Luke barely existed on government databases and he worked hard to keep it that way. Most people wouldn't finger a wheelchair-bound nineteen-year-old sufferer of Lou Gehrig's disease as a likely candidate for the country's preeminent hacker, anyway.

Nina nodded, satisfied. "What's going to happen with those nukes?"

Some things Wyoming wasn't able to answer, because there was no answer. "They're safe where they are now. We're certainly never going to use one. The question is, what was the administration planning to do with them?"

She smiled. "Got to go. This is going to be fantastic. You do watch my show, don't you, Wyoming?"

"Now that you're one of us, I'd never miss it."

CHAPTER 33

NEAR RENO, NEVADA
DECEMBER 5, 2021—8 AM

BENJY ROBSON STOOD in the underground room and stared at a computer screen over the shoulder of one of the men. The image in shades of gray showed buildings outlined from far above, a grid of city streets, cars and trucks moving in straight lines or rounding corners in an orderly fashion. The digital numbers blinking in all four corners of the screen meant nothing to him. This was the view from a high altitude drone.

"Meet the team," John said, moving slowly over taped cables, extending his hand to take in the entire room.

"These people control the drones?" Benjy asked. Around the long table in the middle of the room sat ten men and women, staring at their screens and talking into headsets. They swiped their fingers on pads on the table in front of the screen, talking in hushed voices.

"So many?" Raine asked.

John nodded, then motioned them through a doorway into another room with a small conference table. He beckoned them to sit down.

"This was our backup command and control center until Homeland Security took out the one in Palo Alto."

"Now there's no backup?" Benjy asked.

His stepfather smiled. "Oh no, we would never let that happen. I probably shouldn't reveal where the new backup facility is located. We don't have all the drones based in one place, either."

"I'm guessing the other drone base is near the East Coast somewhere," Benjy said.

"How do they know how to do it?" Raine asked.

"Most are former military," John said. "They earned their stripes. Once discharged, they have a very specialized skill and nowhere to put it to use except computer games."

"Don't you worry about..." Benjy didn't know how to phrase the rest, but his stepfather immediately understood. One thing about John, he was really smart.

"We pay triple what they earned in the military," John said. "And we put them through a long and rigorous training regimen to see if we can convince them that March22 has only the best intentions for this country. Those folks are believers. You're right if you're thinking that's a much stronger motivation than money, Benjy, even triple pay. The ones who don't pass the test never come anywhere near this facility."

"Are there any situations going on right now, like back in San Francisco?" Benjy asked. He remembered vividly the scene at San Francisco Airport, taking off in Wyoming Ryder's second jet as missiles rained down from March22 drones, taking out the tanks at the north end of the field.

John Carney checked his Jetlink. "Right now there are ten drones in the air, over different parts of the country. No situations. We're just watching over things, and keeping skills sharp."

"Who decides when to shoot the missiles?" Raine asked. Benjy had wanted to ask the same thing, but wouldn't have dared.

"That's the job of March22's leaders," John said. A grim look came over his face. "None of us would ever take that responsibility lightly."

"Do you control them?" Benjy asked.

"I'm not authorized," John said. "We have strict command protocols. The actual command has to come from one person. All those controllers are in direct contact with Luke."

"Luke?" Benjy was shocked. Luke was a genius, sure, but he was nineteen.

John shrugged. "There is a logic to it, I can assure you. Besides, Luke built the whole system on which this is based. I'm strong in certain areas, but overall I'd be lost. Technically speaking, Luke is the right person."

"Can you follow Matt?" Raine went on. "Can you help protect him?"

The wrinkles deepened in John's brow. "It's unclear where he is. Whether he's still in Ann Arbor or not. We're keeping a bird over that part of Michigan, just in case he needs us. We'd like to support him, but without knowing where he is, it's difficult, even with this technology."

"Have we heard anything from Dark Fiber?" When John shook his head, Benjy went on. "What are they holding him for, all this time?"

"The last time I heard from him was yesterday," Raine said. "Then he was still in Ann Arbor."

His stepfather looked at Raine sharply, saying nothing.

"What possible benefit do they get from kidnapping Matt Carney?" Benjy persisted.

"The administration decided to put planes in the air again, starting December tenth," John said. "This means less reliance on big rigs for shipping goods. It puts pressure on the militias. Now, we think the militias were responsible for the shoulder-fired missile attacks of 2019, specifically Dark Fiber. If they have the feeling their business is threatened, they may try to use Matt as a bargaining chip with the administration, to keep their business afloat. We know Homeland Security is looking for a silver bullet to get at the heart of March22."

"That's sick," Raine said. "You mean they would turn him in to Homeland Security?"

"Apparently that's what they told Matt when they kidnapped him," John said. He looked directly at Raine. "When do you think you'll speak with him again?"

"I never know when he's going to call. I don't like to call him, because I never know if he's in the middle of saving someone's life or something."

John smiled. "Well, when you do, just tell him hello from me."

It was a nice sentiment, Benjy thought. He hadn't seen that side of John in a long time.

CHAPTER 34

WASHINGTON, DC
FACE THE POPULATION TALK SHOW
DECEMBER 5, 2021—9 AM

THE PANEL OF three representatives and two senators represented five of the nine parties. It must have made sense to someone, Dan Donovan thought, as the young man worked on his makeup. He looked in the mirror. His white waves spray-frozen in place befitted a member of the House of Representatives. The paunch bespoke too little time on the cross-trainer and too much time hunched over a desk with a burrito beside his tablet.

A few minutes later, the panel members took their seats on a stage. Ohio Rep. Randy Kelleher of Anonymous—or March22—sat to Donovan's right, while California Senator Oswald Tormichael of UMC took the chair on his left. Georgia Rep. Jamaica Warner of the Bible Party was here, as was New York Senator Kenneth Uhland of the Corporates.

To Donovan, it would've made more sense to have two or, at most, three parties represented. This had the potential for a free-for-all, especially with Jamaica Warner's famous rapid-fire tongue. All five of them were good for a speech or two. Each knew their party's talking points cold, but Jamaica Warner was a cut above the rest. She mesmerized people. When Jamaica Warner got going, you almost felt the oxygen being sucked out of the air.

Moderator Chauncey London took his seat as the producer cued thirty seconds to live broadcast.

"Welcome, esteemed senators and representatives. I'm going to make sure everyone gets their two cents in. Nobody talks more than ninety seconds. You'll see Marcia there—" London pointed toward a blond producer, who looked like a homegrown version of Lady Diana. Marcia used her arm to make an exaggerated hatchet motion—"if Marcia makes that signal, your time is up. If you keep going, I'll break in. Deal?"

"Ten seconds," Marcia said.

Chauncey licked his lips, practice-smiled, then raised his face to the drone-mounted camera nearest him.

"Good morning, citizens. Welcome to *Face the Population*." As Chauncey introduced the guests, Donovan had another chance to study Jamaica Warner's face. Her milk chocolate skin had a slightly reddish tint that he found attractive, along with her prominent nose and full lips.

An ordained minister and mother of four, Warner had honed her rhetorical skills in an Atlanta mega-church. From there to the House of Representatives was a logical jump and the woman had the world in her hands. She was at least ten years younger than he. The Bible Party was on a roll, unlike the UN Party, which had lost its own visionaries on November 15, when President David Burns and Vice President McKinley had been assassinated, along with four others. How quickly fortunes could turn. It remained to be seen how the UN Party would recover from the blow. Some party stalwarts were actually hoping for war to break out in Russia, or some other international calamity, just to raise the profile of the UN party once again.

"Representative Keller, in ninety seconds," Chauncey was saying, "can you state the objectives of the momentous changes we heard about last night?"

"Glad to, Chauncey. Anonymous doesn't really exist anymore in its original form, because we're always evolving. We caucused with constituents and thinkers, including March22, and discovered that we have much in common. March22 is the future, Anonymous is the past. Both parties stand for and are committed to fighting for the restoration of those basic rights that have been degraded for all Americans in recent years and the maintenance of other basic rights, which seem more endangered every day. For example, the first article of the Bill of Rights lays the basis for a clear separation of church and state. Yet one of our most powerful parties today is the Bible Party, whose members openly base their votes on interpretations of the Bible. This is a clear contravention of the law of the land and the will of the founding fathers."

"I beg to differ, if you are suggesting that Bible Party's elected representatives to Congress aren't capable of making rational votes in the best interests of this country while keeping God's word in mind," retorted Jamaica Warner. "You're out of touch. There's a reason why we've gained more seats in the House in each of the last four elections, Congressman Kelleher. We listen to the people of this country and we truly represent them. For you, true representation is only a pipe bomb — excuse me, I meant a pipe dream, of course. The founding fathers envisioned a government of the people, for the people, by the people, and no party fulfills this vision better than the Bible Party today."

The woman had a Machiavellian streak, Donovan thought. He saw others grinning at Jamaica Warner's blatant insult.

"The founding fathers and the early settlers of this country ran for their lives from religious persecution in the old world," Kelleher rebutted. "Their houses were burned. They were beaten and driven from their homes, all because of the way they chose to worship. They knew firsthand the dangers of the church residing in the seat of lawmaking, which is why they insisted on keeping a strict separation. As the power of the Bible Party grows, we will see all the new laws passing through a religious filter. We already have schools in districts where the teaching of evolution is illegal. Teachers instructing their pupils not to *believe* in evolution, as if it were a choice anyone could make. That's like asking us to believe or not believe in gravity, my friend. I don't see anyone walking over the edge of the Grand Canyon because they don't *believe* in gravity. The more we become a Christian Evangelical government, with laws that meet the Christian Evangelical moral standard, the more the laws will discriminate against Jews, Catholics, Muslims, Hindus, nonbelievers, homosexuals, and last but not least, thinking people."

In the second half of his speech, Kelleher had to shout, because both Jamaica Warner and Oswald Tormichael of UMC were talking over him. Marcia repeatedly gestured, but was ignored until Chauncey interrupted.

"Senator Tormichael of UMC," said Chauncey, "your party recently entered into a coalition agreement with the Bible Party. The political benefits for both are obvious, but what about the separation of church and state?"

"UMC embraced the Bible Party precisely because it's not just Christian Evangelical, it's a big umbrella encompassing many churches and many ways of interpreting God's word. Anyone who thinks we're using the Bible to create laws is crazy. We're trying to straighten out the serious problems this country has gotten into through the leadership mistakes of the past. The rise of March22 and the fact that Anonymous is admitting its true identity worries me. March22 is a known terrorist organization responsible for bombings, killings, and many other crimes. The leader or leaders are a shadowy group whose identities are mostly unknown. I worry a lot more about ordinary people feeling tempted to throw their support behind a group that's committed to violence."

"March22 has never been linked to violence—" Kelleher shouted, but he was immediately drowned out by the four other participants. Now everyone was shouting. Donovan heard himself shouting along with the rest, and when Chauncey pointed at him, he started over.

"March22 has a long, stained record of suspected violence and heinous crimes," Donovan said. "Most recently, the Golden Gate Bridge, the theft of over a thousand armed drones, and the baseball bombings. How can you sit there and say they've never been linked to violence?"

"You're forgetting the militias, which are controlled mainly by UMC," Kelleher shouted over him. "How many of those—?"

"That's a cowardly lie!" Oswald Tormichael shouted.

"March22 is committed to wiping out the militias in order to help get the country back on its feet," Kelleher shouted. "The militias control the food supply. The militias blow up bridges and get into shootouts at their shadowmarkets. Our lives are controlled by militias!"

"Why don't the leaders of March22 come out of hiding and defend themselves?" Tormichael continued. "If they're so squeaky clean, what are they afraid of? Instead they're all on the FBI's most wanted list."

"We're here to represent March22," Kelleher retorted. "Talk to me or any of our other elected representatives."

"Armed violence is not the solution," Jamaica Warner said. "March22 is committed to fighting is what you said. What ever happened to debate and discussion, followed by a roll call vote? I second Senator Tormichael's suggestion. If the March22 leaders have nothing on their conscience, why do they have to hide behind you? Why can't we hear from them directly?"

"Anonymous changed its name to March22 precisely to give March22 the opportunity to participate in government processes in the time-honored way," Kelleher said. "Your problem lies with the militias, not March22."

"What ever happened to driving down the highway without having to cross through an armed checkpoint every fifty miles?" said Kenneth Uhland, the Corporate Party senator from New York, getting the floor for the first time. "For four years in a row, our economy has contracted. Goods can't be shipped from one place to another because of hijackings and bridges blown up." He pointed at Donovan. "It was your party that let this situation fester while you wasted time and resources trying to fix all the other problems around the world. The president has just announced that he's going to get commercial aviation up and running again on December tenth. We support his efforts wholeheartedly."

"I just told you we stand for wiping out the militias," Kelleher said. "It's obvious that they're responsible for the heinous acts you were talking about. Why is the administration focused on March22 when the militias are the real scourge causing the biggest problems? You want to know why? I'll tell you why. The militias have the UMC, Corporate, and UN parties in their pockets throughout the country, that's why."

Tormichael started, "I don't know where you get your information—"

Suddenly Jamaica Warner screamed, not talking over the others, but really screaming.

Then Donovan saw, in the darkness beyond the glare of the lights at back of the studio, the bursting flame of rapid-fire shots. As the barrel of the weapon rolled sideways, Donovan threw himself on the floor. His cheek banged the wooden parquet, and the wires and cables crisscrossing it dug into his ribs. Dust rose into the studio lights as screams filled the air all around him.

Donovan remained motionless and flat on the floor, unscathed, wondering if the shooter would assume he was dead. Everyone knew it was dangerous going on talk shows these days. The Secret Service couldn't be everywhere. The assassins were clever and persistent. Now other people were shooting from the stage. Single shots, and automatic fire as the Secret Service aimed at targets somewhere in the back. The initial barrage would have been carried on live TV. Donovan kept his eyes closed, and prayed. *Dear God, let it pass over me. Let it pass over... .*

CHAPTER 35

AFTER HIS NIGHT of paradise, this had been one of the lousiest days Ike could ever remember. At dinner in the big tent, Nasreen had completely ignored him. She always sat with Pastor Peaches at the far table, but he had managed to get in behind her in the cafeteria line. She'd kept her back turned as if he didn't exist.

Much as he hated to admit it, Tranny's theories were beginning to make more sense. It didn't help that Tranny stared the whole time while Ike followed Nasreen through the line like a lovesick puppy.

"She don't look like she got the hots for you," Tranny observed when Ike came back with his tray. He'd lost his appetite. His stomach felt like it was tied up in giant knots.

"Would you shut up? I don't want the whole world knowin'." Luckily, they were a few feet away from the next group of people.

"She didn't even look at you, man," Tranny said. "Not givin' you the time of day, I'd say."

"If you don't want this coffee down your front, just shut your trap," Ike said. He knew his anger should be directed at Nasreen, not Tranny. How could a woman be so tender and kind one day, and so cold and distant the next?

The thought jogged an ancient memory of his ex-wife, Tula. Her parents had named her Tulip, but everyone called her Tula. Now that he thought about it, Tula had sometimes done the Jekyll-and-Hyde act, too. He remembered one time, probably their anniversary, he'd brought home a bouquet of flowers and she'd prepared a nice dinner. That night they'd had sex on the living room couch in in front of the TV, then later in bed.

The next day, Tula had turned away when he started pawing her in the morning. She'd woken up bitchy. They were young then, in their twenties. In those days, he'd wanted sex all the time. She'd left the bed, and he'd given up. Later they were having breakfast in silence. When he'd complained about his eggs being too runny, without saying a word she had snatched his plate and hurled it across the kitchen. The plate ended up in twenty pieces, egg coating the walls.

You never could tell what made a woman tick.

After dinner was quiet time, and Ike's next shift wasn't until six a.m. He wondered how he was going to sleep tonight, fretting about Nasreen's personality change. He couldn't stand Tranny's needling. He was one step away from volunteering as Tranny's private punching bag. Breathing in the cool evening air, Ike strolled along the wooden traffic barriers he and Tranny had set up when they arrived in Denver two weeks ago. All the pink and green cars were parked inside the barriers, with the big tent in the middle. The three big buses and a couple of trucks were parked on the other side. Nasreen would've gone back to her bus after dinner, unless she had business to take care of.

He gazed at the stars, so many of them tonight, some fainter, some brighter. Seeing the stars was a luxury they'd had to do without most of the time in prison. The night sky always seemed like such a beautiful thing. Never again would he take the stars for granted.

"Hi, Ike," a voice said. "Over here."

He was standing by one of the big trucks. Nasreen's voice seemed to come from behind it. He found her in the narrow space between two trucks.

"You kinda startled me," he said.

"I saw you looking at the sky. Do you like the stars?"

"Yeah, I really do. What about you?"

"I could watch them all night long."

"Me too."

"Ike, have you got plans for the night?"

"Me? Hell no. Tranny's watchin' something on TV. I didn't feel like watchin' no police drama tonight."

"What about... well, last night was really sweet, Ike. Do you want to spend the night with me again?"

They were standing face-to-face, three feet apart. She made no move to come closer. He saw the sweetness of last night in her eyes again. He felt torn in two with this sudden reversal in her mood.

"Yeah, I'd really like that a lot, Nasreen. I mean, are you sure?"

"Why wouldn't I be sure? I told you I had my eye on you."

"Yeah, but today..." He didn't know what to say exactly. He didn't want to be like the old Ike with Tula, chasing her around, pawing and begging for sex.

"Why didn't I hold hands with you? Why didn't I kiss you in front of all the guys?"

"Well, no, not that," he replied.

"Ike, you've got to understand. This is a professional organization with important work to do. I can't let my private life interfere with my work. We've got to be discreet, at least for a while. Can we have an understanding?"

"What kind of understanding?"

"During the day you're nothing special. I ignore you, I even call you out if you step out of line, like this morning. I need you to do your job well. You're not going to get any special commendations, either. And during the night, I'm your woman. You're my man."

"Really?"

"I mean it. Really."

"You're my woman?"

"I want to be your woman. I want you to be my man. As long as we can be discreet."

When he reached out his hand to shake, Nasreen didn't take it. Even though they were hidden between these trucks, he realized she was afraid someone would see. He smiled.

"You got yourself a deal, woman."

"Come back to the bus at ten."

Ike strolled back to the camper with a cushion of air under his feet.

CHAPTER 36

NEAR ANN ARBOR, MICHIGAN
DECEMBER 5, 2021—4 PM

AS CLAIRE MAXIMIZED one screen after another, trying to choose a program while avoiding Nina Nardelli, Matt proudly recalled something he'd seen on the news. Anonymous had changed its name to March22. The bluebird drones he'd proposed to Sander had actually been used in the House of Representatives to announce the change.

Claire left *Face the Population* maximized on the screen, one of those boring talk shows with panels of people yelling at each other. Better than *Faking It with the Nardelli's*, at least. A bunch of senators and representatives were ganging up on Kelleher, the March22 representative, who had one of the bluebird drones in his hand.

More than ever now, Matt wished he were digesting this news with other March22 people, instead of here in some forgotten Dark Fiber safe house. As the politicians shouted back and forth, he thought he would give anything to be together with Raine tonight, instead of this tomboy Dark Fiber leader.

Just then, Kelleher held up the bluebird drone while making a point.

"See that," Matt said.

"What?"

"That drone he's got. It was..." he stopped short, not knowing whether he should confide that it had been his idea. Claire might get the impression he was an important figure in March22 after all. "I suggested that design. You know, the bluebird."

"What a cool idea to make a drone that looks like a bird."

The people on TV were all shouting at the same time again.

"How can you watch this garbage?" Matt asked. "When they talk over each other, you can't even follow what they're saying."

"You like things nice and orderly in your world, don't you?" Claire assessed him with her intense brown eyes. He looked at the screen again, bothered. Who didn't like things orderly? Who liked chaos, and people all talking at the same time?

Suddenly a familiar sound met his ears—the sound of assault rifle fire—and, one after another, the politicians jerked in their chairs as angry red splattering wounds appeared on their clothes. The African-American woman pitched forward and hit the floor, blood pouring from her mouth, her eyes wide. Two others were thrown backward. The moderator actually stood up before collapsing, his torso riddled with spurting wounds. It all happened in just a few seconds.

"Oh my God!" Matt yelled.

"This is terrible," Claire said, her eyes glued to the screen.

Abruptly, the image changed to the logo of *Face the Population*. Then a commercial for gasoline came on.

"What just happened?" Matt cried. "Who was that?"

"No idea. They didn't turn the cameras around. I've always wondered how assassins can even get into TV studios like that. Especially with all those political big shots. Don't they have special security?"

"I thought so."

"Maybe someone paid off the security," Claire said.

"But why? Why does anyone want to mow down a bunch of politicians?"

"Five different parties," Claire mused. "UMC, March22, Corporate, UN, and Bible. Pretty broad spectrum, but not all the parties. Maybe it was one of the other parties, like the Occupy Party."

"But it doesn't make sense. You can't just shoot people because they represent a certain party. I bet it was your people, Dark Fiber."

"Why would we do a thing like that?" Claire's face turned bright red.

"I don't know. Why would you?"

"We wouldn't, that's what I'm saying. Stuff like that is senseless. It could've been some crazy person, unaffiliated with any group. An anarchist. Or some mentally unstable person."

Matt shook his head. "Someone who's mentally unstable does that in their workplace or school, and most of the victims are random. This was someone with an objective. We just don't know what it was. What the hell can you accomplish by murdering five senators and representatives from different parties?"

"Create fear," Claire said. "You can make people frightened and panicky, so they want more control, more security, more surveillance."

"I don't know," Matt said. He felt shaken up inside, even a little queasy. It was a reminder of all the horrifying events he had been a part of so recently.

"IT'S BORING JUST sitting around in this house," Matt said that evening. They'd done another round of shooting, this time throwing pennies up in the air for each other, and shooting them out of the sky, but it wasn't enough to keep him happy. "I can't stand wasting all this time."

"Half of life is spent waiting for something," Claire said. "The other half is spent cleaning up messes."

"You guys made a real mess kidnapping me."

"We lost some good men in that firefight five days ago," she said. Sadness was written her face, and she sighed. "I should be rebuilding my organization. I should be training new leaders."

"Why aren't you?"

She fingered her coffee mug on the table. "Sometimes you know you have to do something, but you just don't feel like it."

"That's how it always was for me with my homework."

"You compare this to homework?"

He realized she was suffering. Maybe she was as depressed as he was, only for different reasons. "Look, I'm sorry you lost people you cared about."

"It's part of the job. You know that when you wake up each day, but still I have trouble with it."

"Anyone you're especially going to miss?"

She looked at him. "Nothing like that. I don't do the boyfriend thing. But, you know, I worked with those guys. We planned operations. We trusted each other."

Matt had killed people on his way out to California, and he'd seen many more die in explosions. They hadn't been people close to him. They'd all been his enemies, most of them trying to kill him. Still, he felt rotten whenever he thought about it.

"We need to make it so the world isn't so dangerous. Just going outside, just driving down the road, you're risking your life nowadays."

"I guess you're not talking about car crashes," Claire said.

"People shooting each other."

She nodded. "Why did you hate school so much?"

"I just never got motivated. Besides, I was in charge of food for the family. My dad put me in charge of the ration coupons so my stepmom wouldn't drink so much. And I hunted."

"What, like deer?"

"Exactly. Lots of deer around Chicago still. Less than there used to be, but plenty for our family. I avoided shadowmarkets as much as possible, but my stepmother's a regular at those alcohol markets."

"Probably Dark Fiber Chicago," Claire said.

"If you say so."

"Then your dad recruited you."

"What do you know about my dad?"

"He was one of the founders of March22, right?" When Matt didn't answer, she went on, "When all those bombings started happening one after another, the baseball bombings—"

"My father had nothing to do with that."

"Well, it certainly wasn't Dark Fiber. Who else could've done it?"

He wasn't prepared to tell her it had been a faction of March22, the original Anonymous members. He wasn't going to tell her the leaders of March22, including his father, had made the agonizing decision to make them pay with their lives for violating orders not to commit pointless acts of mass murder.

"All I can tell you is my father had nothing to do with the baseball bombings in 2019."

"Now March22 is a proper political party," Claire said. "Maybe your dad should run for office."

Matt had to smile. "I don't think that's his kind of thing."

"He's more of a fighter, like you and me." When Matt said nothing, Claire stood up. "He's obviously grooming you to be a leader in the future. That's probably why Dark Fiber decided to grab you."

"They should've done their homework a little better. I'll never be a leader."

"What makes you so sure? I think you'd make a good leader. I never planned to be a leader, yet here I am. We had a good thing going in Ann Arbor, till now."

"Your alcohol shadowmarkets?"

"Absolutely. There's a ton of money in it. The way we do it, it's almost pure profit."

"You hijack the trucks, steal the bottles, and then resell them. Is everyone a volunteer or do you pay yourselves something?"

"We get our expenses reimbursed, but we also have other costs," Claire said. "We buy our protection."

"Oh. You mean like the police?"

Claire was hunting in the fridge again. "The police, the mayor, the aldermen—basically everyone has his hand out. I have people who do nothing but go around handing out cash."

"Is that how it works?" Matt was surprised, but then it was logical. The police didn't often raid shadowmarkets. Now he knew the reason why.

"It can't last forever," Claire said, returning to the table with a bowl of potato salad. "Could you maybe get us a couple of plates and glasses? I don't know about you, but I'm hungry."

While they were eating, Matt asked, "Why did you say it can't last?"

"For one thing, there are plenty of honest cops," Claire said. "There are constant internal battles among the authorities. Whenever an internal investigation gets rolling, our shadowmarkets have to lay low. It's happened more frequently in the last six months. We have to stay underground for two or three weeks at a time, sitting on inventory. All that time, we're at risk of attack or police raids."

"And no money coming in, so less money to pay for protection."

She nodded. "Vicious circle. And, the word is, people are getting tired of all the disruption in the grocery business. Don't forget it's not just Dark Fiber. We may be the biggest, but there are thirty or forty other big militias doing the same thing in different parts of the country."

"Are all your members trained in shooting, like you?"

She grinned. "All of them are trained. They don't all shoot like yours truly."

"You have a high opinion of yourself."

"No I don't. I'm a good shot, that's just a fact. If I were good at painting pictures, you'd see it in the paintings. I happen to be a good marksman."

"We probably do a lot of the same kind of training as you."

At that moment, a loud knock came on the door. Three knocks and a few shuffled steps, as if someone were moving into position. Claire put her fork down and sat straight in her chair. "That's weird. Gram doesn't get packages delivered here."

"Don't you have a drone out there?"

Claire was already checking her Jetlink and keying in commands. From a distance, Matt saw an image resolve on her screen. Her face went pale.

"Six dudes from Black Widow," she said. "I can't believe they found us here."

"Okay, how do you want to play it?" Matt said.

"Three are staying there, three are going around the back. Can you take the ones in the back?"

"How serious is this?"

Claire was already headed for the front door, but she turned to fix him with her eyes. "I figure we have about fifteen seconds before they start setting timers on firebombs. Take them out before they blow up Gram's house."

He opened the back door in time to see three men rounding the corner from his right. An image of the cabin blowing up five days ago came to his mind. Maybe these were some of the same men. He had the Beretta up before the men could draw. They didn't have a good angle, even as they ran and spread out, ignoring their lack of cover. As bullets from the first man thwacked into the wood of the kitchen door, Matt buried three rounds in his chest. The other two men sprinted across the back yard forty feet away, heading for the cover of a woodpile.

He hit the lead man in the thigh, bringing him down. The second man kept running, so Matt put a bullet in his leg as well. The second man, wearing a dark blue down vest, lay on the grass panting and moaning.

They couldn't have known what a good shot he was, but still. The stupidity of it all threatened to overwhelm him for a moment. He forced himself to focus. The first man was sitting up, facing him. Matt kept his gun trained, letting the doorframe shield most of his body.

"Throw your weapons toward me," Matt said. "I'm gonna count to three and then I'll start shooting."

"Don't shoot!" the dude said in a high voice. "I'm already hit. Here! Here's my gun!"

The device in the Black Widow man's hand was not a gun, not even close. From this distance, Matt couldn't tell exactly what it was, but it looked like a small rectangular box made of black metal or plastic. He shot the object out of the air the moment it left the man's hand.

A twenty-foot fireball erupted in the yard, well away from the house. Over the roar of the superheated air, Matt heard the screams of both men as they were engulfed in flames.

"Idiots!"

What a disaster. So much for making an effort to spare their lives. He slammed the kitchen door and ran through the house to check on Claire.

Claire had hit two men. Maybe she'd shot them through the mail slot. The front door stood ajar and the dead men, eyes wide and staring like deer you'd find in a ditch, lay on top of each other.

Matt peeked around the door, looking for Claire. Maybe the other dude had run into the trees around the driveway and she'd chased him. He wondered if she would do something that dangerous. The two Black Widow pickup trucks stood empty in the driveway.

Off to the left stood the big red barn. They could be in or behind the barn somewhere. Beyond the barn, three other outbuildings occupied a patch about three hundred feet back.

He had no cover between the main house and the barn, except for the Black Widow trucks. He didn't like the idea of being picked off while running across the wide front yard. An idea formed in his head, and Matt returned through the house to the kitchen door. The fire was still burning in the back yard. The revolting smell nearly knocked him over. The first man he'd shot lay in the yard five feet away, still not moving. Three men dead in the back, two in the front, and one missing, along with Claire. He didn't like it.

After removing the pistol from the dead man's hand, and getting no response, he stuck his fingers in the man's right front jeans pocket. His lucky day—a set of truck keys.

Returning through the house to the front door, Matt scanned the perimeter once more. Still no sign of Claire. He kept thinking he would see her round the corner of the barn any moment now, marching back across the yard with gun in hand. No sound reached his ears, except for birdsong from the distant trees. On the count of three, he sprinted down the steps and ten paces to the cover of the two trucks, keeping them between him and the barn.

The keys didn't fit in the first truck, a big Ford. He crept around and fitted a key into the other pickup, also a Ford, but an older model. The rumble of the engine as he pressed on the gas pedal made a couple of crows take off from an elm tree by the driveway. The truck would give him cover as he hunted for Claire. He drove slowly toward the barn, scanning for movement, any sign at all of either Claire or the sixth Black Widow dude.

On the far side the barn, the doors stood wide open. He drove up to the opening and flicked the high beam on, lighting up the dark interior. Fifty feet away, near the far wall, his eyes fell on the sight of a man with his jeans down around his boots and a half-naked Claire Tenneman on the dirt beneath him.

Matt leapt from the cab as the man straightened up. He saw the gun coming up in the man's hand, but he was quicker, filling the man's belly with five rounds. The man fell back in the dirt as Matt ran closer, then lay without moving, his pecker limp and the soles of his boots neatly lined up with Claire's feet.

Claire lay on the dirt floor without moving, naked below the waist. The sight of her bleeding private parts brought tears to his eyes. At first, Matt thought she might be dead, but Claire's left arm slowly rose from the dirt and curled around to cover her eyes. Then she started shaking. He realized she was sobbing.

He crouched down beside her and laid his heavy army jacket over the lower half of her body. He touched her shoulder with his left hand.

"It's over, Claire. He's dead. I'm sorry I took so damned long to find you. God, what a dirty son of a bitch."

She didn't say a word. She lay with her arm over her eyes. He saw her body quaking, but she made no sound. He crouched beside her for at least five minutes, wondering what to do. With six dead bodies, this farmhouse wasn't going to be safe much longer. There were no neighbors nearby, but that fireball might've been seen from the road.

Hearing a movement behind him, Matt spun in his crouch, raising the gun. He still had four rounds, and he had two extra clips in his pocket. But the figure in the barn doorway was Gram.

"What happened?" she said, not coming closer.

Matt stood. "Claire is here. One of the men raped her before I could find them. Can you help?"

Gram hurried over. The woman looked older than she probably was. She knelt down, stroked Claire's hair, and took her hand. She spoke soothing words, but Claire didn't remove her arm from her eyes and didn't speak. Matt stood back twenty feet and watched, turning often to check the barn doorway.

Why did that Black Widow asshole have to do it? What kind of sick bastard took a girl out to a barn and raped her?

"Claire, I'm going to have Matt carry you inside," Gram said. Claire gave no answer. "We'll get you fixed up, okay?"

Gram stepped back to give him space. Keeping the coat in place over Claire's belly and legs, he worked his right arm under her thighs and his left under her back, with her head resting on the crook of his elbow. Claire still kept one arm over her face. It would've been easier in a fireman's carry, but Claire was so light it didn't strain him.

Gram hurried ahead, stepping over the bodies on the porch. By the time Matt reached the living room, she had towels covering the couch.

"Lay her down here and leave the rest to me. Close the door on your way out. Maybe you could start doing something about those bodies."

Matt went out without a word, hoping Claire would be all right. It was shocking enough what had happened, but her muteness disturbed him. She was ordinarily so talkative. *I don't do boyfriends,* she'd said. Maybe she had never had sex in her life. Now this.

He dragged the two men from the porch across the front yard and into the barn, where the other man lay. They were a lot heavier than Claire, and he couldn't easily lift them, so he dragged them in the dirt, one after the other. Their heads bumped along on every uneven clod of earth.

When he was finished, he went around to the back porch. Gram didn't even know about this body. He dragged the dead man around the house and laid him out in the barn beside the others.

Finally, he went behind the house and steeled himself for a look at the two burn victims. Their clothes and shoes were all burned off and their bodies a mess of sticky reddish, blackish charred skin and flesh. The smell assaulted him from thirty feet away. He'd hoped there would be less remaining of the two men, after that fireball, but the flames had died down too quickly to consume them entirely.

He left them there, deciding the only thing he could do was to tell Gram and let her figure out what to do.

CHAPTER 37

NEAR ANN ARBOR, MICHIGAN
DECEMBER 6, 2021—3 AM

MATT HUNKERED AT the kitchen table for hours, sipping green tea and waiting for the living room door to open. He wasn't much of a praying man, but that short week with the Bible Party must have left an impression. *Please God, let Claire be okay.*

Visions of what that Black Widow bastard might have done to Claire, in addition to raping her, kept running through his mind. Claire was so feisty, the man must have clobbered her, at the least, to get her pants off. But rape, for a woman, must be the worst nightmare of all. Worse than dying, worse than torture. He couldn't imagine how awful it must feel to have a man force himself on her, force himself *into* her, hitting her again and again if she struggled. That was the battle Claire must've fought, and lost.

With that fireball and all these bodies, the place would be crawling with police by morning. Who would they find? One of Homeland Security's most wanted, Matt Carney. He itched to leave *now,* but first he had to know if Claire was okay.

What was she going to do? Her safe house wasn't safe. Those dudes had come here to kill her. They hadn't cared who else got killed along with her. Dark Fiber was powerless to protect her. Her apartment building had been torched. Maybe all the Dark Fiber members in Ann Arbor were going through the same soul-searching process as Claire. Dark Fiber was in pieces in Ann Arbor. Black Widow was taking over the town, it seemed.

At that instant, he realized he would be leaving with Claire.

Six men had come to murder her, and none had come back. The other Black Widow members must know by now that something had gone wrong. They might show up before morning. They might be outside right now, looking in the windows, setting timers on firebombs.

Suddenly, the living room door opened. Claire led the way, with Gram hovering close behind. Claire sat at the table, not meeting his eyes. She picked up his mug and drank from his tea. She drank half of it.

"Thank you, Matt." Her voice was soft, a breathy voice he'd never heard from Claire.

"You're taking my car," Gram said. She handed Matt the keys. "Leave the rest to me. Let me just pack you a bag of food. I want you out of here in two minutes."

"Gram, there's something I've got to tell you." Matt joined her at the fridge. "Out back there are two more men. Two bodies. Burned. They tried to firebomb the house."

"And the rest?"

"Four more in the barn. It's not a pretty sight."

"All right. We've had situations before. The important thing is you two get out of here before the police show up."

"Listen, I've got a confession to make," Matt said. Gram cut him off.

"Keep the money. You're going to need it, and the ration coupons, too. I've got plenty."

"You're not safe here," Claire said in that soft voice.

"I've got my shotgun," Gram said, putting food into a bag. She obviously knew the police were not the only threat. "I've got a drone out on the driveway. I'll give you an hour's head start, then call the police. Get up, Claire. Matt will take you someplace far enough that you can get some rest and heal your body. Those cuts are superficial, but you need to take it easy for a day or two. Remember to use the cream against infection."

"Are you okay?" Matt asked.

"I'll make it." Claire slowly rose to her feet.

"I got extra clips for our guns," Matt said.

Out of instinct, he kept the lights off as they rolled down the driveway in Gram's white Impala. Matt's eyes had adjusted and the stars were out. It was just after three in the morning. On the main road, no cars were coming from either direction, but a hundred yards to the south he saw a car parked on the shoulder. It was too far away to tell what make or model.

He left the lights off and turned north, going light on the gas to make as little noise as possible. No point in throwing gravel, with that car parked there. With any luck, the surveillance dude was napping.

"You recognize it?" Matt asked.

"Not really," Claire said. "I'm getting the feeling Black Widow expanded in the last few weeks. I didn't recognize most of those guys last night, either. New members, or else people they brought in from out of town."

"I'm heading out of town. You can think about where you want me to drop you off."

"I know some Dark Fiber people in Chicago, but—"

"We're going to steer clear of Chicago," Matt said. "Big cities, in general. We have to stay on county roads like this."

"Until they lift the checkpoints."

"I doubt they're going to do that anytime soon."

"I saw something on the news. They're starting with commercial flights again on December tenth. They think the drones will provide enough protection for normal planes to fly again."

"What's that got to do with checkpoints?" Matt checked his rearview mirror. Still no one following, and they were entering the long curve directly before entering the city of Ann Arbor. After his escape attempt and returning on the back of Claire's motorcycle twice, he knew this road by heart. He put on the lights.

"If they start up again with commercial flights, a lot of cargo will travel by air, like it used to. The reliance on big rigs hauling valuable goods will decline, and there won't be so many hijackings. They won't need checkpoints anymore," Claire said.

"I sure hope you're right."

"It means they're putting the militias out of business."

"Well, if people can buy food at normal grocery stores again instead of having to risk their lives at shadowmarkets, I'd call that progress."

Claire looked out the window as they rode through the city, past dark storefronts and apartment buildings. No other cars approached. They rolled up to a stop sign, on the other side of which was a marker for Route 12, the western route out of town. The last time he'd covered this stretch with Claire, he'd been forced to ride behind her on her motorcycle, blinded by helpless rage.

"It was Dark Fiber that got those shoulder-fired missiles," Matt said, coming back to one of Luke's objectives. "You must have a huge supply of them still."

"Some of the guys down south were in the military," Claire said. "Apparently it was easy to make a few thousand missiles and launch assemblies disappear. The military only discovered the theft when the weapons were used."

Claire suddenly seemed chatty and willing to reveal information about Dark Fiber. At the moment, talking helped calm his jitters.

"Dark Fiber shot down those planes in 2019?"

"I didn't know about that when I joined, you know."

He looked at her across the dim interior. "That was a horrible thing."

She nodded. "It was."

"With the planes going up again, you think they'll do it again?"

"I hope not. That was one of those events that changed the country forever, it seems like. Even if it helped Dark Fiber get established, it was wrong."

"How does it work in Dark Fiber? Are there just a few who would decide a thing like that, and everyone else has to live with it?"

"Of course. Do you think it's a democracy? It's more like a company," Claire said. "When Wal-Mart decides to close on of its stores somewhere, do you think they take a vote among all the employees?"

"I guess not."

"The managers decide and then they do it, whether the workers like it or not. Since a lot of them lose their jobs, you can be sure they don't like it."

"Do you know those guys?"

"Which guys?"

"The ones with the shoulder-fireds."

"I know two or three. They go around visiting people like me, around the country. Thomas is one of them. They call it support, but they're collecting suitcases full of hundred dollar bills. We've also had some online chats. The more I think about it, those guys are probably planning a new attack right now. That's how stupid they are."

"Why stupid?"

"The new policy is that if there's an attack on a commercial plane, Homeland Security will use drones to take out the attackers. It's supposed to make the attackers think twice. But they won't care. They'll just train some retards to carry out the actual attacks. The leaders wouldn't risk their own lives."

"You sound pretty sure. Like you're sure they'll do it again."

She nodded. "From what I know of them, the more I think about it, the more I think it is a sure thing."

"How do you feel about that?"

Claire made a face. "I didn't sign up for shooting down planes full of innocent people. I only understood it was Dark Fiber maybe six months ago. They don't go broadcasting it. I figured it out from some offhand comments they made. I was totally shocked. It's one thing to have rivalries and fight with other militias to protect your turf. It's another thing altogether to kill innocent people."

Matt's mind was racing. He needed to talk to Luke. Claire was in the right frame of mind to divulge everything she knew about the shoulder-fired missiles, and she was convinced that another attack would follow. March22 would surely do everything in its power to stop that.

Route 12 took them on a slow journey westward as the darkness deepened. Matt wondered if Luke was even awake.

Hey super geek, how're you doing?

Wake me out of a sound sleep, why don't you?

You sleep in that wheelchair?

Don't be an idiot. What's the latest?

Dark Fiber has the shoulder-fireds for sure. Claire told me the Dark Fiber leaders are planning a new attack when they start up with commercial flights again on December tenth.

Holy shit, you might actually be worth the resources we're investing, after all. How sure is this?

Luke sounded wide awake now. *You think I could make something like that up?*

Where are the missiles? Luke asked.

I don't have details like that yet, but I think she knows. We left Ann Arbor.

You and the chick are together?

Long story.

I'm telling Raine.

It's not like that, geek, and you'd better not tell her anything about this.

They tell me she's pretty mopey, with you contacting her so infrequently.

I'll call her later today. How secure is it?

Not secure. Don't say anything that could compromise you. Nothing about the stuff you just told me.

I'm not a total idiot. I need to know what you want us to do.

Where are you now?

Headed west on Route 12 in Michigan, an hour west of Ann Arbor. Headed for Indiana, Illinois, and points west. Staying off the Interstate. Raine's in Nevada, right? She said she and Benjy had to move.

You didn't hear it from me, Luke said.

Why so secret?

The camp in Montana got raided. Everyone got out in time, but the folks at Homeland Security are ramping up the pressure, raiding all sorts of places. We're tightening our security, and we want to keep them out of the rest of Montana.

For obvious reasons, Matt said, thinking of the drones, and also the dirty bombs.

Get off the road before sunrise. Find a motel and pay cash. Let the girl do the talking, you don't show your face. They've got facial recognition everywhere hooked up to Homeland Security. Find the grungiest motel you can, less likely to have working cameras. Are you wearing a cap?

It's not that cold.

To hide your face, dumbass. When you stop for gas, have her buy you a baseball cap and keep your head down. God, this stuff is so basic. It takes a handicapped person to teach it to you. What does that say about you?

Everyone has their own handicaps, I guess. He hadn't intended to wax philosophical. Luke ignored the comment anyway.

Don't give any information to our father, in case he contacts you. I'll get with the other leaders in the morning. You find out where the missiles are stored, buddy.

CHAPTER 38

BOZEMAN, MONTANA
DECEMBER 6, 2021—10 AM

"Jes' THINK, PHIL, we're gonna be on TV." Mel Grady sat with his brother enjoying a breakfast of fried eggs and bacon at Big Sky Base. They'd been living here almost two weeks now. They didn't have to train with the others on account of their advanced age, but just for fun Phil had joined the defensive driving course on his motorcycle. Two days ago, Commander Winter had told them they were going to go on TV to tell the world about the attack on their hog farm.

"Lil' Lena ain't never been on TV before," Phil said before stuffing another two strips of bacon in his mouth.

"That remind me o' somethin'," Mel said, putting his fork down. "We ain't talked about it much since I found out, but seein' as we're gonna be on TV."

"I knows what you're gonna say, and you might as well jes' let it be," Phil said.

"How's that bunny?"

"Doin' jes' fine," Phil said irritably.

It was a thorny topic between them, but one way or the other it had to be settled. Mel didn't know *how* it could be settled, exactly, but he had to try. Back in Denver, on a visit to a pet shop where they'd convinced the owner to go along with their *Prove Your Patriotism — Eat Bacon!* program, Phil had bought a pet rabbit. When Mel remarked how unusual a *brown* rabbit was, Phil had dropped his bombshell. Mel still remembered his brother's exact words:

"Lil' Lena been goin' with a white man all these years, she wanted a brown rabbit."

Mel had been stuck dumb to find out his brother's imaginary woman friend was black. They'd battled it out with their fists in a Dunkin' Donut shop. From that moment on, the topic had been taboo. That had been two weeks ago, but now they were going on TV.

"I jes' wanna say it ain't right you're hooked up with a black woman," Mel said. "There, now you heard it, so deal with it."

"Lil' Lena sez she ain't black, she's *African*-American," Phil said.

"That's jes' another way o' sayin' black, and everyone knows it."

"Well she ain't black, and you're hurtin' her feelings with every damn thing you say."

"How come you got to speak for her the whole time, Phil? Can't she speak for herself?" He figured that was below the belt, but Phil always had an answer anyway.

"She kin speak for herself jes' fine," Phil said. "She sez she don't care to speak with no racist motherfucker like yourself."

"I ain't racist," Mel said. "I'm your brother, man. I want your happiness, and a white man's always happier with a white woman. White men that hook up with a black woman got nothing but problems."

"What the hell you know about them things anyway?" Phil demanded. "You ain't got nobody, and never did have."

He let the hurtful comment from Phil sit for a while, for there were no words to come back with. Their work on the hog farm had always kept them so busy he'd never had much inclination to go into town to one of the bars where women went to get picked up. Once, it was true, he'd had a little fling with one of the Mexican women who worked in the hog houses. Consuela had exercised him good for about two weeks, showing up in his bedroom in the middle of the night. Her breasts had flopped around like melons while she rode him like a bronco. He'd had the time of his life those sweaty summer nights. Phil had never gotten wind of it.

Then one night there'd been a knife fight in the yard, which Mel never did get to the bottom of. Consuela had gotten in the middle, trying to separate the two workers. One of them had stabbed her in the heat of the battle, and that had been the end of Consuela.

After breakfast, Mel and Phil squeezed into the rear seat of a blue Subaru headed for Bozeman, two and a half hours up the road. The driver and his March22 buddy were young muscular types. They carried the guns. Mel and Phil were being treated like some kind of elder statesmen, what with their gray hair and their sensational story. The men in front were responsible for getting them back to Big Sky Base safely. The March22 leaders thought the risk was worth the benefit of publicizing the destruction of their hog farm.

After their tense breakfast, neither was in the mood for talking. Mel had even been tempted to leave Phil behind, but he figured Winter wouldn't like it if he changed the game at the last minute.

"Lil' Lena always wanted to be on TV, right, girl?" Phil said at some point as they neared Bozeman.

"Now you know what they said about not mentionin' your girlfriend on TV." Mel caught the driver rolling his eyes in the rearview mirror. Everyone at Big Sky Base had "met" Lena, but they hadn't lived with the fantasy for all these years the way Mel had.

"It ain't polite not to include her," Phil said.

"All we have to do is tell our lil' story. That's what Winter said."

"An' she was there. She saw the whole thing too," Phil said.

"Listen, bro. Let the TV audience look at her. Jes' don't let her talk. It's bad enough you're hangin' out with a black girl. Don't say what she says all the time. Think you kin do that?"

"She ain't black, I told ya. She's African-American."

"I don't go 'round tellin' everyone I'm *English*-American, do I? Get that through your head, brother."

"You just one jealous old fuck," Phil said.

Mel didn't feel calm when they arrived at 9:30, even with his tummy full of coffee he'd drunk from a thermos. He wished to hell Consuela hadn't died that night. Maybe he would've ended up with a Mexican bride and a bunch of cute brats instead of an ornery loony bin brother.

"Ever worn makeup before?" the attractive stylist at the TV station asked. The two brothers sat side by side in a room with a mirror along one whole wall. The woman ran a hand through Mel's bush of gray hair, smiling. "What're we going to do with you?"

Mel wasn't sure he'd heard right. "Ain't makeup for pretty women, like yourself?"

"Relax," the woman said. "You're going to be on TV. This is for sure going to get picked up by the national networks. Those lights are so intense, you'd look like a ghost without makeup."

She went to work on his face, powdering and painting him, while another woman did the same thing on Phil. She put powder on his cheeks and forehead. She went over his lips with pink lipstick and made him pucker up. Mel watched the girl in the mirror. She didn't look older than early twenties. She sure was pretty, with her long brown hair and big smile. He'd much rather have a real woman, like this one here, than some imaginary black girl who only lived in his head.

"Ten minutes," another woman said, popping her head in the door.

"Okay," the stylist said. Now she was working on his hair, spraying it with two different cans and brushing vigorously.

"You gonna give me a trim?" Mel asked.

"I'm not trained for that," the girl said, laughing.

"You live here in Bozeman?"

"Sure do. What about you?"

"I live up the road a ways," Mel said. "Don't take much time at all on my motorcycle."

"I love motorcycles," she said.

Much too soon, the other woman came back. Mel would've liked to stay and flirt with the stylist a while longer. Maybe he could stop and see her afterwards. Grudgingly he followed the new woman down a long corridor, through a door, and into a room where he saw drones hovering around with cameras and lights, wires running across the floor, and about ten other people. He broke out in a sweat just looking at it all.

"My name's Nancy, and I'm the producer," the woman who'd brought them said. She indicated two swiveling chairs. "You two sit there. Lolo will be sitting in that other chair, there. We're going to practice now." Nancy sat down in the chair to Phil's right.

"Mel, could you tell us who you are and where you come from?"

"Sure, my name's Mel. Me and my brother Phil are hog farmers from Missouri. We had an operation we took over when our daddy died and built it up to twelve thousand hogs." He looked at the camera lens that was pointing at him. It sat on top of a drone that hovered about six feet away.

"One thing, Mel, don't look at the camera. Look at me when you're talking."

"I don't look at the camera?"

"No, always look at me. I mean, you know, when Lolo's sitting here, look at her." Nancy checked her Jetlink. "One minute, everybody."

A slender woman with dark brown hair piled on top of her head and cascading down her back bent and shook his hand. "I'm Lolo. How are you, Mel?"

"A little nervous, I guess."

"And you must be Phil. Very pleased to meet you."

"Likewise," Phil said.

Mel could tell Phil had a frog in his throat. He decided it wasn't his problem. Whatever Phil said, even if he mentioned his imaginary girlfriend, well, what the hell did it really matter? No one watching TV had to know she was a black woman.

"Just be yourselves. Tell your story like it happened. We've got some real good video we'll be showing along with the segment. You're going to knock their socks off."

"Ten seconds," Nancy said. "Ready to roll? Sit up straight, Mel. Phil, you look smashing. Look at Lolo. And, action."

Then Lolo was speaking. "I'm Lolo Anderson, and this is *Viewpoint*. We're here today with Mel and Phil, hog farmers from Missouri. For their security, we're not revealing their last name. Thank you both for joining us on *Viewpoint*."

The red light on the camera blinked on, and the studio lights blazed in Mel's eyes. He tore his gaze away and looked at Lolo. "Thanks for inviting us."

"Mighty proud to be here," Phil said.

"Where is your hog farm located, Mel, and how many hogs did you have?"

"Right near Warrenville, Missouri," he said. "Me and my brother Phil built her up to twelve thousand hogs."

"How long have you been running your hog farm?"

"We're sixty-three, and Daddy died when we were thirty-three. Guess that makes thirty years."

Lolo smiled, then turned to his brother. "Phil, can you tell us what happened on your hog farm a few weeks ago, on November sixteenth?"

"Sure thing. My brother and me, see, we like to shoot down them little drones when they come snooping on our farm. Animal rights groups, the neighbors, they're always flying their little drones right over our property. So that day we shot down this little drone, like we always do."

"When you say you shot it down, what do you mean, with a gun?"

"Sure, we live out in the country. One bullet is all it takes with them contraptions."

"What happened next?"

"Mel and me didn't think much of it. We went in for lunch, and then we had our siesta. We always sleep for an hour or two after lunch."

Lolo Anderson smiled, showing all her teeth. "Then what happened?"

"Something woke me up, sounded like an explosion," Phil said. "I thought a plane crashed in the backyard. Like an earthquake, then another one, and another. I sez to Lil' Lena, I sez—" Phil stopped abruptly, looking helplessly at Mel.

"One explosion after the other, boom, boom, boom, boom," Mel said, making grand gestures. "Phil and me come running from different ends of the house. We go out on the porch, and it look like something out of an ol' war movie. All the hog houses on fire, smoke everywhere, hogs screamin' and whinin' like they do when you stick 'em with a knife. Only ain't nobody was stabbin' 'em, they was all burnin' up. When the smoke cleared, our hog houses was in ruins, nothin' left. No walls, no roof, just charred hogs everywhere you look."

"What caused these explosions and fires?" Lolo asked.

"Our foreman, his name is Felipe," Mel went on. "He come runnin' outta the forest with a coupla others. They said they saw somethin' streakin' outta the sky. He said it was some kinda missile hit our hog houses."

"What did you do?"

"Well, me and Phil don't take too kindly to someone wreakin' death and destruction on our place. We never done nothin' to no one. Ol' Phil, he rigged up the waste tank. We figgered whoever done this might come in the driveway and want to have a look at the damage, you know? So when we saw them comin' up the driveway a coupla hours after the explosions, Phil opened up the runoff valve. That's thirty thousand gallons of hog piss, you know. We let that hog piss spill out on the driveway to meet whoever was comin' up the hill to get us."

"Who was coming up the driveway?"

"Goddamned US Army jeeps," Phil said. "They got a three-foot wave of hog wastage coming down the driveway in their faces. That stopped all but one o' them jeeps. The one jeep drove through it and got up into the yard."

"And then?"

"We rigged up our car to drive across the yard by itself. When the soldiers started firing' on it—shootin' out all the tires and the windows—we knew they jes' come to kill us. So, we set off a little explosion of our own from a hundred yards away. Our car blew sky-high, an' that was the end of those folks in the jeep. Then we high-tailed it outta there on our bikes."

"Can we show the pictures, first?" Lolo asked, pointing at Nancy, the producer. On a wall-sized screen over to the side, Mel saw giant, blown-up pictures from his own camera of the charred and smoking hog houses.

"Yep, that's what it look like that day. I took them pictures," Mel said.

"This ABC affiliate has come into possession of the official government drone video of the drone strike on a Missouri hog farm on November sixteenth," Lolo said. "We are now going to run the drone footage, taken by the same Homeland Security drone that destroyed their farm with air-to-ground Hellfire missiles."

Mel had never seen this video before. It took a few seconds for his eyes to adjust to the stark gray images on the screen. Then, with a shock, he realized that the six long rectangular structures in the middle were the hog houses, seen from up in the sky, while the bigger one at the top was the main house. The square building off to the right must be the workers' bunkhouse. Little digital numbers played in all four corners of the video, and the voice of a controller could be heard, though he couldn't follow what the man was saying.

What happened next made him sit up straight. The first hog house in the row erupted in a giant white ball of flame. Then the second hog house was hit, and one after another, until all of them had received direct hits. You didn't actually see the missiles.

They streaked in too fast. You only saw the gigantic fireballs.

Mel felt his throat tightening and his eyes filling.

"What you've just seen," Lolo said when the video ended, "is official Homeland Security video of their drone strike against a working hog farm with twelve thousand hogs in Missouri. This strike occurred on November sixteenth, the first full day the drones were put into deployment by the US military."

"That was a terrible day fer us," Phil said in a gravelly voice.

"How did you gentlemen feel when you realized your farm was destroyed, that you had built up over so many years?" Lolo asked.

"I felt really sad, like someone died," Mel said. He'd gotten hold of himself and wiped away a tear while the moderator was speaking. His voice cracked. "That inferno you saw there was our whole life, up in smoke."

"I also felt angry," Phil said. "All we done was shoot down one of them little drones, like we always done. Even if that were a government drone, they got no right to come snoopin' on our property. This is America."

"An' they got no right to destroy our whole farm jes' cause we shoot down their little Viper, or whatever it were," Mel added.

"And now you're fugitives from the law," Lolo said. "How does that feel?"

"I don't feel like we done nothing wrong," Mel said. "Nothin' more than what they done, anyway. They kill twelve thousand hogs in one go."

"Do you feel the government has the right to conduct drone strikes against American citizens in this country?"

"I don't think so, but they sure as hell doin' it," Mel said.

"Can you tell us how you ended up in Montana?"

"We was plannin' to go up to Canada but along the way we joined up with some of them March22 folks that were sympathetic about what happened. March22 don't think the government should be shootin' missiles outta the sky at farms across the country."

"How did you happen to find your March22 contacts?"

"That weren't too hard," Mel said. He remembered what Winter had coached him to say. "March22 folks is jes' about everywhere around the country now. We even got a political party in Washington to fight for our rights that's been taken away."

Lolo Anderson looked at the camera. "This has been *Viewpoint,* featuring a live interview with Mel and Phil, two brothers from Missouri whose hog farm was destroyed by a Homeland Security drone strike using live missiles on November sixteenth. You will find a transcript of the interview, pictures and the video on our website. Thanks for tuning in."

Nancy the producer said, "Cut," and Lolo Anderson stood up. She came over and offered her hand.

"You did great, Mel," she said, shaking his hand. His hand trembled in hers, like he had the shakes. He could really use a shot of whiskey right now. Then she shook Phil's hand. "Thank you, Phil. I wish you gentlemen Godspeed."

"Thanks." Mel's mouth was dry as ashes. He was glad it was over.

"It's time to get you out of here," Nancy said. "Even though we said it was live, the show was taped and will air in about an hour. It's better if you're well on your way by then."

They followed Nancy down several corridors, then down two flights of stairs. She led them through a door that came out on a loading dock. Mel would've liked to go back and chat with that friendly stylist, but not with this case of the jitters. Maybe he come back and give her a ride on his bike someday. The two March22 men stood beside the Subaru smoking cigarettes.

"Let's go," said the driver, clapping his hands once. He held the door for Mel.

Mel's hands were still trembling as they drove off. Phil looked calm.

"Listen, boys," Mel said, leaning forward. "Stop and get us a bottle of Jack Daniels for the trip home." The driver nodded.

Phil smiled for the first time. "Good idea. I never let Lil' Lena drink much, but she likes a drop now and again, too."

CHAPTER 39

PRESIDENT JAMES JEFFERS sat in the Oval Office with Dave Knopfler from Homeland Security, Hal Holsom from NSA, and Tom Underwood, his chief of staff. They had just watched a TV report on the hog farmers whose farm had been obliterated. The rest of the country would be watching it as well, as it would certainly be replayed on dozens of channels.

"It's simple," Knopfler said. "Put the blame on March22 for that attack. It wasn't our drones. It was theirs. We can take the high road on this one."

"The army came in two hours later to investigate the incident," Tom Underwood said. "As they normally would, if a missile attack were detected. Maybe Dave's right."

"What about the chain of command? The drone controllers who overreacted?" Jeffers asked.

"Loyal soldiers. We can depend on them to keep quiet," Knopfler said.

"How the fuck did those oafs get their hands on our video?" President Jeffers demanded. The national news had just carried a video with genuine Homeland Security timestamps, lifted straight off of secure servers. The people in this room had seen the same video the day after the strike. Appropriate measures had been taken to make sure no drone controller could overreact in the future. Now, it was national news.

"Their hacking abilities are formidable," NSA Chief Holsom said. "The man admitted he's with March22, but he's no hacker. Those kinds of videos would be very difficult indeed to pull out."

"We've got to hold a press conference," Underwood said. "There's an outcry in social media. It's too late to own this one, but we need to get our spin on it."

"These people killed five soldiers that day, and we haven't caught them?" Jeffers glared at Knopfler from Homeland Security.

"That was a military operation, Mr. President," Knopfler said, shoving the blame on Reese, who wasn't in the room. "My understanding is they determined that the farmers must have died in the explosion."

"Well, they were fucking wrong," Jeffers said, pounding the table. "I want those men arrested and the book thrown at them."

"Yes, sir, Mr. President," Knopfler said, turning to an aide.

Jeffers looked at his chief of staff who seemed deep in thought. Underwood was his idea man.

"This was the hog farm we talked about two weeks ago," Underwood said. "We already saw it. As I recall, the neighbor ratted out the hog farmers. This happened the day after the nationwide prison break. One of the affected prisons is located only three miles from the hog farm. The neighbor told the local authorities they were hiding a large number of inmates in the hog houses."

"Get to the point," Jeffers said.

"We can't possibly put this on March22," Holsom interrupted. Everyone looked at him expectantly. "It's a government stamped video. The revelation has come through a member of March22. Nobody in his right mind would believe us."

"Comments?" Jeffers said.

"Besides, it's public knowledge that we can't see their drones," Holsom went on. "The *Post* article spelled that out. We can only see our own drones, so how could we have a video—"

"Stop calling them *their* drones. Those are stolen drones," Jeffers said.

"They shot down a government reconnaissance octocopter," Knopfler interjected. "That joker, Mel, said it himself. So okay, we take the heat for the missile strike. The message will be, don't mess with ongoing law enforcement operations."

"Goddammit, do these men have a last name?" Jeffers said.

"Grady, Mr. President," Knopfler said.

"People will see a drone strike as way too harsh," Underwood said. "Congress is already in turmoil with the drone bill in committee. This can only hurt us."

"Very harsh, though personally I like it," Jeffers said. "But you're right. We've got to get that bill through. But if we can't put it on March22?"

"We shift the focus to the escaped convicts," Underwood said. "You know, from that nearby prison in Missouri. Find some real hard cases. Legitimize the urgency of the strike."

"Go on," Jeffers said.

Knopfler turned to his aide. "Get profiles on the escapees from the prison in Warrenville, Missouri. Focus on the ones still at large. Bring me the ten nastiest, most dangerous ones you've got. Real scary-looking types."

"Yes, sir." The aide left the room at a jog.

"How long does he need?" Jeffers asked.

"Give him an hour," Knopfler said. "He'll have something in time for the press conference."

"We suspected some of our worst specimens of the inmate population were holed up in those hog houses, and therefore gave an exceptional one-time order for a strike," Jeffers said. "Is that what you're suggesting? It sounds risky."

"Maybe we could credibly say we had information that they had rigged up an explosion," Underwood offered.

"There was a booby trap," Holsom said.

"After our reconnaissance octocopter was shot out of the air," Underwood summarized. "The hog farmers were actively sabotaging a government operation. We had information that explosives were rigged. Explosives that ultimately killed five soldiers. This justifies the hostile reaction, after the fact."

"Jesus, I see how that could work," Jeffers said. "Okay, if we don't think of something better, that's what we'll go with."

"The TV report was shot in Bozeman, Montana, Mr. President," Knopfler said. "Melvin and Philip Grady were gone by the time the police and Homeland Security got there. We had helicopters covering the highways in every direction. There aren't so many ways they could've gone. But we didn't find them."

"Facial recognition?"

"We know who they are, but they're not in the database."

"How can they not be in the database?"

"Some of these people live out in the country, Mr. President. They don't renew their driver's licenses. They don't vote. We'll never get all of them. That's my guess."

"You've got people on the ground in Montana," Jeffers said. "Light a goddamned fire under their asses. How hard can it be to track down a pair of sixty-three year old hog farmers named Melvin and Philip Grady?"

"Make contact with that neighbor of theirs in Missouri," Knopfler said to another aide. "The one who told us they were harboring escaped convicts. We'll need his sworn testimony."

"Mr. President, sir, I found the Gradys when I was preparing for the meeting," one of his own aides said. The man turned his laptop around, showing a Facebook page. The page was called *Prove Your Patriotism* and showed a smiling picture of the two brothers, Mel and Phil. Sprinkled across the top of the page were several March22 bluebirds. "These are the guys who started up the whole *Prove Your Patriotism — Eat Bacon!* movement. Now it looks like they have..." the aide looked up. "Over a million likes."

Everyone started talking at once. Every man in the room had been offered bacon treats at shops and restaurants around the capitol.

"Those two gray-haired jokers are behind Prove Your Patriotism?" Underwood marveled. "This is not good."

"That's a fast-growing movement," Holsom said.

"Some damned patriotism," Jeffers stormed. "So find them. I want them in prison, I want to know everything they know about March22, and when they're done talking I want them to fry in the electric chair."

"March22 is bigger than anyone thought," Underwood said.

"Maybe not, actually," the aide went on. He had been trying to get their attention. "I analyzed those million likes on their Facebook page. Over seven hundred thousand are from click farms in Bangladesh, Pakistan, Malaysia, and Indonesia."

"What the hell is a click farm?" Jeffers asked.

"Low-paid workers paid to spread out likes over as many pages as possible," the aide said. "They typically get one dollar for every thousand likes, but they don't really engage. The point is they don't represent true interest in the movement."

"Good work, but that still leaves three hundred thousand genuine likes," Holsom said.

"I still don't like it that March22 has those drones," Knopfler said. "Not to mention the bombs."

Jeffers turned to Underwood. "Get with Petra Bedrosian and brief her for the press conference. That's the last time those March22 assholes are going to get in the way of our operations. It's time they knew what real pressure feels like."

CHAPTER 40

WASHINGTON, DC
WHITE HOUSE PRESS ROOM
DECEMBER 6, 2021—6:30 PM

PETRA BEDROSIAN FACED the unruly crowd of reporters knowing tonight's press conference would test her abilities. But then, every press conference was a test. Drones swarmed the room, capturing video and audio. In a strange way, the din of everyone talking at once calmed her. She liked talking to crowds. She liked hostile questions. She liked being attacked.

"Can I have your attention please?" Her voice reverberated in the packed room, swiftly resulting in an expectant silence. Every one of these people had seen the hog farmers' interview and the video. "I'm going to read a statement. Then I'll take questions," she announced.

"Mrs. Bedrosian, what are the rules of engagement for drones in our airspace?" a male reporter shouted. She ignored him. *Questions later, moron.*

"You have all seen the report out of Bozeman, Montana," she began. "As you know, when the American Prison Corporation had a computer glitch on November fifteenth and approximately two million hardened criminals walked out of their jail cells in all fifty states, the president authorized the use of Homeland Security drones in American airspace to provide local law enforcement with an extra tool for rounding them up. The executive order gave us ninety days to accomplish the mission. The program has worked. To date, thanks to the use of drone technology and the heroic efforts of law enforcement officers, ninety-six percent of the escaped convicts have been caught."

"How many escaped convicts were killed while resisting arrest?" shouted a female reporter.

Although she had prepared the answer, Bedrosian ignored the question. Questions came later.

"Because we were in a hurry to protect law-abiding Americans in the towns and cities of America, the president authorized the activation of the drones in the early hours of November sixteenth, less than eight hours after the mass escape. The risk of a huge spike in violent crime was high. Our foremost duty is to protect Americans.

"Because of the urgency of the situation, the decision was made to get the first few drones in the air with their normal armaments loaded."

"How many drones were activated in total?" shouted a male reporter.

Would they ever learn? She ignored him and went on.

"Local elements of Homeland Security worked closely with the drone operations of the US military in seamless cooperation. The hog farm that was destroyed on the morning after the breakout is located three miles from one of the affected prisons. Homeland Security sent in a small reconnaissance octocopter to investigate a neighborhood watch report from a concerned citizen. The neighbor told the authorities that a large number of escaped convicts were being sheltered in the hog houses. When the octocopter was shot out of the air by the hog farmers, Homeland Security rated it hostile. They relayed the event to the drone controllers, who then launched six air-to-ground Hellfire missiles, destroying the suspect hog houses."

"How many convicts were killed in the attack?"

Petra Bedrosian took pleasure in pretending she simply didn't hear these questions. They were out of order.

"Two hours after the attack, a unit from the nearest US Army base arrived to assess the damage. One of their jeeps was blown up in a booby-trap left by the hog farmers, killing five servicemen. The administration therefore feels justified in pursuing Melvin and Philip Grady to the full extent of the law."

"Mrs. Bedrosian, how about the stolen drones and March22?"

Again, she ignored the question.

"After an internal review, despite the presence of booby traps which cost five soldiers their lives, the missile attack was determined to be overzealous. The responsible operators have been removed from their duties and reprimanded. No other such attacks have occurred since the drones were activated. Fair compensation would be offered to the hog farmers if they were ultimately found innocent of the charges pending against them.

"One other thing," Bedrosian continued, stifling the din that had again started up. "We thought it would be fitting to give you some idea of the gravity of the situation concerning the convicts still at large. These are profiles of just a few of the inmates who were serving sentences at that one prison in Missouri who are still at large today."

On the wall behind her, a giant image of a gray-haired, big-bellied inmate in an orange jumpsuit appeared.

"Meet Ike Mullin, serving twenty years to life for bank robbery, second degree murder, kidnapping, and tax evasion."

A second photo flashed on the wall, showing a thickly muscled Asian man, approximately forty years old, with longish black hair and an angry look.

"Meet Tran Ng, also serving twenty to life, for bank robbery, assault with a deadly weapon, kidnapping, and forgery."

She showed three additional dangerous-looking individuals.

"I could go on, but you get the picture," she said. "Law enforcement is not an exact science. We have to weigh the benefits against the risks. We concede that taking out a hog farm with missiles was bad judgment. This was never the intention of the administration. It was a chain-of-command error. We have taken the necessary steps to ensure it doesn't happen again. In this case, twelve thousand hogs were killed and six people are missing, but there were no human remains found in the hog houses. We have unconfirmed information that the missing persons were undocumented aliens who may have simply left the area. Now I am available for your questions."

She pointed at a familiar reporter from the *New York Times.*

"Mrs. Bedrosian, what safeguards have been put in place to make sure homes and businesses where Homeland Security suspects criminal activity will not be hit with missiles?"

"No homes or businesses or individuals will be targeted by the drones, even if there is criminal activity," she said. "The Homeland Security drones are only used for reconnaissance. When the convicts are spotted, using electro-optical sensors and facial recognition technology, the drone operators speak in real time with local law enforcement. Local police do the rest. In a few days, when commercial aviation starts up again, the drones will also be used to help keep that safe."

She pointed at a female reporter. "Yes, Marie."

"Mrs. Bedrosian, thank you for your statement. How many drones in the air are still armed?"

"We will have sufficient armed drones in the air to safeguard commercial aviation in this country. The rest will be unarmed."

"Can you give us exact numbers on those?"

She decided to answer the out-of-order question before it spiraled out of control. "That number is classified, I don't know it, but it's a Homeland Security issue working in tandem with the FAA."

She pointed at a man in the crowd. "Pierre, nice to see you."

"Thank you, Mrs. Bedrosian," the reporter said. "How much compensation was offered to the hog farmers in the video?"

"Fair market value for the hogs and the buildings plus a generous goodwill payment for the emotional distress."

"What's the dollar figure, please?"

"I'm not at liberty to give you the dollar figure. It's a private matter. And please note it's only offered on condition that the men are found innocent." She pointed at a female reporter at the back of the room. "Cindy, you're next."

"Mrs. Bedrosian," the woman said, amplifying her voice through her drone. "The hog farmer stated he and his brother had joined March22. Does this mean the government is offering financial support to March22?"

She smiled at the innuendo. "The drone operators overreacted in this case, and the administration saw fit to make amends. The administration was prepared to compensate the hog farmers for their tangible and intangible losses, should they ultimately be found innocent. That does not constitute support for March22."

She pointed at Jonas, from the *Village Voice*.

"Mrs. Bedrosian, there's a bill being rushed through Congress to make the use of military drones in US airspace permanent. Doesn't this mean the use of the US military forces on American soil is being legalized? What guarantee do the American people have that they won't be targeted?"

"Let me be perfectly clear," she said. "The American people are not being targeted. The drones are there for surveillance for the purpose of *protecting* the American people. The drones are flying under the aegis of Homeland Security for the support of local law enforcement and the FAA. This is an important distinction."

She pointed at a man in the front row in a bow tie.

"I have two questions, Mrs. Bedrosian. First, escaped convicts and criminals are American citizens, too, are they not? Don't they, therefore, have equal rights for protection from government attacks under the First Amendment? Second, will the drones be used for reconnaissance efforts in finding pockets of March22 terrorists?"

She smiled. "No American citizens will be targeted by the drones except in cases determined by Homeland Security working with the FAA to protect commercial planes. Apart from that scenario, they are doing reconnaissance, that's it. I don't have any information in regard to your second question."

She pointed at a woman waving her hand in the middle of the throng. "Yes, Linda."

"Mrs. Bedrosian, two days ago you announced that the drones will be used to help safeguard commercial aviation after it starts up again on December tenth. How likely is another attack of shoulder-fired missiles, in the assessment of this administration, and what progress has been made to find the missing missiles?"

"I wouldn't want to speculate about the likelihood of a new attack," she said. "To your second question, although the missing missiles have not yet been located, Homeland Security has installed massive new security features in the perimeters around this country's airports. Together with the drone coverage, air travelers can once again feel completely safe, starting on December tenth."

She pointed at a male journalist. "Two more questions. Yes, Bob."

"Mrs. Bedrosian, if the Homeland Security drones shoot missiles at terrorists who have attacked a commercial plane, doesn't the plane blow up anyway? How does this make commercial aviation safer?"

"As I told you two days ago, it's meant as a deterrent. Last question, please?"

She pointed at an older woman in a green dress. Martha Dempsey from the *Washington Post*. "Hello, Martha."

"Thank you, Mrs. Bedrosian. As we are all aware, March22 is in possession of armed drones as well. Does this administration foresee a showdown in the skies between the two sides?"

"I'm not here to discuss hypothetical scenarios," she said. "I leave that to the people who are paid to do it. Thank you for your attention."

As the din instantly started up again, the last question unsettled her. The *Washington Post* journalist, Martha something, stood there with a smug smile, as if satisfied just to have asked the question. She looked like a courtroom prosecutor who knew that questions themselves could do damage, even if no answer were forthcoming. Now every reporter in the room would start thinking about that scenario. In addition, the *Post* happened to be the newspaper that had that special source. That could not be a coincidence.

Petra Bedrosian didn't like hypotheticals in general, but what she really didn't like was that nightmare image of a showdown in the sky over America.

CHAPTER 41

DENVER, COLORADO
DECEMBER 6, 2021—9 PM

SHIPTON ARRIVED IN a brown Lincoln at nine o'clock one night.

"Got an emergency, boys, right here in Denver. You're just the men for the job."

Ike Mullin stood in the camper doorway. He didn't return Shipton's cheerful grin. He'd been looking forward to another night with Nasreen.

"I ain't doin' another one o' them jobs like last time," Tranny said from behind him.

"We owe the man, Tranny," Ike said. "Besides, you remember what he said the pay was."

"Different kind of job this time anyway," Shipton said. "Come on, fellas. We've got to be somewhere."

"What's it all about?" Tranny asked, throwing his leather jacket over one shoulder as they walked with Shipton back to the car.

"Does Nasreen know you're takin' us?" Ike asked.

"I checked it out with her. She's informed, and I'll have you back here in three hours," Shipton said.

At least that, thought Ike.

When they got in the car, Tranny again asked for more information. Ike rode in front with Shipton in the buttery soft passenger seat.

"We're on a rescue mission," Shipton explained. "Tonight we're going to save a life."

"Glad we ain't takin' a life, like last time," Tranny said.

"Stop your bitchin' and moanin'," Ike said. "This here's the boss. He tells us what we gotta do, we don't get to choose."

"I ain't bitchin' an' moanin', just sayin' what I will and won't do," Tranny said.

"Well, cut it out, whatever you're doin'," Ike said.

"Glad you see it that way," Shipton said. "All of it is God's work, anyway. He's the real boss. I'm just a middleman."

Shipton laughed as if he'd made some kind of joke. Ike joined in to be polite, although he didn't really have much of a connection with God. Even after two weeks with the Bible Party, he didn't feel the feeling. He was just happy they were going to be back before the night was over.

"So who the fuck're we rescuing, some doctor?" Tranny asked after a minute or two of driving in silence.

"We're almost there," Shipton said. "It's a young woman. She's inside her house watching TV with her husband. The two little ones are sleeping."

"How do you know all this shit?" Tranny interrupted.

"We've got our little drone in there with 'em," Shipton said. "Now listen real carefully. We know about this little lady because we've got our eyes in those abortion clinics all over, too, see? She's had her mandatory consultation, and she wants to go through with it. Her appointment is tomorrow."

"That's why we're goin' in tonight."

"Exactly, Ike," Shipton said. "Our objective is to stop her from going through with it."

"How the hell're we gonna do that?" Tranny asked. "Talking to her, or something else?"

"We subdue the husband, restrain the little lady, and then take her with us," Shipton said. "We've got a place about thirty miles from here. She's going to stay there for a few months."

"No shit?" Tranny said. "Like a prison?"

"It's like a very nice prison," Shipton agreed. "Only we're not really out to punish the little lady. We just want to save the child."

"Better not punch her in the stomach, Ike," Tranny said.

"I wouldn't punch a lady in the stomach anyway."

"Because she's pregnato, you know."

"You don't have to tell me," Ike said. "He just explained it."

Ike sighed as the car rolled slowly through a neighborhood of small houses, Shipton scanning for a number. Tranny always wanted to argue about the smallest things. Ever since Ike had connected with Nasreen, he felt such calmness, he had no need to take the bait.

"Here we are," Shipton said. "I'll go in first. You boys keep out of sight in those bushes till I'm in."

Shipton got a brown box out of the back seat. It had *Amazon* printed on it, and he put on a brown cap with the Amazon logo sewn into the front.

Shipton only had to ring once. From where he stood in the bushes at the side of the porch, heart pounding, all Ike saw was the house owner's bare feet.

"Yes?" the man said.

"Package for Mrs. Lisa Watkins. Need a signature."

"I'll sign," the man said.

"Sorry, she's got to sign it herself," Shipton said. As soon as Shipton went through the door, Ike moved to the porch. Shipton was three steps into the living room, and the house owner's back was turned as he spoke to his wife on the couch across the room. The man had one hand on the door and was pushing it closed when Ike put his foot in the way.

Ike saw Shipton putting down the box and talking to the woman as the house owner spun around. He was six inches shorter than Ike, and skinny, besides being barefoot. With his left arm, Ike banged the door open. At the same time, he slammed his right fist into the skinny man's bugged-out eye, sending him staggering backward across the carpet. Ike was aware of Tranny coming in behind him, and he heard the front door latch.

"What is this? Who are you?" the woman on the couch screamed. She was tussling with Shipton.

"Keep it quiet, boys. Don't wake the little ones," Shipton said, breathing hard. He had plastic handcuffs in his right hand and, with his left, he was trying to subdue the woman. But she was in a frenzy, batting and slapping her arms all about and kicking out with her feet. Shipton couldn't get a handle on her.

"Go help him," Ike directed Tranny. "Jes' don't hit her."

"You don' have to tell *me* that," Tranny said.

The skinny man, sitting on the floor, was breathing hard, still dazed. He had on jeans and a T-shirt. Ike couldn't be sure, but it didn't look like the man had a weapon.

As Tranny and Shipton chased the woman around the living room, Ike put a set of plastic handcuffs on the skinny man's wrists. He slipped the man's Jetlink off, then went through his pockets, producing an old fashioned cell phone, a set of keys, and a wallet. He placed the phone in his own pocket. He'd once had a collection of old cell phones. Maybe he could start a new one.

"You got any duct tape?" Ike asked Shipton.

"Fuck you," the skinny man said.

Tranny and Shipton had the young woman on the carpet on her back. She was screaming and kicking and wriggling like a fish. Not good for a pregnant woman, Ike thought. You couldn't see any baby bump. Tranny held her down while Shipton tried to get hold of both of her wrists at the same time. Finally he succeeded, but both men took a lot of kicks in the process. Tranny was sidestepping her the whole time to keep his balls out of the way of her strong feet.

"Who are you assholes?" the woman shouted. "Let me go. Police! Help!"

Once her hands were restrained, Shipton wadded up a handkerchief and stuffed it in her mouth. The woman tried to bite him, but he got his fingers out in time. He carefully stuffed more and more of the handkerchief in her mouth until she was gagging. It looked like Shipton had done this before. Shipton now slipped the woman's Jetlink off her wrist and slid it in his pocket.

Tranny held the woman's ankles on the ground, keeping all his weight on them, while Shipton, breathing heavily, went back to the couch. He unrolled a strip of duct tape and bound the woman's ankles. Then he tossed the tape to Ike.

"Wrap up his ankles like I did her," Shipton said.

"What the hell do you want from us?" the skinny man said. He hadn't moved from his position on the carpet. His left eye had swollen up till it was almost closed.

"We're taking the little lady," Shipton said. "She made a poor choice."

"We don't have any money. We're almost out of ration coupons and we have two kids sleeping upstairs. What the fuck is wrong with you people?"

"You take care of those other little ones," Shipton said. "We'll have your wife back in a few months, safe and sound, big and round."

"What the—?" The skinny man stopped, something dawning on him. "A few *months*? What do you mean, a few months?"

"We don't want your money," Shipton said. "We're a rescue organization. Don't worry, we'll take good care of her."

The woman was groaning and grunting and trying to head-butt Tranny, but Tranny kept one heavy hand on her shoulder, pinning her to the carpet.

"I don't get it. What are you going to do to her, you sickos?"

"Maybe there's something your little lady didn't share with you," Shipton said. "That happens. Did you tell him your secret, sugar?"

The woman growled into the gag like a cornered tiger, eyes flashing fire, fixed on Shipton.

"Hmm, that explains it," Shipton said. "Well, not our problem. Fact is, she's going to have another baby."

A much larger tiger growl shook the woman's entire body.

"What?" The skinny man looked surprised. Slowly his lips curled into a smile. "Honey, that's wonderful. Why didn't you tell me? How do these strangers know about a thing like that?"

The woman made no sound now. Ike noticed she didn't look at her husband.

"I'll let you two sort that out six months from now," Shipton said. "You got his Jetlink?"

"Here." Ike patted his pocket.

Shipton took the man's Jetlink and went through a doorway into another room. Ike heard a drawer opening and closing. Then Shipton came back into the living room.

"Might take you a while to find it, but you'll live," he said to the skinny man. "Boys, let's go. Can you get her by yourself?"

Tranny looked at the woman wriggling on the floor. "Sure thing."

While Ike grabbed the Amazon box and Shipton rummaged in a closet for a coat for the woman, Tranny bent and slid his arms under the woman's body.

"Guess you're going to ride in the back with me," he said.

The woman growled again, eyes bulging. She bucked a little with her knees, but it was nothing Tranny couldn't handle.

A minute later, they were driving back down the residential street. Ike and Tranny rode in back with the woman sandwiched in between. Shipton didn't want the woman throwing herself around, possibly injuring the baby.

"We need to put this on her now," Shipton said. He handed them a pillowcase. Tranny unfolded it and slipped it over the woman's head.

Ike wondered as they drove along in silence what Nasreen would make of all this. Did she know what Shipton's organization did? She must know, because Shipton had checked it out with her. The arrangement was that Ike and Tranny would be loaned to Shipton whenever he had a job for them. A few weeks ago, Shipton had arranged for them to shoot one of those abortion doctors coming out the back door of his clinic. They'd sat in a car three blocks away, pressing buttons on a Jetlink that activated a sniper rifle set up a hundred yards from the clinic. The aiming capability had been provided by a small drone. Despite bodyguards and other security, they'd nailed that doctor with deadly accuracy. Now they were kidnapping some young pregnant woman who had planned to have an abortion tomorrow. Shipton's group sure had everything figured out.

Thirty minutes later Shipton pulled off the two-lane road onto a gravel driveway that led into some trees. The pregnant woman had gone quiet. They'd taken the highway north from Denver, then exited on this local road. The gravel track went on for a couple of minutes, winding through pine trees on both sides, before opening into a large clearing. A large, four-story mansion rose through the darkness in front of them. Shipton parked by the front door.

"Welcome home," he said to the woman, and got out.

Shipton reached into the back seat and removed the pillowcase and the gag. The woman was crying now.

"What is this place? Who are you people?" she pleaded.

"Now, now, you're going to like it here," Shipton said. "Come on, let's get you inside and settled."

"You want I should carry her in?" Tranny asked.

"Keep your hands off me, you big ape," the woman said.

"Lisa, isn't it?" Shipton said. "Now listen. We took off your gag and your blindfold. Would you like to walk in like a lady, or be carried in?"

"You people are going to go to jail, if it's the last thing I do."

Shipton sighed. "I guess you're carrying her."

Ike laughed as the woman wriggled and tried to evade Tranny's big paws. "Remember what we said back there," Ike said, just to irritate his friend.

"I ain't punchin' her," Tranny retorted, settling the load in his arms. The woman was small and skinny, but ninety pounds was ninety pounds. Tranny was breathing hard by the time they got up the porch steps.

A light came on and the door opened. A big lady with a scarf on her head and an old-fashioned dress that came down to her ankles stood waiting.

"It's been a while, Gerald," the woman said.

"Mamsie, meet Lisa Watkins, your new resident."

"Right. Well, nice to meet you, Lisa."

"Fuck you, sideways and backward," Lisa said.

"She's got a mouth on her," Tranny offered.

The woman named Mamsie smiled wider. "You'll fit in just fine. Come on in, boys. Anyone want a cup of coffee?"

They stood in a large entry hall with a ceiling that went up about twenty feet. Ike stared at the wooden stair railing, the chandeliers, the mirrors in ornate gold frames, and couches made from carved wood. When Mamsie pushed the front door shut, she touched her Jetlink. Ike heard bolts being thrown in the door locking mechanism. Good security, he thought. Like a prison.

Another woman appeared, younger and thinner than Mamsie. "Hello, my name's Mary. Please come with me for a coffee," she said in an accent Ike couldn't place. The woman's red hair hung down her back in a long, thick braid.

"I'll be along in a few," Shipton said, heading up the stairs with Mamsie and Lisa. Ike noticed how Shipton stayed behind Lisa on the stairs. Maybe he was afraid the woman was going to throw herself down.

The kitchen also had a high ceiling, though not two stories high, like the entry. Mary set mugs in front of them and poured steaming coffee.

"Milk and sugar?" She wiped her hands on her apron.

"You got any whiskey?" Tranny asked. When Mary laughed, he added, "I like whiskey in my coffee at this hour of the day."

"Me too, but we haven't any alcohol here. None at all."

"That accent," Ike said. "Like you come from somewhere."

"I'm from Dublin."

"Oh? Never heard of that," Ike said.

"It's in Ireland, dumbhead," Tranny said. "Everyone knows that."

"Right," Mary said with a big smile. She sat down with them while Ike stirred sugar into his coffee.

"Can't know everything, I guess," Ike said.

"I saw it on a TV program once," Tranny said. "Real pretty place, all green and everything."

"That's why we call it the Emerald Isle," Mary said.

A little silence ensued as they all looked at each other.

"Have you been working here long?" Ike said finally.

"Two years."

"What's it like?" Tranny said.

"We have about twenty girls."

"Twenty?" Ike was surprised. It was a big house, but still.

"I had my own baby here," Mary said. She spoke matter-of-factly, showing no emotion. "A little baby boy. His name is James. I gave him up for adoption."

"That must've been tough." Ike didn't know what else to say.

"Most girls don't have their babies here. I was special. I didn't have any place to go home to."

"Because you're from Ireland?" Ike asked.

"I'm illegal. They'd deport me if they found me."

"You don't want to go back?"

"My family disowned me."

"All because you got pregnant?" Tranny asked.

"I come from a small village, actually, not the city. But even in the city you'll have your sweet trouble."

"What about the dad?" Tranny asked.

Mary dismissed him with a wave. "He was a no-good drunk that I never should've given the time o' day. Everything's clear in hindsight, ain't it the truth?"

"That's for sure," Ike said.

"This girl we brought in, she gets to go home after a while?" Tranny asked.

"At thirty weeks. When she's nice and big and round and has learned to love her baby instead o' hatin' him, they'll take her home again."

"Sorta like a reverse kidnapping," Ike said, which made the Irish woman laugh.

"How do they know when it's thirty weeks?" Tranny said.

"Jes' look at the calendar, buddy," Ike said good-naturedly.

"She means thirty weeks in the pregnancy," Tranny said.

"Right. Sometimes the girls tell us openly. Sometimes the doctor here can wheedle information from the clinics. They can also tell by the ultrasound."

"Do them girls ever try and escape?" Tranny asked.

Mary smiled. "All the time, but they never get far. It's the drones in the hallways, cameras in the rooms, drones outside, not to mention guard dogs. We're a long walk from civilization even if you did get off the property. In my two years, no one's ever succeeded."

"Like a jail," Ike noted.

"But a very fancy and nice one," Mary said. "We have a bigger problem with suicides. They can be quite ingenious, you know. No matter you take away every conceivable thing from the girls, there's always a new inspiration."

"That ain't so fancy and nice," Tranny said.

"Yes, because if they succeed, they take two lives at the same time," Mary said. "It's happened twice since I got here. Poor me. Four people dead."

"How'd they manage it?" Ike asked.

Mary's smile disappeared. "I'd rather not talk about it, if you gentlemen don't mind."

CHAPTER 42

DENVER, COLORADO
DECEMBER 6, 2021—11 PM

"It's one of our less publicized activities, for obvious reasons," Nasreen said when Ike asked her about the kidnapping. "We've got people working in all fifty states, doing those rescues every single day, but it's still only the tip of the iceberg. Ike, I really need to show you something," she went on. It was after eleven and they were in her little room on the bus. She opened a compartment in the wall, exposing a small TV wall.

Ike saw a noisy press conference, the kind that always made him switch the channel. A lady stood at the podium, and reporters were shouting questions that she answered in a fast monotone.

Suddenly, his picture filled the screen. He saw his own mottled skin, his big nose, his gray hair, and the old jagged scar around his eye. It was strange enough to see a picture of yourself, but this was frigging national TV. Ike's mouth went dry. His heart hammered in his chest.

"Meet Ike Mullin. Twenty years to life for bank robbery, second degree murder, kidnapping and tax evasion," the woman at the podium said. Ike's full name was written in block letters at the bottom of the screen.

He looked at Nasreen, his world shattered. Nasreen smiled. Ike felt his legs giving out, but she took a step forward, took his face in her hands, and kissed him hard.

"Ike was a bad boy," Nasreen said. He searched her eyes. Still smiling, she didn't look away. "You and your friend did a good job keeping out of sight since the breakout, didn't you?"

"But now... but now..." he stammered.

"Now everyone will know? I don't think you need to worry about Pastor Peaches or the rest of the crew," Nasreen said. "Everyone's got a secret, you know. We seem to attract people like that."

"Yeah, but they'd lock us up again in a second. They're lookin' for us. Now we've been on TV."

Nasreen helped him sit in her little desk chair. She knelt on the carpet beside him.

"You're not safe here," she agreed. "We have new people wandering in every day, lots of visitors. Someone would recognize the two of you."

He felt the panic infiltrating his muscles, paralyzing him. The prison in Missouri, nine long years... nine years without a woman. The thought of losing Nasreen struck him like a sledge hammer blow to the heart.

"I don't know what we're gonna do." Ike sat there shaking his head, feeling numb and powerless.

"I should've waited to show you the video," Nasreen said. "I thought you might've actually seen it already. I thought we needed to talk about it. We need to make a plan."

"Tranny watches a lot of TV," Ike said. "I kinda got my fill of it in prison. We had it on just about all the time in there, sometimes all night long."

"He's probably seen it then. Did you talk to him?"

"We were working different shifts today. I didn't see him at dinner. Must be back in the camper by now."

"Well, I spoke to Pastor Peaches and we worked something out. Shipton's coming back early in the morning. He'll bring you someplace safe. Do you want to climb up first, or shall I?" Nasreen pointed at her bunk. Ike's mind was working very sluggishly. He looked at her.

"I don't want to go away from you."

"It's close, Ike. It's where you were earlier tonight."

"That house for pregnant women?"

Nasreen smiled. "Doesn't get much safer than that."

He thought about that strange house with all its three-bolt locks, drones, dogs, and twenty pregnant women. Women that often tried to escape and sometimes killed themselves. It might be better than going back to jail in Missouri, but it didn't sound like paradise, either.

"I'd rather stay here with you than go to that loony house," Ike said.

"They need security there, too," Nasreen said. "Once you get over there, we'll make some changes to your appearance, both of you. Otherwise, the girls could turn you in once they're sent home. Here, people have already gotten used to your appearance. You'll have work to do. I'll come and visit whenever I can."

"Wait a minute, what kinda changes?"

She smiled. "Your hair, maybe. You'd look good in glasses, Ike, don't you think?"

She pulled him close, this time kissing him long and softly on the cheek, which he had shaved carefully four hours ago. She wanted him to wear glasses? Four hours ago, he'd had no idea his face would be on TV and all his crimes exposed for the world. Bank robbery and second-degree murder. Him and Tranny both. How in the world was she going to change his appearance?

He lay on the bed, the ceiling just three feet above him, while Nasreen tugged at the tail of his shirt. "I want to see that tummy." She knelt beside him on the bed, taking off his clothes. He glanced her way and got an eyeful of delightful cleavage. To think he might lose this!

She fiddled with something on her Jetlink. "Hey, what would you say to a fire in the fireplace?" Next he heard a crackling and popping, and the low roar of air being sucked into a fire. When he turned to look at the TV wall, a perfectly blazing fire filled the screen.

"How did you do that?" he asked.

Nasreen answered by undoing her bra. The view of those gorgeous curves wakened something in him. If the shit was going to hit the fan tomorrow, it was no reason to spoil his last night as a free man. He started to respond as Nasreen continued to sprinkle kisses across his chest. He took her hand in his and kissed it right up the arm, making her giggle. She made him take off the rest of her clothes, one article at a time.

Afterward they lay there for a long time. Over the relaxing sounds of the fire, he heard distant voices through the bus wall, a car engine starting, a car driving away. He pictured himself and Nasreen in some little house somewhere, a couple of kids sleeping in their beds. Kids that looked like a perfect mix between him and Nasreen.

Ike sighed. "They're gonna find me. They're gonna take us away. Too many people here seen us."

"Stop worrying, Ike. We're taking care of it."

He straightened up and looked at Nasreen, this gorgeous woman who seemed so determined to solve his problems.

"Why are you sticking your neck out for me like that? I don't get it."

She gazed at him, a small smile playing on her lips. At first, he couldn't read the meaning behind it. Suddenly, like a flash, he understood it as clearly as if she had said it out loud. He and Tranny belonged to the family. He had those words in his mind. He saw them, clear as letters printed on a piece of paper. That the words came from Nasreen, he had no doubt, but how she had placed them in his mind was a mystery. What was more, he *believed* it with all his heart and soul. His doubt had left him. Nasreen smiled again, and he felt his eyes filling at the thought of *belonging*.

Once again, he saw those little kids running around, maybe with Nasreen's hair, eyes, and the beginnings of her long legs. Little Nasreens. She leaned forward, and the smile turned into another kiss.

SHIPTON PICKED THEM up at six a.m. sharp. The only wrinkle was when Rocker, one of the other security men, who was standing guard as they walked across the compound to Shipton's car, ran and caught up with Ike.

"Hey, man, saw you on TV last night," Rocker said. "You didn't tell me you was one of them *escaped* convicts."

"Ain't the kinda thing people go talkin' about," Ike said. He kept walking as Rocker tagged along. Something in Rocker's tone was making him nervous.

"Ike, man. I could use a little dough. You 'member what I was tellin' you about my home situation?" Rocker put a hand on Ike's shoulder. Ike brushed the man off and kept walking.

"Five hundred bucks, man. I won't tell a soul."

Ike spun around when they reached Shipton's white Lincoln. "I thought you was my friend, man. Friends don't go rattin' each other out and demandin' money not to."

"I need the money, man. Otherwise I'd never—"

All at once, Tranny stepped between them and slugged Rocker in the throat. Rocker staggered sideways, banging into the car and wheezing. While Rocker tried to get his breathing back to normal, Tranny advanced a step.

"You ever hit on my buddy again, I'll kill you. Got that, you Okie pussy?"

Rocker took a swing, but so weakly Tranny caught his arm in one hand. Then Tranny's boot came up and connected with the man's balls. As Rocker screamed in pain, leaning over and holding his privates, Ike removed the assault rifle from the strap around his neck. He brought it with him.

"Let's go, boys, before he gets mad," Shipton said.

"Too early in the morning for this shit," Tranny agreed.

Ike got in the car, too rattled to speak. When was he going to see Nasreen again?

CHAPTER 43

"WOULD YOU IDIOTS get your drinks and sit down so we can get started?"

Kyle Cedric Pluess had learned a thing or two about leadership since taking over the reins of Pluess Farm Implements when his father died two years ago. It was hard exerting pressure on the same guys who'd given each other whirlies back in junior high, who'd all had sex for the first time within one month of each other, and sworn eternal friendship by marking their faces with each other's blood.

"Pipe down, Cedric. We're getting there," said Will Hutchins, his tall redheaded friend. Hutch was just filling his goblet with an Italian Brunello di Montalcino. These three hundred-dollar bottles didn't always sell at the shadowmarkets.

"Hard day at the office, Hutch?" said Thomas Paine, wearing his trademark Hawaiian shirt. The guy actually fantasized about the old *Hawaii Five-O* episodes from the 1970s.

"Ladies, can I remind you this is not an ordinary meeting? We have serious business."

"But we all agree. What is there to discuss?" Hutch said, finally settling his lanky frame into one of the plush chairs. They sat in the Pluess headquarters conference room. The rest of the office staff had departed an hour before. Most of the secretaries would stop to barter their daily bottle of surplus wine for other household needs on their way home.

"He needs to prove he's still got the biggest balls west of the Mississippi," Paine said, sinking his ass into the chair opposite Hutch. The three huddled at one end of the long table, their wineglasses in front of them.

"He already proved that many times," Hutch said with no irony.

Pluess touched a button on his Jetlink, lighting up the wall with a map of the United States. Though they had all studied this map repeatedly over the previous forty-eight hours, the twenty yellow starbursts still grabbed your attention instantly.

The symbols were spread out over the lower forty-eight states—four in the Northeast, four in the South, four in the Middle Atlantic states, four in the Midwest, and four more on the West Coast.

"We're going to put their moronic idea to the test, and see if they still want to fly," Pluess said. "Random geographic spread. No link to Iowa. Totally compartmentalized. Now, to the problems."

"When?" Hutch asked, having gone serious. "I'm going to need to make sure it doesn't conflict with the Hawkeyes schedule."

"Fuck your Hawkeyes," Pluess said.

"They're not playing on the tenth. I checked," Paine added.

"We're not doing anything on the tenth," Pluess said. The other two stared at him. He had been the one who proposed at least one token demonstration of rocket-propelled fireworks on the day commercial aviation was relaunched. "Two reasons. Logistics work against us. We're not going to have men ready in all those places that quickly. And we can't use FedEx to get the missiles there, either."

"And the other reason?" Paine asked.

"Commercial aviation starts again on December tenth," Pluess said. "After a hiatus of more than two years, there'll be kinks to work out. Flight crews, pilot shortages, equipment problems."

"Air traffic controllers," Hutch added.

"That's probably the one area they're okay," Pluess said. "But anyway, we'll give them a couple of weeks to get everything running smoothly. Get back up to eighty or ninety percent, then pow!"

"So, you're thinking..." Paine left the question open.

"Christmas Eve," Pluess announced. He watched the faces of the others.

"Yes!" Hutch jumped up in enthusiasm. "Planes filled to the max, people rushing to get home in time for Christmas."

Paine was equally impressed. "I can see the headlines. *Christmas Attacks Paralyze Air Travel*. I love it!"

"I'm glad you agree," Pluess said. "I just wish I could take one down myself."

"Too risky," Hutch said, the grin gone.

"It must be quite a rush," Paine said.

"You ain't kidding," Pluess said. He raised his wineglass. "To my father, may he rest in peace."

"Or burn in the eternal fires of the place you sent him," Hutch said.

Pluess thought back to that night in the cornfield, a mile from the end of runway five at Des Moines Airport. The twin-engine Otter slowly barreling over his position in a rickety old duck blind, climbing out of one thousand feet.

His father, he knew, enjoying a stiff drink of scotch as he headed for Nebraska, on his way to visit customers early the next morning. The last drink that would ever pass his lips. It had been easy to smuggle a drone into the plane to record his father's last moments. The missile had left the chute and headed straight for the heat of the plane's engines. The fireball had been awesome to behold. Inside the plane, just an instant of smoke and flames before the connection died, the drone itself immolated.

Some members of the board had found him too young to take over after the tragic death of his father. He'd been working at the company for seven years. Within a year, he'd ousted those board members and installed men who were friendlier to his vision. As if Cedric Pluess didn't know how to run a company. He ran the company and still found time for a very time-consuming hobby, thank you very much. With over a billion dollars in sales so far in 2021, and nearly two hundred million in profits, Dark Fiber dwarfed the company his father had built.

"When can I start moving the merchandise?" Hutch asked. Hutch's people had valuable connections in the rail industry. Because of that, and since railways were the least vulnerable to the prying investigators of Homeland Security, they had already decided to move the shoulder-fireds and launch assemblies around the country on trains. All the starbursts lay within twenty miles of a rail depot. From there, the crates could easily be hauled away in an ordinary pickup truck.

Pluess turned to Paine. "How's your team doing on lining up the personnel?"

"That is a challenge," Paine said. "I'm glad you're moving back the date. We've reached out to our most trusted leaders in all the specified locations. They'll make a choice from among their members. One by one, they're getting back to us. Once the merchandise is delivered, they'll do the training, and then we'll be set."

"That all takes time," Pluess agreed.

"Did you get any blowback till now?" Hutch asked.

Paine shook his head. "It's amazing, you know. They all seem to have two or three members who are ready to die trying. Or who are convinced they can outrun a Hellfire inferno."

They all took a sip, reflecting. "Death is part of life," Pluess said.

"They'll die for a good cause," Paine added. The three clinked glasses.

"There is one situation we need to talk about," Hutch said.

"Ann Arbor, Michigan," Paine said.

"You got it," Hutch said.

"Matt Carney's dead," Pluess said.

"That's what we thought," Hutch said. "However, Claire somehow got Carney out of the cabin that was torched by Black Widow. I have a sleeper contact in Black Widow. He said Black Widow went to another safe house yesterday to try and kill Claire, and lost six men. Claire is alive, as is Carney."

"Hasn't she checked in?" Pluess asked.

"Not a peep. They got away from both Black Widow attacks. At this point, we have to assume she's on the run with Carney."

"Claire took out six men? I knew she was a good shot, but Christ," Paine said.

"What the fuck does she go AWOL for?" Pluess said.

"With Carney," Hutch said. "My contact said the lady's car was gone. The lady that lived in that safe house."

"Make and model?"

"He got it, and we're on it. I took it over."

"So we've got an implosion in Ann Arbor with Black Widow filling the vacuum," Pluess said, "and we've got Claire on the run with our trump card. What is this shit?" In an organization this large, you always had some kind of situation to deal with. He just wished it hadn't been Ann Arbor. Still, it was good news that Carney was alive.

"I told you guys she was too young," Paine said. "The situation got out of control and she panicked. Sounds to me like she and Carney are working together."

"On the run together, anyway," Hutch said.

"When did this happen?" Pluess demanded.

"Sometime last night." Hutch met his fiery gaze.

"I want her stopped, and I want that March22 idiot somewhere safe, where we'll have him when we need him. Because we *are* going to need his ass."

"Let me work with you on this," Paine said, looking at Hutch. "Do we know how much she knows?"

"She knows nothing," Hutch said. "She joined up eighteen months ago. Ran a good ship in Ann Arbor till now. Good with a gun. The combination of the Black Widow power play and having to keep watch on Carney must've gotten to her."

"You should've given her more support," Pluess said.

"Black Widow increased their presence in Ann Arbor just as we decided to stash Carney there," Paine said. "It's a coincidence. Those dopeheads don't know anything about Carney."

"I'm not worried about Black Widow," Pluess said. "It's even okay if we forfeit Ann Arbor, for the time being. I don't like it that Claire Tenneman hasn't called in. And I really don't like it that Carney's gone."

"Let's break this up and get working on it," Paine said. He turned to Hutch again. "Shoot me the information on that car, will you? I'll get my people started on that."

CHAPTER 44

"MATT HAD TO leave in a hurry," Luke reported on the secure chat. He felt himself bristling. It irritated him just to know his father was listening. His father who had handed Matt on a platter to those Dark Fiber idiots. He always had to filter everything he said. "He's with the Ann Arbor Dark Fiber leader. Apparently, he saved her life, so she's feeling beholden to him. She confirmed that Dark Fiber has the shoulder-fired missiles."

"It was Dark Fiber?" Winter said.

"Did you ever doubt it?" John Carney said.

"I'll be damned," Sander said. "I always had it in mind that was our old Anonymous compatriots."

"They would've taken credit for anything," his father said. "That's probably where you got the idea."

"Luke, did he say anything more?" Sander said.

"The Ann Arbor woman is sure that with the reinstatement of commercial flights, they'll carry out a new attack. If the planes get back in the air, the militias are out of business, and quickly. Shadowmarkets will be a thing of the past. A new attack is the best way to ensure that the country remains at their mercy."

"They're crazy," Sander said.

"We always knew that," his father said.

"Where are those damned shoulder-fireds?" Winter put in.

"Matt's working on that," Luke said. "He'll try to have that information soon. It's extremely tricky getting information out of the woman. Let's assume we're going to get details on the location. We need to finalize our strategy."

"Where is Matt now?" his father asked.

The man honestly had a screw loose. *Does he think I'm going to forget? Does he think I'm stupid?*

When Luke didn't answer, Sander jumped in. "Luke, can you tell us where Matt is now?"

"Left Ann Arbor heading south," Luke said. He lied, knowing his father would try to circumvent the other leaders and contact Matt. He could inform the others later concerning the disinformation.

"One thing is clear. We've got a chance to end Dark Fiber's reign of terror," Sander said. "Not just because they kidnapped Matt. If we can take them down, the rest of the militias will be severely weakened. We can take full credit for it, too."

"Once we know where the damned missiles are stored," Winter agreed.

"I just need some indication of where they are. Something to start with," Luke said. "We can steal the missiles and then hand them over to Homeland Security while proving that Dark Fiber had stolen and used them back in 2019."

"That would go a long way toward sanitizing our image," Sander said. "We do it very publicly, of course."

"Exactly," Luke said.

"I just hope they don't bill us for that bridge in San Francisco," Winter growled.

"If they do, we can pay off the debt with a few dirty nukes," his father said. Luke considered the comment batshit on several different levels. Surprisingly, no one called his father on it. The others were focusing on the problem at hand.

"Stealing six thousand shoulder-fireds from Dark Fiber is not going to be a walk in the park," Winter said.

"That's exactly why I favor another solution," his father said. "Once we find out where they're stored, we simply destroy them. A giant pillory. For example, with a few Hellfire missiles."

"Wait a minute. What about the collateral damage, John?" Sander asked.

His father's age-old problem, Luke thought. John Carney cared nothing about collateral damage. That was precisely where he differed from the other leaders. Always a new idea, never thought through.

"Precise strikes," John said. "We get everyone out of there before the strike. That would be the cleanest."

"This is sounding more and more complicated," Sander said.

"You light up the shoulder-fired missiles from above, you'll have some of them launching spontaneously," Luke put in. Maybe this argument would silence his father.

"Plus we would be tagged as bomb throwers," Winter said. "Just what we're trying to get away from, with this operation. Now that we've got our own political party, we said we would clean up our act. If we can steal the missiles and hand them over intact, I'd much prefer that approach."

"Let's walk through this," his father said. "Because stealing them is close to impossible, if you ask me. Dark Fiber is an awfully tough bunch. I'd like to go with a lower-risk approach."

"I worry about the risk to our reputation with missiles raining down out of the sky, then going off every which way, maybe killing folks," Winter said.

"John, you have to consider he has a point," Sander said. "Although it does partly depend on where they're being stored. If they're in a cave or underground somewhere, John's idea won't work anyway. If they're in some isolated barn out in the country, no innocent people get hurt."

"We want to wipe out Dark Fiber, right?" his father went on. "One of our primary aims is to end the disruption in the food industry and get rid of these goddamned ration coupons."

"Right," Winter said.

"So we document the attack, while destroying the missiles, and we make sure the responsible members of Dark Fiber get caught, right up at the highest levels. That's the surest way of putting them in the death chamber for the attacks back in 2019."

"They might already be moving the missiles," Winter pointed out. "December tenth is just around the corner."

"We need to act quickly," Sander agreed.

"Stopping them through some trickery is probably impossible and, in the best case, very high risk," his father countered. "If you fail, you have nothing. Planes start getting shot out of the sky, Dark Fiber doesn't get caught, and maybe we get the blame. We're back to square one, with the militias ruling the roads under the comfortable protection of the major parties."

"I see it differently," Winter said. "We make a foolproof plan to steal the missiles as soon as possible, making sure they can't carry out a single attack. We're capable of an operation like that. We've done more complex ones. We document the whole thing so March22 gets the credit while Dark Fiber gets the blame, and we hand over the missiles to Homeland Security. We're heroes. Just like Luke said."

"Yes," Luke said simply.

"Returning the missiles would show our goodwill," Sander said. "But we have to make sure it's clear we stole them from those Dark Fiber fanatics."

"Piece of cake," Luke said. "I've got their emails going back three years. It's all there."

"You guys are busy building sand castles without good sand," his father said. "We don't know where they are. We don't have any idea how to steal them. March22 could easily get caught red-handed with a few truckloads of shoulder-fired missiles when the authorities move in. Is that what you want to see on TV?"

"It's three to one, John," Sander said quietly. "Have more faith in our own men to do a good job. You're outvoted."

"I'm not giving up so quickly," his father said. "You guys are deluded and staking our whole future on this. Everything we've worked for. It's too dangerous."

"Luke, report back after you've learned more from Matt," Sander said. "That Dark Fiber woman he's on the run with seems to be the key right now."

"Sure thing," Luke said.

The worrisome thing is, Luke thought after cutting the connection and permanently deleting the network they had used, John Carney was still a renegade within the group of leaders, even after all his many fuckups. The man didn't learn from his mistakes.

CHAPTER 45

JEFFERS ADMITS DEADLY DRONE STRIKE ON MISSOURI FARM
Several Missing, Presumed Dead

After an exclusive ABC News report, President James Jeffers has admitted that one deadly drone strike has occurred in the U.S. This contradicts previous assurances by the administration. On November 16, at least six Hellfire missiles were fired from Homeland Security drones. The missiles reportedly destroyed a hog farm near Warrenville, Missouri, killing an unknown number of people.

The hog farm belonged to Melvin and Philip Grady, both 63, who are now fugitives and are suspected of harboring escaped convicts on their property. The security agency has publicly stated it was operating on information that the hog houses were booby-trapped. When the farmers, who are brothers, shot down a small Homeland Security reconnaissance drone in their yard, government drone controllers acted on orders to attack the farm.

According to the farmers, the government's missile strikes destroyed the hog houses and approximately 12,000 animals. The number of people in the hog houses at the time of the strike has not been verified, but six individuals are listed as missing and presumed dead.

A unit of soldiers from the nearby Fort Leonard Wood army base was dispatched to the scene to assess the damage. One vehicle was destroyed as it approached one of the ruined structures. The five soldiers in the vehicle died at the scene.

"They rigged redundant booby traps," said an informed government source speaking on the condition of anonymity.

Until yesterday's TV interview with ABC News, Melvin and Philip Grady had been presumed dead. In the interview, Melvin Grady admitted to being a member of the terrorist organization, March22. The Gradys also launched the Prove Your Patriotism — Eat Bacon! movement, which has a Facebook page with more than one million likes.

The Gradys have been added to Homeland Security's most wanted list for the deaths of the five soldiers, allegedly harboring escaped convicts and sabotaging a government reconnaissance operation.

"We deplore the use of missiles against American citizens in the homeland, for any reason," said Orson Twillers of the American Civil Liberties Union. The ACLU filed a lawsuit today against Homeland Security to end the deployment of drones over America.

March22 has been accused of firing missiles at military tanks and other vehicles at the Battle of San Francisco Airport on November 23. More than thirty soldiers died in that battle, for which no group has claimed responsibility.

After two years of flight restrictions, the administration has announced that the Homeland Security drones will be used to help guarantee the safety of commercial aviation resuming December 10.

CHAPTER 46

STURGIS, MICHIGAN
DECEMBER 7, 2021—6 AM

THE RATTLING AIR ventilator in the motel kept Matt awake despite his exhaustion. The room had two double beds, and Claire appeared to have gone right to sleep. In the dim light, he thought of Raine and of what he was going to tell her. If March22 wanted him and Claire to steal those missiles, it was going to be a dangerous operation, even if March22 provided local help.

But then everything was dangerous, now. Everywhere was dangerous.

Claire had paid sixty dollars cash for the room, and she said the hotel clerk hadn't asked for identification. Matt hadn't seen any cameras when he got out of the Impala and snuck into the room, but that didn't mean there weren't any. He'd worn his new Detroit Lions cap with the brim pulled low, and kept his head down. If the authorities nabbed them here, should they shoot their way out? He was considered armed and dangerous, a *predator,* and they wouldn't try to take him on with just two officers. It sounded like a good way to die.

Sleep finally came at some point, a sweaty, frazzled, unsatisfying sleep in which he never felt quite unconscious. He woke to the sound of the rattling air clicking on. Sun streamed through cracks in the drawn curtains that felt like plastic when he reached across to touch them. He went to the sink and washed, wishing he had a toothbrush. He hesitated, then used Claire's — what the hell. Looking at himself in the mirror, he noticed the lines around his eyes and mouth, the three-day scruff on his chin and sideburns, the exhaustion in his eyes. He looked older than nineteen.

When he came out of the shower with a towel wrapped around his waist, Claire was dressed and sitting on the side of her bed, studying her Jetlink. She smiled.

"Hungry?"

"Starving. What about ordering pizza?"

"That should work," she said. "Get dressed while I take care of it. Any preferences?"

Red hair and green eyes, Matt thought.

"Just get two different kinds," he said. "Then we can share."

They had the TV wall on while waiting for the pizza, but Matt wasn't interested in any of the shows. Claire maximized one window after another, never staying more than thirty seconds on one.

"I was thinking about that attack you said your leaders are planning," he said. "I was thinking someone has to stop them."

Claire looked at him. "They're totally ruthless. Nobody can stop those guys. They're organized, smart, and fanatical. Once they decide to do something, it's as good as already done."

"You don't think we'd have a chance?"

There was a lot that Claire didn't know. She didn't know about Luke's hacking skills, for example, or their communications link. She knew March22 had stolen government drones, since that was public knowledge, but she didn't know how they could be used to support an operation. Matt had seen it firsthand.

"Not a chance in hell," Claire said.

"Why not? Explain it so I can understand."

"Mainly because I know those guys. They don't make mistakes. That's why Dark Fiber is the biggest and most powerful militia, and rolling in money."

"How many simultaneous attacks was it in 2019 when they shot down those planes?"

"Twelve. Something like a thousand people died, even though two of the planes were just cargo."

"So this time you think it'll be less? Like maybe six planes?"

"Knowing those guys, they'll make it twice as many, not half as many."

Matt said nothing, watching her face. She wasn't looking at the TV wall now. Slowly she turned to meet his gaze with her intense brown eyes. A little of the old Claire had come back.

"We have to try, don't we?"

"I want to try," Matt said. "But we won't be alone. We'll have March22 supporting us."

"Supporting us how?"

"People, weapons, vehicles. Like what if, say, we managed to find out where the missiles are and stole them?"

"We'll never get them out of there."

"Let's just say we manage it somehow. Then we've got to get them on trucks, right? We'll have trucks. We'll have manpower. We'll have computer support and firepower and our asses covered."

"You think March22 can do all that?"

"I don't think so, I know it," Matt said.

"You thought they would come and rescue you, too."

He shrugged. He couldn't very well tell her the only reason he hadn't been rescued was because they'd ordered him to stay. He wasn't about to tell her they had demanded that he obtain information from her. Surprisingly, he'd already accomplished some of it. It felt good to be out of that safe house.

"We have good people. We have good hacking capabilities. We have lots of people all over, trained and ready."

"Including Iowa?"

"Is that where they are?"

Claire nodded. "One of the leaders runs a family business, like tractor parts, combines, farm machinery. They have warehouses. The missiles are in one of the warehouses. Or at least they were."

"How do you know this?"

"They got drunk when two of them were in Ann Arbor three months ago. We have the alcohol business, you know, so they're all so convinced they can hold their liquor. A group of us, we were partying at one of the safe houses. The guy with the farm implement business in Iowa started blabbing. Everyone in the room was a trusted lieutenant, you know, so I guess he didn't think too much of it."

"What's that guy's name?"

"I only know his first name. Those guys only go by first names, like Thomas. I don't even know if they're real names."

"Doesn't matter. Thomas Paine, by the way. What's the other guy's first name?"

"Cedric."

"Okay, so where in Iowa?"

"That I don't know."

A knock came on the door. Matt drew his gun and went in the bathroom while Claire peeked through a crack in the curtains. With her own gun in her right hand and two fifty-dollar bills in her left, she spoke through the door.

"Who's there?"

"You ordered pizza?" said a male voice.

She opened the door a crack, pointing her gun at the lone man in the pizza uniform. The little chain wouldn't keep someone from busting in, but it could slow them down enough for her to fill them with lead.

"Set the pizzas on the ground," Claire said. "Here's your money. Keep the change."

"You have a nice day, too." The man spun around and walked away quickly.

While they ate their pizza and Claire watched TV, Matt channeled Luke.

The shoulder-fireds are in a warehouse somewhere in Iowa. Are you there, geek-head?

Is she cute?

Cut it out, Luke. Did you hear what I said before?

There are probably a thousand warehouses in Iowa. If not ten thousand.

Guy runs a family business, according to her. Tractor parts, combines, farm implements. His first name is Cedric, no last name revealed. Might not be a real name.

Ah, a puzzle, Luke said. *The kind of puzzle my computer loves.* After a short silence, during which Matt supposed his brother was thinking, Luke came back. *I have a single hit, which means we have localized our man.*

What, already? Where is he?

Head for Des Moines, junior. Pluess Farm Tech Corp. One headquarters building, four warehouses, three in one location, one in a separate location. Kyle Cedric Pluess is your man. He's the CEO, twenty-eight years old. It'll take you a day to get there, meanwhile I'll start learning more about the warehouses. Maybe get some plans and security codes, stuff like that.

What about support and logistics? If we can get into the right warehouse and steal the stuff, we're going to need a truck or two, and some men.

Does your girlfriend have any idea if all the stolen shoulder-fireds are stored in this location, or just some of them?

I'll ask her. Not sure if she knows that.

If yes, I can figure out the volume and organize the right number of trucks and men.

They'll have monster security, according to her.

No security is a match for me, Luke bragged.

I'll believe that when it's over.

Believe it. Now do you think you can get over there without getting yourself hosed?

We'll leave when it gets dark, drive all night. The only real challenge is getting across the Mississippi.

Why? It's just a river, Luke said.

Matt recalled crossing the river three weeks before. All the bridges had heavy security and were closed to private traffic. The kind a wanted man like Matt Carney wouldn't have a chance getting through.

Their one-car ferryboat had nearly been run down by a military barge cloaked in image-cancellation technology. They'd only seen it in time because Benjy's drone had picked up a vibration signature. Soldiers on the bow of the military barge had started shooting at them. Matt had taken out the two soldiers with his AR-15 assault rifle, one after the other, but not before their captain had taken a fatal round.

How the hell were they going to get across the river this time?

CHAPTER 47

STURGIS, MICHIGAN
DECEMBER 7, 2021—6:30 PM

MATT PULLED THE Lions cap low over his brow and followed Claire out the door to the Impala, which was parked in front of their room. She'd made a deal with the front desk, paying another thirty dollars to be allowed to stay till 6 p.m.

"We need to head south leaving this town," Claire said. "After ten miles we pick up Route 20, which will take us as far as South Bend, Indiana, without running into an Interstate."

"What happens at South Bend?"

"Then we have to jog south on Route 31 till we pick up Route 30. That gets us all the way across Indiana and into Illinois, south of Chicago, where it turns into Route 52. It's the most direct route to Iowa, keeping off the interstate."

Twenty minutes later they were cruising west on US Route 20. They traveled in silence, the dangers and challenges ahead of them weighing on Matt's mind. He tried to think of Raine, remembering suddenly that he'd meant to give her a call.

"I was wondering something," he said some time later, looking away from the lights of oncoming cars. The darkness in the Impala interior hid his blush. "You don't have to say anything if you don't want to. What exactly happened with that Black Widow dude back at Gram's house?"

"He got the jump on me while I was shooting the other two." Matt heard Claire breathing faster. His own heart started pounding at the memory. He'd been calm as the events unfolded, but the memory of it made him break out in a sweat. "He came out of nowhere, must've hit me over the head. Pistol-whipped me. The next thing I knew I was lying in the dirt with my pants off, and he was hanging over me with his schlong out."

"That must've been horrible. I'm really sorry."

"You don't have to be sorry, Matt. He obviously would've killed me afterwards. You saved my life."

"Just wish I'd got there sooner," he said huskily.

"He hit me again before I could grab his dick. He wanted me unconscious. I would've torn it right off for him, you know?"

"Jesus."

"That would've been a first. Well, the whole thing was a first for me. I mean being raped."

"Let's hope to hell it's the first and last time."

Claire was silent for a moment. "All I could think when he hit me that last time, because I didn't go unconscious, you know, just... paralyzed. I guess it was a kind of panic. All I could think was how I was going to kill him. I felt his big ugly thickness plowing into me, cutting me, hurting me. I'm no pansy when it comes to pain, you know, although pain down there was a new experience. I just focused on all the bullets I was going to fill him with. The way he was fucking me, I would fuck him back, only with greasy, smoking hot bullets. He violated my body, I would put holes in his body wherever I felt like it. I was going to perforate his body if it was the last thing I did."

"Man, what an experience," Matt said. "What a sick dude he was."

"I know you shot him, but I was a little incoherent at the time."

"I shot him all right. He went down."

"I hope you shot his dick off. Tell me you shot his dick off."

Across the dimness, Matt momentarily met her eyes. Part of him wanted to laugh, but it wasn't funny. The whole thing was the opposite of funny.

"He had his gun up. I didn't have the luxury. I had to kill him, not just stop him. Otherwise he would've returned fire for sure."

"I see," Claire said.

"At least he's dead."

"But the asshole didn't suffer."

"He couldn't have suffered long, the way he looked."

"That's a disappointment." Claire sighed. "But then, life is full of those, don't you think?"

In the silence that ensued, Matt thought back to when his father had been hauled off by the FBI, leaving him alone in the house with his alcoholic stepmother and her worthless kids. Worthless except for Benjy. The arrest had turned out to be a staged March22 operation to get his father out, a fact he hadn't known at the time. He'd been left with such a feeling of mourning, as if someone had died. His father's departure had left him feeling hopeless and alone.

Or when Raine had broken up with him, shocking him with a simple message while he journeyed to California to rescue her.

Raine had given up hope of ever seeing him again. She'd actually started shacking up with some guy from the university, she was so convinced it was hopeless. When he'd finally gotten the truth out of her, he'd felt like walking out into a cornfield and blowing his own head off.

The only thing that stopped him was that his father had given him a mission. He had to do it for his father. That mission was to save Raine.

Now, his father had handed him over to Dark Fiber so that they could kidnap him. What kind of a father did something so crazy?

Claire looked at him expectantly, but he didn't feel like telling her details about his disappointments. They hardly knew each other. Even if they'd saved each other's lives, he couldn't really confide in her.

An hour later, when they stopped for gas and Claire got out and left him alone in the car, Matt dialed Raine.

"Matt, where are you? I've been waiting and waiting for you to call."

"I'm safe," he said. "I'm sorry I didn't call. It's been a little hairy, the whole time. I miss you."

"When are you coming back? Are you still a captive? Did you escape?"

"I escaped, but Raine, you can't tell anyone about it. Just keep it to yourself, okay?"

"Sure, I can do that. I'm training every day. You should see my arms. You should see my shooting scores."

"I can't wait to have your arms around me."

"Oh, Matt, don't make me crazy."

"I hope it won't be too long."

"Don't get caught, that's all I ask. If you get caught, who knows when I'll see you again?"

"I'm being super careful, don't worry. Hey, I've got to go now." He saw Claire coming across the parking lot, stuffing change into her pocket.

"I love you, Matt."

"Love your bones, too." He disconnected as the door opened.

Why was he so itchy about Claire not knowing about Raine? They could've gone on talking even after Claire got back to the car. He thought about it as they drove away from the gas station. Some things were just private. Maybe he didn't want to share it because Raine was the most special thing he had.

"One thing I'm not clear about," Matt said as they drove on, puncturing the deep Illinois darkness with the Impala headlights. "You're basically turning on your own group. Like you're ready to betray them."

"My loyalty only goes up to a certain point," Claire said. "When I thought about the shoulder-fired missiles again, I said to myself, this new attack can't happen. If we can stop them, we have to do it. We have to try."

"What if they find out about it? What would they do to you?"

"Number one, they know by now that I'm gone. I started getting messages yesterday, even though I haven't answered any. Somehow, they found out we survived and they'll be looking for me. I have to be careful. Number two, what do you think they'd do?"

"They'd see you as a traitor, and also a threat," Matt said. "I guess we're not talking about life in prison."

She shook her head with a grim look, then said, "Hey, you were talking on the phone back there. Was that one of your March22 bosses, or were you wishing your father a good night?"

"It was a March22 person," he said. He laughed at the idea of wishing his father good night. He had no idea what he was going to say when they finally spoke again. *Did you ever think of asking me? Maybe you didn't feel like sharing your ideas with the leaders, but what about me? I'm your son, for God's sake.*

When he didn't elaborate, Claire scoffed, "So much for trusting me. I was just making conversation. Look, Matt, we decided to do this thing, and we need to trust each other. With our lives. I know I can trust you. I feel it. What about you?"

Claire's intense brown eyes searched his soul in the dimness. It felt good to hear her say she trusted him. The only people he had ever trusted were his father, Raine, and, most recently, Benjy from their travels across the country. He trusted Luke now, too.

Raine had betrayed his trust, but they'd straightened that out. When something like that happened, you talked about it and tried to put it behind you. He felt sure it wouldn't happen again.

Suddenly he knew Claire was right. She had sacrificed and given more than her share so far. He had shot her attacker dead, and then covered up Claire with his coat. If you couldn't trust a person after what he and Claire had been through in the last few days, you couldn't trust anyone.

"It was just my girlfriend," he said. "She's with me in March22. The last time I saw her was the day you guys kidnapped me."

"She's in Montana? What's her name?"

"Raine." Claire didn't need to know Raine's true location.

"That's a pretty name. I like that name. I never knew a Raine before."

"We've been together a long time."

"How long?"

"Four years."

Claire whistled. "Man, you're only nineteen and you've had the same girlfriend for four years? Respect, man."

Matt's breast filled with pride. He'd never thought of their relationship as an accomplishment. *I don't do boyfriends,* Claire had said. Maybe she would do boyfriends if the right one came along.

A little after five in the morning, while it was still dark, they stopped at a motel in Monmouth, Illinois, ten miles from the Mississippi River. He was exhausted, and it was too late to try and figure out a way of crossing. They could sleep all day. The crossing would have to wait till nightfall.

CHAPTER 48

AT THE MOTEL in Monmouth, Claire negotiated at the hotel desk while Matt waited in the car. His Lions cap pulled low, he slid from the car into the room behind Claire and closed the flimsy door. It felt as light as if it were fashioned of cardboard.

This room had no noisy ventilation system, but the shower had a network of brown cracks that made you think twice about touching them with your bare feet. He'd come so close to getting killed in the last three weeks, he decided not to worry about catching a foot fungus.

They ate the rest of the chips and beef jerky out of Gram's food bag while watching the TV wall, then immediately stretched out on separate beds.

"Let's sleep till sunset, okay?" Matt said across the dimness. When Claire didn't answer, he figured she was already asleep.

The early risers were already moving around in rooms around them. A shower running, doors slamming, engines starting. A few minutes later, the noise of someone revving his engine was so loud, it almost sounded as if the car were right in their room.

Claire let out a soft moan, and Matt's muscles went stiff as he caught his breath. He turned to look, and she lay on her side with her back to him. She moaned again and again. He couldn't tell if she was having a bad dream or was arousing herself. Which seemed pretty unlikely, after what she'd been through only three days ago. To his embarrassment, his body was responding as if it were Raine making those sounds. Nothing turned him on more than the sounds Raine made during their lovemaking. He shifted to his other side, faced the light-filled curtains with his eyes wide open, and tried not to listen as Claire moaned again.

When he could stand it no longer, Matt flopped on his back once more and said, "Hey, Claire, are you okay?"

"Hmm?" came the answer.

"You woke me up. I thought you were having a nightmare or something."

"Actually it was a nice kind of dream."

"Uh huh." He didn't know what to say to that.

"Hey, Matt, if you want to come over here..."

She didn't go on. She didn't need to. This was definitely a situation he was not prepared for. Last night he'd told her about Raine and their four years together. Was she putting him to a test?

"I don't think so," he said at last.

"Come on, Matt. I want you to come over here."

"Claire, I really like you, but I don't want to." It felt lame, somehow, but it was the truth. The whole discussion was making him blush.

"Please."

"No."

"Is it because of Raine?"

"Yes, actually."

"We could be dead by tomorrow."

"We're not going to get ourselves killed."

"I hope not, too, but it's possible."

"Even if you're right, it's not a reason. Not for me. But listen, I'm glad you're feeling healed up."

A few moments went by, as he stared at the ceiling, purposely not looking at Claire. This was the risk when you shared a room with a woman. Given their situation, they couldn't very well get separate rooms. He felt her eyes on him. Claire thought she could entice him with those brown eyes, but she was wrong.

"You're really lucky, you know," Claire said. "And Raine's lucky too. I hope I get to meet her."

"Maybe you will," he said. "What do you say we get some sleep?"

Mercifully, Claire let it go at that, and sleep came soon after. When he woke, he could tell by the light in the room that it was late afternoon. He heard the shower running. He blanked out the sound and closed his eyes again, relaxing his mind.

Luke, are you there?

Always, bro. I've got stuff you need to know.

Like what?

The first thing you need to know is, the Dark Fiber gang is hunting for Claire. They know you're driving that white Impala. I hope you've ditched it by now.

With a pang of terror, Matt thought of the car parked outside their door, in full view of anyone who drove into this lot.

They went to that safe house you were at, murdered the lady who lived there, and put two and two together. They've got friends in police departments all over, Matt. The police are helping them look for the car. Get far away from it ASAP.

Dark Fiber had killed Gram. The reality swept through him like darkness falling. The strong lady who had taken control after the rape, helped Claire, and then decisively gotten them out of there before more thugs came back. How in the world was he going to tell Claire?

Got you, Matt said. *They'd have to steal another vehicle.*

Second thing, Luke went on. *Our moron of a father is dead against the March22 operation.*

What? He's the one who handed my ass over to these idiots. How could he be against it?

I'll spare you the details. Just know that he's planning a rogue operation to stop you from doing what we're planning.

Christ, you mean he would literally put obstacles in my way? After handing my ass over to these people? The more he heard, the more it seemed like there were two different John Carneys: the one he'd grown up with — the man who'd taught him everything he knew and gotten him out of that hellhole in Chicago — and the one who'd cast him into a deadly situation hoping for the best. He wished everyone would stop messing with his brain.

Exactly, Luke said.

How could he do that to his own son?

One thing you've got to remember, Luke said. *March22 is more important to him than anything else, even us. His vision for March22. Always has been. Not very much of a team player, in my humble opinion. He was outvoted three to one, and he still goes off on his own tangent.*

Let's come back to that. What's the layout? What's the plan?

Where are you now?

Monmouth, Illinois. About ten miles east of the river.

How are you going to get across?

We'll have a look tonight. Not sure exactly.

Your friend Claire grew up with boats. If you can steal a boat, she would know how to drive it.

You looked her up?

I spend my whole day looking things up, and sometimes half the night, too. This brings me to the next morsel. Our friend Cedric in Des Moines. I figured out which warehouse the stolen missiles are stored in.

How the hell do you do this stuff?

It's a puzzle, like I said. People are careless with their email. I plowed through his emails of the last three years and deciphered their silly little code. I found out which warehouse the missiles are stored in, which corner of the warehouse, how they're packed, how heavy the crates are, and so on. All the missiles and launch assemblies are right there, buddy. I've got four trucks with five men each, ready to go.

What about Dad?

I put him on a false scent. Told him you were headed south out of Ann Arbor, let him think everything was going down in Alabama. But you know he's a sly fox. I can't exclude the possibility that he'll see through it.

You lied to him?

All the time. You should try it.

Matt was shocked. He couldn't remember ever lying to his father. Of course, things had changed now. Luke was probably right to be cagey.

This situation with Dad is really tearing me apart, Luke. You don't know him like I do. I grew up with him. We did all kinds of things together, and he's always been a good father to me. I never lied to him before. Up until yesterday, I'd have done just about anything for him.

We just have to be extra careful, that's all. You'll have to figure out all that stuff afterwards.

What about security at the warehouse?

Oh, this is going to be the fun part. You're going to have to put in some codes and shit on-site. Nothing too complicated. It's really important that this moves through you, so we can keep the local men squeaky clean and out of the loop. That way, when they get arrested, they'll know nothing about the bigger picture.

You make it sound easy.

Those Dark Fiber goons decided if they made the security state of the art, workers and shit would get suspicious about what they were storing, so they have the same security on the warehouse for the shoulder-fireds as they do for the others. The missiles are in a special storage area at the back with its own code, but that's no problem. They do have quite a lot of guards strolling around. We've been watching them for the last twelve hours. It's going to get hairy when we start the diversion.

If they've got all those guards, there's sure to be a firefight, Matt said. For some reason, he thought of Claire.

I need to know when this is going to go down, Luke said. *All of our people are working on their own preparations and waiting for the green light. Would tomorrow night suit you?* Luke asked as if it were an invitation to a casual dinner party.

Tomorrow night is fine as long as we can get across the river tonight. If we don't get across the river, we'll have to put it off for another night.

We can't put it off another night.

Why not?

They're preparing to ship some of the shoulder-fireds. Looks like your girlfriend was right on the money with her assessment.

She's not my girlfriend, idiot. He felt himself blushing at the memory of declining Claire's little invitation. Luke never needed to hear about that.

Where's that Impala?

Right outside our motel room door.

Jesus, Matt. Get the hell out of there. All it takes is one patrol car pulling in for a looksee, and you're toast. This whole operation is up for grabs without you and her. But especially you. You're my feet on the ground. Especially with this situation with Dad.

We're going, we're going. It's not dark yet. Claire was in the shower. We'll be leaving shortly.

In the shower? Tell me, is she hot?

Shut up, Luke.

No really, is she stacked? Tell me what she looks like naked. Have you slept with her yet?

You are such a pathetic, hard up geek, you know that? For your information, I wouldn't think of doing something like that to Raine.

What a prude you are, Luke said. *Check in when you've gotten across the river.*

Will do.

"Matt, I was talking to you, and you're, like, staring into space the whole time. Do you always do that?" Claire stood with her hand on one hip, staring at him. Her hair was combed wet, but she was dressed.

"Sorry, daydreaming, I guess," Matt said. "Listen, we've got to get out of here. The Impala was reported stolen. They're looking for it—and us. Dark Fiber and the police. It's way too hot, and we've got to get away from it right now. Are you ready to go?" He left out the part about Gram. Now was not the moment.

"How do you know it was reported stolen?"

He held up his Jetlink. "Secure link with March22. I just got a little update. That's what I was thinking about."

"How can we get around without a car?"

"I can hotwire a car."

Five minutes later, they snuck out the door. Claire left the car keys in the ignition of the Impala. She unlocked the doors, and ran the driver's window all the way down. Maybe someone would steal it and drive fifty miles in another direction.

Rather than walking through the parking lot and out to the street, they snuck to the back of the lot and cut through a straggly hedge, which led to a deserted strip mall. Darkness had descended on the town, and there was only one light in the middle of the strip. They kept to the vacant storefronts as Matt eyed the cars.

He was getting interested in a large Ford pickup when a man in coveralls and a jeans jacket came out of the electronics store opposite, the only store that appeared open, and unlocked the truck via remote control. When the man slowed his steps, staring right at them, Matt looked down, letting the cap brim hide his face. How guilty can a man act, he thought, feeling very stupid.

"What about a motorcycle?" Claire asked as they cut across a grassy ravine that led to another street. Matt had a bag of extra clips and drones over one shoulder. Claire had a bag with some clothes in it.

"I wouldn't know how to hotwire it," Matt said.

"Maybe between the two of us."

They walked to the other side of the street, and eyed a tall apartment building.

"No outdoor parking," Matt observed. "They must have an underground garage. That means good cover. Let's see if we can get in." Walking around the building, they found a ramp leading down into the garage.

It took half an hour, but finally the garage door opened as a car rounded the corner and rolled slowly down the ramp. Through the darkness they watched from just inside a stand of trees to the north of the building. When the car disappeared into the garage, Claire ran across the pavement and walked fast down the ramp, holding her body erect and looking straight ahead, like a person who belonged there.

Matt waited as the garage door closed. Claire would be inside now, hiding in the shadows as the recently arrived driver got out of his car and went inside. Or she was being attacked, and... Matt banished that thought from his mind. Claire had her gun, and she knew how to use it.

When the garage door opened again, Claire waved from the bottom of the ramp. He walked purposefully across the pavement and down the ramp while she waited inside.

"Look what we have here," Claire said, fingering the seat of a big Suzuki bike with a yellow lightning bolt decal on the gas tank.

He scanned the garage and estimated about twenty cars. The door to the building lobby lay about thirty feet to their left. A large metal storage cabinet stood against the wall, between the motorcycle and the door to the building lobby, and would give cover in case anyone walked in. The bigger danger was someone coming in the garage door, in which case they would probably be seen.

Claire was already down on her knees, tugging at some wires. "These are the ignition system," she said. "What do I have to do?"

At that moment, steps sounded outside the door to the lobby, then the door opened with a bang. Matt crouched in position behind the storage cabinet while Claire squeezed behind a pile of tires. If the person headed for any of the cars around the garage, they probably wouldn't be noticed in the dim light, keeping perfectly still.

The young man suddenly stood before them, his back to them. Wearing motorcycle leathers and boots, he prepared to get on the bike. Just their luck. His helmet sat balanced on the seat. Well, maybe there was another way to steal this bike Claire wanted so much.

Matt caught her eye, and he knew she understood his meaning.

He took two silent steps toward the young man, then cracked him over the head with the butt of his Beretta. Matt caught the man as he crumpled and fell where he stood.

"Get the damned keys," he whispered. The young man couldn't be much older than he was. He was sorry to knock the dude out, but this was sort of in the interest of national security, wasn't it? There was no way of telling how long he would be unconscious. Only a minute or two, maybe— and then he would surely call the police. Matt slipped the man's Jetlink off and put it in his pocket. That would slow him down once he woke up.

Claire rifled the man's pockets, came up with the keys, and got on the bike. "Let's get out of here."

Claire put the bike in gear, and they raced across the garage. It seemed like a whole minute passed as they waited for the garage door to rumble open. Matt stole a glance back at the figure on the floor. The dude hadn't moved yet as Claire took off up the ramp, throwing Matt back into the backrest. He tossed the Jetlink into some bushes as they hit the top of the ramp.

"Head west to the river," Matt shouted.

Claire certainly knew how to maneuver a bike, even a big one like this. They had no trouble finding Route 164. Broadway turned into the highway going out of town. Once into the cornfields, she sailed along at sixty miles an hour, and less than ten minutes later, they found themselves entering a tiny river town called Oquawka.

The road took them around a bend, and they passed block after block of small wooden houses set closely together. Bicycles, trampolines, and lawn furniture lay scattered around the yards, but few people were in evidence. Oquawka looked pretty quiet.

"Turn right, get off the main road. We've got to get down to the river," he said.

They headed down a residential street, past a park with a white stone monument to Abraham Lincoln and Steven Douglas. Matt read the gold lettering as they rolled by. He knew who Abe Lincoln was, but no idea about the other dude. History had been one of many subjects in which the teachers always handed back his tests with a big frown, as if they took his failure personally. Even the thought of picking up those heavy history textbooks used to make him drowsy.

Well, he was way beyond that now. He breathed in the Suzuki's tangy exhaust and let the vibrations ripple through his muscles. He felt alive.

After two more blocks, they glimpsed the murky water of the Mississippi, and turned right. Boats were moored all along this stretch of Marine Drive, which turned into North First Street.

After five or six more blocks, First Street curved to the right and started a gentle incline going away from the river.

At the back end of town, perhaps ten blocks uphill from the river, they came to a cemetery. The parking lot had quite a few cars in it, as if maybe a funeral were taking place inside the long, low building fifty feet down a brick pathway.

"We can ditch the bike here," Matt said. "Park it between those two cars."

"I hate to give up this bike," Claire said. She was breathing hard. "This was so fun."

"That guy must've called the police when he came to."

"This town is so small, I doubt they have any police."

She left the bike between two parked cars and they headed back toward the river on foot. The quiet street sloped gently downhill as they walked past quiet houses. Few lights were on, but here and there the blue glow of a TV wall shone through curtains.

"You know anything about boats?" Matt asked as they reached the waterfront. They turned left and headed back toward the section where all the boats were tied up. It was too early to steal one now, but they could have a look, and then decide where to spend the next few hours.

"My dad has a boat," Claire said. "We always had a boat, growing up. He taught me how to work on engines. I'd say I know a thing or two."

"Good, because that's about the only way to get across this river, unless you want to try swimming."

Claire smiled. "Skinny dipping with Matt Carney, I'd be up for that."

He stared, for a moment uncomprehending, because he was focused on the challenge of how to cross the river. Then he remembered the scene with her moaning in the motel room. It was like she wasn't giving up.

"Listen, Claire, it's really sweet of you to come on to me like this, but I already told you how I feel."

"I was only joking, Matt. Loosen up."

"Well, we're on a mission. We've got to defend each other. It could get really dicey and dangerous tonight, getting across this river."

"All right, I got the point. You sound like an old man sometimes."

That was the first time anyone had said *that* to him. He felt a little stiff and artificial as they walked slowly along the boats, like two young people out for a stroll, only one of them was like an *old man* sometimes. Was that what Claire thought of people who remained faithful to their partner?

Not that there were many people around to observe them. The whole town seemed deserted, even though it was only seven in the evening.

"Have I told you about the first time I crossed, a few weeks ago?"

"Tell me," Claire said.

"I was with my younger stepbrother, Benjy. He's fourteen. We had left Chicago and we had to get out to California as fast as possible."

"What for?"

"Well... to get Raine out of a dangerous situation she was in." He hadn't thought ahead, and didn't know how much he should divulge about March22's involvement in the Battle of San Francisco Airport, as it was now called on TV.

"Dangerous situation? What from?"

"Look, I wanted to tell you about crossing the river, okay? I'm like an *old man*. I have to stick to one subject at a time, otherwise I lose my train of thought. Maybe I can tell you about the rest another time. We've got to cross the river tonight, and it'd be good if you knew what we're up against."

"Whatever, Matt." Claire sounded sulky.

"Well, see, a lot of the bridges got blown up—"

"By Dark Fiber and other militias."

"Really?"

"Who did you think?"

"I... ah, actually thought that was March22, but—"

"March22, March22, what are you, some kind of March22 groupie? Why would March22 blow up bridges? We did it to make it easier to hijack trucks and steal their cargo. Duh!"

Claire was acting really weird, gesturing wildly, implying he was stupid. He hadn't really thought about who blew up all the bridges. He'd never asked anyone from March22 about those events, either. Now that she said it, it made sense that it had been the militias. He wished she would just let him tell the story.

"Anyway, all the bridges still standing are closed to private traffic. Super high security. Since Benjy and I were wanted by the police, we had to stay away from them anyway."

"What was he wanted for? He's only fourteen, you said."

"They thought I kidnapped him. He's officially listed as missing, kidnapped. I'm supposedly the kidnapper."

"Really?"

"It was just a story my stepmother made up. Benjy ran away right after I left. He caught up to me at a checkpoint outside Chicago, and in the end I had no choice but to let him come with me."

"Where is he now?"

"In a March22 training camp."

"Cool. So the two of you crossed the river together?"

"Yeah, we found this guy who had a ferry boat. We paid him to take us and the car on his boat, and he brought us across."

"Is that the end of the story?"

Matt scoffed. "It's just the beginning. You also have to know it's against about ten different laws to take a boat across the river."

"I saw that somewhere, but I never understood why."

"The military uses it for huge convoys of materiel going up and down. Apart from that, I don't know," Matt said.

"A lot of things got put in place where we didn't really get the reason, don't you think?"

"Like what?"

"Well, like those drones they've got flying around spying on us."

"We've got a few drones, too, you know."

Claire looked sharply at him. "Stealing a thousand drones out of the sky makes stealing a few shoulder-fired missiles and launch assemblies look like small potatoes."

"I didn't have anything to do with it, but I know the people who pulled it off."

"You do?" Claire said.

"I know them pretty well in fact." If she only knew it had been his twin brother, the super-geek.

Claire had stopped. Matt saw her eyeing a long, low motorboat with a small pilothouse, big enough for one or two people. A huge engine hung off the back, and there was about fifteen feet of space between the pilothouse and the stern.

"This looks exactly like the boat my dad has," Claire said. "It's the same engine."

"You'd know how to start it?" Matt looked around, but nobody was anywhere near them. One man a hundred feet down the street was walking slowly toward them, smoking, and looking up at the sky. "We've got to keep moving," he said.

"That's our boat," Claire said, starting to walk again. "You know what I was thinking?"

"I'm not sure I want to know."

"We come back here at three in the morning, right? We put the bike on the boat."

"I knew you were going to say that."

"No, wait. Anyone looking for that bike would be on this side of the river. The police would never look for it on the other side, right, since no one can cross the river?"

"We're not taking the risk," Matt said.

CHAPTER 49

MONMOUTH, ILLINOIS
DECEMBER 8, 2021—10 PM

"WE FOUND THEM," Paine reported. He stood in a gas station in Monmouth, Illinois. Three local Black Fiber men waited in his car.

"Where?" Hutch asked.

"Western Illinois. The cops found the old lady's car, stolen. They contacted me. They also had a report of a Suzuki 850 being stolen here."

"So?"

"Claire Tenneman loves bikes. This is a small town. Somebody saw the Suzuki headed west out of town with a woman driving and a male passenger. It's got to be her."

"Who saw them?"

"The brother of the guy whose bike got stolen. The bike has a yellow lightning bolt on the gas tank. He saw it and called his brother. His brother had been knocked out, didn't see the attackers. They called the police, and the cops told me."

"That does sound like our Claire," Hutch said.

"Now, west of here, there's nothing," Paine said. "Nothing but the Mississippi River, really. They're probably going to try to cross and head west."

"Sounds like that bitch really has gone rogue," Hutch said.

"I'm lining up some more help. On the river, there's a couple more little towns, and we're going to ask around till we find them."

"I'll inform Cedric," Hutch said. "Keep in touch."

WHEN HE GOT back to the car, Paine found it filled with the sweet fumes of high-grade marijuana. All three men were also guzzling beer out of cans.

"Damn it, this is a rental," Paine said, holding his door open to air out the car. "Besides, we've got a job to do."

"You're the designated driver," said Victor, the man in front, as he passed the joint to one of the guys in back. "Feel free to join in, though."

"You guys know anybody in Oquawka?" Paine asked, getting in. He ran down the two front windows and started moving.

"Oquawka?" croaked one of the guys in back. "What the hell's that?"

"Over on the river, limp dick," said the other man in back.

"I know some guys over there," Victor said. "What's up?"

"Our girl was spotted leaving Monmouth on Route 164 headed west. They're going to cross the river. The only town over there for ten miles north or south is Oquawka."

"Oquawka, Oquawka." The two guys in the back were chanting and giggling.

"Let me make a call," Victor said.

"Suzuki 850 with a lightning bolt on the gas tank," Paine said. "Yellow lightning bolt."

"Oquawka's not very big," Victor said. Then he spoke into his Jetlink.

After less than fifteen minutes driving through cornfields, they were cruising down the main street of tiny Oquawka and looking at a line of tied-up boats. Opposite the boats, a row of dingy bars and probably a whorehouse or two, from the look of it, threw feeble light on the street. A few men stood outside one of the bars, smoking and eyeing them. They circled the town twice in five minutes, slowly driving up and down residential streets. The whole town was only eight streets wide, with a big cemetery on higher ground at the eastern end.

"I've seen three bikes, but no Suzuki 850," Victor said.

"Oquawka," chanted the men in the back seat. "Man, I'm hungry," one added. "Where could we get some hamburgers and fries?"

"Yeah, man," the other said.

"Are those guys fit to shoot?" Paine asked.

"They're good," Victor said. "Look, there's our backup."

A red pickup stood parked in front of the bar with two men standing out front. Paine pulled in behind it, and the four men got out.

After introductions were made, he agreed that the others could go in to the bar and get some food to go. At this hour, nobody would be foolish enough to try and cross the river, let alone steal a boat. Interestingly, this bar didn't seem to have a security guard. This place was really out in the sticks.

While the others got the food, Paine decided to see if he could find out anything from these locals standing outside. He approached a man in a Caterpillar cap.

"How you doing?"

"Just fine, and yourself?" The man stared back with reddened eyes.

Paine gazed out over the boats. "Looking for someone. Guy and a girl on a big Suzuki 850. Lightning bolt painted on the gas tank."

The man blew out a rope of smoke. "I seen 'em. Came along here lookin' at the boats."

"When was this exactly?"

"You some kinda cop or somethin'?"

"No, but it's my bike," Paine said. "My brother gets his kicks that way."

"I hear you," the man said. "Guess it was maybe an hour ago."

"You said they were looking at the boats?"

"Ain't much else to look at."

Paine checked up and down the street, making sure the Suzuki wasn't parked somewhere and he'd missed it. If they had been checking out the boats, they might try to cross the river here. "You see which way they went?"

The man pointed off to the north. "They took a right on Schuyler Street, right there. That'll take 'em right outta town."

"He knows what I'm going to do when I catch him," Paine said.

"Bikes're a real turn-on for chicks, ain't it so?" the man said, a sly smile curving his lips. "Only thing is, your brother let his girl drive. Prob'ly the only reason I noticed 'em in the first place."

Paine nodded. "He's funny like that."

"Oh, she knew how to handle a bike, I could see that."

When the other men came out of the bar with bags of burgers and fries, Paine gave orders.

"We're heading up the river to Keithsburg," he said. "We'll lead the way. Stay together. Any of you guys know anyone in Keithsburg?"

One of the guys from the red truck piped up. "I got a coupla friends over there."

"Give them a call," Paine said. "Ask them if they've seen the bike."

Twenty minutes later, Keithsburg turned out to be half as big as Oquawka. They crisscrossed the town in two vehicles, Victor keeping in touch with the men in the red truck by phone. None of the men's friends had seen the bike. Paine interrupted two men arguing over ration coupons to ask if they'd seen the Suzuki. One of the men pulled a hunting knife from the sheath on his belt and stared at him with wild eyes.

"We ain't seen no motorcycle," the other man said.

After Keithsburg, as the darkness deepened, they headed another ten miles upriver to New Boston, an equally small village perched on the riverbank. Paine made two enquiries, but no one had seen the bike.

This search party was turning into a major pain in the ass with a shitload of driving around on empty roads in empty towns. It might be his imagination, but the other five men were beginning to eye him with annoyance. Who would've thought Claire Tenneman and that stuck-up March22 punk, Matt Carney, could create so much trouble?

"We're headed back to Oquawka," he said, getting back in the car. The only place the Suzuki had been seen was there. Maybe they hadn't left the town at all. With no prompting, the man wearing the Caterpillar cap had given a believable description of what could've been Claire and Carney casing the boats. Their best bet was to head back there and keep an eye on the waterfront.

Halfway back to Oquawka, Victor's phone buzzed. "Yeah, Justin?" Victor listened for half a minute, then hung up. "That was one of my good buddies in Oquawka. He only heard my message now. He lives up by the cemetery and saw the bike riding by up there."

"The cemetery?" Paine echoed.

By the time they arrived, it was almost one in the morning. The grumbling in the back seat had stopped, but maybe those two had gone to sleep. Victor pointed the way, a quick turn off Route 164. Then they were gliding by a large, dark graveyard filled with headstones and little private mausoleums that, from a distance, looked like marble outhouses.

Paine pulled over at the curb, gazing across the darkened space. "Anybody here got a drone?"

After a minute, he had provided images of Matt Carney and Claire Tenneman to the two drones the men carried. They released the drones to search the cemetery, and got out to stretch their legs.

PART 3

CHAPTER 50

OQUAWKA, ILLINOIS
DECEMBER 9, 2021—1 AM

"OH, SHIT," CLAIRE said.

"Who are they?"

They sat in the middle of the cemetery. Matt hadn't gotten bored watching the stars, even with long silences in between bits of conversation. Claire had wept when he told her about Gram. No matter what he said, she felt responsible. As they went on talking about it, even though Black Widow had carried out the attack, he'd sensed a new level of anger and determination from her to destroy Black Fiber and to turn her back on militias forever. Life was too fragile when people you cared about were murdered. They agreed completely on that point.

Two cars had stopped on the street three hundred feet away, and Claire peered at the men getting out. Matt counted six. The men stayed standing by their cars, studying their Jetlinks.

"I only recognize one. It's Thomas, one of the Dark Fiber leaders. This is very bad."

"Thomas Paine. Is it your Jetlink? Can they track you?"

"I've been powered off for hours."

"So, they can't track you?"

"I bet they found the Impala and started asking around. Someone from Dark Fiber must live in this little town. Maybe the motorcycle got reported. Maybe someone saw us heading this way."

"If I were them, I'd be sending a couple of drones around the cemetery."

"You're right. Come on," Claire said. Matt rose from the gravestone he'd been sitting on and followed her on hands and knees. If drones were searching the cemetery, they were sure to be found. They kept low, the rows of grave markers hiding them from the men.

Matt knew what Claire had in mind, and he didn't like it. She wanted to make a run for it. But it was either that, or try to shoot six men across a dark graveyard. They might hit two or three, but the others would scatter and find good cover, and their chances of survival would sink dramatically.

The men were still standing in a group studying their Jetlinks when Matt and Claire reached the cemetery parking lot.

"Are you ready?" she said.

"Go."

Claire threw her leg over the seat and switched the bike on. Matt barely had time to settle in the seat behind her before she peeled out onto the grass. All the men stood ramrod straight, staring at them. Claire sped across the park headed south, away from the Dark Fiber group, running hard between picnic tables and trash cans as the men ran to their cars.

Even over the sound of the motorcycle, Matt heard them shouting, then the sound of rubber biting into pavement and engines screaming. With a bang, one of the Dark Fiber cars crashed into the other, but then both were executing U-turns in the road along the east perimeter of the cemetery.

Claire hit the road at thirty mph and hung a right onto one of the streets that led down to the water, accelerating sharply. The first block had only six houses, and she took the first left. Looking back, Matt saw the first Dark Fiber car coming around the corner behind them. He also saw a drone over his right shoulder. He couldn't do anything about the car, but he could sure take care of that drone. On the next straightaway, in one graceful movement, he raised his slingshot and let a one-inch ball bearing fly. The drone splintered into eight or ten pieces on impact.

"Speed it up, lose them!" he yelled.

She turned at every corner, zigzagging down to the waterfront. Matt looked for other drones, but saw none. Momentarily, they'd lost the cars. He had no doubt Dark Fiber would quickly catch up with them in this tiny town.

They came out at the waterfront about one block north of the boats, and Claire turned left. Ten seconds later, she slowed and gauged the distance from the concrete sidewalk to the stern of the boat.

"No!" Matt yelled.

Claire ignored him, gunned the engine as she came out of her turn, and aimed for the boat. The sidewalk was probably three feet above the stern of the boat. They took off from the edge smoothly. He gripped the chrome bars under his thighs with both hands, holding his breath. In the water below he saw the psychedelic swirls of leaked fuel, and a duck started quacking and flapping. The rear tire of the bike clipped the stern rail of the boat, throwing the front end down. Then it was all a chaos of bumping and twisting and smashing against hard surfaces. He was aware of his shoulder striking the wall of the pilothouse. When he opened his eyes, he saw ropes lying in coils, and the hot motorcycle pinning his leg. Claire lay on her stomach on the other side of it.

"Are you okay?" Matt asked. Claire groaned. Bruised and battered, he lifted the bike up enough to scramble out. "Stay low. Maybe they won't see us."

Headlights appeared two blocks up the street. Two cars.

"Quick, you untie us," Claire said.

Matt took one look at the knots on the cleats, and unsheathed his hunting knife while Claire yanked on the starting cord. The engine didn't start.

The cars moved slowly up the street toward them. Matt was sure they hadn't been seen, but it wouldn't be much longer.

Claire ran to the pilothouse. "Damn, it's locked."

"Shoot it," Matt said. Both ropes were cut. He used a gaff to push the boat out away from the wall. He pushed as hard as he could, and the boat moved out through the water. Anything for a little distance.

Claire's shot echoed off the storefronts. Within three seconds, the two cars hit the gas and floored it, heading their way.

In the pilothouse, Claire pulled out the choke, then ran back to the engine and yanked the cord again. On the second try, the engine roared. She sprinted back to the pilothouse, and then the boat leapt forward, headed out into the river. The men had come to a screaming stop on the dock just opposite and were pouring out of their cars. Matt saw guns in their hands.

"Get ready for shooting," he yelled, and drew his own gun. He clicked the safety off and took aim. They were a hundred feet out and churning steadily away from the dock. "Compensate for that wind."

"Don't tell me how to shoot," Claire yelled.

He and Claire hunkered on either side of the boat, staying low, firing off shots under the cover of the prow. The corners were reinforced with extra fiberglass supports, and offered more stopping power. Holes opened in the stern of the boat as the men's bullets clustered in the center. Maybe they were aiming at the engine.

Matt squeezed off two shots, targeting at a man in a red jacket shooting an assault rifle. He was the only one with an assault rifle. The others all had pistols. The man was thrown backward, and fell to the ground. The Dark Fiber men fell one after another as Matt and Claire picked them off. Over the whine of the engine, Matt heard one man screaming. The last two scurried behind the cars, diving for cover.

When the shooting stopped, Matt found Claire lying face down on the floor on the piles of ropes, her body quaking.

"Hey, are you hit?" He scrambled over, still keeping low, and lifted her. No blood. She opened her eyes and stretched out her arms. In a crouch, he hugged her.

They were both wet from random waves slopping over the sides, and he felt her warmth. Scanning around them, he saw only dark water, no other boats upriver or downriver. For the moment, as the boat motored straight out into the river, they were safe. She rested her head in the crook of his neck and quieted. "I thought you were hit for a minute there."

"I'm okay. Usually I don't go to pieces in a fight. This was—"

"Maybe it's because those were your own people."

Claire didn't answer, just looked at the floor.

Less than a minute later, with Claire standing at the wheel in the pilothouse, the engine sputtered. It coughed a few times, then died. Matt peered out across the water again, checking for other boats. The last time he'd crossed this river, they'd nearly been run down by a string of army barges. Nothing was moving out here, tonight, luckily, and the chilly breeze on his face was peacefully quiet without the engine.

Claire yanked on the cord over and over. After five or six tries, she went back to the pilothouse to fiddle with something, then tried again.

"They must've hit something," she said. "It's not flooded. You don't smell gas, do you? I'm not sure I can get it started again."

"This is bad." They were out in the middle of the river, and the current was pulling them southward at an alarming pace. The boat had turned in the water and faced upriver. It felt like they were going backward, which made him feel queasy and helpless. What was worse, they might drift back to the Illinois side, where Dark Fiber thugs might be waiting with their guns. Or they might float down as far as the next lock and crash into it.

"Luke," he said out loud, without thinking, and closed his eyes to concentrate.

"What? Who's Luke?" Claire said, still tinkering with the engine.

Hey, buddy, we're in trouble here. I need your help, real fast.

You and your hot babe forget to use a condom? Some things I just can't help with.

I'm serious, Luke. We just left the Illinois side in a boat. We were taking fire from some Dark Fiber idiots, and they shot out our motor. We're drifting downriver.

Not good on the mighty Mississippi, Luke agreed. *Where did you put in?*

Place called Oquawka. Matt spelled it out.

Sounds like a duck in heat, Luke said. *Give me a minute.*

"Matt, I'm talking to you," Claire said. "You're just sitting there staring into space again. This is not the time for daydreaming."

"Sorry, I was working on a solution."

"I can't get this engine started. I checked the fuel line and it's intact. It also has plenty of gas. They hit something else, something inside."

"I guess if they had hit the fuel line, it might've exploded."

"I guess so. Anyway, it didn't blow up."

"Listen, I need a moment to think in peace. You keep watch for other boats and make sure we don't get run down."

"We're drifting God knows where and he wants to think in peace," Claire said. She turned her back and walked to the rail to scan for other traffic.

Are you there, junior? Your current is pulling you downriver at 1.2 miles an hour. There's a bunch of islands and shit, but if you're really in the channel, you should be able to stay clear.

I see an island. We're missing it.

Okay, here's what I'm working on. Sander knows a guy with a boat in a place called Keokuk. I know it sounds like an anagram of Oquawka, but it's not. It's in Iowa, fifteen miles downriver from you. Sander's trying to get hold of him. If we can get that guy out of bed, he'll find you and lash on. Then he can bring you in on the Iowa side.

And, if he can't?

You're so impatient, Matt. Have faith in our Iowa organization. Ah, there he is now. Sander reached him. The guy is getting dressed. He'll be out on the river in fifteen, looking for you.

What's this guy's name? What's his boat look like?

He'll find you, Matt, stop worrying. He'll come upriver looking for you, by the way. He's not gonna wait all night for you to drift down to Keokuk. You're probably the only thing floating helplessly downriver this morning. Good-looking flotsam, that's what we'll call you from now on.

Very funny.

You do know how to swim, don't you?

I was wondering something else, Matt said. *What do you know about our mother?*

What do you wanna know?

Like where does she live? After a moment he added, *And what's she like, anyway?*

She's stupid, like you. Anything else?

Come on, what do you mean?

How intelligent can a person be to separate identical twins? Luke said. *Did our father tell you the story?*

He said they had some kind of big fight, and she decided to leave with both of us. Take us away somewhere. Just before she left, I came down with meningitis or something and had to go to the hospital. She left anyway, but she only took you. We've been separated since we were two.

I rest my case, Luke said.

What was the big fight about? Why'd she leave him?

Politics, what else? Dad was already going radical seventeen years ago when this happened. She got scared.

How can politics get scary?

He tossed a few bombs in his time, in case you were too blind to see.

Our father?

A real terrorist. Now a grownup terrorist, but still a terrorist. Mom didn't think that set a good example for the kids. She voted with her feet.

Sounds like you see her side better than his, but here you are working for him.

Wrong, wrong, wrong.

Aren't you working for March22? Did I misunderstand something?

Something pretty basic actually. He works for me, not the other way around. I don't speak to the idiot.

What?

Why don't you stop deluding yourself, junior?

I knew you guys weren't on speaking terms, but you said he works for you?

You heard it right.

"Matt, there are no boats, and we're just drifting down this river. Don't you think we should try and swim it?"

"No way," Matt said. "The river could very easily do Dark Fiber's job for them. I'm not joking now. We have to wait."

"Wait for what? A miracle? This current is so strong it'll pull us all the way to New Orleans. It's not even very far."

She meant the Iowa side of the river wasn't far. Probably no more than five hundred feet. But the current was strong, and filled with strange eddies and whirlpools that could drag a swimmer down. They certainly couldn't call for help if one of them floundered.

"Not a chance. It's too dangerous."

"I'm going to try." Claire started taking off her jacket.

"Claire, no, wait." Matt stood up. "There's a boat downriver that's going to help us out."

"What boat? What are you talking about?"

"In Keokuk, Iowa, fifteen miles downriver. There's a guy getting in his boat right now. He's going to come up and meet us as we drift down, and he's going to tie on and pull us in."

"Who is this guy? How do you know this?"

"I just arranged it, okay? It's a March22 guy."

"How did you just arrange it? I don't understand."

Matt put his hands on Claire's shoulders to calm her. He looked into her fiery brown eyes. The boat had turned sideways in the water now. They were drifting down the river sideways. It was enough to send anyone into a panic. Because he knew the rescue was already in progress, he was feeling calm.

"The current is so strong, it'll keep us in the channel," he went on. "He'll be out there with his boat, waiting for us. It's all taken care of."

"But how, Matt? I was watching you. You didn't even look at your Jetlink."

He hadn't told anyone about his special communications link with Luke. He hadn't even confided it to Raine. The problem was that it made him feel like a freak. No one understood how a thing like that could work, not even Luke, who had been researching the question since they discovered it less than three weeks ago. Most identical twins had some special link that made them think in tandem. Identical twins growing up in different countries had been known to marry on the same day, choose partners with the same name, choose the same careers, have children with the same names, and all without having any contact with each other. Other twins felt an identical pain when their twin in a different place was injured, just as Luke had experienced when Matt had been struck hard on the back.

Luke's theory was that their being separated at the age of two just at the moment when Matt was in the hospital with a case of meningitis had somehow activated a special link between their brains. At age fifteen, Luke's disease had begun to waste away his muscle fiber, but at the same time, his brain had taken off in a frenzy of new directions. One of them had been this special gift, according to Luke's theory.

It was all just a bunch of mumbo jumbo to Matt. The main thing was that it worked, and they could communicate.

Claire's wild look meant he had to tell her something. Otherwise, she was going to dive headfirst into the roiling waters.

"There's something I've never told anybody. If I tell you about it, you have to swear you'll never reveal it."

"We'll probably be dead before I could reveal it anyway, the way things are going," Claire said.

"Do you swear?"

"All right, I swear I'll keep your little secret. What is it, some newfangled device no one's ever seen before? Are you guys running a beta-test or something?"

"I have a twin brother," Matt said. "An identical twin."

"Whoa, does he have a girlfriend, too?" Claire asked.

Matt turned away. He walked to the railing and looked out across the river. Iowa looked so close, and yet remained stubbornly unreachable. Raine waited somewhere far away on the other side.

It bugged the hell out of him that Claire couldn't leave that topic alone.

"I'm sorry, Matt. I couldn't help it."

"It's all right."

He imagined Claire's face when she learned that Luke was a wheelchair-bound super-geek who talked through a voice synthesizer and happened to possess wicked hacking skills. She'd already had to digest Gram's murder tonight, a motorcycle crash, and a shootout with her own people. This definitely wasn't the time to tell her what Luke really looked like.

"We keep drifting down this river," Claire prodded. "a few minutes ago you said there's some boat down there that's going to tie on and pull us to safety."

"Yep, that's right."

"And you were telling me how you managed to arrange this when I so rudely interrupted. Your identical twin brother, Luke."

"We were separated when we were two years old," Matt said. "My mother wanted to kidnap us and run away from my father. The night she chose to do it, I got this super high fever and had to go to the hospital with meningitis. So then she took off just with Luke."

"Wow."

"Skip to the present. I didn't even know I had a twin until a few weeks ago."

"How could you not know?"

"Complicated family story," he explained. "Anyway, we were reunited a few weeks ago, age nineteen. Suddenly we're standing in front of each other, and he's talking to me."

"Luke?"

"Yeah, Luke. Only not talking normally. No sounds. More like words popping up in my brain."

"What do you mean, in your brain? You mean telepathy?"

"I guess you could call it that."

"You guys can talk to each other just with your brains?"

Matt couldn't help smiling. He knew it looked foolish, but it felt good to let go of the secret. It felt good to know his brain was good for something after all. Really good. "That's about what it is, yeah."

"That's a bunch of bullshit, is what it is," Claire said, one hand planted on her hip. She held out her other hand. "Come on, empty your pockets. Show it to me."

"Show what?"

"You must have some new kind of communication device. I want to see it."

"I don't have any special device. Just this." He held up his Jetlink.

At that very moment, Raine chose to make an appearance. He almost laughed at the timing of it. He turned away so Claire couldn't see her face.

"Hey, how are you?" Raine asked.

"A little wet, actually, but not bleeding."

"Wet? How come?"

"I'm on a boat in the middle of the Mississippi River. Oops, I probably shouldn't be saying that. These things aren't exactly secure."

"You got to the river?" When he nodded, Raine smiled excitedly. "Oh, Matt, that's fantastic. Are you coming back?"

"Soon I hope. There's something we've got to do first."

"We? Who are you with?"

"It's... ah, I don't think I should identify her on this line, Raine. We've got, like different sets of bad guys trying to kill us."

Raine grew serious. "It's okay, Matt, I understand. Just be careful, okay?"

"How's Benjy? Is he there with you?"

"We've had so many good talks, Matt. He's such a great kid, and I really had no idea what you went through to get out to California."

"Why, what else did he tell you?" She had talked about this a couple days ago, and he still didn't know how he felt about it.

Raine hesitated, obviously not knowing what she should reveal. "Let's talk about it when you get back, okay? I just want you to know... how much I admire your courage and your intelligence."

He gulped. Raine had never put him down for being dumb, like most people, but she had never openly praised his intelligence, either.

"What the hell did he go and tell you? He's probably making up half of it."

"I'm sure he didn't make up a thing, Matt. I love you."

"Me too."

They cut the connection at the same time. Then Matt realized Claire was behind him, looking over his shoulder.

"She's beautiful," Claire said.

"Oh, that's great. Now your image is probably on the call as well. Do you want them to track you?"

"I stayed hidden behind you. My image is not on the call."

Fifteen minutes later, Matt picked up the sound of a motor. They craned their necks looking downriver. The river's curve didn't allow them to see beyond a certain point five hundred feet away, where an island with trees at crazy angles blocked the view. Suddenly the dark form of a boat came into view from around the trees.

"That could be him," Matt said, getting up. He tried to ignore the funny way Claire was staring at him. Oh yeah, now you're gonna believe me, he thought. "Come on. Let's prepare some ropes."

The boat motored against the current toward them as they drifted slowly toward it.

"On a boat they're called *lines*," Claire said.

CHAPTER 51

"YOU'RE MATT, RIGHT?" yelled the giant in the black jacket and ski cap. Another man stood ready with a coiled rope in his hand. A coiled *line*.

"Yeah!"

Lines were thrown, and within a minute the two boats were lashed side by side, with the other man's engine churning the water. Claire went first, then Matt clambered over the railing. Suddenly he was shivering.

"You two come inside," the man said. He led them into his pilothouse, which was three times the size of the one on their boat. It wasn't exactly hot in here, but there were chairs, and they were out of the wind. "My name's Hank." He extended a huge gloved paw.

"Thanks for the rescue," Matt said. "Don't know what we would've done without you."

"I had my alarm set for four anyways," Hank said with a grin, checking his Jetlink. It was quarter to three.

"I can't believe this is happening," Claire said. She looked questioningly at Matt. "It's really true, isn't it?"

Hank had turned to work with the throttle and the wheel. His back was to them.

"We'll talk about it later," Matt said in a quiet voice. He got up and stood next to Hank to get away from her inquisitive eyes. They were pointed downriver again, the second man standing out on the bow, keeping watch. "Where are you taking us?"

"I'd say back to Keokuk. That's what I talked about with Sander," Hank said. "Unless you got other ideas."

"Anyplace on the Iowa side that's safe is good with me," Matt said. "We had some Dark Fiber idiots that sent us off with a hundred rounds from their guns. That's what did our engine in."

"So I heard," Hank said. "You're thinking they've got people on the Iowa side, too?"

"We know they do."

"We can handle them, if they show up," Hank said. "But I reckon they'll think you got straight across, and they'll start off looking for you upriver. Did they know you got stranded?"

"No, we killed three or four of them. Two ran for cover. We were too far out for them to see when it conked out."

"They'll assume you made it across up there. You can get some rest at my house. Sander thought you might need wheels, too."

"We've got a stolen motorcycle in our boat. You think they'd be looking for it on the Iowa side?"

"Why take a chance?" Hank said. "I'll line up some new wheels while you're resting. We'll get you some food, and you can be on your way by afternoon."

Matt sat with Claire while the boat continued down the river. All at once, lulled by the steady vibrations of the boat's engine, a wave of exhaustion swept over him, leaving him shivering again. By the time they finally got to Hank's house, he was just going through the motions of walking, carrying bags, closing doors. He didn't want food, just a bed. Since there was only one bed for the two of them, Matt ended up on a couch, rolled up in a blanket, with a pillow for his head. He could've slept on the floor if necessary.

CHAPTER 52

OQUAWKA, ILLINOIS
DECEMBER 9, 2021—3:30 AM

"WE LOST THEM, and four men in the process," Paine said on the secure link.

"You fuckwads," Pluess said. "Tell me what happened."

Paine described the search process briefly, then the chase from the cemetery down to the waterfront, and finally the gun battle as Claire and Matt had motored away across the river.

"You know what a good shot she is. We lost four men. Carney was shooting, too."

"Where the hell are they?" Pluess shouted. "Why the hell did they want to get across the river, anyway?"

"He's probably trying to get back to Montana."

"Why Montana?"

Pluess obviously had a lot on his mind. "He came from there. We grabbed him over there, remember?"

"What if you're wrong? What if they're headed here?"

Cedric had always been the most paranoid of the inner circle. His mind was constantly spinning doomsday scenarios the others didn't even think of. "Why would they head to Des Moines?"

"I'll give you one guess, Paine."

Cedric only called him by his last name when he was furious. "You're paranoid, Cedric, relax. She knows nothing. How would she know anything about Des Moines?"

"Those March22 bastards stole over a thousand drones from the US fucking army," Pluess retorted. "I wouldn't put it past them to know more about us than we'd like to believe."

Paine had to admit his friend had a point. "Our security is intact. They can't touch us."

"What if they took out the warehouse with a couple of those air-to-ground missiles? Then where would we be?"

"I see what you're saying, I just think it's super unlikely," Paine said. "What do you want to do?"

"We need to get the merchandise moving right now. Spread it out. I want to get started even if we don't have the men in place yet. Each crate will take a week to move across the country anyway."

"Tonight?"

Pluess nodded. "I'll get my team and the merchandise prepared. I'll have trucks ready. See if Hutch's people can move up the bookings of the rail space to tomorrow or the next day. They know the destinations. We'll get the merchandise moving, crate by crate."

"What's the official content designation?"

"Tractors, spare parts. Combines, spare parts. Balers, spare parts. How many do you need?"

"That'll do." Paine repeated to himself: tractors, combines, balers. Hutch's people probably had all this anyway.

"Have you called your contacts in Iowa?" Pluess went on. "I want those two schnooks caught, and I want to chain Claire to a post and whip her myself until she's breathed her last. This is totally unacceptable. We need to make an example of her."

"I agree," Paine said. "I misjudged her."

CHAPTER 53

BENJY SAT AT the breakfast table in the underground facility near Reno. They had been here for four days and it fascinated him. John Carney had let him shadow one of the drone controllers. The drone controls were relayed by satellite from here to wherever they were in the country. His stepfather, who he knew used to work for Motorola, was the satellite expert. He had showed Benjy how he booked capacity for March22 on satellites under the names of several front companies.

"I've got my own private space on all of those babies, too," John had said last night. Benjy hadn't fully understood the comment, and wanted to ask more about it today.

Raine walked into the kitchen with wet hair.

"Morning," Benjy said.

"Don't look at my hair. There aren't any hair dryers here."

"In this climate it'll dry in fifteen minutes anyway," he said.

She gave him a wry look, and placed bread in the toaster. At that moment, his stepfather walked into the room.

"Any coffee left?" John said. "Morning kids."

"Oh, I talked to Matt last night," Raine said, her face brightening. John stopped in the middle of the kitchen. "He said he was on the Mississippi River. They were in the middle of crossing it."

His stepfather's face showed a ghost of a smile. "I hope he was okay. Did you tell him hi from me?"

"Sure," Raine said. "He sounded stressed out, but he was fine."

"How did he get across the river?" John asked.

"He just said they were on a boat."

"He and the Dark Fiber leader from Ann Arbor?"

"I guess so."

Benjy moved his chair to the left, and made space, as John Carney seemed to want to sit right between him and Raine. His stepfather drank from his mug, looking at Raine.

"Did he say where he was going? It sounds like they've traveled from Ann Arbor to the Mississippi River, heading west."

"He didn't say," Raine said. "We never talk very long."

"That's good," John said. "He could be headed to Montana, but you had to come here. Does he know you're here?"

"I wasn't supposed to tell him," Raine said. Benjy noticed she hadn't really answered the question.

His stepfather sat for a moment steeped in thought. Benjy wondered what it must be like to be a March22 leader, in charge of such dangerous weapons and so many people, when so many people depended on you to make the right decisions. John was obviously also concerned for Matt's safety. Benjy knew how much Matt looked up to John, and when you saw the inner workings in this high-tech control center, the feeling of power was contagious.

"You did the right thing, Raine," John said at last. "When you talk to him again, be sure to ask him which way he's headed. Maybe we can steer him in the right direction without actually giving him the exact location, just in case the call isn't secure."

Benjy thought it sounded like a reasonable request.

CHAPTER 54

KEOKUK, IOWA
DECEMBER 9, 2021—3 PM

SUNLIGHT STREAMED THROUGH the living room window when Matt woke. It was three in the afternoon and the house was quiet. For a minute, Matt had to reconstruct where he was: Keokuk, Iowa, wherever that was.

They had a job to do in Des Moines. He had to find out about those wheels and get an update from Luke.

Suddenly an image appeared on his Jetlink.

"Dad?" He sat up and breathed deep, rubbing sleep out of his eyes.

"Matt, we've got to keep this short," John Carney said. "Are you safe?"

"No thanks to you. What the hell were you thinking, Dad?"

"Son, March22 has got you on a suicide mission. I couldn't convince the others. My prime concern is your safety."

"I wouldn't be on any mission at all over here if you hadn't sent that anonymous tip to Dark Fiber."

His father frowned. "So they told you. I'm sorry for not consulting with you about it, Matt. That's neither here nor there now. We're on the verge of a big success, but you've got to work with me."

"What do you mean, Dad? Is this secure?"

"Secure enough," his father answered. "They want you to steal the shoulder-fired missiles and hand them over to Homeland Security. There's a high risk that March22 will get caught with our pants down in possession of those weapons. That would be the end of March22."

"But we're going to turn them over to the authorities. We can prove it was Dark Fiber that had them up till now. It was Dark Fiber that stole them from the army in 2019."

John Carney shook his head. "They'll turn it all around and make it look like March22 did it. We'll never win in the court of public opinion."

"What are you asking me to do?"

"Abort the mission, Matt."

"What?"

"Just between you and me, I've got control over two drones, son. If you can find out where the missiles are stored, we'll blow the place to kingdom come and destroy them. Then we can provide the authorities with proof that Dark Fiber was in possession of them, and carried out the attacks two years ago. Then the missiles can't be used by anybody."

It was clear that Luke was somehow keeping their father out of the loop on key details, like the location of the warehouse in Des Moines. The news that his father had control over two drones shocked him.

"How does that control over the drones actually work?" he asked.

"That's not important, Matt. When will you know where they're being stored? Where are you now?"

"I don't know," he replied, unsure. His father sounded dead serious. Like he was really going against the other leaders—again. Matt remembered Luke had told their father he was heading for Alabama.

"You don't know where you are?"

"She blindfolds me." The lie came out so easily. He was shocked at his own behavior. He felt the blood rushing to his face and wondered if his father would notice on his Jetlink screen. This was probably the first time he had ever lied to his father, and it wasn't a good feeling. "All I know is we're in a house."

"Are you in Alabama?"

"I don't think so. It would be warm in Alabama, wouldn't it?"

"Matt, I know you're in Iowa." His father suddenly spoke in a different, lower voice. Matt felt a tingling in his arms and legs. How the hell did he know they were in Iowa? "When can you find out where they're stored? This is a matter of the highest urgency, Matt."

"You can't ask me to work with you on your rogue operation." Matt's face was on fire. The words came out almost on their own, without forethought. Lying to his father was so painful, it felt like he was speaking through a filter. He noticed his hand was trembling as he looked at his father's deep frown on the screen.

"You lied to me just now, Matt."

"You're asking me to disobey orders. You handed me over to Dark Fiber. You want me to lie to all the others. How do you expect me to do that?"

"It's for the good of the country, son. They're wrong. I've been doing this a long time, you know. Their plan is too risky."

"Why did they all sign off on one plan, and you're all alone with yours?"

His father sighed. The contorted look on his face told of his own inner turmoil. "I know it's a lot to ask, Matt. Trust me on this. I'm your father, damn it."

"I don't know."

He felt torn. It had been his father who revealed that Raine was in danger. Because of his warning, Raine was safe. Because of his father, Matt had escaped from his dreadful existence in Chicago. His father loved him. Yet when he recalled Sander's wise face, or Commander Winter, or Wyoming, who Luke had mentioned was sitting in an FBI lockup in San Francisco somewhere, not to mention his super-geek brother—they were all counting on him. The thought of betraying all of them was too much.

"Matt, tell me where the missiles are stored."

"I can't, Dad."

"So you know?"

"Ask Luke. If you can get Luke on your side, then I'll do it."

His father swore. "Christ, that's like praying for rain in the desert. Luke is the one who convinced the others on this crazy plan."

Matt watched as the screen went blank again, the connection ended. Rather than continuing the discussion, his father had simply hung up. His mind had gone blank. His hands trembled, and the rotten feeling weighed on his stomach. He felt like throwing up. It was just as Luke had said. Their father had worked out a different plan and wanted him to work against the others. How could he even imagine Matt would go along with it?

So, you made it, junior, Luke said. *How's the babe?*

Oh God, it's you. Matt felt himself calming.

Your better half, as it were.

That reminds me. Do you know which one of us is older?

You are, Luke said. *Two minutes ahead of me. Beauty before brains.*

Very funny. Thanks for the helping hand last night.

Thank Sander. Thank Hank. I'm just a lousy go-between.

Claire wanted to swim it. I had to restrain her so she wouldn't jump in the river.

Bet you'd have liked to see her in a wet T-shirt, Luke said.

Speak for yourself.

So you just had a chat with our father, Luke went on.

You listened in?

Piece of cake.

Is it true that he has control over two drones?

That was news to me, Luke said. *Something I'll be checking on. I didn't consider it possible, but you never know. It would complicate matters.*

Why does he say it's a suicide mission? Is there something you're not telling me?

A favorite tactic of John Carney. He uses fear to motivate people.

It's not a suicide mission?

I'd be lying if I said it wasn't dangerous. Suicide mission, no way. We've got a lot of cool stuff lined up.

I wasn't sure what to tell him.

You did a good job, junior. He's totally out of line.

I couldn't believe he tried to recruit me for his rogue plan.

You're beginning to see what he's capable of. Don't say I didn't tell you.

How did he know I was in Iowa?

Raine.

I didn't... oh my God. I talked to her last night, when we were on the river.

She didn't know any better. I talked to Benjy. Our father coaxed it out of her very cleverly. They both have no idea.

I don't believe this, Matt said. It was a sickening revelation that he had to work against his own father, after all his father had done for him. He didn't like it that his father had used Raine to get information.

I can't stay on too long. I need to make sure he doesn't control any drones. If he does, I need to do something about it.

So what's new with Cedric?

You're in luck. Cedric is invited to a party tonight. I saw some emails. The man is a drinker. If he goes, he'll probably get soused. This is a good night to move in.

We're in Keokuk. How far is it to Des Moines?

Three hours, all on county roads. You think tonight is a go?

Damn straight.

What about your woman, how trustworthy is she?

She's not going to turn on us.

You done the dirty, yet?

Fuck you, Luke.

Just asking, man, settle down.

I guess the only kind of thrill you'll ever know is, like, through other people, Matt said.

A, the word you were looking for is vicarious. B, I get plenty of thrills in that department. Although I am rather curious about the actual dirty.

Spare me the details.

No really, what's it like, junior?

What?

You know, when you slide your John Thomas right in there, where it wants to go. What's it feel like?

I am not having this conversation with you.

Tell me what it feels like, Luke persisted.

Fuck you, all right? Tell me what's going to happen tonight.

I'll tell you everything you need to know about tonight as soon as you give me the information I just asked for.

Would you cut it out? This is not helping.

When Luke went on pestering him, Matt decided to cut the connection. Luke was truly disgusting sometimes. He went to the kitchen to find something to snack on, and a platter of roast beef awaited him on the table. Within five minutes, he had two thick sandwiches prepared and a glass of milk.

Claire emerged from the guest bedroom as he was finishing the second sandwich. She had sleep in her eyes, and gazed at him for a minute from the doorway.

"Welcome to Iowa," he said.

"Jesus, everything's been happening so fast, I didn't know where I was."

"It's going down tonight," Matt said. "Hank's going to get us some proper wheels. Everything else is being arranged. Now you need some food."

Claire smiled. "You March22 people sure are organized."

He wished it were really true. The rift between his father and the rest of the group worried him. Luke hadn't even known about their father stealing control of two drones. At this very moment he was probably trying to figure out what to do about it. When you had two sons forced to conspire against their own father, you couldn't call it organized.

CHAPTER 55

WASHINGTON, DC
DECEMBER 9, 2021—9 PM

"MR. PRESIDENT, WE'VE got two stolen drones on our screens."

Jeffers was sitting in the Oval Office reading the night's briefing on March22. The timing of Knopfler's call couldn't have been more exquisite.

"Where? What's happening?"

"Over Des Moines. They're circling at fifty thousand feet, plain as day. Suddenly they appeared on our screens."

"How do you know they're stolen ones?"

"Mr. President, each bird has a unique identifying signature. Our systems are alarmed. The second they showed up, we had alarms going off in the whole area—Iowa, Nebraska, Illinois, Wisconsin."

"Where did they come from? Why two? What the hell does this mean?"

"They just appeared on screens, sir, at cruising altitude. We don't know where they took off from or who's controlling them. We're not controlling them. We can see them, but we can't get in."

"Shit. Are they armed?"

"Definitely."

"Situation room, sixty minutes," Jeffers said. "I want Knopfler, Reese, and Tom there. Why Des Moines? Get your people on standby in Des Moines."

"Already done, sir," Knopfler said.

CHAPTER 56

DES MOINES, IOWA
DECEMBER 9, 2021—9:30 PM

THE TWO BROTHERS wearing black clothing carried backpacks filled with accelerants and tools. They had AR-15 assault rifles and hunting knives. The taller one was bald. His younger brother had a full head of hair and did most of the talking, but tonight they would keep conversation to the minimum.

They walked through the industrial park about five miles outside the city, keeping to the shadows in dark loading docks. Most people should have gone home for the day hours ago, but every one of these warehouses and factories had at least one guard patrolling outside all night. They produced everything from fertilizer to high-tech precision instruments to soybean meal for animal feed.

The Pluess Farm Tech headquarters building stood opposite their position — six stories of aluminum and glass. Generally, paper and furniture and curtains filled office buildings — things that would burn. All these militias were renowned for their firebombs. For once, they would get payback in-kind.

The brothers watched a pair of guards strolling along the north perimeter of the Pluess building, one of whom eyed the ground floor windows while the other scanned the parking lot. A recycling dumpster provided the perfect cover. The dumpster lid was open at a forty-five degree angle, and they watched the guards through the crack between the lid and the container rim.

Sixty seconds after the guards had rounded the south end of the Pluess building, the brothers jogged across the open pavement. They reached their target — a side door — in twenty seconds. The taller brother held the lock gun against the lock. An ashtray overflowing with cigarette butts stood beside the door. The office workers probably stood out here for their breaks.

Once inside, the taller brother pulled the door closed behind them. They stood for a moment in the dim green light of the emergency exit sign, getting their bearings. This side hallway led to the main lobby, where they could access the stairway.

The lobby guard should have already left, since his shift ended at nine o'clock, unlike the guards outside. The accelerant would be placed in eight places on each of the second, fourth, and sixth floors. They would start at the top and work their way down.

CHAPTER 57

DES MOINES, IOWA
DECEMBER 9, 2021—9:55 PM

KYLE CEDRIC PLUESS sat with Thomas Paine and three other men at the kitchen table in his house on the north side of town.

"Hutch hasn't booked the rail space yet," Paine said. "He's probably working on it right now."

"How hard can it be?" Pluess said. "I was supposed to be at a party tonight, too, but some things are more important. All we need is ten crates of missiles. Make sure to get launch assemblies for each one, too. We can bring them here and store them in my garage."

"I've got one of the trucks ready to go," said one of the other men.

"All right, we move in ten minutes," Pluess said.

He checked the call coming in on his Jetlink. "What the hell? Yes?"

"Kyle Pluess?" the man at the other end said. "This is Wes Jones from the Des Moines Engine Company Five. We've got a three-alarm fire at your building here in the West Loop Industrial Park. You better get on down here, sir."

"A fire! Which building?"

The fireman gave the address of the headquarters building, then added, "It's not under control yet. All signs point to arson."

At least it wasn't one of the warehouses.

"I'm on my way," Pluess said. The men in the room looked at him expectantly. "We've got a fire at the corporate office. Get the truck and load the crates out of the warehouse while I deal with the situation up front. Christ."

Maybe he had been right about Claire Tenneman heading for Des Moines, after all. He had hoped it wasn't true. But was a girl like that capable of burning down his headquarters?

CHAPTER 58

DES MOINES, IOWA
DECEMBER 9, 2021—9:45 PM

MATT CARNEY SAT in the rear seat of the old-time fire engine from Ames Company Seventeen. Through a friend of Sander's, March22 had laid their hands on four of these old buggies. The trucks had been modified long ago to haul cargo in their giant water tanks, which were accessed by a double-wide loading door at the back.

The convoy of antique fire trucks waited in a far corner of the industrial park, behind the Conrad Medical building. The first responders from Des Moines had already arrived at the headquarters fire, sirens wailing, and Matt heard more arriving continually. Luke would give the signal when they should move.

Fortunately, Claire sat in one of the other trucks. Matt didn't feel like hearing any more innuendos. She had spent the whole drive to Des Moines pestering him about Luke, as if they didn't have more important things to think about. What he was like as a person, why he didn't have a girlfriend, what he did for fun—she inquired about everything except his physical appearance. He was looking forward to telling her Luke hardly resembled him at all, a super-geek with a taste for large breasts, his body forever molded to a wheelchair.

Beside Matt and in the front seats, the men cradled their assault rifles and reflected on the mission. Nobody spoke.

It'll be a few minutes, Luke said.

What about Dad's drones?

They're up there. Maybe you're going to see some fireworks up in the sky.

Why, what's happening?

That asshole hacked my satellite, Luke said. *So I changed a few settings and put his lousy drones on full view to the administration.*

You mean they're detectable now?

His drones are. Ours aren't.

What if he launches the missiles before we get out?

If I see him arming, I can probably mess with his drone guidance. Throw his birds off course. I'd prefer to let Homeland Security do the job for me. I honestly don't know what the hell they're waiting for.

Probably?

Working on it. Be patient.

Wait a minute. How sure are you?

Have faith, little brother.

You're my little brother, you nerd. So stop calling me junior. If he shoots a missile, how long do we have to get out?

Approximately thirty-seven point nine seconds, at their present altitude.

I don't like this.

Best I can do, Matt. Just do your job, and let me worry about control of the skies.

Obviously, you don't have control of the skies. That's what worries me.

Don't worry about things you can't control.

Speaking of control, how'd he get two of the birds?

It's a little embarrassing.

I probably wouldn't understand it anyway.

He hacked into my protocol from the back end, from the satellite.

What satellite?

The signals to and from the drones are relayed through geosynchronous satellites, dickhead. That means they're stationary above a certain point on earth. We have a few of these satellites where we've got secret real estate. Now, unfortunately, Dad might not know his way around computers in general, but he does know some tricks when it comes to satellites. He got in.

What if he has more than two drones?

How could he have more than two? He's only got two hands.

Ha, ha. Are you sure?

It's a good question, actually. Pesky parents.

Matt felt his stomach twisting up like a rope inside him, tighter and tighter. His father obviously knew where the warehouse was, given that he had positioned his drones over Des Moines. He might not know March22 people were down here right now, ready to steal the shoulder-fired missiles. He might launch the Hellfire missiles while they were in the warehouse. If he knew they were inside, would he hold off from firing?

"Okay, you need to get over to the warehouse now," Luke's synthesized voice came over the comm, so that everyone heard it.

"Move it out, Greg," said Tristan Hines, the operations leader. Hines sat in the passenger seat in the front of Matt's truck, his lower lip jutted out from a wad of chewing tobacco. The tangy smell of his breath permeated the interior, and every minute or two he spat a long stream out the window.

The driver started the engine and all four Ames Company Seventeen fire trucks made wide turns and started down the driveway around the Conrad Medical building. Matt wondered if he should inform Hines about the impending danger from his father. Where would he even begin? How would he convince him it was true?

If Matt put himself in leader's shoes, Hines could only decide to carry on with the mission in spite of the danger, since none of what Matt knew could be verified. They had their mission now. They just had to do it.

"They've left you a good corridor to the far end of the industrial park," Luke went on, speaking on the comm. "Just drive past the headquarters fire as if you want to position the trucks farther on. The warehouse is three hundred yards west of the fire, the third warehouse in the row. There's a big 3 painted on the side of the building, so you can't miss it. Most of the warehouse security guards appear to be up in front watching the headquarters burn. Be ready to take them out if they come back to your position."

"Got it," affirmed Hines.

As they drove by, they had front row seats for the blazing conflagration that was the Pluess headquarters building. Flames leapt high above the six-story structure. Two of the fire trucks had extended long ladders, on which firefighters perched, spraying the flames from twenty feet back. It looked like they weren't going to save the building.

The four old-timer trucks roared past at least ten fire trucks, five or six police cars, and three ambulances. Dozens of emergency responders stood around, while others hustled to fight the blaze.

Nobody gave the antique trucks a passing glance.

When they pulled up at warehouse 3 ten seconds later, two guards emerged to meet them. Each of the old-timer trucks carried five men, with Claire riding in one of them. The March22 men jumped out of the trucks, leaving the engines running. Matt was close enough to hear the exchange between Hines, another March22 man, and the two guards.

"You can't park here," said one of the guards.

"We need access to the power supply in that warehouse," said Hines.

"What?"

The March22 men had continued to move closer to the guards during this short exchange. Then both swung their fists practically in unison. They sent the two guards staggering backward, but they were tough and neither fell. As they reached for their assault rifles, five or six March22 men piled on each one. They had trained for this exact scenario earlier this evening. Four men wrestled each guard and pinned him to the pavement while one March22 man focused on prying the assault rifle away. Another March22 man searched for other weapons. They removed the guards' Jetlinks at the same time, so that no alarms could be sent. The two guards were bound and gagged and pulled off to one side.

While this was going on, the rest of the March22 team secured the perimeter around the front of the warehouse.

"You got those codes, right, Matt?" Hines called. "I don't know why he only sent them to you. I'm the one leading this operation."

Hines spat on the pavement, close enough to splatter Matt's boots. They stood at the massive warehouse door, and Matt held his Jetlink up to the keypad. Luke had sent him two security passcodes, one to open this door, the other for the special storage area where the shoulder-fired missiles were hidden. When his Jetlink had flashed the code to the keypad reader, the doors opened with the grinding sound of wheels on metal tracks.

Hines had his Jetlink up as well, and the code transferred to his device at the same time.

"It's not just because we're brothers. It's supposed to be compartmentalized for your protection," Matt said. He couldn't very well tell Hines that they had instant communication capability if anything went wrong. Hines didn't know anything about the two rogue drones circling above and looking for this warehouse.

As the warehouse doors opened, two more guards came sprinting toward them across the wide interior space.

"What the hell is this?" one guard yelled, reaching for his gun. They were too far away for any March22 man to engage in hand-to-hand combat. The first four March22 men in line let out a deadly burst from their assault rifles. One of the guards screamed as he fell to the concrete floor. The other was thrown backward and lay still as smoke from the shots curled upward from Matt's gun.

"Make sure there's no more. You four take that side," said Hines. "Carney, I'll get that other code from you when we've secured the interior."

Matt was one of the designated men. His squad spread out and jogged into the cavernous warehouse, moving up the left side. Large crates were stacked on metal shelving that reached up to the forty-foot ceiling. Matt jogged behind three other men, checking row after row. He heard more commands from Hines and he observed Claire jogging with a unit of March22 men up the right side. Behind him he heard the grumbling diesel engines of the old-timers as they backed into the warehouse. Half of the March22 men stayed outside, guarding the front.

Then two giant yellow forklifts sped past him, driven by March22 men. He knew the shoulder-fired missiles were stored at the back of the warehouse on the right-hand side.

"The building is clear," Hines announced a minute later on the comm. "Let's go get our merchandise."

Matt headed to the corner at the rear right, where the missiles were stored. Hines stood with a group of March22 men in front of a tall metal door the size of a truck garage.

Steel walls extended straight up to the ceiling of the warehouse. Luke had said the missiles were stored in this special storage area.

"Okay, let's have that damned code," Hines said, holding his Jetlink up.

"Here you go." Matt held up his Jetlink to the keypad reader. He waited three or four seconds for the reader to pick up his Jetlink signal. This time, the door didn't open.

"I'm not getting it," Hines said.

"The door didn't open," said another March22 man named Jared.

Luke, it's not working. The damned code for the special storage room.

Fuck you, junior, it's the right code.

Well, it's not working.

"Try it again, Carney," Hines said. Engines idling, the forklifts waited ten feet away, prepared to pick up pallets and load them into the fire trucks.

Matt heard the sound of assault rifle fire coming from the front. The March22 men were probably being confronted by more guards. Maybe an alarm somewhere had been tripped. He tried to stay focused.

Why isn't it working? Luke said.

I'm holding my Jetlink up to it. Nothing's happening.

Goddamn him, Luke said. *Matt, input the code manually. He's blocking your Jetlink. Shit!*

What do you mean, manually? You mean, type in the numbers?

Quick, before he deletes it or something. Christ, why didn't I think of this?

"Hey, Jared, can you read off that number and put in the code?" Matt's hand was shaking so badly, he didn't trust himself to do it. Jared started inputting the long sequence of numbers and letters on the keypad.

"What is this shit?" Hines said. "It won't transfer."

"Let's just get the damn thing open," Matt said. Jared continued inputting the number on the keypad.

What do you mean, delete it?

He's hijacking your Jetlink, Matt. He's blocking the transfer. As soon as you've got the damned door open, do me a favor and power off your Jetlink.

Why, what's the point of that?

Father John knows where you are with that damned thing on. His drones have your location down to within inches.

If he knows where I am, then he won't launch.

When Luke didn't answer, Matt felt the sweat blossoming on his brow and upper lip. His father certainly wouldn't launch Hellfire missiles with him and all the other March22 men in here, but still. It was unnerving just to think that he could, if he were that crazy.

Once Jared finished inputting the code, the door unsealed with a hiss. When the men pulled the doors open wide, a burst of frigid air wafted in their faces.

Matt powered off his Jetlink as the forklifts rolled up.

Inside the storage area, the crates were stacked eight high on pallets, and each crate was six feet by four feet by four feet. The forklifts ran their forks up to the highest position. Each grabbed the top four crates in the pile, then ratcheted the loads down as they backed up and swung around to bring the crates to the waiting fire trucks.

Matt, power on again. Dad's trying to reach you, Luke said. *Try to buy time.*

"Okay, now we're cooking. Out of the way, everybody," Hines said, and spat out another long stream of tobacco juice.

Matt touched the power button. Almost immediately his father's face appeared.

"Matt, you're in the Pluess warehouse. Pluess is a Dark Fiber leader. I know what's going on. I need you to get out of there right now."

Several possible retorts occurred to him at the same time, leaving Matt stammering. Finally, he managed to speak coherently. "There must be some mistake. What makes you think I'm in some warehouse?"

His father's face wrinkled in exasperation. "Matt, there isn't time for a long discussion, here. Get out of there. The whole place is going to blow!"

The forklifts were coming back for another load. The men inside the fire trucks were shoving the crates forward and stacking them to fit.

"I'm not getting out till the job is done," Matt said.

"Don't do this to me," his father said. "Those missiles have to be destroyed."

"If you launch your Hellfires, you'll take me with."

"I can't do that, son. Don't force me to make that choice. Get the hell out of there so I can finish the job."

Hines was staring at him. Matt walked toward the other side, where no one could hear the conversation. "I have my official orders from March22, Dad. I'm not taking orders from you. I'm here with twenty other March22 men. We're here, and we're carrying out our mission. If you want to stop us, you'll have to kill us all."

Tears streamed down his father's cheeks. His father was shaking his head, and looked unable to speak. It seemed unthinkable that a man could even consider sending his own son to a fiery death. Luke was convinced that their father would be capable of it, but Matt knew it was impossible. He knew it in his heart. He knew it when he saw how much pain his father was in.

As the forklifts took their third load to the old-timers, Matt watched his father on the screen. It looked like his whole body was shaking.

"Accept it, Dad," he said. "You could be wrong. The leaders made a decision to do the mission this way. We all just have to accept it."

John Carney's face was a network of wrinkles. "I'm launching in sixty seconds," he said. "Get them all out, for God's sake, Matt."

"No!" he yelled. "We're completing the mission."

"Matt, what's going on over there?" Claire was walking over, an assault rifle cradled in her hands. Matt held up his hand, stopping her ten feet away.

When Matt looked down again, Benjy's face filled the screen on his Jetlink. Then Benjy moved back and Raine came into view behind him. Behind the two of them Matt saw men struggling. The shapes blurred and went in and out of the picture. He couldn't tell if his father was one of them, but he heard men shouting in the background.

"Benjy, what's going on there?" he cried.

Benjy had a worried look on his face. "They dragged him away from the console," he said.

"Who?"

"Security, Matt. They're tying him up. Luke told us we had to do it. Four security guys are here. I don't exactly know what's happening. Luke said he was about to launch a missile."

"Did he launch it? I've got to know if he did it."

Benjy's eyes were glued to the console. "I think he didn't launch anything," he said. Matt heard more yelling in the background. His father had been ready to launch, but Luke's quick thinking had stopped him. It was too much to comprehend.

"Jesus, Benjy. What happened?"

"We have Marcus and three others here. Luke told me I had to stop John. They snuck up behind him just as he was reaching for the launch button."

Matt closed his eyes, trying to shut out the sound of the forklifts and the diesel engines of the old-timers.

Luke, Benjy said security has tied up our father. Can you check and see if he got the missiles armed or launched?

Checking now, Luke answered curtly.

Matt stood in the middle of the warehouse floor, still holding Claire off with one hand, and waited for the report from Luke. The forklifts ran back and forth from the special storage area to the antique fire trucks. Either Benjy had really succeeded, or a Hellfire missile would come ripping through the warehouse roof in the next few seconds, ending all their lives instantly.

Matt had lost count of the number of trips the forklifts had made, but the first two fire trucks were full and the others were backing into position. He hoped Luke had calculated the space requirements correctly. It looked like half the crates were gone from the special refrigerated storage.

At least the machine-gun fire out front had quieted.

The men are holding Dad on the floor, Luke said. *He armed a missile but didn't launch.*

Thank God for that.

Guess what's happening now?

I give up.

We've got FA-18s scrambling from the Des Moines National Guard. Homeland Security and the army are finally getting their butts in gear.

Do they know about us?

They don't know about you, but they picked it up loud and clear when he armed the Hellfires. It won't be long till they shoot down Dad's drones. How long till you guys are done?

Ten minutes, tops.

"Matt, why are you just standing there?" Claire came closer. "Are you talking to Luke right now?"

"I was," Matt confirmed.

"Why? What's happening?"

"Just some last minute details." He wiped sweat from his brow, avoiding her gaze.

"Why don't you ever trust me with anything?" Claire asked.

"I do trust you," he said. "We're here, aren't we? March22 arranged this whole operation in just a few days, and here we are." Why was he trying to placate Claire? She got on his nerves sometimes.

"But what is your brother's role? Is he involved in the operation, too?" Claire persisted.

Matt looked around nervously, but no other March22 men were standing close by. "Listen, Claire, I told you we have to keep all that secret. Now is really not the time, okay?"

She made a face, then turned and stalked away again, almost getting hit by a forklift speeding by. His father had been ready to launch a Hellfire missile, even with him and all the other March22 men in the warehouse. Was he crazy? Why did it take four men physically overpowering him to prevent him from killing his own son?

Hines spat another long stream of tobacco juice as the forklifts went by again. Matt didn't like the way Hines kept looking at him, as if he'd intentionally prevented the ops leader from getting the code. But there was no way to explain the whole thing without giving Hines information that he shouldn't possess.

Matt stood alone, far out of the way of the forklifts, tormented by random thoughts swirling around in his mind. Suddenly Luke's voice came in again, loud and clear on their private channel.

Matt, Matt, we've got a launch! Luke screamed. *Drop everything and get everyone out.*

How did – ?

Just get everyone out. You've got thirty-five seconds!

"Everyone listen!" Matt yelled.

Instinct took over, and he ran toward the others. Luke wouldn't shit him about a thing like this, and the seconds were ticking. Two forklifts were just going by, headed for the fire truck. Hines turned, an angry look contorting his face, as if he'd expected another problem from Matt.

"In thirty seconds this whole place is going to blow!"

"What are you talking about?" Hines demanded, lower lip jutting.

"Just believe me. We have to leave the rest of the crates!" Matt grabbed Claire and a March22 man who was standing there. "Run up front and get the trucks moving out. The trucks have to get out. Get the trucks out! Get everyone clear of the warehouse, now!" He gave them a shove, and they ran.

"Tell me what the hell is going on, Carney," Hines demanded. Matt was watching the others as they started ambling toward the front when Hines punched him hard in the shoulder. "I'm talking to you. You seem to think you're the leader here."

"Just get your men out," Matt yelled. "Incoming Hellfire missile."

Luke, get on the comm and tell Hines. He's not listening to me.

Doing it, Luke said.

Ignoring Hines, Matt ran over to the refrigerated storage, where six or seven men still stood around. The forklifts were coming back for another load.

"Everybody, listen up!" he yelled. "Just listen to me! We've got an incoming Hellfire missile that's going to smoke this whole warehouse in twenty seconds. Leave the rest right NOW and run out the front." They hesitated. Some men started to walk, while others just stood there. Matt screamed at them. "Are you listening to me? If you don't want to die, get moving. Incoming missile!"

He pushed the nearest group of them, then started running himself. When he looked behind him, he saw his genuine panic had touched a chord. The others were running after him.

"Everyone out of the warehouse NOW," Luke said on the comm. "Incoming Hellfire missile in 18 seconds. Repeat, incoming Hellfire missile."

When Matt looked back, he saw many of the March22 men sprinting out after him. Luke's order had done the trick. But Hines and one other man had gone back in and were getting on the forklifts, which had been vacated. Those idiots were going back into the refrigerated storage for another load.

The first fire trucks were out of the warehouse and came to a stop a hundred yards away. Two trucks still stood in the warehouse. Matt slapped the door of the truck on the left, making the driver sit up straight.

"This place is going to blow in about ten seconds! Get this truck out of here. We're leaving!"

"But we haven't got all of them!" the driver answered.

"Incoming missile! Just do it!" Matt ran around the front of the truck. As it pulled out, a second truck nearly ran him over. Claire had gotten that driver moving. Matt heard Luke counting down on the comm. Nine... eight... seven... . Everybody heard Luke on the comm, so why was Hines still in there? Claire joined him as they ran for the doors, following a group of men. The last truck followed them out the door and passed them as they ran to where the other three trucks were parked.

"We still had twenty crates left to go," said the March22 man sprinting alongside Matt. Ahead of them, the Pluess headquarters building was still burning brightly, the area filled with the flashing lights of emergency vehicles.

When Matt looked over his shoulder, still running, he saw deep in the warehouse the two forklifts coming out of the refrigerated storage, each with four crates loaded. They made it about halfway to the front doors.

It was the last thing Matt saw before a giant explosion ripped through the night. The fireball at the warehouse sent plumes of fire shooting high into the dark sky, dwarfing the headquarters fire. The shock wave surged to where they stood, but everyone in the March22 group had hit the deck anyway.

"Goddamn you, Hines," Matt said, kneeling and staring at the collapsing inferno of the warehouse. His vision blurred and he felt his throat tighten.

"That was Hines?" said the man next to Matt.

"The idiot wouldn't listen," Matt said.

"And Freddy," said another man. "Where the fuck did that missile come in from, anyway?"

"Had to be US Army," said the first man. "Freddy was my friend, goddamn."

Matt didn't have the heart to tell the men the truth—that the Hellfire had been launched by a March22 leader. A friendly fire incident, they called it.

He felt sick and retched, but nothing came out. He waited for the next spasm.

His own father. His own goddamned father had launched a missile, knowing he was in its path. He and all the other March22 men as well. The heat of the fire was burning his face. His face, he realized when he touched it, was wet. He had to stifle a sob so the others wouldn't see.

His own father, goddamn it!

A hand was moving in slow circles on his back. A warm hand. When he looked up, through blurred vision, he saw Claire.

"Let's get out of here," one of the March22 men yelled. "Probably got their attention now. We had a mission and we're not done yet. Find your truck and let's deliver this cake to the party."

CHAPTER 59

DES MOINES, IOWA
DECEMBER 9, 2021—10:30 PM

THE ANTIQUE FIRE trucks raced past the still-raging Pluess headquarters fire without slowing, avoiding the first responder police cars rushing toward the burning warehouse. Still in a daze, Matt watched as police at the headquarters fire shouted into their Jetlinks and pointed at the warehouse.

The antique fire trucks exited the industrial park and headed into the city. Now it was time to put the second part of the plan into action.

What the hell happened with that Hellfire missile? Matt asked Luke as they sped down a road. The motion of the big truck was helping to calm him.

Dad had set a timer for four minutes. The timer was cloaked and I didn't see it till the missile actually launched. The idiot was determined to destroy that warehouse even though you and all the others were in it.

At least he gave us extra time to get out. The words felt lame as soon as he said them. Why was he making excuses for his father? His father had come very close to killing all of them.

No one got hurt? Luke asked.

Are you joking? Hines is dead, and a guy named Freddy.

No shit? Luke sounded shocked.

Hines wouldn't listen, even when you said it on the comm. He dragged his buddy back in to get another load.

What a moron.

I feel rotten. I couldn't convince him the place was going to blow. The dude wouldn't listen to me.

Dad's drones have now been shot out of the sky. Someone didn't like him launching that Hellfire. So at least you don't have to worry about more friendly fire attacks.

Where is he now?

They locked him in a room with no Jetlink or anything. You and Claire drive to Sander's. Can you find it?

Halfway into town, the fire trucks pulled up at a stop sign. Matt recognized the corner from the image Luke had sent him this afternoon. A green Honda motorcycle was parked on the street to the right.

When the driver of his truck turned in his seat and gave Matt the thumbs up, Matt opened the door and climbed down. Claire was getting down from the truck just ahead.

CHAPTER 60

PRESIDENT JAMES JEFFERS watched two split screens on the wall-sized projection. In the screen on the left, a Hellfire missile slammed into a structure in some industrial park in Des Moines, Iowa.

"You're saying that missile came from a stolen drone?"

"That's correct, Mr. President," Knopfler confirmed.

"One of those two that suddenly showed up on our screens?"

"Correct," Knopfler said tersely.

"Well, who the hell is controlling those damned things? Who launched that goddamned missile?"

Everyone avoided his eyes by keeping theirs on the screen on the right, which showed views of two Predator drones. These views were courtesy of Homeland Security drones flying overhead. No one knew who exactly had launched, but they all knew without doubt it had to be March22. The operative question was in fact not who, but *how*.

"Request permission to shoot down the stolen drones before they launch another," Secretary of Defense Reese said.

"Do it," Jeffers said. Reese spoke into his Jetlink, and they all watched the screen on the right.

"We've activated a shelter-in-place robocall in greater Des Moines," Knopfler said. "Just pray the wreckage doesn't smash through someone's roof."

Less than sixty seconds later, both stolen drones were hit by Sparrow air-to-air missiles launched from scrambled Iowa National Guard FA-18s. The flaming wreckage rained down harmlessly in fields.

"I want to know what they destroyed down there," Jeffers said.

"It was a warehouse belonging to Pluess Farm Tech Corp.," Knopfler said, reading new information off his Jetlink. "Spare parts for tractors, combines, balers."

"Why the hell does March22 send a Hellfire missile into a warehouse full of tractor parts?"

"How did those drones suddenly become detectable?" Reese growled.

"We're studying the protocols," Holsom said, exasperated.

"Why only two of them?" Jeffers added. "Why Des Moines?"

"Mr. President, I've just received a call from our Homeland Security chief in Des Moines," Knopfler said. "I want to put him on speaker. Roy Budge, you're talking to the White House Situation Room. The president is listening."

"Ah, thanks, Deputy Knopfler. Mr. President, we just got a call from some people who identified themselves as March22. They told us to meet them at the events center in downtown Des Moines. They said they've got about five thousand shoulder-fired missiles and launch assemblies they want to hand over to us."

"Holy Jesus Christ," Reese said.

"The stolen missiles?" Jeffers asked. He shared a look with Reese. What the hell was March22's game? Maybe things were turning around, here. Was it too much to hope it would go this way with the dirty bombs and the drones, too, if they played their cards right? He chastised himself inwardly. Only a fool would think so.

"What is that events center?" Knopfler asked. "Sports arena?"

"We've got our football stadium and the convention center," Budge replied. "But it's quiet tonight, nothing going on."

"Thank God for that," Knopfler said.

"Damn those March22 criminals," Jeffers yelled. "Lock them all up when you get there, and get their story." He turned again to Reese. "How many of those missiles were unaccounted for?"

"Six thousand, Mr. President."

"Mr. President, we are two minutes from the events center," Budge continued. "I've got about thirty of my men en route, plus police and FBI converging. If they've got a large quantity of missiles, sir, we're going to need some help handling them safely."

"Just sit tight, Budge," Reese said. "I'm the defense secretary. We'll get some trucks down to your location within sixty minutes, and you can hand those missiles over to the US Army."

"Yes, sir, will do," said Budge on the speaker. "One more thing. It wasn't very clear to me, but the March22 man said three different times they had just stolen the shoulder-fired missiles from a warehouse over in one of our industrial parks. They said they stole the missiles from the Dark Fiber Militia."

"March22 snatched the missiles from a *militia*?" Knopfler asked.

"That's what he said, sir," Budge said. "We're arriving here at the event center now, and I see four old fire trucks parked in a row with about twenty men standing in front of them."

"Get us video," Jeffers said.

Fifteen seconds later, they had live video of a vast parking lot, in the background a lit stadium outlined against the night sky. Jeffers saw what looked like four antique fire trucks parked side by side, with a row of men standing in front of them, hands in the air.

"Are they armed?" Knopfler asked.

"Well, I see a lot of automatic weapons on the ground in front of them," Budge said.

"Keep your hands up high where we can see them," said a loud, drone-amplified voice in Des Moines. "Two men step forward. Any threatening action will be met with deadly force."

Two of the March22 men walked forward, keeping their arms high. Twenty or thirty Homeland Security agents stood behind car and truck doors, aiming all manner of weapons at the men.

"That's close enough," said a Homeland Security official in a white down jacket. The two men stood about twenty feet away. The sound of a helicopter hovering nearby made it difficult to hear the whole exchange. "What's in those goddamn fire trucks?"

"About five thousand shoulder-fired missiles with launch assemblies, stolen from the US Army by the Dark Fiber Militia in 2019. We're a March22 squad. We discovered Dark Fiber stole them. We found out they were being stored in a warehouse belonging to Pluess Farm Tech Corp. in Des Moines, and the CEO is Kyle Cedric Pluess. He's one of the Dark Fiber leaders and responsible for the theft from the US Army. We stole them tonight from Dark Fiber in order to return them to their rightful owner."

"Who the hell is that?" Jeffers asked.

Knopfler answered. "Facial recognition IDs him as James A. Sizemore, from outside Des Moines. He, ah, works at a bank downtown. Served in Iraq. No police record. Married, two kids."

"And the one next to him?"

"Stuart H. Barclay, age forty, gym teacher at a high school in Des Moines. Also served in Iraq, but twenty years ago."

"What the hell are people like that doing with our goddamned missiles?" Reese thundered.

As more and more emergency vehicles screeched to a stop at the events center, the March22 men remained standing with their hands up. Homeland Security agents moved in and started handcuffing them. The arrests proceeded without incident.

Jeffers watched the scene with growing disbelief. If the March22 man was to be believed, the Dark Fiber Militia was responsible for the shoulder-fired missile attacks of 2019. Not March22.

"What was the name of that company?" Jeffers asked. "The one where the warehouse got taken out by the Hellfire from the stolen drone?"

"Pluess Farm Tech," Holsom confirmed.

"Do you think any of this is more than hogwash?" Jeffers asked the group.

"Mr. President, I've just received a very curious message," Knopfler said. He held out his Jetlink and projected an image on the sidewall. The sender was identified simply as March22. The reference was *Evidence against Dark Fiber and Pluess*.

"You got a message from March22?" Holsom said.

Knopfler opened the FASTBACK file. On the wall, a list of emails opened up before their eyes, the first twenty or so plainly visible. The emails dated back to the summer of 2019. Quickly scanning the first sentence or two of a few of the emails, Jeffers understood the bigger message.

"You'll go through that with a fine-toothed comb," he said to Knopfler. "Pick up this Pluess idiot and his associates, if you can find them. And I want to know the results of your interrogations with these March22 people in Des Moines."

"Of course, Mr. President."

Jeffers looked at Reese as Knopfler started giving orders on his Jetlink. He knew they were both thinking about the dirty bombs. It was nice to have the damned shoulder-fired missiles back, but what about the bombs?

"Mr. President, Mr. Knopfler," Budge from Des Moines broke in again. "We've got secondary explosions going off in that inferno over in the industrial park. The warehouse is burning to the ground, but it looks like they left some missiles behind in there. One of them just took out a couple of our local squad cars."

"Keep your people at a safe distance, Budge," Knopfler said.

"Yes, sir."

CHAPTER 61

MATT GAVE DIRECTIONS for Sander's farm and Claire drove them fifty miles north to Ames. The woman loved her motorcycles. The winter cornfields on either side of the road, with straggly cut stalks sticking up out of the uneven ground and a wispy covering of thin mist, looked haunting in the moonlight. As the wind whipped in his face, he thought the world looked like a forlorn place when your own father was prepared to send you, nineteen other March22 men, and Claire to an early death.

What did it mean for their relationship as father and son? His father had set the timer and then *hidden* it. Only through Luke's ingenuity had Matt been able to save the others—and himself. And then only *most* of the others.

What did it mean for March22, when one of the leaders pig-headedly worked against the others, secretly took control of drones and launched a deadly missile, even after his plan had been rejected? His father had had to be subdued physically, and even then he'd come perilously close to succeeding. He had killed two of their own men. What was going to happen to him now?

Matt wished the answers would appear in his mind as easily as the unending questions, but no answers came. These seemed like problems for which there would be no easy answers.

Buddy, Claire and I are almost there. You around?

Can't a guy get some sleep once in a while?

Sorry. You want me to check in later?

No problem. How's the girl? Did you at least cop a feel?

You have a one-track mind. Get yourself an inflatable doll or something.

Sometimes I feel like I'm the inflatable doll, Luke said.

This business with Dad, Matt said. He didn't know how to continue. Luke picked up the thread without further prompting.

They locked him up in a proper cell. Benjy, Raine, and the others are out of the equation.

What does that mean?

The other leaders ordered our internal security to lock him up.

Including you?

Of course. I'm one of the leaders, aren't I?

What's going to happen to him?

Don't tell me you're feeling sympathy, Matt. The monster would've killed you if we hadn't stopped him. And all the others. As it is, he killed Tristan Hines and Freddy Burton.

I know.

But, he's our father, right?

Well, you know he wanted what's best for March22.

Don't confuse that with the underlying logic, Matt. He didn't accept the fact that he was outvoted by three other people who also only want the best for March22. Part of being a leader in any organization is going along with the consensus, if you're outvoted. We can't have people working at cross purposes to each other.

What I can't get over is he would've knowingly sacrificed me.

Trust your gut feeling. You're right to be tortured by that. It's sick for a father to come that close to sacrificing his own son for a political aim. Because that's what this boils down to. Plus he already did it once before, when he handed you over to Dark Fiber. We're talking about a sick pattern.

What Luke said was shocking, but true. *In addition to risking the lives of so many others,* Matt answered, at a loss for what to say about the pattern.

This will be examined by the leaders. We'll have to make a decision about what will happen to him.

We're not going to execute him.

I don't think that would be proportionate to the crime, personally, Luke said. *It's a close call. Two of our men are dead. It could easily have been more.*

I don't think I'm going to be able to sleep.

We have to watch Nina Nardelli tomorrow. She's got a special. I'm told it focuses on March22, and it's dynamite.

I hate Nina Nardelli.

You are a strange specimen. Are you sure you're even straight?

Claire likes her. Maybe we'll have a look.

We can do it together.

Why? Are you at Sander's?

Sure thing.

When they arrived at the farmhouse where Matt had first visited less than three weeks ago, Sander McIntyre, the gray-haired March22 leader, was standing on the front porch. Finding out Luke was here had picked up his spirits. He was eager to see his brother again.

"This is Claire Tenneman."

Sander extended a hand. "I understand you saved Matt's life. Welcome."

"She officially wants to join us," Matt said.

"That's fine. Come on in and get something to eat. I'll fill you in on the latest information from Des Moines."

They sat at the table and dug into large portions of beef stew while Sander poured himself a cup of tea. At first, Matt had no appetite. But after one bite, he realized how hungry he was. The bulb over the stove cast a dim light that didn't reach the corners of the large kitchen. Sander took a chair across from them.

"They arrested the whole group of March22 men, and brought them to the Des Moines County jail. The US Army took possession of the missiles."

"That's a relief," Matt said.

"I hope they write a thank-you note," Claire said.

"What's going to happen to all those men?" Matt asked.

"They're all locals," Sander said. "They'll say they work for the local March22 chapter and discovered the cache of shoulder-fired missiles through local contacts and rumors. They decided to launch an operation to steal them and return them to the US Army. They'll all say they did the whole thing on their own."

"You mean they won't be tied to you or the rest of March22?"

Sander shook his head. "Totally compartmentalized. Any links that existed have been wiped clean by Luke. They won't find anything linking these local guys to our national organization. They're all upstanding citizens with good references and no police record. We'll get the media on our side, and the men will be out of the lockup within forty-eight hours. We want to make political hay out of this."

"That's amazing," Claire said.

"I understand you provided key information that enabled us to carry out this operation," Sander said.

When Claire blushed, Matt answered for her. "She knew they would use the missiles again as soon as the planes started flying."

Sander nodded. "They were planning a Christmas Eve attack. Twenty locations around the country."

No one said anything. Matt felt the blood draining out of his face. Twenty planes around the country on Christmas Eve. Families with children, rushing to spend the holidays with grandparents. Kids his age coming home from college, able to fly for the first time in more than two years. If each plane carried a hundred passengers on average, that would've been two thousand innocent people losing their lives.

"Homeland Security and the FBI are looking for Kyle Cedric Pluess," Sander went on. "The headquarters building burned to the ground. They seem to have bought the story that March22 snatched the shoulder-fired missiles from the Dark Fiber warehouse belonging to his company."

"Well, it's the truth," Matt said.

"We had some concerns that no matter how transparently we handled it, March22 would still get the blame," Sander said. "But it seems to have worked."

"The operation was creative and everything went smoothly," Claire said. "Dark Fiber looks like a bunch of amateurs, in comparison."

"Luke sent the Homeland Security chief in Washington a FASTBACK file containing more than two years of Dark Fiber emails," Sander said. "All relating to the shoulder-fired missiles, including many that prove Dark Fiber's involvement in the attacks of 2019."

"Luke, that's your twin brother, right?" Claire asked.

"Yes, and that should erase any doubts about March22," Matt said.

Sander nodded. "A few missiles went off in the warehouse fire, but no one else was injured."

"And what about the rogue operation?" Matt asked. The food suddenly tasted sour in his mouth.

"That's the only wrinkle." Sander had a grave look as he shook his head, looking at the table. "We've locked up the person responsible. The authorities are interrogating our men about the Hellfire missile that hit the warehouse. Those men knew nothing about it. We're confident that they won't catch hell for it."

"What rogue operation?" Claire asked.

Matt shared a glance with Sander.

"One of our leaders had a different idea about how to deal with the shoulder-fired missiles," Sander said. "He was the one who launched that Hellfire."

"We weren't even finished loading," Claire said.

"And two of our men died because of it," Sander said. "More would've died without your quick actions, Matt."

"I was just doing what Luke told me."

He saw an image in his mind of shoving the other March22 men toward the warehouse door, screaming at them. He saw Hines and the other man going back in the wrong direction and getting in the forklifts. If only Hines had listened! This was going to give him nightmares.

"It's a tragedy," Sander said.

"I should've insisted," Matt said. "I should've made them get out."

"You did the right thing getting Luke to give the order on the comm," Sander said. "Luke told me about it. You couldn't do more than that."

"I still don't understand," Claire said. "What exactly happened?"

When Sander explained the betrayal in more detail, step by step, Claire's eyes went wide as she looked at Matt. He avoided her gaze.

The sensation of her pity made him feel even worse than when she'd been coming on to him. But she surprised him.

"I really want to meet Luke," Claire said. "When do I get to meet your brother?"

"You can meet him anytime you're ready," Sander said. "Luke arrived here a few days ago."

At that moment, a door opened to the kitchen. Luke entered the room on two wheels, continuing the wheelie all the way across to the kitchen table, as his aide, Corinne, followed close behind. The timing of his entrance made Matt feel sure he had been listening.

Matt watched Claire. She stared as Luke's front wheels came down with a bang. He sat about four feet from her, but it was impossible to tell if he was actually looking at her. His head, with long greasy hair the same shade of dark brown as Matt's, pressed sideways against a long, steel support rod, with a pad to cushion it. Luke's eyes only stopped to focus for brief fractions of a second before rolling up in their sockets. His sticklike arms hung limp and his bony forearms rested on the padded arms of the wheelchair. Luke's mouth hung open most of the time, saliva pooling in one corner and dripping down his chin. His T-shirt proclaimed, "Fuck Google. Just ask me."

"The courageous and beautiful Claire Tenneman," Luke said in his metallic synthesized voice.

"Who are you?" Claire said. Matt noticed her back was pressed hard against her chair. He felt like laughing, but fear made him keep silent.

"Claire, meet Luke Carney, Matt's brother," Sander said.

Claire's face went pale. Her lips moved, but no words came out. Her hands came up and gripped the chair arms as she stared at Luke. Then she turned to look at Matt.

"Identical twins. This is your idea of a joke?"

Matt laughed. He couldn't help it. Even as Claire's eyebrows bunched together and her lips curled down, he couldn't stop. "It's no joke, really. We're identical twins."

"You're about as fucking identical as me and Nina Nardelli," Claire said. Matt watched astonished as she stood up and hurried across the room. She stopped at the first door she came to, a bedroom where he and Benjy had slept two weeks ago, opened the door and shut herself inside. It actually looked like she was about to cry.

"She's worn out," Sander said after a few moments of stunned silence.

"She's no Nina Nardelli," Luke said.

"You could be nice," Matt said. "She's been through a lot. And she proved herself over and over, in the last few days."

"Saved your tender ass," Luke said.

"Why don't you tell us about it," Sander said.

Matt related the story of arriving at the cabin in Michigan, only to have it attacked and firebombed by Black Widow militiamen. He told them how, without Claire's quick thinking, he would've died in that basement. He told them about the laundry room, and the secret tunnel leading outside. From the first moment, when she cut his binds and handed him a loaded Beretta 9mm gun, she had trusted him. He left out the part about her liking him a little too much.

"Seems like the girl's got a functioning brain," Luke said.

"Matt, go and find her," Sander said. Ten minutes had gone by. "She's had a shock. I want her to feel welcome here."

Matt found her sitting on a bed in the guest bedroom. Claire's face was in her hands. He walked over slowly and sat down next to her.

"Sorry for laughing, Claire." He had his hand on the small of her back. "I guess I was nervous or something. I didn't even know Luke was here. I thought he was still in Montana somewhere."

Claire straightened up and threw her arms around his neck. She kissed him hard, on the cheek. Matt kept his face turned away. Her hot breath made him start feeling aroused, but he made no move in her direction. She was so thin and... needy, somehow. She made him uncomfortable. Finally, she took down her arms.

"Matt, what the hell has he got?" Claire had to clear her throat. He could tell she had been crying.

"It's called Lou Gehrig's, or ALS motor neuron disease. He has no control over most of his muscles."

"Since when?"

"Since he was about fifteen, I guess. We didn't grow up together."

"When you said you had an identical twin, I assumed he would look just like you. Like a clone or something."

"I guess I should've told you."

"You're a real asshole, you know that?"

He looked at his feet. "I guess maybe I am, if you think about it."

Claire stood up. "I didn't mean to be impolite before. Come on." She led the way back to the kitchen. Once they reached the group sitting around the table, Matt took his seat again.

To his amazement, Claire went right up to Luke and kissed him on the cheek. "That's for saving our asses when we were drifting backward down the fucking Mississippi River. I was freaking out until Matt told me what you'd arranged. All I could think was we were going to get ground up into hamburger in some giant hydraulic lock somewhere downriver."

"Nice to meet you, too," Luke said.

She knows? Luke asked, using their special link.

Had to tell her, Matt answered.

"Matt tells me you're good at things like DNS spoofing and packet sniffers," Claire said.

"I sincerely doubt Matt told you that," Luke said. He actually sounded surprised.

Claire smiled and looked at Matt. "Actually I guessed. And now I think I know how you got into Gram's safe."

Matt smiled.

"Piece of cake," Luke said. "You know about DNS spoofing?"

"Piece of cake," Claire said.

"What the hell are you guys talking about?" Matt asked. It was as if Claire had suddenly become a whole different person. He was tired, but it sounded like they were speaking a different language.

"What I don't get is how you guys are identical," Claire said. "You must have the same DNA, but can differences this extraordinary come out in the expression? I mean, how else can you explain Luke having this horrible disease while you're so healthy? Shouldn't you both have the same genetic destiny?"

"Genetic destiny," Luke echoed. His shining eyes actually focused on Claire for about two whole seconds. "I like that, but then your variable expression theory will have to be broadened to account for him getting the brain of a fish."

"Matt is brilliant in his own way," Claire said. "So maybe that's one of the things you two have in common."

"He certainly has proved himself adept at surviving," Sander said.

"He certainly is good at blowing opportunities," Luke said.

An unearthly tinny growling sound emanated from Luke, and Matt realized it was his brother laughing through the synthesizer. The strange sound was comical in itself. Claire looked from one to the other, not getting the joke. It was probably better that way. Matt realized he himself was laughing just to see Luke so happy.

MISSILES RECOVERED IN TIME FOR AVIATION START
Stinger Missiles Used in 2019 Attacks

More than two years ago, the U.S. Army could not account for 6,000 shoulder-fired Stinger missiles and launch assemblies. According to government officials, similar missiles were used in attacks on commercial planes on September 11, 2019, which killed 1,024 people. In an operation with cooperation among Homeland Security, local police and army elements, the remaining missiles were recovered yesterday in Des Moines, Iowa.

Petra Bedrosian, the president's press secretary, called the Des Moines operation "courageous, creative and decisive." An anonymous tip led Homeland Security to a suspected March22 warehouse in an industrial park in Des Moines. By the time authorities arrived, according to Bedrosian, most of the missiles had already been loaded onto modified antique fire trucks in preparation for their removal. Twenty active members of March22 were arrested.

When a March22 Hellfire missile slammed into the warehouse with no warning, government investigators were forced to retreat from the uncontrolled inferno. No one was injured. Missiles March22 had left behind continued to spontaneously detonate during the night. Two Predator drones, previously stolen from the government, were blamed for the attack on the warehouse. They were shot down over Des Moines by FA-18 fighter jets from the Iowa National Guard, based in Des Moines.

With yesterday's arrests, the March22 organization has taken responsibility for the missiles stolen in 2019 and the missile strike on the Des Moines warehouse. Whether March22 carried out the attacks on commercial aviation in September 2019 remains under investigation.

"We're extremely pleased to have eliminated the threat of future attacks with these stolen weapons in time for the resumption of regular commercial flights," said David S. Knopfler, Deputy Chief of Homeland Security, at a press conference. The administration and the FAA had previously announced that commercial flights would start again on December 10, after an unprecedented two-year grounding.

"This is a significant victory over the criminal forces that are the scourge of our country," Knopfler said, referring to March22. On December 4, the Anonymous Party changed its name officially to March22. In his own press conference, March22 Representative Dan Creighton denied the version of events presented by Homeland Security. "We provided the authorities with evidence that the Stinger missiles were stolen by the Dark Fiber Militia in 2019 and used by them to carry out the attacks," Creighton said. The administration did not respond to requests for a response to Creighton's statement.

THE AGENTS SITTING across from Wyoming Ryder looked like they'd been up all night. He recognized Riley Johnson, from Homeland Security, and Knight, the FBI chief. Wyoming was flanked by his two lawyers, Karen Vixen and Mark Knox.

"You're free to go," Knight said.

"What?" Vixen said.

"Sensational." Wyoming stood. "We're not going to argue, are we?"

His lawyers stood with him, but Karen Vixen wasn't finished. "What is your finding, for the record?"

"Our searches of your computers and files in Malibu and your duplex in New York turned up no incriminating evidence, as far as we have been able to determine. Mr. Ryder remains a person of interest and has to surrender his passport. However, he is free to go."

Wyoming met the cold blue eyes of Johnson and had the distinct feeling that Homeland Security had made the decision. They could've pulled authority on the FBI. They were surely going to watch him closely. They probably thought he would lead them to the heart of March22.

"Which way are you headed, Mr. Ryder?" Johnson asked as the lawyers put away their papers.

"Is San Francisco Airport open today?"

"Very funny," Johnson said coldly.

"Guess I'll head down to Malibu and check out some new scripts. My agent wants my head on a platter."

"You do that," Johnson said.

A knot of journalists with drones were waiting on the steps of the FBI building when he came out, led by Mark Knox, who stood six inches taller and helped shield him from view. Karen Vixen moved to his left side, the side on which most of the reporters were bunched. The reporters all stood up and started shouting when they glimpsed him.

"Don't answer," she said as she kept a grip on his arm and kept moving.

"Mr. Ryder, now that March22 is a political party, how do you plan to vote?"

"Using my brain," Wyoming said.

"Will you be seeing the First Lady again?" asked another.

"She has my number," he said. "I'm just glad she's safe."

Knox had called a VIP car service from the conference room, and the SUV pulled up as they got to the bottom of the steps. The reporters crowded around as he got into the rear seat. He closed the door without answering any more questions, keeping a photogenic smile on his face. The smile of an innocent man.

CHAPTER 64

AMES, IOWA
DECEMBER 10, 2021 AT NOON

"MATT, TIME TO get up. There's a surprise for you in the kitchen." Sander stood in the doorway. Matt sat up groggily in bed, having only caught the last few words. He had to think for a moment to remember he was back in a familiar March22 safe house.

He pulled on his camouflage pants and sweatshirt, both of which really needed washing, and headed to the kitchen in bare feet. The sun streamed through the windows. Floating on a sunbeam he saw a vision. He could've sworn Raine was standing there, her long red hair tied in a high ponytail, the wide smile lighting up her face and her eyes.

"Don't you know me anymore?"

His throat tightened and tears filled his eyes. Raine stood there in a pair of ripped jeans and a white T-shirt, with her green Converse All Star shoes.

"You're here?" It came out as a croak.

"Got here a half hour ago. I told Sander to let you sleep, but he insisted."

"Oh my God!"

Matt ran the last three steps and crushed her in his arms. Her warm hands pressed into his back, and they found each other in a deep kiss. She felt so solid and warm, but the reality of it only began to take hold as their tongues devoured each other. Matt had dreamed of this moment so many times, not knowing when it would happen again. He didn't want to ever let go. They went on hugging tight for a long time as he breathed in her familiar jasmine scent.

"Good morning, good morning," Luke's synthesized voice came out of nowhere.

Startled, Matt unwound his arms from Raine and opened his eyes. Luke sat in his wheelchair across the table. "Where the hell did you come from?"

"I've been up since six."

"What the hell did you get up so early for?" Laughing, Matt collapsed into a chair and pulled Raine down on his lap.

"Gotta get my kicks any way I can," Luke said. Just then, Claire walked into the kitchen, her short hair wet from the shower. "Ah, speak of the devil."

Claire walked straight over to Luke and, to Matt's amazement, gave him a long kiss on the mouth. Without explanation, Claire then turned and held out her hand to Raine, who stood. "You must be Raine. I'm Claire."

"Hi," Raine said.

"I'm the former Dark Fiber leader from Ann Arbor," Claire said.

"Oh!"

"I caught a glimpse of your face when Matt was on the phone with you," Claire explained. "When we were out on the river."

Raine looked at Matt.

"She saved my life," Matt said. "She's with March22 now."

"He saved mine, too, so we're even," Claire said. "How great that you were able to come here and join him."

"Yeah, how the hell did you get here?" Matt asked.

"They wanted to get me and Benjy out of there because of the situation with—" Raine glanced at Claire, clearly unsure about how much she could say.

"It's okay, Raine," Matt said.

"Your dad really went postal," Raine went on. "Like he wanted to kill us. Winter had to get back to Montana. He thought it best to get us out of there. We left last night. They brought us here in a helicopter during the night but we had to stop four times to refuel and didn't get here until this morning."

"I had them covered from above," Luke said. "Thirteen hundred miles at a thousand feet in a chopper. Pretty tricky."

"Winter decided that for me? For us?" Matt felt overwhelmed with gratitude that the March22 leader had made it a priority to reunite them. Winter always seemed like such a crusty old prick.

Benjy appeared from another door. His face lit up in a smile. "Hey, Matt!"

"Benjy, old friend." Matt stood up and they bro-hugged. "Hey man, thanks for taking care of my woman."

Benjy turned red. "We took a helicopter all the way from Nevada. Did you know a chopper pilot has to work with both hands and both feet at the same time?"

"Ah, that feels good," Luke said. Claire had her hand down in deep between the small of Luke's back and the material of the wheelchair, rubbing softly.

"I slept through most of it," Raine said.

"Benjy, this is Claire," Luke said. They shook hands, after which Claire returned to massaging Luke's back.

"You were with Dark Fiber," Benjy said, his eyes shining.

"I got out while the getting was good," Claire said.

"You're taller and bigger," Matt said, sizing Benjy up. Benjy drew in a deep breath, his chest bulging.

They cooked brunch together, making a huge mess on all the kitchen counters. Soon, platters of pancakes, scrambled eggs, bacon, and toast crowded the table. Luke sat between Benjy and Claire, who fed Luke small bites.

"I gave Corinne the day off," Claire said as the others stared.

"And the night," Luke added. When Claire tried to hush him up, Luke went on, "Corinne's becoming a real bitch, sometimes."

"Luke, zip it and eat," Claire said, placing a bite of pancake on his tongue. Matt was astounded to see how this was working. Claire seemed to have taken over. "You, sir, have a really big mouth," she went on.

"I guess she doesn't just mean for eating," Benjy said, grinning.

"He talked till five in the morning," Claire said. "Then he was up again at six. How's a girl supposed to get any sleep?"

"She finally figured out a surefire way to shut me up," Luke said. He and Claire looked deep into each other's eyes.

"That's enough on that topic," Claire said. She had gone red to the roots of her hair.

"At last, a woman with a brain," Luke said.

Matt looked at Raine, and they both burst out laughing. Who would've thought Luke and Claire would like each other?

"DO YOU REALLY think she likes him that much?" Raine asked. They'd gone on a walk in the late afternoon. Now they were sitting on a little hill at the back of Sander's property. At the bottom of the hill, a forest blanketed the countryside. Oak trees mixed with red maple, birch, hickory and white pine. The sun had sunk to a point halfway below the horizon, and the clouds were aflame in shades of pink, purple, blue, and orange.

Matt understood the question, or at least he thought he did. How could anyone feel romantically inclined toward a person in Luke's condition, the way Luke looked?

Knowing that his disease was incurable and would probably only get worse as he got older. Knowing that he was incapable of doing things like taking her for a walk, like this, or hugging, or making love.

"He does have a wicked sense of humor."

"What's she like?" Raine asked.

"I only spent a few days with her. But when I think of what we went through, well, it showed how tough she is. She likes motorcycles and guns — turns out, she's a great shot."

"Better than you?"

"About the same. We did some shooting. She didn't miss any."

"You don't miss any either, according to Benjy."

Rained didn't know yet about the Black Widow killers who had arrived at Gram's safe house a few days ago. Matt shuddered at the memory of those half-charred men out in the back yard. And their stench. He felt exhausted just thinking of all the people who'd tried to kill him, and paid with their lives for it. How had it ever come to this?

Just then a plane crossed the sky off to the right, slowly banking to the west as it ascended. The loud jet noise startled him, and for a moment Matt could only stare. It was a big commercial jet. Probably it had taken off from Des Moines, fifty miles south, and was headed somewhere north and west of Iowa.

"It's really happening," Raine said, following his eyes and staring at the receding plane in wonder. "They started flying again."

"It's kind of amazing, isn't it," Matt said. "Today's the day they set for starting up again."

"You said they tried to kill her," Raine said. When he looked blankly, she added, "Claire."

"She was in a militia. They had to fight rival militias trying to steal their territory. It's like a continual gang war."

"She's a survivor, like you."

Maybe someday he would tell Raine about the events at the safe house. Just not the part about Claire being raped. He didn't think he could ever tell Raine about that.

"She's been through a lot, yeah. Enough to know she'd had enough of that militia life. I guess she'll make a good addition to March22."

"Matt, when you were kidnapped, I nearly lost it," Raine said. He pushed a strand of her hair back behind her ear, and looked in her eyes. "I was afraid we'd be separated for a long time, all over again."

"Me too."

"I've been training, you know, and I'm going to go on with it. I left California to go to Montana with you because I want to be with you. I don't care about college right now. I just don't want us to be separated anymore."

"We're not going to be separated again," he said. "I'm going to talk to Sander about it. And Luke."

"Why Luke?"

"Apparently, he's the true leader of March22."

"When your dad told us that Luke was the only one who could launch missiles, I almost didn't believe him," she said.

"I guess it's for a good reason."

Raine stared out at the forest. "Why can't we just live our lives somewhere? Why can't we just forget about all this fighting and kidnapping and killing people?"

Matt shrugged, not knowing the answer. His father had made it clear that they had to fight. But now March22 was a political party, and the shoulder-fired missiles had been returned to the US Army. With his father locked up, he probably wouldn't be part of the leadership anymore, so maybe the fight was over. Maybe his father was more a part of the problem than the solution.

"I don't know any reason why we can't do that," he said. "I think we should give it a try."

Raine was pointing at something in the forest. Then he saw it. A flash of bright blue, like the color of the lightest part of the sky. A tingling feeling surged through his muscles. He wanted to look at Raine as the bird skipped off a branch and took flight, but if he looked away, it would be gone.

"It's our lucky bird," Raine said.

The bluebird flew directly toward them before turning and flapping a greeting with its wings. It displayed flashes of its stunning blue back before returning to the forest.

"He came to say hi," Matt said.

"I can't believe we saw one."

"I saw one in Illinois, you know. When Benjy and I were on our way to come and get you. Now I've seen them in Illinois and Iowa. You know what I'd love?"

"What?"

"Someday I'd love to see a mountain bluebird. You only see them high in the mountains, in the Rockies."

"What was this one?"

"This was an Eastern bluebird. They have that brownish breast. Mountain bluebirds are blue all over."

"That must be fabulous," Raine said.

"The males, at least."

"Do you know what I read?" Raine looked at him without smiling. The bluebird had disappeared into the forest, and hadn't come back. "People hunt them."

"Bluebirds?"

"Bluebirds, cardinals, yellow finches, red-winged blackbirds — anything with a spot of color. Some people are crazy enough to use them as target practice, just thanks to their bright colors."

Matt felt his face going hot. "They should be thrown in jail."

When they got back to the main house, the others were sitting in a group in front of the TV wall. Sander and his wife Leisl were also there.

"*Faking It with the Nardellis* is starting in half an hour," Claire said.

"This is a special show on March22," Benjy added.

"Matt and Luke and I have a meeting now," Sander said, getting up from his chair. "We'll be back in time for the show."

"We do?" Matt asked. Sander waved him along without further explanation, leading the way toward the back of the house.

CHAPTER 65

AMES, IOWA
DECEMBER 10, 2021—5 PM

MATT SAT AT a laptop workstation with a headset on and watched the screen. One after another, the images of the others on the secure chat appeared, and automatically minimized to fit. Sander, Winter and Luke appeared, but his own face did not. To Matt's surprise, Wyoming Ryder's face appeared on the screen.

"Welcome to the group, Matt," Sander said. "And welcome back, Wyoming. What the hell are you doing here?"

"Luke invited me," Wyoming said.

"He got sprung a few hours ago," Luke said. "They think they can watch him."

"This is good news," Winter said.

"He's secure?" Sander asked.

"Piece of cake," Luke said.

"Your surprising release is another order of business, then," Sander said. "But first, we need to talk about John, and we also need to talk about the media treatment of what happened last night. Has everybody seen the *Post* article?"

"What article? Matt said. Nobody had said anything to him about a *Post* article.

"The *Washington Post* reported that March22 stole the missiles from the army back in 2019, instead of Dark Fiber," Sander said. "There is the suggestion that we shot down those planes. Hardly any mention of Dark Fiber at all, except for one quote from Dan Creighton. The whole thing makes March22 look like the bad guys."

"That's outrageous," Matt said. "How could they do that?"

"It's what John was afraid of," Winter said. "Luke, didn't you send them that FASTBACK as corroborating evidence?"

"Sure did," Luke said. "But who has time to read, these days?"

"How could they lie like that?" Matt asked. March22 had stolen the missiles out of a Dark Fiber warehouse. The article, as Sander was describing it, was so far from the truth, he was at a loss for words.

"We definitely need to improve our public relations," Wyoming said.

"I've got a theory about this," Winter said.

"Which is?" Sander replied.

"They fed false information to the media in order to provoke us. They want someone from March22 to come forward and fight in public."

"Sounds plausible to me," Wyoming said. "In which case, we will need good legal representation. In any event, we need to make our PR more professional."

"I like the idea of Wyoming being in charge of PR," Winter said.

"I can't be in charge of it, but I know a few people," Wyoming said.

"Luke, are those emails in a form that we can make public?" Sander asked.

"Sure thing," Luke said.

"I'll get my PR people to provide a press release including sections from the emails," Wyoming said, picking up on the idea. "Luke, I'll look up a couple of contacts and tell you after the chat who to send them to. You can send them from an encrypted March22 address."

"All right, so we'll have our rebuttal in a couple of days," Sander said. "We'll let the administration build up a nice sense of false confidence in their untruthful accusations, then hit them where it counts."

"Rub their nose in the doo-doo," Winter added.

"Now to our second order of business," Sander went on. "Matt, we decided to get you in on these discussions because you've been at the center of things in recent weeks. The gift that you and Luke have is a kind of secret weapon for March22. It's therefore especially painful for me to introduce our next topic. Your father committed an atrocity that we cannot take lightly. You are all informed about what he did."

"I'm sorry," Wyoming interrupted. "I just used my get out of jail free card and missed the action."

"John somehow got control of two of our drones," Winter said.

"What?" Wyoming exclaimed.

"He was against our plan of stealing the shoulder-fired missiles from Dark Fiber and handing them over to the army," Winter continued. "John wanted to smoke the warehouse with a Hellfire or two. In the middle of our operation to remove the missiles, he got a missile launched."

"Holy Jesus," Wyoming said.

"Luke was following the situation electronically, Matt on the ground. Due to their special communication ability, Matt was able to get most of our people out of the warehouse before the missile hit."

"Most of our people?" Wyoming echoed.

"Two of our local men were killed."

"Oh, Christ," Wyoming said.

"Those deaths are on his head," Luke said.

"We retrieved five thousand of the missiles and most of the launch assemblies before it happened," Sander said. "John is locked up at Desert West, and frothing at the mouth. He still doesn't see what he did wrong."

"He's unfortunately going to feel vindicated by the *Post* article," Luke pointed out.

"Nevertheless, we made a consensus decision on the strategy," Sander said. "He was obligated to support the group decision even if he disagreed. Instead, he carried out a rogue operation all on his own, and wound up killing two of our men."

"It would've been a lot more without Matt's quick thinking," Winter growled.

"And Luke," Matt said.

"Firing off a Hellfire at this stage didn't exactly help our image, either," Wyoming said.

"Right, so here's the question," Sander went on. "What role, if any, does John Carney have in March22 from here on out? And linked with that, how do we choose to sanction him?"

Matt felt the heat rising in his face as the silence lengthened. Less than a week ago, he had felt only love and admiration for his father. Those feelings had been submerged in a blinding vortex of rage, bitterness, and confusion. Two men were dead now. If the missile had hit only a few seconds earlier, he himself would be dead—murdered by his own father.

"A long prison sentence in a regular penitentiary," Luke said, breaking the silence. "We turn him over to the authorities."

"That's impossible," Wyoming said. "Think of what he could reveal. John knows everything."

"Not everything," Luke said. "But it's true we would have some major reconfiguring tasks on our hands."

"We have all the drones in two locations," Winter pointed out. "Big Sky Base and Georgia. He could lead them directly to those. And you know what else we have at Big Sky Base."

"Where else would we store all the drones and the bombs?" Wyoming said. "We can't turn him in, even if we wanted to."

"Listen, there's something I've got to say," Wyoming said. "We can't ask the man's boys, his flesh and blood, to come up with a solution. It's inhumane."

"I agree," Sander said. "But they are with us in this group. Even if the rest of us come up with an approach, they should have a vote. I suggest we all give it some more thought. We need to take our time with this, even if it takes days or weeks, and get it right. In the meantime, we hold him."

"Sounds about right to me," Wyoming said.

"If you don't like my idea, I'm going to take control of two drones and shoot Hellfire missiles at your children," Luke said. When no one said anything, he added, "Just a little joke."

Matt had the feeling Luke had a new lease on life since last night. Claire's attention seemed to have worked wonders. All this cheerful joking around was different from his usual sarcasm.

"Wyoming, you're my next piece of business," Sander said.

"Those were the exact words of my second ex-wife," Wyoming said.

"You're going to get that email package out to the media in the proper form?"

"I'll put our trusty friend Luke in contact with a PR firm," Wyoming said.

"Of course, they won't be able to identify or locate me," Luke said.

"Right," Wyoming confirmed. "And I'm an arm's length from the PR firm myself. The firm I have in mind is in New Jersey, by the way. This will be a March22 thing, not a Wyoming Ryder thing."

"Good," Sander said. "And we all have to watch Nina Nardelli tonight."

"I hate Nina Nardelli," Matt said.

"You do? Why?" Wyoming said.

"It's all just about big breasts and everything."

"Those are fake," Wyoming laughed. "I knew her when she was a B-cup."

"Are there any women left you haven't known?" The teasing sounded especially funny in Luke's metallic voice, and Wyoming laughed hardest of all.

"Let's keep on track," Sander said. "Wyoming, what can we expect from the Nina Nardelli show? I have to confess, like Matt, I'm not exactly a regular watcher."

"The only thing to expect is the unexpected," Wyoming said. "But seriously. I think we can count on Nina to dramatize our version of events in a memorable way, winning the hearts and minds of sixty million viewers."

"I just hope she doesn't get arrested," Winter said.

"I'm told the show starts in ten minutes. Are we done?" Sander asked.

"Hold on. Hold everything," Winter said. Then he swore. In the image on his screen, Matt saw Winter studying his Jetlink.

"What is it, Douglas?" Sander asked.

Winter's face stared into the screen, all the humor erased. "I just got a message from Rory MacGregor at Desert West. They went to check on John a few minutes ago, and he was gone."

"What?" Sander exclaimed.

"He escaped?" Wyoming echoed.

"MacGregor said a motorcycle is missing, too. They've got vehicles going after him, but they don't have a chopper there right now. They think he may have a head start of an hour, but that's just a guess."

Matt felt his muscles tense as he stared at the men's shocked faces. Wyoming, Sander, and Winter were agape. They had all worked so hard to bring March22 to the point where it was now. They dreamed of solving the country's problems, cleaning up corruption, and making the streets safer. They had found ways to work together, only to have one of their own rise in rebellion against the very group he had created.

Only Luke's expression remained unchanged. Then again, Luke's expression never changed for anything.

"I'll try to pick him up from the air. At least we know where he's headed," Luke said, breaking the silence.

"You know? Where?" Sander asked.

"He won't come here," Winter said, referring to Big Sky Base. "He knows he'd never get through our defenses."

"Where, Luke?" Matt demanded.

"Assume his prime motivation is the furtherance of March22's aims, as he sees them," Luke said. "Because he managed to commandeer two of our drones, assume he thinks he's found out how to rule the skies. If he doesn't go to Big Sky Base, what's the only other place we have drones?"

"Georgia," Wyoming said.

"Right," Luke said.

"We need to warn Abba," Wyoming went on. "Luke may be right. John could activate the network from there if we don't stop him. There's no telling what he might do."

"He can't do that, can he, Luke?" Sander asked. Matt was sure he heard a note of desperation in Sander's voice.

"Working on it," Luke said. "I didn't think he could do what he did in Des Moines. He has his strengths."

"Wyoming, you know Abba best," Winter said. "We need to make sure John doesn't turn him, and we need to make sure John doesn't get in there and light it up."

"I can't take my plane there," Wyoming said. "I can't shake Homeland Security and the FBI for the moment, realistically. I don't want to lead anyone right to our door in Georgia."

"You concentrate on our PR," Luke said.

"I'll go," Sander said. "We've got a chopper here."

"Matt has to go with you," Luke said.

"Me? Why me?" Luke's suggestion caught Matt completely by surprise. He had just gotten back from his kidnapping ordeal. He wasn't about to take off somewhere again. "I don't know anything about computers or controlling drones. How could I possibly contribute anything?"

"We might need you to reason with him," Sander said quietly. "Luke is right. Between you and me, Matt, we might have a chance to get through to him."

Matt saw the logic of it, at least in theory, but the whole idea felt like a mountain rising up in front of him, rising higher and higher as he looked for ways around it. They thought he could reason with his father. How could you reason with a man who'd handed your ass to a vicious militia, then nearly killed you with a missile shot out of the sky?

All the leaders seemed to be waiting for an answer from him.

"I don't really see how I can help, but I'll go on one condition," Matt said. "If I can bring Raine."

"Well, now, Matt, we're not used to having folks set conditions," Winter said immediately.

"It doesn't matter," Wyoming said.

"It's fine if you don't agree," Matt said, relieved. "I just won't go. I've been separated from her long enough. I just got back from being kidnapped. Handed over by my father to those Dark fiber assholes. In the last three weeks, I've been nearly killed about ten different times. I don't care if I have to do this mission, but I'm not going without Raine."

"Maybe we can make an exception," Sander said.

"Second," Wyoming said.

"Let him bring his squeeze," Luke said. "Turns out she's a natural good shot."

"I don't agree, but I'm not John Carney," Winter said.

Sander smiled grimly. "But we need to leave tonight, pretty much right away. Luke, will you inform Abba of the danger, and tell him we're coming to give him some support?"

"Jesus, this is all we needed," Winter said.

"Contacting him now," Luke said.

"Douglas, I agree with Luke," Sander went on. "But still there's a chance John would head north. You'll need to be watchful."

"I'm on it," Winter said. "We'll increase the security massively, with John's capabilities in mind."

"If I can spot him from the air, we'll get confirmation of where he's headed," Luke added.

"Everybody, we need to think like John thinks," Sander said. "We need to assume MacGregor's men won't find him. Any questions?"

"Don't forget to watch Nina," Wyoming said. "It's starting in one minute. I promised her."

Matt observed as the leaders' faces disappeared from his screen, one by one. He had a heavy heart at the challenge that lay before him. He wasn't looking forward to leaving tonight. What could he possibly accomplish with his father? Raine's words came back to him: *Your dad really went postal. Like he wanted to kill us.*

He wasn't looking forward to watching Nina Nardelli, either.

In the kitchen, everyone was still grouped in front of the TV wall. Raine got up from her chair and, without a word, settled on Matt's lap. When he circled his arms around her tummy, and she rested her arms on his, no one gave them a second look.

Claire sat in a chair right next to Luke's wheelchair, her face glued to the TV wall.

Normally Matt would never watch Nina Nardelli. Raine couldn't stand her, either. But being with Raine made everything all right. Even Nina Nardelli. He could tell her afterward about the new mission. He kept his arms around her during the whole show.

CHAPTER 66

NINA NARDELLI SLEEPS in her bed, but she's tossing and turning. Her sleep is disturbed by a dream. Her bedroom is dark, the satin sheets reflecting some soft light. The picture shimmers, signifying that she's still dreaming, as Nina slowly sits up, then rises from the bed. Nina stands next to her bed, wearing only her low-cut nightgown. Her eyes are open, but it's clear that she's in the middle of a vivid dream.

"You!" she exclaims.

President James Jeffers stands just inside her bedroom door. The fucking president of the fucking United States of America.

Jeffers bares his lips in a lascivious smile, then laughs out loud at the prize that awaits. One night with Nina Nardelli, just one night! One wild, unforgettable night burying his face in those gorgeous melons! Every man's fantasy!

He needs to take three steps, then he can throw her on the bed and have his fill of her voluptuous body. When Nina Nardelli says no, even *screams* no, you know it doesn't *mean* no. Because Nina Nardelli *wants* it.

Everything going through the president's mind is written in his face.

The actor playing the president could be a body double, he looks so much like James Jeffers. The actor's name is Ronald Wingsley. Ron was made for the part—a similarly shaped suntanned face, iron gray hair, and broad, stooped shoulders. He wears a duplicate of Jeffers' standard dark gray suit, a crisp white Oxford button-down shirt, and the already familiar arresting blue silk necktie that is Jeffers' trademark.

Jeffers starts toward her, reaching out his hand. "I want you, Nina. I want you for one unforgettable night."

"Wait!" she says, and he stops.

"What?"

"Why did you shoot it down?"

"What? Shoot what down? Please, Nina, don't make me wait."

"My friend, Wyoming Ryder. You shot his plane down."

The actor's face contorts in a grimace. "Don't bother me with business. I don't want to talk about work. I worked most of last night and all day today. Now it's time for my wild night of passion."

"Not until you've told me."

"I'm not telling *you* anything."

"Then you can forget about your wild night, Mr. President. Tell me about shooting down Wyoming's plane."

"Oh, all right. But you can't tell anybody."

"Me? I would never tell anyone."

Jeffers looks relieved. "You know, he had March22 people on board. The command and control elements."

"What's that, Jimmy? Speak English."

"The stolen drones, you know, Nina? You know they stole our drones. There are certain specialists who can oversee the control of all the stolen drones. We zeroed in on them in Palo Alto. But they slipped through our fingers."

"Slipped through your fingers?"

Jeffers nods. "They escaped and fled to the San Francisco Airport. They created a diversion at the north end of the field so they could take off. The airport was closed, Nina. We had missile strikes on our tanks. Missiles from their goddamned stolen drones."

"You must have been mad when Wyoming took off from San Francisco Airport during this battle. Is that why you shot his plane out of the sky?"

"At least I thought we did," Jeffers says, looking slightly confused. "The man appears nine days later. His plane is intact. No wreckage found." The president brightens, and takes a step forward. "Nina, Nina..."

"Wait, Mr. President."

He stops again in midstride, still six feet away. His face clouds. "What now? You are so mind-blowingly hot, I've got to have you."

"Why did they have to blow up the Golden Gate Bridge?"

Jeffers' eyes narrow. His look grows steely. "Who blew it up? Tell me, Nina. Do you know? Was it March22?"

"What have we come to when someone has to blow up the Golden Gate Bridge to ensure America's security?"

"I don't know what you're talking about. Come off this nonsense. Come on, Nina, let's just have sex."

Nina's hand goes up. "Let me jog your memory, Mr. President. What was that army convoy carrying? Why did the bridge blow up just as an army convoy was crossing?"

"They attacked our soldiers," Jeffers says sadly. "Over two hundred of our own young men and women lost their lives in the attack. A cowardly attack."

"You're leaving something out, Mr. President."

"What could be more important than the lives of two hundred soldiers?"

"What was in the trucks? What was the convoy carrying, Mr. President?"

Jeffers hangs his head. "I'm not supposed to say."

"You can tell Nina, Jimmy."

"No, no, no, I can't."

"Tell your little secret to Nina. Then we can go do some beddy-bye together."

He looks up, hopeful. "Really? You mean it?"

"What was that convoy carrying, Jimmy. Tell Nina."

"Just... some bombs."

"Just bombs?"

"Yeah." He clasps his fingers together, looking at the floor.

"Weren't they a teeny bit special, these bombs?"

"Well, yeah. They were dirty." He looks at her. The word acquires special meaning in Nina Nardelli's bedroom. "Dirty nukes, you know."

"You mean like the kind that fit in a briefcase?" Nina persists.

"Well, I don't know if they fit in a *briefcase*, but—"

"And why was the army moving all those dirty nukes that fit in briefcases through the city of San Francisco and across the Golden Gate Bridge on November fifteenth?"

"It wasn't safe, all right?" The president is beginning to get impatient. "The San Andreas Fault, and everything. We were moving them to a safer place."

"Wasn't the new place in Oakville even *closer* to the fault line than the facility in San Jose, Jimmy?"

"Well, yeah, but we were only going to leave them in Oakville till we found a better place somewhere else."

"Oh, Jimmy," Nina says. "Was Jimmy a bad boy?"

"Jimmy was a bad, bad boy," Jeffers says.

"Come a little closer, Jimmy."

They stand there a moment at arm's length. Then Nina steps forward and plants a kiss on the president's mouth. She wraps him in her arms, while sucking the life out of him in one, long, passionate kiss. By the end of the first kiss, they're both panting. His hands clutch her ass, and they're moving together, grinding against each other. The president can't seem to get enough of the deepest part of Nina Nardelli's mouth.

Suddenly she breaks off, leaving him glassy-eyed and panting. His mouth hangs open like he's just run the fifty-yard dash. He looks like he doesn't know what's happening to him.

"Wait," she says again. "You didn't tell me what happened to the briefcase bombs. We know they went to the bottom of the bay when the bridge exploded. They sank with all the trucks, right? They should've been on the bottom of the bay, right, Jimmy? But they weren't."

"No, they weren't," he confirms. "We went down there with our divers and they weren't there."

"Not a single one?"

"We didn't find a single one."

"What the fuck, Jimmy? I mean, really, what the fuck?"

"That's exactly what I said," Jeffers says.

"I mean, really, first you lose six thousand shoulder-fired missiles, back in 2019."

"We got those back. We got them back yesterday," Jeffers points out.

"No more attacks on American Airlines and United Airlines?"

"No, no, no," Jeffers says, going pale at the thought.

"Then you lose over twelve hundred drones."

"Shot two of those down yesterday over Iowa," he says.

"Then you lose all those truckloads of briefcase bombs. What's going on, Jimmy?"

"We're talking business, here. I didn't come here to talk business. What about my wild night of passion?"

"A girl needs to talk a while first, Jimmy. You ought to know that."

"I know, I know." Hangs his head.

"Just one more question. Who did you get the shoulder-fired missiles back from?"

"Come on, Nina, that's a trick question."

"Why? There's no trick."

"We got them back from some very kind, honest March22 folks in Iowa."

"All right then. But, wait! Do you mean March22 stole all those missiles and also carried out the attacks back in 2019? That's not right, is it?"

"No, we actually found out it was one of the militias that stole the missiles in 2019. They're the ones who carried out the attacks in 2019."

"One of the militias? Which one?"

"Dark Fiber. The biggest militia in the country, damned bloodsuckers. They stole the missiles and shot down twelve planes two years ago, then sat on the missiles all this time."

"How do we know this?"

"We've got... evidence," he says.

"Where did March22 come into it?"

"March22 found out about Dark Fiber doing it. They provided us with all the proof. March22 stole the missiles out of a Dark Fiber warehouse. Then they contacted Homeland Security and handed the missiles over to the US Army."

"March22 stole the missiles from Dark Fiber and handed them over to the authorities?"

"Sure did."

"But the newspaper said it was March22 that carried out the attacks in 2019."

Jeffers shrugged. "I guess journalists make mistakes, too."

"Jimmy, how does that make you feel when you realize March22 is actually helping you?"

Jeffers face puckers up. "Can't we go to bed now, Nina? I've got such an itchy pecker. My pecker wants to—"

"We're talking about feelings, Jimmy. Nothing gets a girl more excited. How did you feel about March22 when they recovered weapons that have been missing for more than two years, and handed them over to you?"

Jeffers thinks about it earnestly. "I'd be happier if they gave back our drones and those briefcase bombs, too, if you want the honest truth. Why do they give us back the missiles but not the drones and the bombs?"

"Do they want something in return?" Nina Nardelli asks.

"They haven't said. I haven't got the slightest idea," Jeffers says. "We don't even know who we have to talk to."

"What about the March22 Senators and Congressmen," Nina suggests. "They're a political party, now, aren't they?"

"You might have something there, Nina," he says, reflecting.

She smiles.

The two come together for another kiss. The kiss deepens into another clutching, groping, oxygen depriving, deep-throat exploration. Their knees weaken and they begin to shuffle in place, struggling to keep their feet.

Just as they are about to collapse sideways on the bed, the door to Nina's bedroom bursts open. Six men in motorcycle leathers and dark helmets jog into the room, carrying assault rifles.

The men spray the lovebirds with enough bullets to bring down a family of grizzly bears. Blood and fragments of skin and bone spatter everywhere, marking the ceiling, soaking the bed, staining Nina's famous white carpet. They fall on the ground, still clasped together, jerking and twitching as the last intact nerve endings send final signals to hands and feet and eyes.

The image on the screen shimmers again, obscuring any view of the bloodbath in the bedroom. As the shimmer ends, Nina Nardelli wakes suddenly, back in her bed, in the satin sheets. She sits bolt upright, breathing in choked gasps, covered in sweat, panic etched in her face. She flings all the covers on the floor, looking around wildly, then screams as her sister Alessandra Nardelli dashes into the room.

"I heard you," Alessandra says. "What happened? Are you all right?"

"I had a nightmare," Nina says, still hyperventilating. "Oh my God, what a nightmare! I was with the president. I was here. I was making out with President Jeffers."

"What happened? What did he say?" Alessandra asks.

"I don't remember. All I remember is we were making out. Ugh!" Nina makes a sour face, like she's eaten something bad.

CHAPTER 67

"I DON'T WANT to go."

"Matt, you have to go. Plus, I'll be by your side," Raine said. "Look you did it, and it's going to be okay. Just what we were talking about earlier. You arranged it so we could be together."

When she kissed him on the cheek with her arms wrapped tight around him, he felt his worries magically melting away. They sat on the bed in their guest room at Sander's farm. Instead of getting ready for a little lovemaking or sleep, since exhaustion was threatening to drag his eyelids closed whether he liked it or not, they had packed the few clothes and toiletries they had into Raine's overnight bag. Sander had popped in and said the chopper was leaving in fifteen minutes.

"We don't even know for sure if he's going to that place. It's like we're always going on some wild goose chase around the country."

"From what I saw, he could be dangerous," Raine said.

"You're damn right he's dangerous. He nearly killed me."

"You have to go because you're his son," Raine said. She was running her fingers through his hair. Matt stared at the door, his mind suddenly blank, like a paused movie. He had to struggle to listen. "You're their best shot at getting through to him. You and Sander together. That's what you told me. It makes sense, Matt. We can't let him get control of that place in Georgia, whatever it is."

"They have six hundred drones stored there," Matt said. "All the ones that aren't at Big Sky Base are at that place in Georgia."

"Sander knows what he's talking about," Raine said. "Luke will be supporting you from here. You know you can depend on your brother."

"I thought I could depend on my *father*." When he looked at her, Matt felt his eyes tearing up. "Why do I have to fight against my own father? Why can't he just work with the group? What ever happened to people working as a team?"

Her green eyes gazed at him and she put her arms around him. A few short weeks ago, he was proud to have learned that his father was one of the leaders and founders of March22. The organization had training camps, safe houses, fundraising programs, and thousands of committed men and women who believed in its purpose. His father had been a driving force in building the organization, and now he was fighting against it, a renegade, an outcast. What could possibly drive a man to strike out on his own and battle against his own people, his own flesh and blood? He knew Raine didn't have an answer for that. No one had the answer, for the simple reason that the answer was hidden deep in his father's tormented brain.

When he stood up, his feet felt as if they were attached to fifty-pound weights. Raine took the bag, keeping one arm around his waist, and they slowly walked to the door.

"Just promise me one thing," Matt said, stopping to face her again. She looked up at him, waiting. "Whatever happens, you'll never leave me again."

Raine's face clouded at the memory. Maybe she was thinking she had already promised it would never happen again. Maybe she was just sorry. Once they'd gotten it behind them, they hadn't talked much about Raine's brief entanglement with a dude at Stanford, just before Matt rescued her and took her to Montana.

"I can only go up against my own father if I know I have your support," Matt went on. "I mean, this isn't just about him. It's about us. I want to spend my whole life with you. You know that. This mission to Georgia, or wherever we find that crazy guy—I have the feeling it's going to be the hardest thing I've ever done. I need you by my side."

She waited till she was sure he'd finished. She reached up and touched his lips with the tip of her finger. "You can count on me, Matt. And that means forever."

Those were just the words he needed to hear.

# # #

ACKNOWLEDGMENTS

The second book in the Drone Wars series would not have been possible without the help and support of many people. My early readers Andrea Dannegger, Simon Jenner, Meredith Newman, and Naznin Azeez gave me fabulous ideas and pointed out areas that needed tightening in an early draft. My editor, Elizabeth King Humphrey, took care of my many blind spots and helped polish the text in a hundred ways. Anne Chaconas and her team at Badass Marketing did a marvelous job with the cover, formatting and a multitude of marketing tasks. Lastly, my deepest gratitude goes to Ebru O. for encouraging me to take new risks with my writing, without which this book would not have been possible. My thanks to all of you.

ABOUT THE AUTHOR

FREDERICK LEE BROOKE launched the **Annie Ogden Mystery Series** in 2011 with *Doing Max Vinyl* and following with *Zombie Candy* in 2012, a book that is neither about zombies nor sweets. The third mystery in the series, *Collateral Damage*, appeared in 2013. *Saving Raine*, the first book in Fred's entirely new series, **The Drone Wars**, appeared in December, 2013.

A resident of Switzerland, Fred has worked as a teacher, language school manager and school owner. He has three boys and two cats and recently had to learn how to operate both washing machine and dryer. He makes frequent trips back to his native Chicago.

When not writing or doing the washing, Fred can be found walking along the banks of the Rhine River, sitting in a local cafe, or visiting all the local pubs in search of his lost umbrella.

Made in the USA
Lexington, KY
05 June 2014